Khalil Nouri

Rattling *the* JEWEL *in the Crown*

PRINCE NASRULLAH & QUEEN VICTORIA
and THE STRUGGLE FOR AFGAN AUTONOMY

First published by Romaunce Books in 2023
Suite 2, Top Floor, 7 Dyer Street, Cirencester, Gloucestershire, GL7 2PF

© Khalil Nouri

Rattling the Jewel in the Crown
Paperback ISBN 978-1-7391857-5-6

Cover design and content by Ray Lipscombe

Printed and bound in Great Britain
Romaunce Books™ is a registered trademark

Khalil Nouri

Rattling *the* JEWEL *in the Crown*

PRINCE NASRULLAH & QUEEN VICTORIA
and THE STRUGGLE FOR AFGAN AUTONOMY

INTRODUCTION

❧❧❧

In July 1880, two months after ascending to the throne of Afghanistan, the representative of the Governor-General of India, Sir Lepel Griffin delivered a letter by hand to Amir Abdul-Rahaman Khan.

"Your Highness has requested that the views and intentions of the British Government about the position of the ruler at Kabul in relation to Foreign Powers should be placed on record for Your Highness's information. The Viceroy and Governor-General in Council authorises me to declare to you that since the British Government admits no right of interference by Foreign Powers within Afghanistan, and since both Russia and Persia are pledged to abstain from all interference with the affairs of Afghanistan, it is plain that Your Highness can have no political relations with any Foreign Power except with the British government."

Then, after three years of struggle to take control of his foreign policy on his own, he received the following letter from the British Governor-General in India:

The Viceroy and Governor-General of India to Ameer Abdur Rahaman Khan.

Fort William, February 22, 1883

Many vague rumours are doubtless afloat, but they are for the most part, without foundation, and need cause your Highness no uneasiness, more especially as, under the engagements of 1880, which are embodied in the Memorandum presented to your Highness by Sir Lepel Griffin in that year, your Highness is in possession of the assurance of the British Government that, if any foreign Power should lead to unprovoked aggression on the dominions of your Highness, in that event the British Government would be prepared to aid you - to such an extent and in such manner as may appear to the British government necessary - in repelling it, provided that your Highness follows unreservedly the advice of the British Government regarding your external relations.

Under these circumstances, your Highness need be under no apprehension but may rest in secure reliance that the British Government has both the will and the power to make good all its engagements with your Highness.

I beg to express the high consideration I entertain for your Highness and to subscribe myself your Highness' sincere friend.

George Frederick Samuel Robinson, 1st Marquess of Ripon Governor General of India.

PART ONE

CHAPTER ONE

~⊙〜⊙〜⊙~

April 1894 -- Afghan calendar month: *Sawr* 1273
Kabul, Afghanistan

Four years into his reign, the British-backed Afghan ruler, Amir Abdul-Rahman Khan, triumphantly claimed his success. The stability of his dominion with boundaries delineated by two empires, Great Britain and Czarist Russia had been brought under his control and he could assure Great Britain that there need be no fear of disturbance or insurgency spilling over into neighboring British Colonial India and that, under his rule, security and stability would be restored to Afghanistan.

The aging Queen Victoria graciously thanked the Amir for his successes and accomplishments: "His Highness, the Amir has answered our prayers for controlling his nation and ensuring stability to our mission in India," the Queen announced from Windsor Castle. "He is a forceful, intelligent leader, capable of welding his divided people into a state." In a final addition to her paeon of praise, she concluded: "He pursued success as a Knight of the Holy Grail."

The British Viceroy and Governor-General of India also marked the Amir's accomplishments as a successful milestone. In his letter, the

Viceroy thanked him: "Your Highness! You have sailed through the world like a white yacht jubilant with flags. Britain is grateful to you, and I have proposed to the Queen an increase in the subsidy for your government."

Indeed, people called him the Iron Amir. By breaking down the power of warring tribes, he had established an absolute autocratic military force and did all he could to establish normalcy in his realm. The Amir's goal was to maintain a firm grip on his state. His management style was severe and his punishments cruel. At the slightest suspicion of disloyalty, he brutally executed or exiled, men whose political influence he deemed a challenge. Disturbances in all corners of Afghanistan were put down without compunction and the unwarranted ascendancy of local chieftains was stopped. Amir Abdul Rahman rid the land of violent crime through fear of torture and death.

Despite this, the Amir was not able to hold power like his grandfather Amir Dost Mohammad Khan, or any of his Barakzai cousins and siblings. He was faced with an almost-destitute treasury, a tough and unsettled populace, a curmudgeonly government, widespread starvation, and contradictory rulings by chieftains in every village and city in the country.

On an April day in Kabul, The Amir convened his *darbar* in his newly built palace and citadel, Arg. Inside this magnificent hall of politics, the Delkosha, he sat twice daily to grant an audience, receive complaints, petitions, personal grievances and to announce births and deaths, or to dole out punishments.

Following Aristotle's saying that the roots of education are bitter but the fruit is sweet, the Amir made it a point of inviting his two sons, Crown Prince Habibullah, aged twenty-one, and nineteen-year-old Prince Nasrullah, to listen and to gain enlightenment from the daily proceedings. The Royal court of justice was their only education; they watched and learned from the interaction of the viziers, muftis of the law, and visiting plenipotentiaries from every tribe and province in the dominion. It was here that criminals were tried; citizens presented their complaints to be heard, and where benisons were rewarded. The Amir, his viziers, and other courtiers listened to the charges, obsecrations, and pleas for mercy. The final decree lay with the Amir, who specified damages to be paid to a plaintiff, to be obtained from an appellant; and handed down judgment and punishment he deemed appropriate.

In the Delkusha, where he received the title of *Zia-ul-Millat-Wa-Ud Din*, Light of the Nation and Religion, the Amir ascended the raised dais and glanced down upon his subjects before seating himself on his throne. Amir Abdul-Rahman was medium-height, stout, and broad-bodied and not much to look at as he sat facing the audience. After a cordial Salaam and an exchange of greetings with the courtiers, the Mullah of the royal court opened *the darbar* with a melodic recital: "*Bismillah ir-Rahaman ir Rahim*, in the name of God, most Gracious, most Compassionate, and then quoted a few short verses from the Qur'an.

"*Malika* Weektorya sent me a letter from *Englistan*," his deep thunderous voice echoed throughout the hall. He stroked his full beard crossed his short legs and rested them on an embroidered pillow. "She thanked me because I surely merited the title and have broken the power of rebellious chieftains and fanatical mullahs."

The courtiers' silence was as fear in a wilderness and their sharp eyes focused as lynxes', but their love for the despotic ruler was like an epidemic, the more they feared him, the more they loved him.

The Amir made it clear to his subjects that the increase of the British subsidy would have no significance in boosting the morale and prosperity of his countrymen but, by far, the greatest desire from the day he was enthroned was to free Afghanistan from British rule.

The Amir, fuming with frustration, slapped his open palm on the armrest of the winged chair.

"*Pa Khodai-Kay!*, By God!" he screamed, pumping a fist defiantly into the air. He shifted his right foot off the embroidered pillow and flinched. The page boy in attendance quietly stepped forward and repositioned the pillow. "I will secure full control of Afghan foreign policy for the sake of the country. I've made it clear to *Englistan* that they must have confidence in me and my leadership. I am fully capable of taking control of my own nation's foreign policy. Yes, I can! I've proved it to the blind *Englees-Ha* but it always falls on deaf ears, and they look the other way. This is our Afghanistan, I don't need to answer to a foreign power! Enough of enslavement and dependency!"

There was an enthusiastic murmur of assent, like the united call of *Ameen* in the mosque.

The unique position of Afghanistan, as the buffer state between the two superpowers, the English lion and the Russian grizzly, was of vital importance, and the Amir's skillful diplomacy between the contenders for regional domination had been remarkable. In the eyes of the British aristocratic class, Amir Abdul Rahman had proved to be the savior of India, which was Queen Victoria's Crown Jewel, the backbone of British superiority on the world stage.

One of the courtiers stood up hesitantly and requested permission to speak to the Amir.

"Permission granted," the Amir replied, unexpectedly.

"Your Highness, we may have no option but to start a third war with *Englistan*, as did your respected grandfather, Amir Dost Mohammad Khan," he bowed his head in deference to the memory of the great man, "when he too was challenged in his mission."

"Sit down, you imbecile!" Amir Abdul Rahman exploded, "War is not the solution!" he spluttered. "No one gives me advice! If I wanted it, I would ask." His fearsome and merciless eyes bulged like poached eggs. The demoralized courtier sat down on the *Toshak*. An eddy of

4

fear swirled around him like a rabbit pounced upon by a lion.

Next to him, another courtier muttered, "You are truly a fool! Have you no fear of death or torture, or hanging in a public square? Keep a low profile before your bones rot in a cage! Do you..." he stopped, not wanting to offend him further.

"How much more Afghan blood must be spilled?" the Amir roared, gesticulating wildly. "What option do we have but to collect subsidies from the Satan *Englees*, to feed the hungry people, and avoid the sort of bloodbath we have seen for decades? I know the *Iblees Englees-Ha* are untrustworthy but we have to accept their demands or lose the county. *Padar-Lanat-Ha*, may their fathers be cursed! They put a boundary-line dividing my people in two. They think they can divide the country however they like and apply their policy of divide and rule. By cutting them out of my dominion they will neither be of any use to you nor me. We will always be engaged in fighting or other troubles with them, and they will always go on plundering. But as long as this government remains strong and our land is at peace, we will keep control." He parted his thick lips and went on to say, "Let me give you an example of how to deal in the politics of this nation," the Amir said in a quieter moment when his passion had faded. He clicked his fingers at his Chamberlain and ordered tea. "When I was still in exile and my followers and I were fugitives in the hills in Northern Afghanistan, we arrived one afternoon at a village in the Kakar territory, where my followers set out their food and prepared to eat. I looked around for a young, fat sheep for myself, I found a nice one and paid twenty *Kabuli rupees* for it and the owner agreed with the price." He took a sip of tea from his goblet handed to him by his chamberlain and went on, "we were just about to slaughter the animal when the owner changed his mind and wanted it back. I shrugged and told him to take it back, but again he changed his mind. We instantly slaughtered the animal. Next thing, he threw my money at me, demanding that I should resurrect the creature. 'I don't have that kind of power,' I said, but if you want the dead sheep, you can have it and the money back. He refused once more, insisting that I should miraculously resurrect his sheep." His courtiers laughed.

"What did you do?" they asked.

"I called a Mullah who was unaware of the ongoing dispute between us and I told him that the owner of the sheep had been cursing his name and the name of his wife.

'Curse me, if you like," I said as the Mullah turned to face the man, "but do not insult this man's wife. He is a holy man and a prophet!" 'The Mullah exploded with rage and called the man a pig for insulting his wife. The man cursed him back and a heated argument ensued. Meanwhile, I took the sheep and the money and walked away, leaving them to settle their differences." The courtiers slapped their thighs and laughed uproariously at this ingenious trickery. "I became aware," the Amir continued, "that half the spectators sided with the owner of the sheep and the other half with the Mullah and they mediated between them. You can see," he added, "how the man who brilliantly applies the strategy, walks away with everything. This is how we must deal with the Eenglesh-ha." He finished his tea and set the goblet down on the table. "Well, my fellow Afghans, knowing that I am the man, you have my word that I am well fitted to match the opposing Afghan factions against each other, and, a far greater task, to strike down the ambitions of the Lion, and the Bear! Under my leadership, we will not only receive the sheep, the throne of Afghanistan, but also hefty subsidies from the British government."

The Amir had not broken free from Britain's bondage, but for the past fifteen years had fought against extreme odds both inside and outside the country. Often, the critical decisions by which he firmly shaped his nation affected both himself and his family. His people were divided by loyalties to a variety of princes and local warlords, and Afghan courts were poisoned with intrigues and conspiracies. By exercising good and bad policies, Amir Abdul Rahman had played an effective role in bringing his country under the rule of his administration, successfully severing unscrupulous and sacrilegious hands from every cluster in his dominion. He was described as genial, strong, clever, and well-informed in all subjects of general interest. He was also eloquent, resolute, logical, humorous, demanding, and possessed no small capacity for cunning and intrigue. Despite living to further his interests, he strove tirelessly to unify his divided people into a solid nation. Conversely, some described him as a tyrant who wielded his power through cruelty and terror - a despotic ruler who used oppression and threats to run the country. As the British described him, "He is a hard and cruel ruler, but he rules a hard and cruel people."

The British and the Amir did not share the same view regarding control of Afghanistan. Britain's hefty subsidy, provision of new arms and ammunition for the Afghan army, and, above all, full and immediate British support in the event of foreign aggression, determined that Britain still held the solution for security in the country.

In Windsor Palace, the Governor-General of India clarified the position to the Queen, "Your Majesty," he said, "Afghanistan is not ready to take control of its foreign policy. If a Russian invasion took place, the Afghans could not defend the country militarily and politically. In our absence, undoubtedly, Czarist Russia would interfere to destabilize the economy and the war machine that India provides us with. Afghanistan is in the forefront of guarding our mighty resources, we cannot afford to lose that."

"I'm tired of Amir's persistence in constantly asking Britain to grant him control of Afghanistan's foreign policy." The Queen spoke coolly but could not hide her misgivings.

"Your Majesty," The Governor-General drew his hands close to his chest, "As I understand Abdul Rahman, he's a man of great strength and he will never abandon something once his mind is set on it. It's hard to trust an Afghan, your Majesty, the Czar could buy him with a few pounds more than what we pay him. Britain cannot take this chance to leave the fate of our colonial India in the hands of Amir Abdul Rahman without Britain's ultimate control. The Amir is walking a fine line," he continued, "he cannot bear the criticism of his subjects if he remains in the service and mercy of Britain. Your Majesty must see that his dignity and stature are on the line and he'll fade precipitously if he doesn't secure independence for his nation. He knows he could lose support amongst his people if he continues to play a subordinate role to Britain, but at the same time, he loves the handsome British subsidies." The Queen, who was listening carefully to the Governor-General's words, nodded.

"I am certain he ponders hard to find a solution," he said. "Abdul Rahman is a man who has had an adventurous career. Despite his present illness, he is a strong and purposeful leader who tries hard to find a resolution for his desires. Indeed, self-confidence surrounds him like an allure. I fear, your Majesty, that he is likely to put forth a plan to attempt to free his nation from the grip of a foreign power."

CHAPTER TWO

～ఌఄ～ఌఄ～ఌఄ～

The Amir groaned as Doctor Hamilton examined him. Dr. Lillias Hamilton, sensing the distress and turmoil that exacerbated his pain, asked bluntly, "Your Highness, have you changed your eating habits, as I suggested?"

"This is nothing to do with food!"

"In which case, I think the restlessness and fatigue you are experiencing, Amir, is not entirely related to your gout," she replied, regarding him quizzically. With the interpreter's help she probed further, "Your Highness, I can see that your condition has worsened. Perhaps you are worrying?" After a brief pause, she added, "It is my job to help."

Dr. Lillias Hamilton had lived in Scotland, trained as a doctor in London and qualified in 1890. Most women doctors faced huge challenges in establishing practices in a male-dominated field and many were forced to leave England to work overseas. Lillias left England, and practiced in Calcutta before being offered the position of personal physician to the Amir in Afghanistan.

"I don't know why. I'm also sleepless and weak," he said, becoming almost child-like as he often did under her control.

"Is there something bothering you?"

"Yes, doctor. *Malika* Weektorya cannot understand that the policies they have instituted are causing me difficulties with my people."

"Please explain why."

"She doesn't believe I can handle Afghanistan's foreign policy and my people are angry with the demarcation."

A few days before, the British Mission under Sir Mortimer Durand, who had demarcated the new boundary line between India and Afghanistan, had left Kabul after the Amir reluctantly agreed to the delineation of eastern and southern boundaries of his dominion.

The fair-skinned doctor stopped the wheelchair and briefly touched the two ornately designed hair clips pinned to the hair piled high on the crown of her head.

"Your Highness, if this problem is making you ill, a solution needs to be found," she said earnestly.

"*Daktar-e-Aziz!*, dear Doctor, my thoughts keep me awake at night, but do not disturb yourself, I will find a solution," he assured her. Lillias gripped the handles of the heavy wheelchair and pushed it forward. The rhythmic rolling of the wheelchair against the gravel combined with sounds of the chirping birds and gushing water fountains created a continual musical symphony. Fresh clear air blew across the city like the flowing glacier waters of the Hindu-Kush, and the turquoise blue of the sky brought to mind a vast field of dense young violets. On the west of the city, the sixth-century stone walls zigzagged like a giant auger, while, from a distance, the mountain tops whitened with snow resembled crests of ocean waves.

Dr. Hamilton stopped the wheelchair near a garden bench. "Your Highness," she faced the Amir calmly. "Do you mind if I ask you more about your anxieties?"

"Please, Daktar Laila, be my guest."

"Is there any other option open to you," she asked, meeting his eyes firmly, "it seems you have tried everything in your power to convince Queen Victoria to accept your plea, but could there be another way?"

"Daktar Laila Jan! I have exhausted all options. I told *Englistan*,

I would be loath to accept any conditions that might blacken me in their eyes, or make me appear ungrateful to them. I would endeavor to be the friend of both Zaar Neekolos and *Malika* Weektorya. But especially of *Malika* Weektorya, who I hope would secure for me the same measure of independence that *Englistan* granted to Iran. The people of Afghanistan also need to be appeased."

"Your Highness, do you feel you should travel and see the Queen in person?" she asked, "I could accompany you, if you prefer."

"Daktar Laila Jan! I'm grateful for your kind offer," the Amir smiled pleasantly, displaying the loss of several teeth. "But I do not think I would cope with the long journey to Landan." He stroked his bushy gray beard with an air of calm dignity.

Lillias nodded, knowing that gout caused him severe pain and there was little she could offer to help the frail ruler. Although she had only been in his service for a few months, she considered herself almost a member of Amir's family and recognized his need for physical and emotional support after the years of war and intense work.

"As forthright as the doctor was inclined to be, compassion was reflected in her blue eyes as she looked at him, "I'll do my best to care for you," she said, "and I have decided to extend my stay in Kabul indefinitely so that I can be at Your Highness's service."

The Amir's brown eyes lit up, and his thick lips relaxed into a vivid smile; for a moment he looked young again.

"Daktar Laila Jan! I'm increasing your pay. I am truly grateful to you for you staying on."

"I'm happy to be of need, Your Highness."

꩜

August 1894 - Afghan calendar month: *Asad* 1273
Kabul, Afghanistan

The Durand-Line agreement sprawled over the entire six-foot-long mahogany desk in Arg Palace. It was enhanced, revised, and signed by the Amir and Sir. Mortimer Durand.

"They finally twisted the arm of *Padar Jan*, father, with this agreement," Nasrullah said with an expression of disgust, "Land grabbing is what the *Shaitan Englees*, Satan English, does - the biggest land-grabber in the entire world! They are here, they are there, they are colonizing everywhere - every country in the world - nothing is enough for these greedy warmongers!" He paced angrily as spoke, "Forcing them at gunpoint - bringing them under the subjection of Britain against the will of the people! They colonize the weak and the vulnerable, loot their resources, and use them as slaves. Can you believe this?" he gestured bitterly towards the agreement set on the table. "They just gobbled up a huge territory on our frontier."

One courtier humbly nodded in agreement, "our territory once extended back to Attock, he said, "but not anymore. They may claim Kabul and Qandahar and Herat if they're not stopped."

"Undoubtedly!" Nasrullah said bitterly. "Habibullah," He turned to his brother who, until then had remained silent, "do you agree that the *Englees-Ha* have an agenda to control Afghanistan entirely?"

"My dear brother, let me say this, if we don't have the backing of the *Englees-Ha* then Russians will rule us. We are better off with the *Engless-Ha* than the grizzlies up north. Please understand! We need subsidies to survive. If the Russians can't even feed their starving population, how could they give us such hefty subsidies as the *Englees-*

Ha are giving us?"

Princes Habibullah, Nasrullah, and two royal courtiers waited for the Amir to join them to mark the milestone of the inequitable Durand Line agreement. The Durand Line extended approximately one-thousand-five-hundred miles, starting from the Pamir Mountain range in Northern Afghanistan to the Arabian Sea. The border-line had proved unpopular amongst the tribal factions who found their territories suddenly severed by it, and themselves unexpectedly subject to British rule. Afghans had hoped for an extension of their border to the ocean, but the *Kochis*, nomadic tribes, now found themselves under British control, and their migration routes possibly blocked. Once Queen Victoria granted the Amir free rein over the territories within Afghanistan, inside the Durand Line, he contrived to push his advantage. The British promise of non-interference became an invitation to seize Kafiristan, the land of infidels, and convert the population of two-hundred-thousand en mass, to Islam.

"Why is the name Dooraand, given to this agreement? Why not *choor-wa-chapawol*, loot and plunder?" Nasrullah demanded loudly.

Prince Habibullah's anxiety heightened noticeably and he rubbed the back of his neck. "You need to be more reticent, *Padar Jan*, our father is due here at any moment. You know he won't tolerate your demeaning of the *Englees-Ha*. Your rhetoric could cost you hugely. Be careful!"

"We need to tell the facts, Habibullah!"

"Go ahead and show him your valor if you consider yourself a tiger, but don't be disappointed . . ." Habibullah stopped as the Amir rolled his wheelchair across the threshold.

"The good news is *Malika* Weektorya finally granted me absolute autonomy without any British interference in our domestic affairs!" he roared cheerfully as he approached his sons. His wheelchair was still being pushed across the colossal *darbar* hall.

'But only over this side of the Line," Prince Nasrullah muttered under his breath. Habibullah shot him a warning glance.

"However, there is disturbing news from India!" the Amir said and his countenance fell. He suddenly appeared subdued and anxious and he leaned towards his sons as he gave them the news.

"A journalist named Radyaad Kilpin published a report that a few years ago two *Englees,* English men, crossed into our territory of Kafiristan - one of them declared himself King there!" Nasrullah shot a triumphant glance at his brother, which went unnoticed by the Amir.

"I sent a wireless to the *Naib-Ul-Hokoma-e-Englistaan dar Kalkataa*, British Governor-General in Calcutta, *Aghai* Booroos, Mr. Bruce. He told me he's unaware of this story and cannot confirm." The Amir snatched the telegram from the pageboy and waved it in the air, "Read it for yourselves, I don't believe a renowned journalist like Radyaard Kilpin would ever publish an untrue story like this!" He handed it to Nasrullah.

"Maybe Kilpin can be contacted in Lahore?" Nasrullah suggested, trying his best to remain respectful.

"So?" Prince Habibullah said, "even if it's true, what stops them from declaring themselves Kings of Kafiristan?" he stuttered slightly over the words, raised both hands, and dropped them as though baffled.

"I will not allow any obtuse and worthless man to declare himself a king—not anywhere in my dominion!" the Amir declared adamantly. "My decision cannot be overruled by anyone. I am the absolute Amir! I will declare a holy war to introduce the unbelievers into purity and cleanse their souls of sin. They will be enlightened once the pure religion of Islam shines on their souls."

A courtier bowed in deference, "May Allah reward you for your good intentions"

"*Alahazrata,* Your Majesty! You're the true light of the nation and religion," the other proclaimed.

"*Padar,* Father!" Habibullah exclaimed, "Why resort to conquest

14

and bloodshed when these phony kings can easily be removed?" he twisted his hands uneasily and his slight stutter became more pronounced, "Let's make the right . . ."

"The entire population of the land abides by the pure religion of Islam, so should those *kafirs*, infidels," Nasrullah interjected.

"Son!" Amir exclaimed, "even if these so-called kings are removed, the entire Kafiristan will remain vulnerable to rule by an outsider at any time. We must change them to Islam before it is too late!"

"*Padar Jan,* dear father!" Habibullah interjected, "This is for you too, Nasrullah!" He scrambled his words as he attempted to make his point, "We h-h-have Hindus living all over the country and m-m-more than seventy thousand Jewish families in northern and western Afghanistan—should they all convert? When Iran tried to force Jews to convert, they migrated to other counties—some even to Afghanistan. Do you want the entire Kafiristan to go into exile?" He paused but continued when there was no response, "The people of Kafiristan are descendants of a Macedonian colony that were brought in and settled there by *Iskandar-e-Kabir*, Alexander the Great. Why force them to convert when they're at peace with themselves and the adjoining tribes?"

"They worship idols, you're utterly ill-informed!" Nasrullah locked his gaze with Habibullah's.

Unlike the Amir and Nasrullah, the liberal-minded Habibullah was far ahead of his time. He understood that every religion had value and none taught evil, but his plea to dissuade his father from the onslaught against the innocent people of Kafiristan was a futile effort. The Amir deployed thousands of his well-armed soldiers and enforced his full authority like a riptide. The curtain fell with complete darkness. Later, rumors of the invasion spread throughout the city squares, mosques, and bazaars. There was talk of horrible repressions, of young *Kafir* boys forcibly sent to Kabul to learn the religion of Islam and being indoctrinated with the false notion that they had emanated from the wandering tribe of Quraish. Finally, the evolution of the region was marked by a distinction in the name: from Kafiristan, Land of Unbelievers, to Nuristan, Land of the Enlightened.

CHAPTER THREE

It had been five months since Lillias Hamilton's stay in Kabul was extended.

She checked her appearance in the mirror, running her fingertips over her high cheekbones and smoothing her chestnut hair. She glanced briefly at the clock on her mantelpiece. It was eight o'clock— later than she realized. She hurried down to the carriage and briefly acknowledged the driver.

"Bostan-Sarai please."

Dr. Hamilton was pale and tired from restless nights spent attending to the Amir. Her commitment to giving full care to her ailing patient was her only responsibility and she was in constant attendance, performing medical measurements and diagnoses, as well as nutritional monitoring. Above all, she was closely watching the crystals of sodium urate that formed inside and around his joints, which was the cause of so much suffering.

"*Salaam* Your Highness! Please forgive me for my tardiness."

"*Salaam* Doctor Laila Jan! Glad you arrived. May Allah grant you long life and good health." He looked up at her from his wheelchair, "You are truly a life-saver and I have no worries when you're here in Kabul."

"You will always have my full attention, Your Highness." Lillias administered some medicine to the Amir to reduce his uric acid and tucked a shawl around his severely gout-diseased feet. "Your

17

Highness, you seem beset by pain."

"I have my days, Daktar Laila Jan."

She could see that the discomfort was almost unbearable; the Amir's face was white and drawn, and he flinched constantly under the relentless torment; shafts of pain knifed through his legs from his throbbing ankles and feet. His fingers made small jittery movements when the Doctor exerted any pressure on his ankle and, as she concluded her examination, he weakly attempted to reach his feet over his stout stomach. He nodded to his page boy who promptly stepped forward and massaged them gently.

With the help of the attending nurse, Dr. Hamilton took him for frequent long strolls in the gardens of Arg Palace. Today, Lillias slowly pushed the Amir, seated in his immaculately upholstered wheelchair, through the smooth dirt-packed paths fenced with ornate iron railings, toward the spacious and superbly manicured gardens, handsomely landscaped to an eighteen-century design. The gardens were green and lush filled with ruby-colored cherry trees; beds of yellow crocuses stood erect like trumpets, flame-like tulips, and crown-imperial lilies bunched together in a frill of green like faded cauliflowers. As the Amir breathed in the perfumed air, his anxiety decreased. A flowing stream filled the marbled fountain pool where ducks, swans, and other waterfowl, paddled and swam. The melodic sounds of chirping birds rang in the air like dropping coins. This touch of paradise rested like a bed of glittering jewels in the heart of Kabul surrounded by gentle hills and towering mountain ranges. Further away were the Northern Hindu-Kush meadows and eastern grassy plains spread out like immense green towels.

Doctor Hamilton and the Amir usually communicated through the Indian-born interpreter, Raj, whose constant mask-like smile, reminiscent of a circus clown, made him appear as though the corners of his mouth are strung up on invisible wires. Occasionally, the Amir would snap irritably at him when his interpretation from Dari became slap-dash.

There were occasions when the Amir wanted to discuss something confidential with Doctor Hamilton, which he would prefer the interpreter should not know, but his skills were needed to translate.

"*Tarjuman!* Interpreter!" he would say.

"*Accha Sahab?* Yes, Master?"

"What we discuss here, or anywhere, remains here. No *shaitanee*, blabber mouthing, or else the punishment will be severe . . . your organs make perfect *maza* for the stray dogs!"

"*Achha Amir Sahab,* certainly, Amir, Master!" He would join his palms together and bow, but his smile never faded.

Amir Abdul Rahman moved his body into a slightly more comfortable position and gestured to Lillias.

"Please, *Daktar,* bring the wheelchair close to that rose bush," he said. He reached over and plucked a flame-red rose and handed it to her, "*Barai Daktar Ma!* For my Doctor!"

"*Tashakur,* Your Highness, she held her blue and white striped dress with one hand and dipped into a genteel curtsy. The Amir smiled briefly tilting his gray Karakul Astrakhan hat.

"Daktar Laila Jan. I wish my wives and concubines had your manners," he said.

As Raj interpreted she smiled down at the Amir.

"Your Highness, I'm honored! If I may be of service to the ladies of the *Harem-Sarai*, I would be happy to share with them anything they want to hear and introduce them to some of my English customs. Some have expressed curiosity at my skin color, my upbringing, and the differences in our cultures. We could learn from one another." Lillias pushed the wheelchair through the pavilion to where a wide variety of flowering stocks, sweet peas, and more gaily-colored roses grew. The air was heavy with their perfume.

"Daktar Laila! How is your novel writing? I forgot the title."

"A Vizier's Daughter, Your Highness."

"What is it about?"

"It's a Tale of the Hazara War, Your Highness."

"Daktar Laila," the Amir said with a guarded look, "do you know why I'd to let Doctor Gray go?" He narrowed his eyes and met her gaze sternly.

"No Your Highness."

"Have you read his books, At The Court Of The Amir, and My Residence At The Court?"

"I'm looking forward to reading them, Your Highness!" Lillias said, then seeing his expression, her hand flew to her mouth, "Did he write something that offended you, Your Highness?"

"Yes, Daktar Laila Jan, he referred to my illness, diagnoses, and symptoms. He publicly revealed my medical status . . . That's exactly why he had to go."

"Your Highness, I would never reveal your health status in my book and you have my word that I will keep your private matters confidential."

"But Daktar Laila Jan, you well know that I ordered the conquest of those revolting Hazaras in Bamyan, I hope there's nothing said to boost their filthy egos and make them more rebellious because I would have to shed more Hazara blood."

"Your Highness, this is simply a story of a Vizier's daughter. I think you would probably be interested in reading it."

"Of course, Daktar Laila Jan, I'll be the first to receive a copy."

"*Ba har-doo cheshem!* With both eyes!" She raised both hands to her eyes in a cordial Afghan saying and gesture she had learned.

Indeed, the Amir's life was dependent upon their relationship, Lillias was able to sense his problems both clinically and emotionally as their friendship grew, they were like two clocks keeping time.

"*Too mara az marg nejat dadee*, you've saved me from death, Daktar Laila!" the Amir wheezed. "I will always be grateful to you. I hope you're happy with your stay in Kabul, for I want you here."

With the few words she knew in Dari, she replied smilingly, "*Tashakur Amir, Sahib! Ma hemesha ba khedmat shoma mebasham!* I'll always be at your service.

During those months when the Amir's life was in serious jeopardy, the palace Hakim, Jon Mohammad, who had jealously served the Amir for many years, fearing Amir's imminent death and mindful of his future, blamed Dr. Hamilton for the patient's turn for the worst.

Dr. Lillias Hamilton was constantly aware at that time that her life was in danger thanks to the well-planned intrigues of the Hakim. If the Amir had died, or if she lost his protection under his waning health and mental instability, the result could quite possibly be imprisonment or execution on the charge of having poisoned the Afghan ruler.

The duplicitous Hakim clad in white robes and a tightly-swathed white turban was suspicious even of the distorted candlelight that cast shadows across his wrinkled face.

"The fancy candle you brought for Amir Sahib from *Englistan.*" The Hakim pointed with his sinewy fingers at the candlestick set in a beveled holder on the mantelpiece. "Some candles from *Englistan* smell strange," he said, his jaundiced eyes challenged the Doctor as she moved around the room and when he spoke, his voice held a hint of mockery. His hands dangled loosely at his sides as he watched her every move. "I hear they are made with a combination of arsenic and other secret ingredients," he continued, not bothering to hide the stinging accusation behind his words. "Supposedly, such candles are poisoned. They can cause terrible ailments, insanity, and death. Untraceable too." There was a sardonic gleam in his eyes. "I need your assurance that there is no harm to Amir Sahib or any member of his family."

As Dr. Hamilton turned to face him down, Hakim Mohammed

averted his eyes from her angry gaze.

"Hakim Sahib! It would never cross my mind to harm Amir Sahib, I'm an ethical and loyal doctor and I am here to ensure the wellbeing of Amir Sahib at all times," she replied firmly. "If those candles contained arsenic, I would be endangered as well! It is preposterous that you would suggest such a thing!"

"I was told *Englees-Ha* are masters in killing covertly."

"Well, that certainly does not apply to me!" she returned sharply, hands on hips, "and I do not appreciate your judgment of me!" She felt her heart pounding against the stifling cage of her tightly laced corset.

"Your lips are dripping with lies, *Bibi Jan*, dear Lady, so-called Daktar." The Hakim pounded the checkered marble floor with his cane as he spoke, causing his long straggly beard to quiver. "I hate to even call you a Daktar, because a woman like you, in fact, any woman, is incapable of practicing my profession."

"Your profession?" Dr. Hamilton replied phlegmatically. "Is it your superstitious profession that causes you to give quince seeds to the ladies of the *Harem-Sarai* to quell their temperament?" she demanded, blinking rapidly as she fought to bring her own emotions under control. "Prescribing one quince seed per day for forty days and telling them not to go in a rage, else it will not work?" She shook her head vigorously, "And then, at the end of the forty-days, when, of course, it fails; you accuse them of having lost their temper during that period! What are your facts, Sir, what is your source?" Pinching her lips together into a thin line, she folded her arms and met his eyes, willing him to back down. "Apart from your bizarre quince remedy, the hemorrhoidal balm you asked me to give you to share with others who suffered the complication, you claimed was your invention! Are you not ashamed to make that assertion?" Lillias was fuming but in full control of the situation. "If I tell the Amir about this, who is he going to believe?" she demanded, "you or me?"

22

He was no longer able to look the doctor in the eye. "Amir Sahib has known me for many years," the Hakim muttered, "I've gained his full trust." He mumbled irritably under his breath and walked away. "We Afghans know every *Angrez*, English, who comes here, sucking every drop of our blood and now killing our beloved Amir." The shuffling of his curly pointed shoes combined with the tap-tap of his cane echoed sharply as he walked away and then faded in the distance.

Despite Habibullah, the Amir's son, personally reassuring her and pledging his protection to the Doctor, Lillias Hamilton kept a fast horse ready near the palace's entrance to flee in the event of the Amir's death.

CHAPTER FOUR

❦

June 1894 -- Afghan calendar month: *Jawza* 1273
Kabul, Afghanistan

Shortly after agreeing to stay on indefinitely in Kabul, Doctor Hamilton received a telegram from her twin sister, Roma Hamilton to say that she was coming to pay her a visit. Lillias's excitement bubbled over into joyful song so that the guard outside her house looked in to check whether all was well. *"Khoob astee Daktar Sahib?"*

"Everything is fine, *Tashakur!*" she responded in her broken Dari, "My sister will soon be visiting me."

She read the telegram multiple times, but the initial pleasure was gradually replaced by a nagging fear. How would Roma cross the Khyber Pass and travel to Kabul on her own? For her sister to visit an extremely isolated country like Afghanistan would be like flying through a smokescreen of impossibilities. Roads were rough and often impassable, there were no trains, and very little adequate security to protect her from robbers. Lillias Hamilton remembered crossing freezing mountain passes and wide-open deserts with an unknown guide—it was like being ushered along by a stray shepherd dog! Suddenly she was petrified at the idea of her sister making such a perilous journey.

There was one person she could ask for advice. Lillias sent a boy ahead with her visiting card and an hour later called for the carriage.

"Deh-Afghan," she ordered.

The driver clicked his tongue and cracked the whip and the two horses trotted forward. The wheels rumbled over the Arg's gravel road sounding like a crockery shop in an earthquake. The faded, black carriage carrying Doctor Hamilton was escorted by multiple mounted armed guards. They all wore colorless top coats and knee-high leather boots. On their heads, they sported shaggy circular caps of goat hair. The men were as filthy as birds of paradise that had spent all night in the mud and rain, while the lack-luster coats of their feisty horses, ungroomed since the day they were born, were mud-splashed and matted.

As the escorted carriage made its way through the crowded streets, Lillias closed the casement window to stop the solicitation of beggars. In places, Kabul smelt like an open drain: the streets reverberated with noise and clamor; horse-drawn carts, the wailing of babies, the cries of vendors, the braying of donkeys, and the clip-clop of horses' hoofs—everything combined to form a maddening cacophony. There were tea shops, tanners, dyers, salt grinders, pot makers, and slaughter shops. Open braziers on the street corners grilled kebabs over the glowing coals. In the milling crowd, pickpockets, thieves, and hawkers rubbed shoulders with businessmen.

The carriage stopped at the foothill of the Asema-Ye-Mountain, close to Martin's house. Dr. Hamilton alighted from the carriage, carefully lifting her skirts as she by-passed a stinking pit. She lifted the heavy cast-iron knocker and let it fall against the wooden door. A servant opened it, bowed briefly to acknowledge her presence, and showed Lillias into the courtyard.

"My dear Dr. Hamilton, please come in, this is a pleasant surprise!"

Chief Engineer, Frank Martin, ran the Amir's arsenal and coinage factories in Kabul. Frank was in his late thirties, tall, well-groomed, and clean-shaven. Lillias smiled to see he was wearing a gray *Perahan-*

Tunban with an embroidered *Koochie* vest. A servant set a tray of tea and refreshments on the low table and Frank dismissed him with a nod.

"Lillias, it is good to see you again," he said. "I am delighted, but I am sure you have come with news? Please, take a seat."

"I have!" she replied. "My sister, Roma is on her way to Kabul to visit me."

Frank Martin poured tea for them both and sat down on a *charpaie*, an Afghan cot, opposite Lillias. "That is very good news," he said with a smile, seeing the excitement in his friend's face.

"I wondered whether I could ask for your help in arranging her travel from Peshawar to Kabul? You know better than anyone that an elegant young English woman traveling alone across from Khyber Pass to Kabul is extremely dangerous. I am desperately worried about her, Frank, and I wondered if you know of anyone else who is coming that may be able to accompany her."

Frank Martin thought for a moment. "Mr. Clemence's wife is also on her way to Kabul," Frank Martin replied setting his cup down on the table next to him. "I'm not sure when she is due, but their travel plans may coincide…"

Lillias met his glance hopefully, "My sister is due to reach Peshawar in a week," she said, "Mr. Clemence's wife would no doubt be accompanied by an armed escort?"

"Certainly!" The Engineer crossed his legs and rubbed his chin thoughtfully, "He mentioned that his wife is on the train to Peshawar," he said, "They could conceivably be on the same train. Mr. Clemence would certainly have made arrangements for her to come here, he might be able to help you better than I."

"Do you have any further details?" she asked anxiously.

"Only that, as we know, the journey from Peshawar will take a few weeks."

"I hope it is not too late! It would be perfect if Roma was able to accompany her." Her eyes shone with excitement. "You have truly been a great help, Frank, thank you so much."

"Thomas Clemence is in Beymaroo, the military compound," he gestured briefly towards the east side of the city, "It is a twenty-minute carriage ride from the palace. He teaches Amir's veterinarian students and maintains over twenty-thousand horses so he is on call around the clock. Like the rest of us, Clemence carries more on his shoulders than he should, to keep the Amir happy. How is Amir? he added. "I heard he had taken a turn for the worse."

"He is still very unwell, but he has improved recently," the doctor replied. "I am more at ease with his situation, but he is still in much pain."

He nodded empathetically. "I suggest you invite Mr. Clemence to see you at his leisure," he said.

"I should be honored if you would come at the same time," Lillias said blushing slightly, "I will organize a dinner."

Hamilton bowed, "I should be delighted."

Martin took Lillias Hamilton by the arm and ushered her to the waiting carriage. They had only taken a few steps beyond his courtyard when they were surrounded by a swarm of children that had appeared like bees from nowhere; imploring hands reached out, begging for food or *Paisa*. Dr. Hamilton noticed, sadly, their infected eyes and matted hair.

"They're here every day," Frank explained briefly, "the servants are instructed to give them bread and leftover food." He opened the carriage door for Lillias and supported her arm as she stepped up and took her seat. Moments later the carriage rolled forward, and the children gave chase until it picked up speed and faded into a cloud of dust.

CHAPTER FIVE

꩜

Since her little cottage was within the Arg premises, Lillias felt it necessary to speak to the Amir before inviting Mr. Clemence and Frank Martin and so she broached the subject when she saw him later that day.

"Daktar Laila Jan, there is no need for you to ask for permission," the Amir replied with a shaky voice.

"Thank you, Your Highness," she said gratefully, "I have decided to deliver the invitation to Mr. Clemence personally tomorrow so that I can arrange a convenient time."

The long gun turrets and high watchtowers of the newly built fortress of Baymaroo could be seen from a long way off. As the carriage approached and the guards recognized the palace insignia, the huge wooden double doors, with rows of metal spikes were slowly opened, rusty hinges screeching like, Lillias thought, London's fishwives. The carriage rolled inside, the clip-clop of the horses' hooves reverberated from the walls of the stables on either side of the long dirt road. The smell of horse dung, sweaty leather, and hay wafted into the moving carriage. Soldiers could be seen as the carriage passed by, leading the Amir's magnificent stallions to and fro between the stables and exercise pens.

Doctor Hamilton did not need to be told that the healthy, well-groomed horses were the result of the labor of veterinarian, Mr. Clemence; she was painfully aware that most stables run by Afghans were filthy and the horses neglected. She could see heaps of saddles stacked in storage rooms between some stables and the tack walls hung with bridles, woolen blankets, grooming tools, and handwoven Afghan saddle pads.

The carriage drew to a halt at the end of the road, close to Mr. Clemence's bungalow. The older man was distinguished from the group of Afghan Army students he was lecturing, by his debonair mustaches and the pipe clenched firmly between his teeth. He handed the bridle of the Arab stallion he was holding, to one of the students and strode across to the carriage. Clad in khaki breeches and tall black boots, a white starched coat open at the neck, to reveal a ruffled shirt with a black, puffed cravat—Thomas Clemence was the picture of a well-attired British gentleman. He waited for the cloud of dust to settle before courteously opening the door.

"Good day Dr. Hamilton. It's a surprise to see you here!" He took her hand to help her alight from the carriage.

"I'm obliged, Mr. Clemence," she curtsied respectfully, holding on with one hand to the straw bonnet that threatened to lift in the breeze. "Forgive me for arriving unannounced, but I heard the happy news that Mrs. Clemence will be joining you here in Kabul."

"Indeed, Doctor," he smiled, "the telegram arrived two days ago, and I am expecting her within a month." He politely gestured her to take a seat under the cool shade of a weeping willow tree where a set of steamer deck chairs and a hand-carved table were placed. He set his pipe down on the table and called for tea.

"*Chai byar!*" A pageboy scuttled off in the direction of the house.

Sitting down opposite Dr. Hamilton, Clemence knocked the old tobacco from his pipe and began methodically to refill it. Lillias, suddenly conscious of her impetuosity, smoothed the flowered fabric of her long skirt and looked down to where the toes of her brown buttoned boots peaked out beneath its folds.

"My apologies again, at arriving unannounced, Mr. Clemence, but I felt my mission was quite urgent," she looked up more brightly.

"You've given these stables a distinctly English feel and the horses are immaculate and well-taken care of."

The pungent, but not unpleasant, smell of hay, horses, and their trappings filled the air with their unique odor.

"Yes Dr. Hamilton, I am employed to work with horses, which is what I love, and in so doing I aim to keep the Amir as happy as possible. As you know, he is not always easy to please, but similar work in England and India is scarce."

The page boy set the tray on the table and poured the tea into glazed china cups.

"You said your visit was urgent?" Clemence questioned as he handed her the cup and saucer.

"My sister, Roma Hamilton will be arriving in Peshawar about the same time as Mrs. Clemence," she said. "I was hoping, if it is convenient, that the two ladies might travel to Kabul together." She added milk and sugar to her tea and stirred it with a sterling silver spoon. "I am here to extend an invitation to have you and Mr. Martin join me for dinner in my cottage in Arg Palace so that we can discuss possible arrangements."

"Thank you, madam, English food would make a delightful change," he replied, with a laugh, "and I hear your cooking is unsurpassed." He glanced at her curiously, "Where are you from, I can't place your accent?" he said. "There seems to be a Scottish twang…"

Lillias laughed. My parents were Scottish," she said, "but they moved to New South Wales in Australia," which is where I was born. Later, we returned to Britain and we lived in Cheltenham."

"So," Clemence replied, "you followed your parents as an adventurer. How did you come to be in Kabul?"

"It is a long story," she said. "I studied as a doctor in England but women doctors don't find employment easily."

He nodded, "It is a male-dominated profession," he said

sympathetically, "but Kabul is a most unlikely place to a woman to have arrived in—and particularly to have found employment as a doctor to the Amir!"

She smiled. "I first practiced in India, but I became ill with cholera during an epidemic in Calcutta. It was a long convalescence and I was forced to give up work. It's well known that the air in Kabul is most conducive to good health, so I made my way here having heard the Amir was looking for a woman doctor for the Harem."

"Remarkable!" Thomas Clemence said. "And I gather you have been here for quite some time?"

She nodded and smiled at the page as he offered to refill her cup. "After the first few months of working in the Harem, the Amir asked me to become his court doctor."

"That would have been after Dr. Gray left," he said.

She nodded. "To be quite honest, I was reluctant to take the position. By that time, I was aware that his nature was erratic and his ways lacked stability."

He laughed. "Dr. Hamilton, that is perhaps the most polite description of the Amir's tyrannical rule that I have yet heard from anyone emanating from outside Afghanistan's borders."

"When one lives within the palace grounds, it is preferable to err on the side of caution," she replied with a lopsided smile. "But it is time I left; the carriage is waiting. Would this Friday evening be suitable for dinner?"

"Certainly," he replied. "I look forward to it."

"Then it is arranged, Mr. Clemence," she said with a smile.

July 1894 -- Afghan calendar month: *Saratan* 1273

Kabul, Afghanistan

In the months since Dr. Hamilton's arrival to serve the Amir, she had spent time training the palace chefs in English cooking, pastries, and desserts. The Amir himself had developed a keen taste for Doctor Hamilton's cooking and occasionally ordered from the menus that she introduced.

The kitchen was in a separate building alongside the Bostan-Sarai Palace. Under the head chef, multiple master cooks scurried around the huge kitchen preparing curries and various other Afghan dishes around the clock. Often, they would prepare for one-hundred-and-fifty to two-hundred members of the household and palace personnel, not including guests. The daily requirements amounted to around a hundred-and-fifty pounds of meat, between a hundred to hundred-and-fifty eggs, and piles of vegetables of all sorts, all needing to be washed, chopped, or sliced. At the end of each day, portions of scraps and leftovers were distributed to palace helpers to take home.

In preparation for her guests, Frank Martin and Mr. Clemence, Lillias asked the head chef to prepare a two-course English meal of mutton cutlets and chicken noisettes. During her stay, she had taken time to carefully demonstrate these and other recipes to the head chef who was quick to learn.

"Please also do a separate course of *mantoo*," the Chef smiled broadly knowing that this dumpling dish, with a meat and onion mixture encased in individual dough wrappers and served with split pea sauce and garlic yogurt, was *Daktar Jan's* personal Afghan favorite. "And for dessert," Lillias went on, "a plum pudding covered with custard cream served with tea or coffee!" Every so often, the Doctor received a small supply of coffee from India. The lack of coffee in Afghanistan was one thing she missed—most Afghans had never heard of it.

In the unbearable summer heat, Kabul was swept by dust-laden winds, but it was the mild evenings and night skies resplendent with stars that Lillias cherished; she imagined those panoramic skies were a huge sheet of clear glass filled with glittering gems. The songs of crickets and frogs enhanced the beauty of the night rising and falling like swelling sails, a symphony beneath those twinkling lights.

From the doorway where the doctor stood, the candle-lit chandelier behind her cast a long, flickering shadow to the end of her private courtyard. She took a deep breath like a swimmer coming up for air, and spoke quietly, " Oh my God, I love Kabul's starry nights—this is like a night in heaven!"

The sound of an approaching carriage drew her out of her reverie. Her guard opened the small, arched door to her courtyard and stood aside to allow them to enter. With the formalities of greeting over, each presented the Doctor with a wrapped gift.

"If there is a servant here, open these later," Clemence warned.

She raised her eyebrows, "Gentlemen, you haven't brought liquor?"

Thomas Clemence grinned, "A gin just arrived from Peshawar, madam, flavored with sloe berries, and Frank has brandy made here in Kabul."

"In Kabul?" Lillias glanced at Frank doubtfully.

"This is the one I make in the *Mashin-Khana*," the engineer replied cheerfully. He sat down on one of the hand-carved chairs.

"We know how cautious we have to be with alcohol here, Amir is a devoted Muslim, he hates it," she said, alarmed. "I am sure you know, that he orders public amputations when his subjects are caught intoxicated."

"Of course, Lillias, we have to be careful when consuming alcohol in Afghanistan," Frank Martin agreed quietly. "But we do produce a fine brandy here in Kabul," he shifted his chair to see her better, "I ask you, of course, to keep it confidential. I monitor one of the distilleries where I work."

"I had drinks with British military officers and Sir Mortimer Durand in Bala-Hisar Palace years ago and the Amir looked the other way," Mr. Clemence said. "I know for a fact, he publicly dismembers or executes his own Afghans for doing the same, but doesn't care if we British drink. Take my word for it and let's enjoy the night."

Both men were smartly dressed in frock coats with frilled white shirts, and Clemence sported a colorful cravat; they lit up their cheroots and Frank poured their brandy into crystal glasses. Lillias also raised her glass with a delightful smile. "To eternity –may it last forever!" she said. The clink of glasses filled the air and they tossed smiles at each other as though they were certificates of trust.

"Martin has also received some great news," Thomas Clemence said setting his brandy glass down. He tapped the ash from his cheroot into the ashtray. Grayish-blue smoke formed a cloud between them.

"Yes, I do, and it is such a coincidence! I received a telegram from Charlotte, my wife, today. She, with our young boy, William, and her childhood friend, Olivia Worth, granddaughter of Charles Worth, the famous dress designer,is also heading to Kabul," he said, smiling broadly. He drew deeply on his cheroot and blew the smoke into the air.

"That is wonderful news!" Lillias said delightedly. "And the granddaughter of Charles Worth is also coming?"

"Yes."

She was at once animated and her blue eyes sparkled. "Considering it will be such a large party, I could ask the Amir to provide a platoon of some twenty-five men to bring them all across the Khyber Pass."

"I am sure he will put men at our disposal," Frank Martin said. The tip of his cheroot glowed red and then slowly faded to black; he leaned forward and extinguished it in the ashtray.

At that moment, the palace footmen began to set the hot food on the six-foot-long table in the small courtyard and the steam from the dishes wafted inside, to where the little group was seated, reminding them that they were hungry. The immaculate silverware gleamed under the brightly lit *torchères* behind every chair, while in their light, dizzy moths fluttered like twirling leaves. Once the servants had left, another toast was offered for the safe arrival of their families to Kabul, to the satisfying clink of the crystal glasses.

They ate slowly, thoughtfully, as if fixing the taste of each spoonful in their minds. It was the taste of English food that the men had looked forward to for so long, reminding them of home and of their loved ones soon to join them.

"It's no secret that the Amir has been invited to visit the Queen at Windsor," Frank Martin said, "he has told all of us of his dilemma. Has any further decision been made?"

"Well," Lillias carefully set her knife and fork down and dabbed her mouth with the starched white napkin, " of course, he is unable to go in his present state of health but he is thinking of sending one of his sons."

"It not going to be difficult for him to decide who to send," Clemence said with a short laugh. He took a sip and set his glass down, "Does the Queen realize the Amir will not manage to travel that distance? "

"Queen Victoria suggested to the Amir that he send either Prince Habibullah or Nasrullah if he is unable to travel," Lillias replied. "Sir Durand told the Queen, regarding the demarcation of the boundary line between his people, that losing the vast Pashtun territory to India has deeply upset the Amir. She has been in full communication with Sir Durand through the Viceroy in India. I did ask the Amir if he would be willing to see the Queen in person," she added, "but we both know he's too frail to travel the long journey."

"I have an idea the Viceroy is not communicating with the Queen effectively," Martin commented bluntly. He stopped talking while the next course was being served and kept his voice low when the servants stepped out of the room. "Just to caution you, Doctor Hamilton, the Amir deploys all sorts of informants, and you never know if the footmen speak fluent English." He continued where he left off, "Indeed, I strongly doubt whether he would make it to Karachi, let alone Windsor. He would die before reaching Peshawar!"

"So, presumably, the Amir will ask Prince Habibullah to go in his place?" Mr. Clemence asked, glancing first at Frank Martin and then at Lillias.

Habibullah was the obvious choice to represent his father being the more mature of the two princes; his manners were considerably more stately and he was endued with a greater sense of reason and diplomacy than his younger brother. He was, undoubtedly, the best candidate to convince the Queen to accept his father's request for representation in the Court of St. James.

"Well," Dr. Hamilton replied, "Prince Habibullah is the oldest and the most obvious choice, so I am sure, the Amir would send him. In any case, this is a golden opportunity for one of his sons to take the long journey to Windsor, it will be a life-changing experience. Just imagine, an Afghan Prince seeing the wonders of the world for the first time—the Pyramids, the Sphinx, and the Suez Canal. And perhaps on his return trip, he might visit Paris and other European cities."

The two men continued eating. They were both silently considering the possible scandal either of the princes might cause in Victoria's court.

"Is there anything we can do to aid the Amir?" Clemence asked.

Frank Martin set his knife and fork neatly side by side on his plate, "There are many imponderables," he said dubiously. "The conflict of cultures . . ." he trailed off.

"No doubt we will be able to assist," Dr. Hamilton replied firmly, taking a sip of her water. "I can assure you, much can be done to prepare whoever goes, but it will require patience." She looked at the men thoughtfully, "Perhaps I should suggest to the Amir that you gentlemen could prepare a letter for Prince Habibullah to deliver on behalf of the Amir to Queen Victoria? You would be far more suited to the task than his secretary."

"A splendid idea, don't you think, Martin!" Thomas Clemence exclaimed.

The footman removed the empty plates and changed the top tablecloth before laying out dessert plates and teacups.

"I believe Habibullah would be easy to train in the etiquette of the court. We could all help prepare him for his meeting with the Queen and the royal household in Windsor!" Lillias added eagerly as she prepared to take a spoonful of the plum pudding.

"Train Habibullah in the etiquette of the Royal Court?" Frank asked, stupefied.

"Yes, of course. He's well-mannered but still needs a few things to be explained before he appears before the Queen."

"We all know the one who *really* needs training," Frank laughed, "Nasrullah! He's a long, long way from civilization!"

"We'll deal with that when the Amir decides who should go," Dr. Hamilton said politely.

"Doctor Hamilton," Clemence said as he lifted his chin, removed his napkin, and placed it on the table, "A fine meal, madam, thank you."

"Wonderful!" Frank Martin agreed, contemplating a second helping dessert.

"I recommend you ask Amir to send an escort for our family across the Khyber Pass before we propose anything regarding the prince's trip to London," Clemence said. "That would be our priority."

Lillias smiled, "I totally agree, Mr. Clemence, I'll make every effort to ask the Amir when I see fit. Because he is in pain, his mood has been somewhat erratic lately."

A few days later, when Dr. Lillias Hamilton climbed the marble staircase to the Amir's suite in the palace of Bostan-Sarai he was in noticeably better health. She found him sitting in his deck chair on the gleaming travertine marble terrace, a cup of tea in hand, listening to the chirping of the birds. He appeared to be deep in thought.

"*Salaam Alaikum!* Your Highness! You seem to be in better spirits today."

He smiled a greeting as she set her medical bag down on the table nearby: it was Lillias's pride and joy, highly polished brown leather monogrammed with her initials and status—L.H. MD.

The Amir noticed with approval her cream full-length dress with its high collar and lacy neckline; the bodice was of draped, filmy fabric over the sleek line of the frock. The foundational garment of the era was the whale-boned corset designed to sculpt even the slenderest of waistlines, such as Lillias's, into an even more perfect silhouette. She had twisted her long brown hair into a bun at the crown of her head and loosed some curls over her forehead.

"*Alaikum Asalaam!* Daktar Laila Jan." Setting the cup and the saucer down on the hand-carved table next to him, he nodded with a smile, "*Khosh amadee!* Welcome! May Allah be praised, for he knows both how to keep me well and how to take me from this earth." He raised both hands in a pious gesture of prayer. "*Parwardegar khodesh meyfama!* The Almighty himself knows."

As the interpreter translated, the Amir cupped his ear to better understand his chattering.

"Slow down," he said irritably, "you sound like an excited blue jay!"

Dr. Hamilton smiled as she checked his pulse and then tucked the glass thermometer under his armpit and read his temperature.

"May I ask a special favor of Your Highness?"

"Daktar Laila Jan," he lifted his full-bearded face to look at her directly, "As I have already said, you do not need to ask for permission.

Please ask me and I'll do my best for you," he smiled.

"Your Highness, I hope this is not too much to ask on behalf of myself, Mr. Clemence, and Mr. Martin. Several of our family members are coming to visit us from England."

"They are coming to visit you here?"

"Yes, Your Highness." She placed the monaural stethoscope on his gray, hairy chest, "Please take a deep breath." The Amir followed her instructions matter-of-factly as Lillias moved the stethoscope to different locations on his chest and back.

He smiled up at her, "that will brighten your eyes and mine as well. They are always welcome to Afghanistan."

"I'm grateful for Your Highness's kind words," she said. "Mr. Martin, Mr. Clemence, and I desire an armed escort for the party across the Khyber Pass to Kabul," she replied. "My younger sister is with the party, and their wives and a child."

She knelt on a cushion at his feet, folding her legs underneath her thighs and placing one foot at a time onto her lap began to massage the curing balm in a circular motion into his rough, cracked skin.

"Of course, it is not too much to ask! It will be my delight to do this with both my eyes," he said with the Afghan gesture of hands to his eyes that Lillias loved to emulate. "I am honored to help them. Please do not worry, Madam. I will instruct my men today."

"Concerning the visit to London," Lillias took a deep breath realizing this was as good a time as ever to raise the other thoughts they had had, "I understand Your Highness, that you plan to send one of your sons to visit Queen Victoria in your place?" He nodded and she continued boldly, "Mr. Clemence and Mr. Martin spoke to me over dinner when we met last week and thought we might help with the arrangements. I have a plan to present for your consideration if Your Highness would permit me to present our thoughts?" She had finished rubbing his feet and had begun to pack her instruments into her medical bag.

For a moment the Amir was speechless and Lillias turned hastily to see if she had angered him. His fingers touched his quivering lips, "I am deeply touched that my English friends should want to help. *Muhtarama* Daktar Laila Jan. Please sit down and explain."

As the doctor recounted the conversation, the Amir carefully pondered all the risks and benefits. In the end, he shook his head. "I cannot allow the Crown Prince to undertake this journey," he said, "Habibullah must remain here at my side. I had already decided to send Prince Nasrullah to present the letter to the Queen. I know my health is deteriorating and I could die at anytime. What you do not see, Daktar, is when I die, Prince Habibullah must immediately step into my place to eliminate any future quarrels amongst my bloodline. There are also many power-hungry men outside the circle of my family waiting to sabotage my government." For a moment, he was silent, and Lillias listened to his heavy breathing and waited, aware he was struggling with pain. "Dr. Laila," he continued at length, using the Afghan contraction of her name, "This is Afghanistan where brother kills brother, or a son, a father—over power." He picked up his cup with unsteady hands and took a sip of his tea.

"I understand, Your Highness, but with your permission, the men could help draw up the letter for Queen Victoria," she said, "they understand the official terminology. And all of us could be of help to Prince Nasrullah in preparing him to meet Queen Victoria. There are differences in culture and the procedures of the Royal Court, that he will need to be familiar with."

Amir Abdul Rahman took Lillias's hand and held it for a long moment. "The help of my British friends would be most gratefully received," he assured her.

Thomas Clemence dropped his head into his hands in a gesture of despair when Lillias gave them the news.

"He is a callow youth!" Frank Martin exclaimed forcefully, "And without much intelligence!"

Lillias Hamilton shook her head unhappily, "I know, but the Amir is as firm and unmoved as a mountain. He was adamant that his decision is final. Prince Nasrullah is to take the journey to England."

"Nasrullah is nothing short of an impetuous fool!" Clemence agreed, "I can almost see the headlines in the British papers already."

"The decision is disastrous!" Frank Martin retorted with an air of disgust, "How can this reckless, ill-mannered youth be expected to deal with such a sensitive matter? How could Nasrullah, of all people, convince Queen Victoria and British royal courtiers to change their position on Afghanistan? Is he likely to convince Britain to place the country's foreign policy into the hands of the Amir? He'll be ridiculed! The Amir will pay a huge price." Martin's rapid breathing clearly showed how angry he felt. "He's disobedient, obnoxious, and lacks manners! Nasrullah is patently unfit to face the Queen, why can't the Amir see that?"

"I agree with Martin," Clemence said. "The Amir should rethink his position and find someone with stature and dignity to represent him, Nasrullah is not a good choice. I've known him longer than any other Brit in Kabul," he went on, "and I've dealt with him casually for years. I have a strong feeling that he'll make a mess of things and damage his father's reputation. He's explosive, erratic, and uncontrollable. It's his nature and I'm not sure there is anything any of us can do to change that!"

"I understand why the Amir does not want to send Prince Habibullah, though," Lillias said diplomatically, "if anything did happen when he was away Habibullah would have to step in to maintain the peace."

"You may not be aware of this rebellious young man's habits," Martin said quietly.

Dr. Hamilton shot a questioning glance in his direction. Martin stood up and checked the doors to his courtyard before replying. "He looked apologetically at Lillias, "I do not want to upset your sensibilities," he said.

She smiled, "You forget, I am a doctor," she replied, "you can speak freely."

"Nasrullah urinates indecently," he measured his words carefully. "He sits anywhere in the palace courtyard to urinate and even does his business publicly. To dry the urine droplets, he uses a piece of dry clay to dab his penis and, worse, he holds the string of his baggy pants with one hand, the clay with the other and continues dabbing it for ten, or even fifteen minutes afterward, while holding a conversation! The other thing, of course, is his habit of nose-picking in presence of others," He shook his head wearily, "I could go on..."

"Yes, I've seen a few of those," Clemence said. "But be aware that some habits may fall under cultural behavior, or even Islamic rules and regulations. When religion is involved one must be extremely cautious. Trying to persuade a devoted Muslim to change anything to do with his Islamic beliefs could have disastrous consequences for us all."

"Specifically, regarding Nasullah?" the engineer asked.

"The crouching to urinate and dabbing his private parts with clay."

"So, it'll be acceptable for him to crouch under a bush at Windsor Palace and urinate, or in some London location, say, Hyde Park, in the presence of bystanders?" Frank asked with a sardonic smile. "I wish him luck with finding dried clay over there, by the way!" he added with a grin.

"Of course not! But how do we make him understand this is unacceptable for a prince of his stature in a foreign culture. I know for fact he was raised to be a devout Muslim; he still prays five times a day," Clemence replied, running his fingers through his hair. He uncrossed his legs and leaned forward in his chair, "I'm sure you have seen him in and out of the Royal Mosque."

Nasrullah was taught the Qur'an from early childhood and knew all the *Hadiths* by heart. As a devoted follower of Islamic law, he was obligated to purify his garments and wear clean clothes before praying. Muslims believe urine and other bodily emissions are filth and God loves those who purify themselves. A devout Muslim was taught not to urinate into water that was not flowing. Squatting when urinating was said to provide more modesty for a man than standing and also avoided any droplets defiling his garments; for which reason, of course, a piece of dry clay provided the necessary blotting. It was said that those who failed to take the steps to cleanse themselves would be punished in their graves. Habibullah, on the other hand, practiced the same Muslim regulations but learned to do them privately.

Dr. Hamilton, who had remained silent during this delicate conversation, looked across at Martin and Clemence. "As you both know, I also was hoping for Prince Habibullah to make the journey," she said sadly. "He is the diplomat, but I understand the Amir's reasons and I would never attempt to go against his wishes. So, it is Nasrullah who is to take the journey, and for his father's sake we must make the best of it." She pursed her lips, "given all you have said about Nasrullah, we have a lot of difficult work ahead of us to train him in etiquette acceptable to the court at Windsor."

"Well, my esteemed friend, Doctor Lillias, I hope he'll cooperate and not rebel or think we are attempting to Christianize him," Frank Martin said.

"I am certain we will need the Amir's help to keep him in line," Thomas Clemence replied.

CHAPTER SIX

❦❧❦❧❦

September 1894 -- Afghan calendar month:
Mizan 1273

Windsor, England

The letter of invitation requesting Prince Nasrullah's appearance at Windsor Palace was sent via the British Viceroy in India and ultimately to Windsor Palace. Queen Victoria was aging and forced to give up reading and writing, and she had become increasingly reliant on her youngest daughter, Princess Beatrice, to read her the political dispatches. Victoria had always keenly read through, commented on, and carefully monitored what was going on in the world—especially in the widespread colonies. The Queen's response to Amir Abdul Rahman, however, seemed to be taking forever.

A Windsor royal courtier was quoted as saying, "We may write a long, precise list of things, but they are often not read to Her Majesty as Beatrice is in a hurry to develop a photograph or to paint a flower."

Finally, Princess Beatrice made the effort to read Queen Victoria the request for the invitation of 'Shahzadah Nasrullah Khan of Afghanistan'.

The Queen was feeling a bit tired and debilitated, "Abdul Rahman is like a train; nothing will turn him once he gets going. He is quite stubborn and persistent! Now," she said, clearing her quavering voice, "Beatrice dear, dispatch a reply to Abdul Rahman. Tell him to send his son and Her Majesty will hear his request on behalf of the Emir."

The conversation thus ended, Queen Victoria struggled from her chair, fumbled as she sought to grasp her thick ebony walking cane, and limped slowly across the room. She struck a weary, and somewhat hopeless figure as she was caught in the sunlight that streamed in from a colossal arched window. Dressed in perpetual mourning black, with a black lace cap and ermine stole around her neck, she stopped, as always, to gaze through one of the multiple square windowpanes at the mausoleum of her beloved late consort, Prince Albert. A flock of birds drew her attention to the serenity of the verdant sweep of the palace lawns. Everything reminded her of Prince Albert. Flashes of the past drifted through her thoughts like bright threads in the design of a huge tapestry—the moment she first met him, their engagement, the marriage ceremony in St. James's palace, the hard days of her reign, the glamorous public appearances, and finally, his death that still grieved her profoundly.

After months of frustration, Nasrullah finally received his formal invitation from Windsor: "Your Highness Shahzadah Nasrullah Khan, Queen Victoria will receive you in Windsor in mid-May 1895," the letter stated.

On this pleasant September afternoon as the Friday prayers ended, Shahzadah Nasrullah stood on the marble stairs of the royal mosque. A thin youth of medium height, with sharp aquiline features, the prince wore his happiness like an advertisement and chirped with all the vigor of a bird in spring. Soon he would become the longest traveled Afghan and the first to visit England. This euphoria fueled his desire to see Queen Victoria and a fervent aspiration to relinquish Afghanistan from the talons of the British. In a spiritually inspired moment, Nasrullah lifted his hands to the heavens and demanded a prayer from his courtiers for his success and safe return.

"Our beloved Shahzadah!" Amir's chief of staff, *Naieb-Salar* Mohammad Hassein Khan, bellowed reverently raising his hands towards the sky and displaying the chain of onyx worry beads wrapped twice around his left wrist. "You are our pride and joy, the first Afghan ever to travel to Landan and the very first to meet the *Malika-e-Englistan wa Hindustan*. Queen of England and India." He stepped forward and gave the prince a congratulatory handshake.

Another courtier, cousin to Nasrullah, *Qomandan-e-Ala* Akram Khan yelled out above the noise of the crowd, "May Allah protect you!" He pushed his bottle-thick glasses up the bridge of his nose, "and may your trip be of *Khair* and your return be of *Khair*."

"Your Highness!" Amir's executioner, the cross-eyed, Parwana Khan, shouted—a man as obscene as cancer. "You will be the one to free us from British hands. You will be the one to secure our independence! May Allah grant you success. Your success is our success."

The voyage was still many months away, but there was huge jubilation among the Afghans of Kabul. It was almost as though Nasrullah was Christopher Columbus preparing to set off on a voyage across the oceans to discover the New World. The whole of Kabul was lit up with joy. In local mosques, bazaars, and private homes, happiness fell on Afghans like a shower of rain out of the sky. In a meadow near the palace, a circular formation of about a hundred Pashtun men brandishing red scarves in the air, synchronously performed the spin dance of *Atan* to the deafening beating of the drums, their oily raven hair flung from side to side with every toss of their heads. Verses of Qur'an were recited in mosques around the country and pious Afghans raised their hands in prayer asking the Almighty for Nasrullah's safe journey and well-being.

With his trimmed mustache and close-cropped beard, Prince Nasrullah appeared calm and controlled as he shook hands with his courtiers and assured them of his intention to convince the Queen to accept his father's request. He talked on and on as if rehearsing for a speech: indeed, this was the essence of the address he intended to deliver in presence of Queen Victoria and the British Royal courtiers at Windsor Palace.

Nasrullah had still to face the imperial rulers, the staunch guardians of British colonial wealth, whose hawkish eyes were focused on maintaining the continuous glorification of Great Britain by draining its colonies of wealth and resources as they had in India for more than two hundred years. Handing over Afghanistan's foreign policy to Afghanistan would be a crack in British policy that could widen further and consequently lose Queen Victoria's crown jewel, India the epicenter of Great Britain's military might and world domination. Those in Windsor would be only too delighted to make a case shunning Amir Abdul Rahman's request and send his young boy back empty-handed to his father in Kabul.

"If the Prince wore a full English uniform he would easily pass as an Englishman," Doctor Hamilton asserted, despite the fact that the prince, although handsome, was of dark complexion. Dr. Hamilton had already done her utmost to instill in Nasrullah a sense that he would be treated as one of Britain's own if only he looked and behaved like an Englishman.

"Poor Doctor Lillias can only do so much," Clemence said, "But a smattering of training and dressing him up for the part doesn't give him the depth of character required for the job."

"I'm very happy for you taking the trip to see *Malika-e-Englistaan*." Crown Prince Habibullah stuttered slightly over his words as he held his brother at arm's length and beamed, "We will be very worried about you every step of the way while you are on your journey to *Englistan*. I'm very happy for you that our *Pa-pa-padar*, father, chose you to see *Malika-e-Englistan* in my place. But as a brother, I have a *nasyat*, advice, for you."

Crown Prince Habibullah was the first in line to assume power in the event of his father's death, a fact that left Nasrullah little choice but to hide his insecurities and jealousies from everyone around him. So far, Nasrullah's hidden animosities against his brother had gone unnoticed by the courtiers and, to some extent, even to his father. But although neither Habibullah nor Nasrullah had the gall to make it obvious to the Amir, he was well aware of the intricacies and frictions in royal households between brothers close in age.

"And what'd that be?" Nasrullah asked, resentful that any advice might be necessary.

"I ask you to r-r-remember," he stammered, "this is an official trip and every Afghan has his ears and eyes on you, so It is your duty to do all you can to convince *Malika* Weektorya to grant us our freedom— an independent Afghanistan."

"And, what makes you think I can't do it?" Nasrullah replied argumentatively.

Habibullah glanced around at the ring of courtiers who were listening in to their conversation.

"Brother, let us move away from the crowd to discuss this," he glanced meaningfully at Nasrullah and indicated with an almost imperceptible movement of his head at the men clustered around them. Nasrullah sullenly followed Habibullah down the steps to the gardens.

"I'm not preaching to you, brother," Habibullah said, once he was certain they were out of earshot, "but because I know you well, your un-un-undivided dedication to the task is vital in *Englistan*. Do not deviate or get consumed by your own pleasures and amusements."

"Why don't you worry about keeping the throne secure here?" Nasrullah interjected. "Our father is frail and old, focus on your role instead of preaching to me how to deal with *Malika Weektorya*." An angry frown creased his forehead.

Prince Habibullah stopped and turned his broad shoulders towards his brother. "You and I are no longer juveniles, but men with responsibilities, two adult men who are needed to help our nation!" He smiled to soften his words and set his hand on Nasrullah's shoulder, "Brother! I love you! And we all know you'll make us proud."

"Let me give you my thoughts," Nasrullah cleared his throat and straightened his Astrakhan karakul hat. "Since the very first moment when *Padar* chose me to take the journey to *Englistan*, I've committed myself fully to ensuring I do not come home empty-handed. I will do whatever it takes to convince that woman in *Qasr-e*-Weenzor, Windsor Palace, to accept our father's demand!" He shrugged, "After all, she's a woman. Am I so naive that I am unable to convince a woman? It would bring shame on us all if I come back without an agreement in our favor." Nasrullah smirked, fully confident of the simplicity of the task. "You worry too much, I'll do my best, Habibullah!" he said airily.

Habibullah took a deep breath of frustration. Sometimes, his manners, while pleasant, could be patronizing but his wisdom and understanding far exceeded that of his younger brother. He was smaller in stature than his father and his physique showed an inclination towards stoutness; apart from a sallower complexion than the Amir, he bore a marked facial resemblance that was emphasized by the trim of his beard and mustache. In conversation, his face would often light up with an engaging smile. The almost imperceptible speech impediment had come about after an attempt on his life when, as a child, someone had tried to poison him.

"What you don't understand," Habibullah said, anxious to persuade his brother of the gravity of the mission, "Not all women are weak and can be subdued. The *Malika-e-Englistan* has a reputation for being uncompromising. She will not be afraid of you."

"What do you know, Habibullah? You have never been there! You don't know what you are talking about!" Nasrullah replied irritably, "I will make *Malika* Weektorya give freedom to Afghanistan. You will see, it will be easy."

The brothers had started to stroll back towards the mosque, but the tension between them was stretched close to breaking point.

"Just mark my words," Prince Habibullah replied, "you are de-de-delusional, for the sake of father and our nation, you must listen to what I am saying!"

But it was obvious that the conversation was closed. Habibullah shrugged in frustration and the two young men wended their way back to where the jubilant courtiers were still celebrating Nasrullah's expected victory.

CHAPTER SEVEN

❦

For over a week now Kabul's teahouses and eateries had been filled with clansmen from every corner of the country. They had journeyed their way on the backs of donkeys or camels, in carriages, or simply peregrinating, for the semi-annual *Darbar* summoned by the Amir.

In the old days, during the reigns of Amir's predecessors, in a *Jirgah*, a gathering of elders, any clansman had a say or plea for his case. The sovereign then would issue a final decree pending a hearing. But, as an absolute ruler who imposed a culture of fear, this Amir heard them attentively but declined to be challenged or questioned by the elders. The consequence of doing so was often death.

On this day, the massive *Darbar* was in session in the Delkusha's Darbar Hall. At the invitation of the Amir, they had gathered to be more deeply informed of the reason for Prince Nasrullah's visit to the Queen of England and were invited to express their painful moments spent fighting the British in the past two bloody wars. The deep wounds of the melees were still felt like hot knives in the cores of their bones.

The noise level in the black and white checkered marble hall where over five hundred clansmen sat crossed-legged in row after row, was deafening. Those who were acquainted with each other chatted ebulliently and ceaselessly—mostly greetings, hugs, and pious praise of loved ones and families.

The noise ceased suddenly as two turbaned guards opened the double mahogany doors and, like a congregation in silent prayer, they waited for the Amir's entrance. Dr. Hamilton pushed the wheelchair up the ramp to the dais while Princes Habibullah and Nasrullah followed close behind. For the first time, their father's symbolic seat of power at center stage remained empty. As a gesture of respect, the elders rose to their feet, bowed, and, as they chanted their Salaams to the sovereign in unison, each stood with his hand to his heart.

"All, sit down!" the Amir said with a broad gesture of his hand and he nodded to the Mullah of the court to open the meeting.

The mullah took the podium and recited melodically, "*Bismillah ir-Rahaman ir-Rahim*, in the name of God, most Gracious, most Compassionate," and went on to read a few verses from the Qu'ran. The gathered assembly solemnly cupped their hands in prayer to the Almighty, and then, one by one, with a self-conscious stroke of their beard, they dropped them into their laps.

The Amir broke the ensuing silence in the hall. "You have come here from as far as the Wakhan and Arghandab valleys and even from the remotest villages and towns whose names most have never heard," he fidgeted under the relentless pain in his legs which was becoming harder to bear despite the deep tissue massage two hours before. "And some of you live a stones-throw away from this Palace," his voice still held a memory of the far younger man they had followed so ardently. "I'm grateful that you joined me in this important milestone of our nation in this freezing month of *Dalwa*," he paused. "I understand there are those who could not cross the towering snow-covered mountains to be here today, but I am confident my words will reach them from this *Darbar* hall." He moved his cane to his other side. "After the *Darbar*, we will feast in the name of Allah, *Insha Allah!* Please join me with a hearty appetite." Those men who knew him well would have noticed the pauses between the Amir's words and the weakening of his once-powerful voice, but only the most discerning would have read the pain in his eyes. Lately, Dr. Hamilton had noticed with alarm, the escalation of his moodiness, anger, frustration, and bitterness. She fervently hoped that no one in the gathering would say anything to enrage him and cause the man to disappear with a nod. The Amir had taken to using a secret code to beckon his special guards to walk someone out and execute them with no due process. Some elders, fearful of his mercurial temperament, would not attend, using road closures due to heavy snow as their cover for not showing up. But those from areas of milder weather had no choice but to join the *Darbar*. Even the thought that their absence may be a cause for suspicion was frightening—so whether one was present or absent, the danger to life and limb was very real and the tension in the *Darbar* Hall clutched at their hearts as though a tiger was about to spring and tear them apart.

The British called him "A man of steel ruling a people of steel," which was how they ensured the fortification of their colonial empire against Russian invasion.

"Let me be clear," the Amir stated, his deep voice so quiet that some in the audience struggled to hear him. "I've given you the chance to bid farewell and give your blessings to my son," he gestured towards Nasrullah who stood to his feet obediently and bowed. "Shahzadah Nasrullah Khan is the first in our nation's history to take the long voyage to *Englistan* and meet with *Malika* Weektorya." He raised his hands in supplication, "Let us pray for his safe return." Hands swayed above their heads like a wheatfield in a breeze and everyone replied solemnly and in unison, "Ameen".

"He will be my representative to meet the most powerful leader of the world," he cleared his voice. "Afghan-*ha* and *Englees-Ha* have been shedding each other's blood for years. For what? For what? For nothing! For no gain!" The Amir's voice weakened noticeably, "Only to lose lives and bring devastation on both sides."

Some seated towards the back of the hall craned to catch his words but no one dared ask him to speak more loudly. "At any moment, the Almighty," and again he raised his hands heavenward, "has the absolute power to end my life. His Gracious, *Al-Kabeer*, has

the ultimate discretion whatever he wishes to do with me or you."
He gestured again, briefly, towards Nasrullah, "However, with the
Englees-Ha, I will push for peace and solid friendship between them
and us." However weak in body, the Amir's countenance was lion-
like as he slowly scanned the audience from one side to another with
narrowed eyes. He ruled them according to his own will and caprice
deliberately instilling the fear he injected into their hearts, which was
intended to depress their spirits and extinguish even the least sense of
ambition in their lives. Indeed, his policy approved the vampires of
liberty in overlooking human values and dignity. In the eyes of his
subjects, he was the type of despot who, when wishing to harvest fruit,
cuts down the tree: with another decade of his rule still to come, many
people were still destined to be cut down.

"The mistakes the *Englees-Ha* made in Maiwand are obvious
and the harm they caused my grandfather, Amir Dost Mohammad
Khan, may peace be upon him. To suit their own ends, they had him
jailed and replaced him with their servant, the most incompetent idiot,
Shah-Shuja, who couldn't even write his name or add two and two."
He called for water from his Chamberlain who stood at his side, the
only man responsible for testing his food and drink, and he handed
him his cup.

"They condemned my grandfather because he didn't accept their
demands and replaced him immediately with that a*hmaq*, idiot,
Shah-Shuja." Perspiration trickled down his face with the effort of
speaking; he sipped his water and continued. "They stole the Koh-i-
Noor diamond from Amir Dost Mohammad Khan that he inherited
from his grandfather Ahmad Shah Abdali and now that huge diamond
graces *Malika* Weektorya's crown." The Amir was suddenly racked
with a spasm of coughing; after a long pause, he wiped his face and
continued, "Then, when they could not keep Shah-Shuja in power for
more than a few years they finally had him assassinated." At a signal,
his pageboy raised his foot on the embroidered pillow and massaged it

gently. "Everything I told you about the *Englees-Ha* and Shah-Shuja pains me profoundly," his voice was hoarse and only those in the front rows heard him clearly, "the pain in my heart runs far deeper than many of you realize. Those of you who represent the Southern areas, mainly the Maiwand district, who lost limbs, loved ones, homes, and land... I know you deeply despise the *Englees-Ha* for what they have done to you, but the past is past—It is time for us to move forward and dispense with hatred, which is exactly what the Almighty wants from us. It is time to forget."

1894 - Afghan calendar month: 1273
Windsor, England

The brightly lit parlor in Windsor Castle reverberated to the sound of Princess Beatrice accompanying herself on the piano, and rapturously vocalizing *Lieder Ohne Worte*. Her long, delicate fingers flew over the shiny surface of the creamy-white and raven-black keys, to the extent of almost magically becoming blurred. Queen Victoria and another of her daughters, Princess Louise, were swept away by the music which brought memories of Prince Consort, Albert, when he sang and taught their youngest daughter to play the *Lieder*. As the thirty-eight-year-old Princess ceased the performance, the strings inside the Steinway piano resonated like the pounding of a giant heart.

"Baby," the Queen's pet name for her youngest, "marvelously done, my child," she said as she clapped approvingly, "I so wish your father had lived longer to hear you playing."

"Very well done, Betty," Princess Louisa agreed, applauding soundlessly in her elbow-length gloves.

Beatrice rose to her feet she curtsied, "Thank you, Mama and

Louisa, I am sure Father looks down on me when I play. It makes me feel quite close to him."

"I recall him saying, 'Baby is practicing her scales like a good prima donna.'" the Queen smiled.

Beatrice's loyalty to her close friends was unwavering and everyone enjoyed her keen sense of humor. The youngest princess had large blue eyes, a pretty little mouth, a fine complexion, and bewitching blond hair. As her mother's constant companion and entrusted secretary, Princess Beatrice performed duties such as writing on Queen's behalf and helping with domestic and foreign political correspondence, and the Queen regularly consulted with her on matters regarding Britain and the empire.

"Baby, do you have any updates that you should bring to my attention?" the Queen asked gently stroking her Pekingese, Looty, who was curled up on her lap. Her greyhound, Nero, lay contentedly at her feet.

"Yes, Mama," Beatrice said as she sat down beside her, "That young Afghan Prince will soon be on his way to meet with you."

"Prince Nosroollah? "

"Yes."

"May heaven help us!" the Queen replied and sighed deeply, "I have never, in all my life, had to receive the child of a potentate!" She adjusted her white headscarf and shook her head wearily, "I presume amusements of some sort must be arranged for him. Perhaps a circus or a ball? she paused. "I have no idea what manner of conversation can be carried out with such an inexperienced young man. I certainly don't want his father in a fury thinking his son was not well-received while in England."

"Mama, perhaps he could join us for rides in the mornings?" the forty-seven-year-old Princess Louise suggested.

"I don't think a woman accompanying a man on a ride would be considered appropriate in their culture," the Queen replied.

"He could ride with my husband, John, and me. I don't see any problem with that, Mama."

"Still, it won't be enough to fill his daily schedule," the Queen said thoughtfully "How about Munshi to amuse him?"

"That's a thought," Princess Louisa replied. "And what about Bertie? I'm sure he would happily show him around London."

"And Mama," Princess Beatrice added, "we all know how you grieved for our fallen soldiers at the Battle of Maiwand in Afghanistan." She tucked a loose tendril of her blond hair behind her ear as she spoke and her diamond earring sparkled as it caught the light from the flickering gasolier. "I recall how Bertie often consoled you when you shed tears over the fallen soldiers. Do you think Prince Nosroollah and his accompanying friends would be interested in seeing the battle from the point of view of our British soldiers?"

"What do you think, Mama?" Louisa asked enthusiastically. " I would say that that is a grand idea of Betty's." She turned to Beatrice, "A tour of the British museum could be arranged for them."

"That is thoughtful, Baby," Queen Victoria, agreed and patted her daughter's shoulder. "I will ensure Munshi shows them the statute of Bobbie as well." She tucked Looty under her arm and, with the help of Princess Beatrice, got slowly to her feet. "Indeed, they should be told that I awarded a medal of bravery to Bobbie." She lightly kissed the cheeks of her daughters and they curtsied as she left on her nightly indoor walk before bed.

Almost fifteen years before, the British had attempted to annex Southern Afghanistan. Intelligence was dispatched that Afghan forces were closing in towards Maiwand Pass, about six miles from the British garrison in Qandahar. The following morning a British brigade decided to move forward and break up the Afghan advance. But they were unaware that the Afghans numbered twenty-five thousand men including Afghan regular troops, and five batteries of artillery, including some very modern Armstrong guns. From a distance, the Afghans noticed a swirling cloud of dust as a mixture of crimson and drab brown battle-uniformed men marched towards them.

"*Amada bash ke Englees-Ha amadand*, get ready the British are coming!" one of the Afghan officers yelled—and the message was passed down the ranks.

In the first phase of the battle, the Afghan guns were brought into action forcing the British to take cover from the relentless bombardment. Following the artillery exchange, the Afghan infantry massed in front of the British line for an assault. In a preemptive move, the British ordered an attack. Under the blazing mid-day sun, the hand-to-hand battle continued for hours as the dead fell around the living. Lances were thrust into bodies and blood spurted in streams. Under the crack of muskets and the vicious rattle of machine guns, heads exploded in a splatter of blood and bone. That Tuesday morning, 6th *Asad*, 1259, witnessed carnage never before seen in the history of Anglo-Afghan wars, as thousands of jaws broke, eyes were blinded, cheekbones shattered, noses were reduced to holes, and limbs were severed. Despite the high number of Afghans, their infantrymen began to lose the will to fight. It was a young woman's ear-piercing scream that jarred them into action once more.

"Young love! If you do not fall in the battle of Maiwand, by God, someone will save you as a symbol of shame!"

Malalai was in her late teens, and that day was said to have been their wedding day, instead, she was in the thick of the battle supporting her fiancé, whose morale had been broken by the carnage around him, He was ready to give up. Like many Afghan women, Malalai was there to help tend the wounded and provide water and spare weapons, but Malalai became the Afghan equivalent of Jeanne

D'Arc, or Molly Pitcher, who fought their enemies side by side with their fellow warriors, exhorting the one she loved and to all who would listen, to push on to victory.

It was said she picked up the Afghan flag and waved it above her head repeating her call over and over again. At last, the flag fell from her hands as a bullet pierced her chest. Ultimately, her call was a sheer inspiration to the Afghan forces and pushed them on to win the war. The British suffered excessive casualties. In that late afternoon, after the guns ceased firing, a mass of tribesman surrounded and then charged the British infantry line. The Afghans cut down numbers of them who were too exhausted and demoralized to resist. Out of some two-thousand-five-hundred British soldiers, about one thousand were killed and another two-hundred wounded. Afghan losses were between two, to two-and-a-half thousand, with one-thousand-five-hundred wounded. Deaths and injuries were suffered by every village in the Maiwand district.

One British soldier wrote: "'To tell you the God's truth, I stood almost petrified. As far as you could see on either flank, the enemy was as thick as bees in a hive. They were in horseshoe formation and, from one end to the other, reached at the very least, two-and-a-half miles and we were right in the center of them. If there was one man, there was thousands. When I seen them all I said, 'My God how is this handful of men going to scatter the horde?'".

In a messy retreat, many dehydrated British soldiers were left to die in the unforgiving Afghan desert. The survivors, under debilitating conditions, reached the cantonment in Qandahar. A diary of one soldier stated: "I never saw such a sight in my life—too awful to describe."

What he could not bring himself to write was the hideous sight of legs, arms, heads, and bodies lying scattered in all directions as far as the eye could see. After the British retreat, approximately one hundred men made a last stand, knowing they would eventually be stormed by the Afghans. They were cut down until there were just eleven men were left—two officers and nine infantrymen. After exhausting their ammunition, they charged the enemy with their bayonets. None made it. The Scottish poet William McGonagall recorded them as 'The Last Berkshire Eleven'. Their valor even impressed the Afghans, as one Afghan officer wrote: "These men charged . . . and died with their faces to the enemy, fighting to the death".

Among the survivors was a wounded dog. The 66th Berkshire had a mascot mongrel called Bobbie, who had traveled from England with the regiment and was in the thick of the battle, barking fearlessly at the foe throughout the hand-to-hand fighting. After the battle, Bobbie was nowhere to be seen and presumed dead. But a few days later a bloodied Bobbie, suffering from a bullet wound in the back, was spotted limping towards the Qandahar fort and rescued.

Some months later, when what was left of the regiment returned to England, Bobbie was taken to see Queen Victoria on the Isle of Wight where Victoria, personally, hung the Afghanistan medal around the little dog's neck.

Sadly, a year later, Bobbie was killed after being run over by a horse-drawn carriage near Portsmouth. Queen Victoria shed tears upon hearing the news: how ironic that a dog, which had survived one of the most ferocious battles ever, should succumb to a simple street accident back home. Bobbie was not forgotten. The dog's fame was such that he now sits proudly in a military museum in Salisbury, along with the medal. Bobbie is also featured in the Animals at War memorial in London's Hyde Park.

CHAPTER EIGHT

❧❧❧

Afghans are attuned to the late autumn conditions when winter can blow in under the cover of darkness. The cool September breeze from the nearby valleys stealthily kills the summer with its softest kiss as the golden-hued willow and birch leaves dance down from the trees and cover the ground with the vivid colors of an Afghan rug. It is the last call to sit in the warmth of the fall sunshine and consume the fire-red watermelons and sweet golden grapes as the tumbling leaves sing the autumn song.

On this mild sunny day, the Amir and his English friends gathered on the marble terrace of the Bostan-Sarai Palace, a fine architectural marvel in the Arg's premises with its Ottoman and Moorish globular domes, to discuss plans for the long journey of Shahzadah Nasrullah. A huge tray of watermelon sweet as honey was set on the table. The weather in Kabul had cooled off and the flies had diminished, but now the palace pageboys, holding large hand *punkas*, shoo the persistent yellow-jacketed bees away from the sugary fruits. Their incessant drone can be heard in the surrounding trees and shrubs, as they gather the last nectar before the beginning of the harsh Afghan winter.

The relaxed appearance of the Amir and his doctor's contented smile has lifted the atmosphere in the palace. There is a sense of expectation as if they are steering towards the sun and casting the shadow of their burden behind them.

"Finally, the letter of invitation arrived from *Qasr-e-*Weenzor," the Amir declared, as a smile spreads across his round, bearded face.

"Congratulations Your Highness, now we can really begin to plan and prepare for Prince Nasrullah's journey," Lillias said.

"Dr. Laila Jan! I hope you will consider accompanying Nasrullah to *Englistan*?" he asked earnestly, placing a hand over his heart.

"It would be my pleasure to make the journey with His Highness the Prince," she replied, her eyes widening, "but Your Highness," she turned to face him directly, narrowing her blue eyes, "in my absence, who will replace me? Your health is crucial and constant monitoring is needed." She touched her high collar nervously.

"Doctor Laila, I will be fine as long as the attending nurses are well trained and know what to do." As was his habit, he gestured devoutly heavenward, "I will be in Allah's hands. Upon your return, I want you to celebrate the outcome of this mission to *Englistan*."

The letter of introduction and recommendation to Queen Victoria had already been prepared by Doctor Hamilton, Frank Martin, and Thomas Clemence, on behalf of the Amir, and was ready to be handed ceremoniously by Shahzadah Nasrullah to Her Majesty. It made bold mention of the Amir's request and Frank Martin was reading it aloud to the Amir when Habibullah and Nasrullah mounted the marble staircase to join them.

"I am certain the letter to the Queen is beautifully written," Shahzadah Nasrullah interrupted.

"Your Highness, I think you should rehearse it as well, in preparation for Windsor," Martin said judiciously.

Mr. Clemence nodded and gave the prince a wide smile, "Your Highness," he said in his Welsh lilt, "It will greatly benefit you to know more about the Queen. She has been on the throne for over five decades now and she is aging and not as cheerful as before. However, her Majesty is experienced and has the best advisers in her court to guide her."

"Do not trouble yourself, I will be ready for her. We Afghans know how to deal with women of all ages," Nasrullah replied condescendingly.

"Nasrullah, *Bechem*! Son!" the Amir reprimanded sharply. "There is a lot for us to discuss before you leave! You are being sent as my ambassador, as a diplomat, these things cannot be done the hard way by being non-compliant and disrespectful. Have you heard of a saying a stiff neck is easily severed but a flexible neck is not? The way to succeed with this mission is to be humble and respectful to a woman whose power is unparalleled in the world. Let us peacefully work with her and not pressure the lioness until she pounces and devours us."

During the past fifty-five years of her reign, Victoria had made few mistakes. But, to avoid the same errors she chose, as her advisers, the wisest, most learned, most capable, and best-equipped statesmen in the realm.

However, Martin and Clemence's greatest fear was that the young Prince and his entourage would be played like musical instruments in Windsor. Whatever the outcome may be, the two Englishmen, for the sake of their continued employment under the Amir, never openly expressed their concerns, choosing rather to assist the Amir as best they could in preparation for the journey.

"I'm hoping Queen Victoria does not receive m-m-my brother," Habibullah stammered, "the same way she received the Iranian Shah Nasser-ed-Deen who was invited to Landan about twenty years ago." He paused as the footman stepped forward to light the gasolier. "I heard people in Landan were shocked at his behavior and Her M-M-Majesty reluctantly traveled from her favorite Escotland castle to see him in Landan. He was given residence in Bokingum Palace which he and his entourage soiled and caused damages."

Britain had announced war on Iran when the Shah Nasser-ed-Deen ordered the invasion of Afghanistan but, as a consequence, the Shah called off his over-ambitious objective and submitted to British demand. To contain Iran, Great Britain proposed a mission to forge a territorial alliance with the handsome Shah against Czarist Russia—

indeed a policy of killing two birds with one stone. Much to Queen Victoria's chagrin, Britain endorsed the Shah as a member of the Order of the Garter, after which, in eighteen-seventy-three, he was invited to London. Stories in the London tabloids surfaced, reflecting the Iranians as worse than barbarians. The Shah spent a few days before his official visit, in France exploring, among other things, the Paris brothels, before being pressured to leave the houses of ill-repute for London where he was accommodated in Buckingham Palace. Queen Victoria allocated a substantial budget to redecorate and cleanse the Palace when the Shah left. The most troubling gossip at the time was related to Iranian servants who had reportedly infuriated the Shah. It was rumored that they were asphyxiated and buried in the grounds behind Buckingham Palace.

Frank Martin and Mr. Clemence nervously recalled the Shah's breaches of British protocol and etiquette, particularly during a concert in Albert Hall, when he had slung his arm over the exposed shoulders of the Princess of Wales and her sister the Grand Duchess Marie of Russia and tried to feed them bonbons.

In another bizarre episode, while taking part in a house party as a guest of the Duke of Sutherland, the Shah is said to have told the Prince of Wales, that the Duke was 'too grand of a subject' and declared, 'You will have to have his head off when you come to the throne.'

For a short time in the early eighteenth century, the renowned Koh-i-Noor diamond had been in the possession of Iranians, and the Shah desired that it should be returned to his home country. His eyes had widened in shock when he saw the Queen wearing it as a brooch.

"So, Nasrullah should be treated like *Naser al-Din Shah Qajar*?" the Amir gazed at Prince Habibullah in annoyance. "That filth disgusted the royal family of *Englistan*, why are you comparing Nasrullah to him?"

"If that filth stayed in Qasr-e-Bokingum, why can't he?" Habibullah raised his hands and dropped them against his thighs.

"We will see what the *Englees-Ha* offer before you assume it should be in Qasr-e-Bokingum Palace."

"That Shah was a *maskhara,* a clown! Who was he to assume the Koh-i-Noor was his? It belongs to us, the Afghans!" Nasrullah interjected loudly, as the main subject of his voyage to Windsor steered another more interesting course.

Dr. Hamilton looked at the Amir, "Your Highness, with your permission can we move forward with the planning of Prince Nasrullah's trip to England?" she interjected cordially.

"*Khwahesh mekunam,* I request you do that certainly, Daktar Laila Jan. Sorry we went off at a tangent."

"Thank you, Your Highness, I believe Mr. Martin wanted to say something."

"Your Highness," Martin looked directly at the Amir, "we all know that you are an asset to Britain, India can only survive if Afghanistan remains as a bastion against Russia."

"Yes, certainly," Mr. Clemence agreed, shifting himself into a more comfortable position on his seat. "His Highness is preventing the expansionist grizzlies in the north from invading India."

"It's flattering to hear you both," the Amir said. "First and foremost, I must protect the interests of my homeland before the interests of *Malika Weektorya.*" He wheezed with the effort of speaking, "Of course, her subsidies play a crucial role in keeping my subjects under my control. So long as I have authority over my dominion, no one dares invade my homeland. Outside enemies can only enter and disturb my realm - if and only if," he raised his forefinger and wiggled it lazily back and forth, "my subjects are divided and rebellious against me. I consider this my first goal, to rule my subjects with an iron fist to prevent Afghanistan from fracturing into fiefdoms, chieftains, and if miniature monarchs rule in every corner." He raised his hands as if seeking unction from Allah himself, "I am under the shadow of the

Almighty," he declared, pointing to the heavens with his forefinger, "who directs me to keep my house in order."

They sipped tea and discussed various ideas for Nasrullah's journey until dinner was announced. The Court Chamberlain ushered everyone to the dining hall and requested they take their seats. Cushions were arranged on a richly colored carpet around which, on the large white cloth *or distarkhwan*, were a steaming assortment of Afghan dishes; goulashes, assorted rice dishes, and kabobs, and the tantalizing smell of assorted spices wafted like incense in the air. The suspended candeliers, lit up like birthday cakes, swayed in the wake of the party as they took their seats, casting light back and forth over the steaming delicacies.

Pain prevented the Amir from joining his guests on the floor, instead, he was served at a table strategically placed to enable him to participate in the conversation. A pageboy pulled the winged chair away from the table to allow him to be seated. With the help of his cane, the Amir walked unsteadily to the chair and grimaced with the effort of elevating his legs onto the embroidered pillow.

Casting his gaze over the feast laid out on the *distarkhwan* the Amir sighed, he was fully aware that such wonderfully rich dishes would cause him great suffering for many hours ahead and, ultimately, such food could cost him his life.

Footmen and page boys were in attendance and, with them, both the head chef and two lower-ranked chefs, each holding his plate and spoon, approached as if to dine with the rest. The Chamberlain ordered the three to eat and they obligingly did so as everyone watched. Each man took a spoonful of every dish onto his plate.

"The Amir doesn't joke," Martin whispered, "he holds his top chefs responsible for any poisoning of the food."

"When I first experienced this three years ago, I was as worried as a pregnant fox in a forest fire," Dr. Hamilton replied softly. "I have become used to it now." She wrapped her scarf more firmly over her head as she spoke, "I also know the Amir hung a taster for offering breakfast eggs that were sprayed with poison. The taster tasted the good egg but offered the poisoned one to the Amir. Perhaps there was something about the man's demeanor that alerted the Amir, anyway, he made him eat that one as well."

"What happened," Frank asked curiously.

"Two hours later he was vomiting and he suffered for days. As soon as he recovered, the Amir ordered his hanging to take place in the scullery so the other kitchen workers were forced to watch."

As the clock on the mantelpiece ticked away the minutes, everyone's eyes were focused first on the Chamberlain for his approval to start the feast, and then on the tasters. The Chamberlain was fully absorbed and it was obvious that he missed nothing; his eyes were fixed on every spoonful. He watched their eye movements, breathing, body language, and facial expressions attentively, every move they made was scrutinized with deep suspicion.

Once the chefs had hastily consumed a considerable amount of food the Chamberlain dismissed them. Meantime, two footmen with *aftaba-wa-lagan* poured water on everyone's hands to wash. The Chamberlain politely nodded his head to the Amir and declared the food safe to eat.

The practice of preparation and service of food in the Palace had changed after Prince Habibullah's poisoning incident. However, suspicion of poisoning remained entrenched in Amir Abdul Rahman's royal court.

In the year eighteen-eighty-two, the Amir had ordered an offensive against the Hazara uprisings. His army marched to the home of sixth-century Buddha statues and camped at a town nearby. Some, including the army General, drank from a spring in the area, but within a few hours, the General experienced feelings of deep fatigue and felt desperately ill. He called off the march and went to bed before his usual hour. Several others, besides the General, both officers, and soldiers, suffered severe vomiting, high fever, and diarrhea that night and none were able to sleep. In the morning, the General saw a swelling beneath the knee on his leg and he was tormented by pain. Still, ignoring these alarming symptoms, he ordered the march towards the city to continue. About six miles further on, knowing he was too ill to continue, he called a halt, slid off his horse and died. Other deaths of men and horses followed. It was presumed that the spring had been poisoned to prevent their advance. The news was delivered to the Amir, and Doctor Alfred Gray was called in to determine the cause of death. His study showed poisoning of the potable water and, as a result, heightened vigilance was exercised on all levels of military and government personnel.

During his reign, the Amir only employed British doctors, whose skills he felt he could trust, to treat his illness. The current Hakim, Jon Mohammad, on the other hand, had been vigorously cross-examined to ensure that his intentions in serving the Amir's royal court, were completely above board, but he was not given the stature of an English doctor who was deemed more knowledgeable than hm. However, no member of the royal household was allowed to accept edible items from anyone outside the royal family, unless cleared by a tester and approved by an adult of the household. Indeed, the Amir took every precaution to avoid death and make everyone in the royal household feel safe about enjoying their food.

Throughout the meal, Raj, the interpreter chattered rapidly, almost without a pause, while his unique way of laying stress on the wrong syllables amused both English and Dari speakers. Having to use an interpreter was often extremely cumbersome as both the Amir and the others had to constantly ask Raj to repeat.

"Daktar Laila," Nasrullah said, chewing rapidly, "I also have a question. How many days is the voyage to *Englistan?*"

"A little over three weeks if there are no delays," she replied, "But now and then there are holdups at ports or waterways."

"So, how do you make sure a sick person is not going to die aboard the ship?" Nasrullah asked.

The doctor glanced at him, somewhat surprised by his odd question. "There is no to worry, Your Highness," she answered calmly, "rest assured, I'll be accompanying you to ensure your wellbeing to London and back to Kabul."

"*Tashakur*, Daktar Laila." He belched like a torn balloon and scooped another handful of rice and meat onto his plate. Habibullah, who was seated next to Nasrullah felt shame for his brother enveloping him like a blanket of steam; he narrowed his eyes and shrugged.

We have some serious work ahead of us, Lillias thought.

❧❦❧❦❧

October 1894 -- Afghan calendar month: Mizan 1273

Kabul, Afghanistan

As the time drew near for the arrival of their loved ones, life for Doctor Hamilton, veterinarian Clemence, and engineer Martin became more heartwarming and the glow of excitement could be seen in their faces. Like children anticipating their birthday party, they estimated their arrival by the day, if not the hour. The long-drawn-out years of separation had led to intense longing, and knowing that the time of waiting was almost over—the inner ache to embrace them, to kiss and snuggle with them deepened with every passing hour. Preparations intensified to relieve their family's long and stressful journey across the oceans, deserts, towering passes, and rugged terrains. Their helpers and servants cleaned and tidied their homes; shook out carpets, fluffed and aired cotton mattresses and comforters, and splashed water to settle dusty courtyards.

Martin and Clemence visited the noxiously putrid livestock market where live lambs , cows, and clucking chickens were sold and they threaded their way between steaming piles of dung to haggle for sheep and chickens. From there they continued to the central covered bazaar, Char-Chatta, to buy flour and necessities for their everyday use. Knots of people walked unhurriedly, clogging the narrow passages.

"This is almost as difficult to get around as the livestock market," Frank remarked.

"But the smell is better," Clemence said with a wry grin.

Lillias Hamilton, Clemence, and Martin waited patiently at Kabul's southern gate, which was shut at dusk and opened at dawn, to greet their families upon their arrival. They had covered their faces with thin scarfs as caravans of men and animals egressed and ingressed through the gigantic access into the city, throwing up clouds of dust in their wake.

The day before, Lillias Hamilton had prepared bouquets of roses in Arg Palace to hand to the newcomers. She gazed into the dusty horizon, covering her eyes with her hand to deflect the sun. Little by little, through the haze, the group of escort riders became visible and before long she could make out waving hands from afar.

"There they are!" she shouted breathlessly.

Martin peered through his binoculars.

"There's my boy!" Frank Martin exclaimed; he waved furiously and shouted, "William!"

The sound of trotting hooves grew closer and closer and at last faces became distinguishable. Little William was the first to alight and run to his father's arms; there was a flurry of enthusiastic greetings. After the long separation, their rejoicing and affection broke through like spring flowers through frozen ground. Amongst the newcomers was Olivia Worth who had accompanied Mrs. Clemence and William from London.

"Good heavens!" Dr. Hamilton exclaimed. They were all disheveled and coated with dust from the journey, but her eyes were on their red, tender faces, and wind-burned lips, and her mind was already on the healing ointment they would need once they were settled. "You all need something to quench your thirst and a hearty meal!" she said.

The train of carriages rumbled through the streets as Kabulis watched them from tea houses, roofs, and bazaars. Chattering children ran alongside tapping the dusty black panels and begging for *bakhshish* and although the heat inside was stifling they pulled shutters down. The carriages snaked through the dirt roads which led to Arg Palace and Lillias's little cottage.

Refreshments were immediately set out on the table - skewered lamb kabobs sprayed with *ghora* and pepper tucked in flat Afghan bread. Happy chatter filled the room as they exchanged stories of their travels.

Summer ended. Dusty hot days ceased as golden leaves began to scatter all over the city. The distant snow-covered Hindu-Kush mountaintops gleamed in the sunlight. Kabulis exchanged their light summer robes for thick cotton-filled *chapan* robes and wrapped themselves in shawls to resist the frigid days ahead.

Doctor Hamilton glowed with happiness now that Roma was with her, but she was so focused on planning Shahzadah Nasrullah's trip to Windsor that she hardly noticed the beautiful Autumn days in Kabul or was able to spend much quality time with her sister.

"I would like to make an announcement," Lillias said to the little gathering of ladies in Frank Martin's courtyard, "The Amir's queens have invited us ladies, Mesdames Clemence and Martin, Olivia Worth and Roma Hamilton to the Harem-Sarai next week!" Roma gave a little clap of delight and smiled engagingly at her sister.

"Mrs. Hamilton," little William said, "I want to see them too."

"Of course, William, you may come. I'm sure the Amir will have no objection if you go with us," Lillias replied affectionately.

"This is unusual," little William's face expressed his confusion, "I have never seen a bunch of queens together." No one could swallow their laughter.

Only invited female guests, immediate family members, assigned eunuchs, and, in exceptional circumstances, elderly men, were permitted to enter the Amir's Harem-Sarai. The building was securely structured and the surrounding gardens were doubly secured. Watchful eyes focused intently on the area, like spiders lying in wait for the flies' last drop of blood, twenty-four hours a day, seven days a week. The Amir was merciless toward any intruder who attempted to enter the compound—the sentence was death. Indeed, the infamous iron-fisted Amir would, for his entertainment, happily extract *bujul*, the knucklebones, from any violator of this rule. He believed death was the only language his subjects understood.

"May I have your undivided attention please," Dr. Hamilton implored, "I will need your help to plan for Shazadah Nasrullah's journey to Windsor," she paced around the room and sighed. "I feel we need to help the Amir and those who are struggling to bring an end to indigence in this country. In short, Prince Nasrullah's visit is a possible means to this end. The problem is, we have a difficult candidate for the task and a lot of work ahead of us in training the prince and some of the traveling Afghans in preparation for appearing in British society. I have promised the Amir that we would complete the plan and move forward before his departure in early Summer next year."

"Good luck training the obnoxious Afghan Prince," Frank Martin said. "I may be repeating myself, but woe betide Afghanistan if you let the moron loose on the court at Windsor, there's no telling what may come of it!"

"If it was up to me . . ." Clemence agreed, "I wouldn't send anyone."

"It's too late now," Lillias replied firmly, "The Amir is determined and Windsor has been informed that Nasrullah is going."

"I believe it would help," Frank Martin said perspicaciously, "if the Prince could be persuaded not to wear Afghan attire."

"Good point," Clemence agreed. "If he wore boots, he wouldn't have to rub the dirt off his feet in the Queen's presence!"

Martin laughed, "I must say it is difficult to imagine Nasrullah in a frock coat, waistcoat, and an immaculate ascot or a four-in-hand necktie!"

"What would be his normal attire?" Olivia Worth asked with interest.

"Usually national dress, the *Peran* and *Tomban*," he replied, "the loose Afghan clothing you have seen most men wearing here. But if he appears at the court as a British gentleman, it may aid his father's request."

"Would it be difficult to persuade the prince in this matter?"

"It might be," Frank Martin said. "Their traditional attire gives them confidence, respect for their culture, and esteem locally. I doubt whether he would change willingly." But both men judiciously reckoned that if the Prince could be persuaded to appear clad as a gentleman, it would be an advantage at Windsor Palace.

Clemence opened his silver cigarette case, offered Frank a cheroot, and leaned over to light it before lighting his own. "Well, is anyone willing to talk to the Amir or Nasrullah about the way he should be dressed for Windsor? I'm not! I'm sure it will be resented."

Frank Martin exhaled the smoke from his cheroot. "There's another problem anyway," he said, "There's not a single couturier in Kabul who knows how to mend or tailor English clothing."

"I would be happy to help," Olivia Worth said with a slight smile. "I was raised in the business. My grandfather and my father taught me the trade. Sadly, my grandfather recently passed away in Paris, may God grant him peace. My dear friend . . . " she smiled at Mrs. Martin, "brought me here to uplift my spirits. The anguish of losing my grandfather was quite unbearable, we were very close. I'm grateful to Mrs. Martin for asking me to accompany her to Kabul."

Charlotte Martin put a hand on Olivia Worth's shoulder. "I am sure you have all heard of Jean-Philippe Worth who runs Charles's couture enterprise now," she said. "Olivia is his daughter. Her grandfather, Charles Worth, is well-known as the 'Father of Haute-Couture'"

"Well," Frank said, "I am so sorry to hear of your loss, but, Miss Worth, that is a wonderful offer!"

Lillias echoed Frank Martin's words and gestured to the pageboys to clear the table. She turned to address the ladies.

"Would anyone else be able to help?" she asked, "it would make such a difference if Nasrullah could go looking like royalty!"

"If I can be of help, please use me as well," Roma offered. She straightened her long khaki skirt and lounged back comfortably on the chair, sighing contentedly, "It is wonderful to relax after such an exhausting trip."

Despite her long journey with all its privations, Roma's gleaming blue eyes and gorgeous long lashes radiated an outer beauty but she possessed an inner strength and loveliness as well. Her countenance and charm were so exceptional that any Afghan man would mimic the fourteenth-century Persian poet, Hafez-e-Sherazi to bestow on her the cities of Samarkand and Bukhara for the allure of her perfectly placed black beauty spot alone.

"Please count me and Mrs. Martin in too," Mrs. Clemence said. She was wrapped like a mummy in a faded, floral shawl with William tucked up next to her, his sleepy hazel eyes threatening to close.

"Your enthusiasm brings me a joy that I'll remember for the rest of my life. You ladies have only just arrived to see your loved ones," Lillias declared cheerfully, "and traveled more than a month to be here! I give you my heartfelt gratitude for offering your help in this regard.

"Of course, we'll help and do our best." Mrs. Clemence said in her

74

soft Welsh accent. "I want us to be remembered for helping the Amir, but," she looked a little dubious, "are we helping England?"

"Sweetheart," Mr. Clemence replied, "Let's leave that to the politicians, we are just here to do what we can to make things run smoothly..."

CHAPTER NINE

∾ঞ৹∾ঞ৹∾ঞ৹

November 1894 -- Afghan calendar month:
Aqrab 1273

Kabul, Afghanistan

The Kabul sky on this crisp October afternoon was as blue as Lapis-Lazuli. The early morning frost had faded away and thin sheets of ice in the puddles melted like vapor in the sun. Clad in their immaculate dresses, the English ladies and little William were on their way to the Harem-Serai in Arg Palace. Some of them may have gone with apprehension, presuming the Harem-Serai would resemble the stories they had heard of a paradise of sensual delight, filled with women of captivating, dreamy eyes, sensuous lips, and voluptuous figures. They may have conjured up visions of the Amir in his younger days, clapping his hands to signal the commencement of seductive belly dancing to sexually entice him. In contrast, this Harem-Serai was more often a snake pit of intrigues, jealousies, and power politics as each wife spent her days scheming as to how to get her son recognized as the heir to the throne. And in pandering to Amir's appetites, they competed among themselves to be first in his favor.

Next to the Amir himself, the chief political factor in the country was Queen Sultana, the favored royal spouse of the Amir and mother of six-year-old Prince Omar. Her style was distinctly more British than

Afghan, so much so, that her Harem-Serai apartment was regarded with almost as much suspicion as the British agency. Queen Sultana, was well-versed in social skills and easily engaged with English women while disdaining her Harem-Serai rivals.

The phaetons halted under the columned portico of the Harem-Sarai.

"We've arrived," Lillias said as she straightened her straw bonnet. "Here, Roma, allow me to pin your veil in place," she stood back critically to check the result and nodded her approval.

Roma's blond hair, almost the color of ripe barley, was pinned at the crown, while loose ringlets formed a glowing frame to her face. Her lovely blue eyes were trimmed by long lashes; her fair complexion, rosy cheeks, and perfectly shaped lips were enhanced by the little mole she had carefully darkened with Kohl. Roma wore a pale blue French silk gown with wide puffed sleeves. The dress itself was cut in graceful lines, slender at the waist and falling full length in a wider sweep from the hips. Observing her up close only further proved that truth—she was quite a beauty.

"I'm ready," Roma said.

Gray-bearded guards opened the arched double doors of the fortified compound.

"*Befarmayed, Khosh ameded!*" the guards formally welcomed the little group of women.

"*Taskakur!*" Doctor Hamilton replied and she led the way.

The mist from the marble fountain streaked the nearby windowpanes with flowing silver patterns. Around the fountain were four equidistant carved marble benches adjacent to the beds of assorted roses and Egyptian and Indian botanical plants. At the far end, handsome peahens and peacocks gazed at the British guests; one proudly spread his tail feathers, rattled them, and displayed the magnificent crescent sheens of bright blue and green.

"*Salaam Alaikum! Besyar khosh ameded!*" Queen Sultana

greeted, welcoming the newcomers as she came down the marble stairs towards them. Her Indian-born translator, Saira, Raj's wife, followed close behind. The Queen wore a dress that would have been fashionable in England some thirty years before. It had an auburn crinoline underskirt that slightly protruded at the hem, a tall neckline with a lacy collar, capacious pagoda sleeves, and a dazzling silk sash at the waist. The Queen kissed their cheeks and Salaamed everyone individually. Her allspice *kyphi* perfume, a mixture of sixteen ingredients such as cardamom, cassia, cinnamon, and lemongrass hung on the air as she continued the convivial welcome. The forty-three-year-old Queen, also known as Bibi Jan, was the cousin and third wife of the Amir. She was the richest woman in the land, of royal blood, granddaughter to Amir Dost Mohammad Khan, twice the ruler of Afghanistan.

Dr. Hamilton curtsied respectfully; her large bonnet with a wreath of flowers and ribbons tilted forward over the voluminous bun on the crown of her head. "Your Highness, thank you for inviting us," she said, as she cordially introduced each of her companions. At that moment, other ladies of the royal household began to descend the stairs and advance toward the Queen and the English guests destroying the moment of pleasure Queen Sultana had enjoyed with the British party. She cast a disdainful gaze in their direction and immediately turned to her guests.

"I am glad you all made it safely. Come, follow me inside it has become a bit chilly out here."

Lillias Hamilton was quite familiar with the Queen's reluctance to interact with her rivals of the Harem-Serai, but it was still embarrassing to see them slighted.

"Dakatar Laila Jan! *Cheshem-hayat-roshan*, may your eyes be bright!" The Queen led the four English ladies towards her apartment and stopped for a moment to draw attention to the arched opening covered with light-blue tiles, calligraphed with verses from the Qur'an.

At the top of the stairs, she held Roma at arm's length and widened her almond-shaped eyes.

"So glamorous and beautifully dressed, *Masha-Allah*! The latest fashion, I am sure . . . I need to catch up! You must tell me what the latest style in Landan is, Roma Jan! I am so glad to meet you. Your sister," she fluttered her long lashes in the direction of Dr. Hamilton, "tallied your arrival date every day." The Queen smiled and touched Roma's elbow with her henna-covered hand, "You are adorable, exactly what I imagined." She dropped her eyes to little William as if seeing him for the first time, "And who is this young man?"

"Your Highness," Charlotte Martin replied, "this is our seven-year-old son, William."

Queen Sultana ruffled his dark hair, "You will like my son, he is our only Crown Prince and his name is Omar Jan." She spoke a few words to a page asking that Prince Omar Jan be brought to meet William.

William was still confused, "Why are there so many queens and another crown prince?" he whispered in his mother's ear.

The Amir's other wives and concubines passively Salaamed the English ladies with a slight bow of their heads. Some were dressed in cream-colored robes and some in long colorful, Afghan dresses; a few shyly covered their mouths with their gauzy headscarves. Queen Sultana, determined not to humiliate herself any further in the eyes of the English ladies decided it was time for her rivals to leave and wait; they were no longer welcome in her apartment. A little while later, she led her guests through a portiere, strung with many lines of precious gemstones, into a huge, vaulted room. Fine Afghan carpets were laid over every section of the marble floor.

"Please sit down!" The Queen gestured to multiple tufted sofas and gilded divans around the room.

The Queen's tense posture, rapid blinking, and quick breathing told Lillias that something was amiss: the Doctor understood the rivalries between the Amir's wives and the years of tension between them and was aware that her demeanor demonstrated her vexation.

"Is something bothering Your Highness? You don't seem to be yourself," she asked quietly.

Saira, the Harem-Sarai interpreter, brightly clad in a magenta and orange sari, translated from English dense with a mixture of rhythm and cadence, melody and sorrow. She wore a gold stud in her pierced nose and a silver chain over her head with a coin that rested in the parting of her hair above the red *bindi* dot between her eyebrows.

"Yes, Daktar Laila Jan," the Queen muttered angrily, "this invitation was only for you five ladies, I wasn't expecting the others to come. I'll make sure this doesn't happen again."

Bright sunlight flooded the room and Queen Sultana gestured to one of the ladies-in-waiting to draw the drapes. The rich shawl draperies cascaded in perfect symmetry on either side of the multiple windows; their soft hue contrasted perfectly with peacock feathered wallpaper.

Olivia Worth leaned closer to Mrs. Clemence until their large glamorous hats touched each other and whispered, "The Queen is exceedingly nice."

"Yes, she's most charming, a fine stylish woman." Mrs. Clemence replied and added quite quaintly, "Her beauty outshines the sun and her figure shames the cypress."

The Queen signaled to the concubines and ladies-in-waiting to fetch the tea and *nashta*, hors d'oeuvres and then turned to engage the newcomers.

"I understand the pain of traveling on horseback for days and nights is deeply exhausting," she said sympathetically. "I have never traveled to India but back and forth from Kabul to Qandahar was more than enough!" Roma, Mrs. Clemence, and Olivia nodded in agreement.

"The hardest part was not being able to cleanse ourselves

hygienically," Charlotte Martin said, "and, of course, watching for venomous snakes and scorpions!" The other women laughed at that. Charlotte glanced around again, marveling at the room, and almost mesmerized by the number of queens and concubines who had joined them for the feast. Little William was still tucked up next to her.

"I'm so appalled that we have no railroads like they have in India," the Queen continued, "else you would not have been burdened with the long haul through mountains and deserts." She turned her gaze to Dr. Hamilton and gave voice to another thought. "Daktar Laila Jan! I'm grateful to you for taking care of us, particularly my ailing husband," she gently rubbed Lillias's shoulder causing her gold bangles to clink like falling coins. "And I am also grateful to you and Mrs. Gray for modeling this apartment. I will never forget your assistance." She changed the subject again, which the newcomers were to recognize was her manner, "I have heard about your commotion with the Hakim. I'm so, so . . . " She was momentarily at loss for words, "upset and angry! I don't know what my husband sees in him, but I deeply despise him! Just don't forget, I'm here for you. Whenever you have a problem with that wicked man let me know."

"I will, Your Highness!" Says Dr. Hamilton. "I'm not only your doctor but a friend, I'll remain at your service at all times." She smiled and changed the subject, "Do you still hear from Doctor and Mrs. Gray?" she asked, not wanting to think about the Hakim at a time like this.

"I haven't heard from them in a while but I trust all is well with them. Have you, Daktar Laila Jan?"

Before Doctor Lillias Hamilton arrived in Kabul, Doctor John Alfred Gray had been the physician to the Amir's court. The position, coordinated by the British Government, was very well-paid but dangerous. Doctor Gray's wife, Isabella, had spent a lot of time re-decorating Queen Sultana's apartment, working tirelessly with an English architect, an interior designer, carpenters, and masonries, who were handsomely paid to travel to Kabul to complete the project. She also coordinated the shipment of the fine furniture, a bedroom suite, and even a Steinway piano, and a brass longcase clock. All were meticulously well packed, loaded, and brought to Kabul on the backs of donkeys and camels. But it was rumored that Doctor Gray was a British spy and his employment ended upon the Amir's suspicion. Dr. Hamilton's arrival in Kabul sometime later seemed to some to be mysterious, and so also aroused speculation among the Afghan people in Kabul.

"We met Doctor Alfred Gray and his wife Isabella, Your Highness," Olivia Worth said. Her shiny hair fell to her shoulders under her voluminous bonnet. "Mrs. Clemence and I saw them last in Bombay as they were boarding a troopship back to Portsmouth." Her eyes filled with laughter as she recalled the memory. "Their steamer trunks were filled with Afghan and Indian antiques and took a long while to load onto the ship; I was made to understand that the ship captain was reluctant to accept such a huge shipment of their goods!"

"I am sure half their trunks contained the fine silk carpets they bought in Mazar-i-Sharif," Queen Sultana said with a smile, "I bought some for them myself." The diamond ring on her finger, a pledge of love and commitment from the Amir, gleamed in the sunlight as she moved her hand. This fascinating jewel was cut and polished to perfection so that, from each facet of its surface, light radiated in every direction drawing attention to the precious stone.

In comparison to the other ladies of Amir's court, Queen Sultana was charismatic and elegant. A poetic description of the times declared: "Her considerable beauty inspires at court, eulogy as extravagant as those applied by the veiled prophets of Khorassan to the charms of Zulaikha." Her large, almond-shaped eyes, fringed with long, beautiful lashes as captivating as a butterfly's wings, were outlined in Kohl in a style reminiscent of Cleopatra. The tips of her fingers, nails, and palms were dyed in flowery patterns with henna and if they could have seen her feet, the ladies would have been astonished to find they were similarly decorated.

Prince Omar Jan, wearing a pair of khaki britches and a gray sweater, entered the room with a lady-in-waiting. He greeted everyone shyly with a Salaam and stood close to his mother, but his eyes were fastened on William and sparkled with excitement.

"There's Weellioom Jan!" the Queen smiled alluringly, "go greet him, he just arrived from *Englistan*." She nudged him gently forward, "Weellioom Jan, this is my only son, Crown Prince, Shahzadah Omar Jan."

"William, go and shake hands with the Prince," Mrs. Martin prompted.

Both boys were delighted to meet one another and immediately bolted off to explore and amuse themselves.

The ladies-in-waiting and concubines brought in trays of *nashta*, warm sweetmeats, roasted pistachios, assorted grapes, peeled fruits of various kinds, and tea: there was a whiff of ceremony and grandeur about it. Trays were extended with both hands, and each English lady was served the fruits and hors d'oeuvres of her choice.

"*Khanum* Gulrez, are you excited about His Highness, Prince Nasrullah Khan, traveling to England?" Lillias asked, smiling at the older woman over the rim of her teacup. Nasrullah's mother, a concubine named Gulrez, twisted her hands in her lap and Lillias perceived she was bewildered by what was happening. She loved her two sons more than anything in the world and believed they would present themselves well wherever they went, but she was deeply afraid that if her young son was to cross the vast oceans and venture where no Afghan had been before, he would probably never return. Gulrez knew what it was to face rivalry within the Harem-Sarai. The competition was intense. Every woman desired that her son would become Crown Prince—jealousies were rife and could flare up at any time.

"Daktar Laila Jan!" She leaned forward on the Gryphon Reine bench, "As a mother, I pray every day and night to Allah for the well-being of my two sons." Her brow was deeply furrowed and she abruptly covered her strong, protruding cheekbones with her headscarf. "I don't even know where *Englistan* is." she continued in her rural Wakhi dialect. "They say it's far . . . far away somewhere way over there," Gulrez gestured vaguely in an easterly direction. "Way on the other side of the world and takes months and months to get there."

"The journey only takes about a month, Gulrez," Dr. Hamilton corrected gently.

"The longest I've traveled was from Samarkand to Kabul," she went on, oblivious. "My husband asked us to come when he became the *Padshah*, King. Our caravan moved day after day for over a month crossing glaciers and packed snow over high mountains. We feared for wolves and mountain lions. Unfortunately, the stillbirth of my twin children was very emotional for me, Daktar Laila Jan, Allah took them away from my womb. I'm very worried about my son traveling somewhere that none of us has been before." She fidgeted nervously, "Daktar Laila Jan, if I may ask you," she rubbed the long braid that hung over her shoulder, "please tell me. What does it look like in *Englistan*? Are there predator animals? Are there thieves and outlaws?"

"*Khanum* Gulrez, there are no predators like here in Afghanistan, maybe a few wolves and plenty of foxes, but nothing you should be concerned about. If there are outlaws, they're mostly incarcerated. There is nothing to worry about, the Prince will be guarded at all times," Lillias assured her.

Before accession to the throne, Amir Abdul Rahman had been in exile in Russia's Central Asia. He married his second wife, the daughter of a prestigious chief in Samarkand, but she was unable to conceive. She traveled for days and weeks to all the most sacred shrines seeking Allah's blessing and devoured every *Unani* herb the Hakims prescribed for her to conceive, but fortune passed over her like the high-flying Siberian cranes. So, she presented him with one of her foster daughters, *Gulrez*, whose name means flower-sprinkler, to become his concubine. Gulrez was of Mongoloid-Kyrghyzi descent from the Wakhan corridor, a narrow strip wedged between Pamir and the Karakorum mountains that extends to China—a shortcut of the Silk Road. From that union two sons were born, Habibullah and Nasrullah. The loss of her unborn twins while en route from Samarkand to join the newly enthroned Amir in Kabul, and the disdain with which Gulrez, as a concubine, was shown by the Amir's other wives, had left her bitter and had also had a deep emotional effect on her two sons.

Gulrez raised her hands religiously and muttered a prayer. "*Aye-Khoda-Yaa*! I seek your protection for the safe return of my son, Nasrullah."

"Doctor Laila Jan! I need some more of the same *Goolee* to relieve my throbbing migraine," she said. The mention of *Goolee* immediately attracted everyone's attention. Whenever there was an opportunity, Gulrez, and the other ladies of the Harem-Sarai would pester Dr. Hamilton, whom they saw as the healer of all diseases and the repairer of impediments—malaria, smallpox, headache, gout, poor vision, bone fracture, emphysema, bronchitis, and even hair loss, and diminished hearing due to earwax. In their view, the only cure was *Goolee*, medicine.

"I'll bring you some medication soon, *Khanum* Gulrez," the doctor replied with a smile.

Queen Sultana's eyes widened and her nostrils flared.

"You need to stop begging the Daktar for *Goolee*," she snapped, gazing coldly at Gulrez, "this is not the right occasion and it's a burden on the Daktar! Sometimes I think you ask for medicine when there is nothing wrong with you. She's already overwhelmed with my husband's gout and you are complaining about a simple headache . . . enough is enough!"

Queen Sultana, also known as Bibi-Halima, was intelligent and well-informed, and, while not always loved by the other women in the Harem-Sarai, she was respected. Queen Sultana was also looked up to within the Amir's court, as more than just a woman of engaging personality. She held a position in Afghanistan akin to the Empress Dowager of China or the Lady Om, Queen to the emperor of Korea, and, as a member of the Barakzai clan, she was by far the most powerful of the wives of the Amir, who married her shortly after he acceded to the throne.

"I'm deeply sorry Bibi Jan!" Gulrez said. Her pretty, feminine face had turned white as frost under Queen Sultana's reprimand. "I wish there were women Hakims in the Arg Palace, to take some of the burden off Daktar Laila's shoulders. But the cunning Hakims are men only and they dare not enter the Harem-Sarai. In their feeble minds, women are not clever enough to prescribe their herbs and opiates."

The Queen changed the subject by praising her English guests. She had no desire to continue speaking of the ongoing intrigues and absurdity of the Harem-Sarai.

"I am staunchly anti-Russian," she said. "I hate my husband's past life associated with the Czarist Grizzlies—such cunning pigs! Nothing pleases me when I think back to his exile in Samarkand! I cannot approve of any of his connections with the people beyond the Oxus River!" She glanced meaningfully in the direction of Gulrez, took a sip of her tea, and set the cup down sharply, onto the saucer. "My utmost respect to you, *Englees-Ha*, despite the mistreatment the done to my grandfather, Ala-Hazrat Amir Dost Mohammad Khan, I don't hold grudges against any of you. You all have a place in my heart." She smiled sweetly.

Nasrullah entered the room at that moment. "*Salaam!*" He nodded in the direction of the visitors and helped himself to *nashta* and tea.

Sitting down next to his mother he whispered in her ear, "Blood-sucking *Englees-Ha!* Why are they here?" while at the same time, throwing a coquettish grin at Roma Hamilton. Gulrez averted her eyes and said nothing, but Queen Sultana stared coldly at both mother and son. The mood in the room had changed almost instantly—everyone felt the rising tension and waited; anxiety flowed through the core of everyone's bones like lava. Nasrullah once again stared licentiously at Roma. Very briefly, their eyes met and immediately Roma looked away dismissively. A complete hush prevailed. The Queen continued as though nothing had happened, "I fully support my husband's policy for a friendly relation with *Englistan*," she said sweetly, "I told my husband that it is our duty as Afghans to prove our absolute fidelity and abiding friendship for the *Englees-Ha*, who raised us from poverty to the throne of Afghanistan." She nodded firmly, "Frankly, no one can deny that, and I'm profoundly grateful to you and your countrymen."

"Well Bibi Jan!" interjected Nasrullah arrogantly. "Do you recall when my father was furious and wroth was flowing out of him like molten fire?" He snorted loudly, "he recommended that you mind your own business!" He shot a triumphant look in her direction and set his bowl full of pomegranate seeds on the table next to him. "The *Englees-Ha* owed more to him than he owed to them. My father accepted their offer to rule Afghanistan only to free them from the misery and entanglement they were in with the *Roos-Hai* Grizzlies," he ignored the Queen's disapproving stare. "Indeed, if it wasn't for him, *Englees-Ha* could have been driven out of India within days." He clenched and unclenched his hands, his voice rising in anger, "It is at the cost of Afghan blood that *Englistan's* throne was defended." His arched nostrils flared, "We will see how *Malika* Weektorya will help us when I go to Weendsaar. I will demand our membership in the court of Sia-Jeems, but mark my words she's going to deny Afghanistan's membership!" He picked up his bowl and devoured a full spoon of pomegranate seeds, his mouth moving as rapidly as the treadle on a Singer sewing machine.

"Are you done?" the Queen asked. Nasrullah looked up and they locked gazes. The silence was so complete that it felt as though the great room was empty. "Wroth flowing out of your father like molten fire?" she mimicked, her countenance deadpan, "the *Englees-Ha* owed more to him? What the hell are you talking about? Who is filling you with all these lies? I have no idea why you're chosen for this mission and not someone reasonable and sane?"

"Nasrullah, *bachem*, my son, please!" his mother pleaded. "Humble yourself and you'll be forgiven. Bibi Jan is always right." Gulrez quelled her son with a soft glance, offering balm to his injured pride.

"Bibi Jan!" Nasrullah spoke using Queen Sultana's family title with a sudden genteel air. "I'm very sorry for my comments, but these are facts that are debated amongst many in the royal court."

"Do you know something?"

"No, I don't Bibi Jan."

"You would not even have the gall to speak in that tone and on that subject to your father! He would shut you up before any more filth comes out of your mouth!" She sprang up from her seat and jabbed a finger in his face and then towards the door of her apartment, "There's the door, you were not invited to be here." The Queen planted her feet apart, "Since you consider yourself mature and manly enough, then why are you here among women? Are there any other men here? *Boro gom sho!* Get lost!" She gazed at him bitterly. Nasrullah exited the apartment with no further argument and the Queen walked quietly back to her seat.

"Gulrez!" The Queen murmured, "Tell him never come here again. Not to my apartment! Am I clear?"

"Yes Bibi Jan, I'll make sure he never comes here again," Gulrez replied, looking almost paralyzed with shock and shame, but managing to order her features into something resembling a smile.

The years of incessant discord were harbored deeply in their hearts and ingrained in the very core of the Arg Palace. Eventually, the flame of intrigues and jealousies would destroy everything in its path. They were egocentric, as greedy as vultures, with little appetite for the betterment of their homeland and people. Their nation would continue on this destructive path for years to come until its demise.

CHAPTER TEN

~~∞~∞~∞~~

November 1894 -- Afghan calendar month:
Aqrab 1273

Kabul, Afghanistan

Immediately after Queen Sultana expelled the irascible Nasrullah from her apartment she humbly apologized to the English ladies, "I sincerely apologize for that acrimonious dispute, unfortunately, such things are everyday occurrences in Harem-Sarai. The ill-mannered prince rudely intruded and spoiled our union." She calmed her anger and tranquility slowly returned to the room. "Would you be interested in visiting my sewing and embroidery academy?" she asked. "It is where I invite the ladies of the Harem-Sarai to keep busy and make clothes for themselves and their children."

"We would be obliged, Your Highness," Dr. Hamilton replied. "You'll be as impressed as I was the first time," she assured the others.

As the Queen led the way through her extensive suite of rooms, she began to engage in conversation with them regarding their fashionable dresses and styles, determined to learn from them the latest European patterns and cuts. In her couture academy, was a row of Singer sewing machines aligned with multiple chest-high tailoring tables, wardrobes and storage shelves, and chests filled with fabrics of every sort. In this field, the Queen was an artist, and the ladies saw immediately she possessed a profound passion for design. It showed in the way her eyes moved, how her hands held the fabric, and how the fabric of the universe held her in return.

In one corner, stood two tall gilded mirrors on mahogany stands. An eye-catching clock graced the mantelpiece, its ticking marking a steady rhythm, it was a masterpiece of craftsmanship, a distinctive lapis lazuli bell curve framing a glossy white face in the shape of an Afghan melon. At the far end of the room, a wall clock proclaimed the passing of each hour with the appearance and call of a tiny golden cuckoo.

"I'm very isolated in Kabul, I hardly have any idea of the latest fashion styles in Landan and Parees," the Queen lamented, "unless fashion-loving ladies like you arrive in this remote part of the world and tell me what's out there."

Her couturière room tranquilized the murmurings of the ladies of Harem-Sarai, like the music of a dream. It is the only place where craftsmanship replaced their feelings of envy, futile gossiping, and virulent intrigues against each other. In addition to the happy humming of the ladies when they were focused on their needlework, hundreds of parakeets chattered and called joyfully in a huge aviary set in a far corner.

"How about a show of skills ladies?" the Queen asked. "We would love to see some examples of English embroidery."

"*Oui Oui Votre Altesse!*" Olivia Worth exclaimed, and continued in her charming French accent." Olivia was raised in Paris after her family moved their fashion business from London and switched comfortably between the two languages. I would love to make something!" Someone offered her an embroidery hoop, needles, and a basket of bright silks.

The Harem-Sarai ladies began treadling the Singer machines and the room was filled with whirring like the buzz of giant wasps. Before very long, Olivia Worth produced a rose, stitched and embroidered with colorful threads and decorated with small shell buttons, stunning everyone with her quick and skillful hands.

"That is dazzling!" The Queen's eyes widened, "*Khanum* Oilevia Jan!" I would love to seek your help to teach us your talent while you are here."

"I would be obliged, Your Highness!" Olivia replied and curtseyed.

"And would you be so good as to join us as well, Miss Hamilton?" the Queen asked.

"I would be honored, Your Highness!" Roma replied.

"It would also be my pleasure to help where I can, Your Highness!" Mrs. Martin said.

The gold bangles tinkled on her wrists as the Queen held Olivia Worth at arm's length as her guests prepared to leave, "I don't know how to thank you for being such a wonderful friend," she said, and then, looking from one to another, "you are all very special and dear to me." Turning to the ladies of the Harem-Sarai she nodded, "Go ahead and thank them."

The queens and concubines bowed their heads respectfully and their "*tashakur*" fell softly as rose petals.

A few days after this visit, Doctor Hamilton hurried to Harem-Sarai to meet with Queen Sultana. She rummaged in her bag for her scallop-shaped watch and flipped up its gold cover, "I'm late!" she muttered.

As she approached the compound, she heard a loud commotion from within the high walls of the premises. The squabbling voices were familiar and even from this distance, the doctor felt something of the tension and intensity in the woman's pleading tone. The gray-bearded guards allowed her to pass through the high double-arched doors, and as Lillias approached she recognized that, as she had suspected, Gulrez was onced again the target of the Queen's rage.

"No!" The Queen was spewing words at the top of her lungs at the unfortunate concubine like a train whistle. "You are not a queen! Just bear that in mind! My child is the direct descendant of royal blood.

My prime duty is to preserve the pure royal dynasty of my family. That is exactly what I intend to do!" Her eyes were narrow slits and her face was unreadable—enraged as she was, fearless. "Mark my words, my son, Prince Omar Jan, will carry on the legacy of my husband and our forefathers. My husband's mind will change about sending your obnoxious and irresponsible son to *Qasr-e*-Weenzor! When Prince Omar Jan is old enough, he will go and see *Malika* Weektorya!" Her dark brows were drawn together, and her soft pink rouged cheeks quivered with anger. "Over my dead body will I see a concubine's son sent to see the most powerful Queen on earth! Go, get lost! Daktar Laila Jan is here to see me." Her eyes flicked from Gulrez to Lillias, and the doctor noticed the suggestion of a smirk in her expression.

Gulrez's hands trembled and her eyes had welled up under the tongue-lashing. She turned and walked away in despair. Her only real pleasure was being alone, hidden in the privacy of her apartment. The other women of the Harem-Sarai were all terrified of Queen Sultana's domineering ways and vicious temper—they feared her demons. When she was enraged, the power of her presence caused their body to become hot, the sweat trickled down their necks, and they could hear the thudding of their hearts against their chests. They feared her rages and thought hard before engaging in conversation with the Queen. None of the ladies dared to challenge her with any hope that she might release them from the tension that had clutched at their hearts for so long, or defy the status quo that enabled her to rule with an iron fist. Such an action could bring about their death sentence—it was easier to exist with fear.

"My sincere apologies Daktar Laila Jan, this is very shameful of us to make you feel uncomfortable every time you are here," the Queen said, still breathing heavily. "That *Ahmaq*, stupid, concubine, asked that new attire should be made for Nasrullah before leaving on his trip to Landan," she crossed her arms angrily and her gold bangles clattered. "I don't want any concubine to demand special treatment just because you, Daktar Laila Jan, and your guests, generously offered to teach them couture skills, that shouldn't allow them to expect special clothing!"

Lillias had hoped to approach the Queen with a similar request using Olivia Worth's background as an entree, but after her furious outburst, she knew that any conversation in this regard hung by a slender thread. If she chose to have some dresses made, she might agree to approve the tailoring of formal attire for Nasrullah and a few members of his entourage as a bargaining chip, but a cautious tactical way of reaching the Queen was now necessary to resolve the issue. Lillias was well aware that the Queen despised Nasrullah and might refuse to allow her couturière room and equipment to be utilized.

"Your Highness," Dr. Hamilton said, softening the expression on her face. "I have something interesting to tell you,"

"Then let's go inside and talk privately, Daktar Laila Jan!" she said, and she took Lillias by the hand.

As they made their way to the Queen's apartment, Lillias Hamilton said, "Your Highness, Charlotte Martin's friend, Olivia Worth . . . " she trailed off.

"*Baley*, Oh yes, I remember Oilevia Worth. Little, petite, nice features."

"She's the daughter of a famous fashion designer, Jean-Philippe Worth, and the granddaughter of Charles Worth."

"I don't know her parents but I know she dresses beautifully and her couture skills! *Wah! wah!*" she exclaimed, lauding Olivia's astounding couture work.

As they sat down, Dr. Hamilton turned to Saira, the Harem-Sarai interpreter, and said, "Will you please interpret word for word, I don't think the Queen understood your translation."

"*Jee Han*, Dear Daktar *Saib*," she cloaked her head with the end of her Sari.

"Your Highness, the dress you so admired was designed and made by her father, Jean-Philippe Worth. She learned the trade of couture from her father and grandfather, both are known internationally."

"*Wah! Wah!*" she cried again in surprise, her almond-shaped eyes widening with delight. "Luck fell from . . . " she peered toward the window and gestured upward at the sky, "We're blessed with the grace of Allah. My dream was to wear the latest fashion dresses from Parees and Landan. I believe God is answering my plea and has sent me the daughter of this world-renowned fashion designer. Here, to Afghanistan . . . unimaginable!" She pondered. "Why did she travel on animal back to Afghanistan, and not somewhere presentable like New York, or merely stayed in India?"

"Your Highness, she happily agreed to accompany Mrs. Martin to Afghanistan, her childhood friend, and family member. Her elderly grandfather, Charles Worth, to whom she was very close, died a few months ago. She could not bear the pain of losing him and wanted a change and to travel to somewhere out of the ordinary. Your Highness, Miss Worth is well-traveled. She has been to New York and many other European and American cities. She has also been hunting with her grandfather on many African safaris. But she had a passion to see Afghanistan. She's a true adventurer."

"I want to make her feel at home here in Kabul," the Queen said earnestly, "I hope she likes it here. What can I do Daktar Laila Jan to make her feel at home? Should I throw a gathering in the royal gardens in Paghman? Or perhaps in Babur Gardens?"

"Your Highness, it's imperative for us to talk before we put a gathering together for her."

"Of course, Daktar Laila Jan. I'll be glad to hear you."

"As you know, His Highness, Amir Sahib, has already decided Prince Nasrullah is to make the long journey to meet with Queen Victoria. I totally understand your antipathy towards Prince Nasrullah, particularly after the way he confronted you the other day. Frankly, I would prefer to refrain from taking part in your household differences but my job is to look after His Highness's health and to keep you, and the royal household, in good health as well. His Highness has asked me to spearhead Prince Nasrullah's journey to England. With Your Highness's permission, could I propose a plea, hoping you would give it your consideration?"

"Daktar Laila, *delbar*, heart-ravisher, you know better by now, I've never rejected anything you proposed before and never will as long as it's within my power."

"Olivia will be happy to design Your Highness's dresses and show you the sketches . . . she will modify them as Your Highness wishes. I understand she is quite an artist! With Your Highness' approval, I'll have her start the work immediately."

"Of course Dakatar Liala Jan, that would be wonderful!"

"But, Your Highness, It is the wish of your husband that Prince Nasrullah should have clothing that will reflect Afghanistan and your royal court in the best possible light when he meets with Queen Victoria."

The Queen was thoughtful for a brief moment as she wrestled with her choices, but as Lillias had perceived, the desire for dresses designed by Olivia was overwhelming and she nodded slowly.

"With Your Highness' permission, can Prince Nasrullah's couture start immediately?"

"Of course, if it must be done, Daktar Laila Jan, but I forbid him to step his foot inside my apartment." She stared at her intently, "And only if Prince Omar Jan's attire is made before Nasrullah's."

"As Your Highness wishes. And if I could humbly propose, all fittings and measurement to take place in Gulrez Khanum's apartment."

"Yes and Prince Omar Jan's too."

❦❦❦

June 1893 -- Afghan calendar month: *Jawza* 1272
Kabul, Afghanistan

On a crisp sunny summer morning the previous year, a loud shriek had filled the air like an icy mist, followed by a crash that seemed to jolt a section of the Harem-Sarai. Anxiety streamed through the core of the ladies' bones as they ran up the three-story stairwell to the rooftop. The access door to the roof was open and a laundry hamper, almost empty, was set under the clothesline. The clothes swayed in a slow breeze.

"Feroza came up to hang her clothes on the line," one of the concubines said, "but she's disappeared!"

They searched behind the chimney stacks, and under the *charpaies,* cots, set for their night's sleep under the summer sky.

Feroza, the nineteen-year-old from Herat, who had recently been admitted to concubinage, was missing. Her skin, the color of wheat, her long, raven curls, her beautifully defined rosy lips, and exuberant dark eyes, had attracted many in the Harem-Sarai and within the royal household. And with her quintessential hourglass figure that swayed as voluptuously as Spring's first rose—Feroza was as exquisite as the jam of Almighty.

Gulrez peered down from the waist-high parapet wall, "There! There she is!" she cried urgently. "Hurry! Down there!" The others pressed close to her, against the wall and a few sobbed at the sight of Feroza's body sprawled motionless behind the compound wall. Some cried out hoarsely like birds sounding a warning of a predator on the loose. Their cries of "Allah!" alerted the guards who ran to see what had happened. The girl had fallen outside the forbidden premises and it was up to gray beards bring her body into the compound. Feroza had plunged to her death onto the hardened ground below. Those who retrieved the corpse later mentioned the red, swollen marks on the inner surface of her arms, bruises on her wrists and neck, as well as the direct blow to her head that had oozed blood into her hair.

"She seemed to have been held out over the wall by her arms before falling to her death," Gulrez said uneasily.

Queen Sultana was not in the compound.

Other heinous crimes had taken place in Harem-Sarai in times past. Attempts had been made on the lives of some of the ladies through poison and other methods, but these were immediately covered up and ignored. Why this new concubine? Was it a murder or an accident? If murder, the culprit was never found. The Amir was immediately notified, and, to appease the terrified ladies he ordered a quick investigation; the official result was said to be an accident. According to the report, the Amir said, Feroza had moved too close to the edge of the roof and lost her balance while hanging the clothes on the line.

The ladies of the Harem thought otherwise; some said that despite being fully aware of the facts, he chose not to reveal them. They spoke secretly of their suspicions, conversing with one another where they could not be overheard; in the confines of their apartments, under the dark skies, trees, bushes, or close to the water fountains that smothered their conversations.

"Never go on the roof alone," Gulrez advised.

"Not only on the roof, but anywhere in the compound," another concubine said.

Feelings of jealousy and discontent toward new concubines often occurred. They were likely to be wooed and enjoyed for a while as Amir's favorites, for sexual pleasure or to produce sons. Generally, those who were shown favoritism for any length of time were closely watched, abused, poisoned, or murdered. Whatever the case with Feroza, the ladies of the Harem-Sarai were terrified, and fear haunted them at every turn.

CHAPTER ELEVEN

❧❧❧

December 1894 -- Afghan calendar month:
Qaws 1273

Kabul, Afghanistan

Once again, Doctor Hamilton led the English ladies to Harem-Sarai where Queen Sultana's sewing machines and couturier rooms were being prepared for their use. As agreed between the Queen and Lillias, they were to customize outfits for *Shahzadah* Nasrullah and six of his courtiers who would be accompanying him to Windsor Palace. The assorted English fabrics had already arrived from India and the measurements had been procured for the ladies to begin work.

They were ushered to the parlor in the Queen's apartment by a rosy-cheeked concubine, wearing a white headscarf and an English dress that was far too large for her.

"Please be seated, Her Highness will be with you shortly," she said.

They were greeted by the familiar squawking of Queen's parakeets. A vast arrangement of red delphiniums and white roses, with the few lupins penetrating the mix, filled the room with a heavenly fragrance. Not a single fallen petal lay on the shiny rosewood table.

"*Salaam!* Good day ladies," the Queen said with a wide smile. The English ladies rose to their feet and curtsied, Olivia Worth was given special attention.

"Oilevia Jan, it would seem you are making a brave attempt to appear cheerful. I hope you do not feel homesick, please let me know if I can be of help." She smiled sweetly at her other guests. As she turned her head her dangling earrings swayed. They were made in three tiers, and in each, a large sapphire was separated by tiny diamonds with dazzling effect. "Bear in mind ladies, this applies to all of you - think of me as a big sister."

"Thank you, Your Highness," Lillias said, "We are much obliged to you for your kindness in allowing us to use the academy."

"Of course, Daktar Laila Jan. If it wasn't for you, Nasrullah would have been wearing his local clothes to see *Malika* Weektorya. You and the rest of your ladies are very special to me. Please follow me."

She led the way to the sewing room where a lady-in-waiting and two concubines were hard at work organizing and tidying up in preparation for their visit.

"Show the ladies all the sewing accessories and anything they need for their work," the Queen told the lady-in-waiting authoritatively. "Also, I'm expecting you to take good care of my guests . . . tea, food, and anything they may need should be provided at all times."

"*Albata*, Bibi Jan, of course, my lady," the lady-in-waiting replied.

She opened every drawer, her chatelaine clinking as she did so, "Here are the scissors, embroidery hoops, embroidery stencils, darning eggs, colored chalks," she said. "And here are the colored threads, pincushions, assorted thimbles, tape measures, buttons of all sorts, satin liners, and so forth. If you need anything, I will be here to help. Let me know in advance when you need the coal irons and please allow a quarter of an hour for heating," she added.

"Oilevia Jan, please forgive me, this couture room may not be quite what your father and grandfather have in Parees, but I'm hoping it will suit your needs," Queen Sultana said seeing that the ladies were ready to begin work.

"*Merci Votre Altesse.* It is a lovely room. Many people in England or France don't have anything close to what you have. It is well-equipped and well-stocked with everything we need. Your Highness and the ladies of the Harem-Sarai must enjoy sewing here," Olivia replied. "In his early life, my grandfather owned a tailor shop in London's East End. My family helped him to make women's and men's clothing, even cravats and all sorts of cufflinks. They found a better opportunity in Paris and moved the business there and thereafter it thrived. *C'était peut-être de la chance. Je ne sais pas,*" Olivia said proudly.

"As you will all be making outfits for Nasrullah and those accompanying him, it is a wonderful opportunity for me to learn and watch your work. *Balay Khanum,* Oilevia Jan, I rarely stay idle," the Queen said. "This place brings solace and bonding amongst the feuding women in Harem-Sarai. We do our best but still intrigues and tittle-tattle cannot be stopped."

"We'd be honored for Your Highness to watch us at work at any time," Olivia said.

"I will retire for now, but should you need anything please notify my lady-in-waiting," the Queen replied, and then added in a cajoling tone, "Oh, Daktar Laila Jan," she reached out to touch her, "if my memory serves me well, did we say *Khanun* Oilevia will be designing a few dresses for me?" she asked with a slightly coquettish tone.

Olivia Worth turned to face her, "Oh yes, Your Highness," she said, "I have a few designs in mind. I will prepare the sketches for Your Highness's approval."

Mesdames Clemence and Worth began to chalk out and cut patterns, while Mrs. Martin and Roma prepared to embroider and hand-stitch. Lillias, who was less experienced in needlecraft, helped wherever she was needed. The machines were to be used for the final work.

"I'll have the courtiers measure each other's sizes," Dr. Hamilton said, "but can one of us volunteer to do Nasrullah's measurements?"

she fiddled awkwardly with her cameo pendant necklace.

"Ladies," Olivia said seeing everyone's obvious reluctance, "taking measurements is part of the family trade, I'll do it." She removed her voluminous bonnet and her dragonfly hair clip and shook loose her dark shoulder-length hair.

Lillias looked relieved, "Thank you, Olivia, that is much appreciated," she said.

One afternoon, a distinctive footfall somewhere between a walk and a shuffle, caused Dr. Hamilton to look up from her needlework. Gulrez entered the room holding the end of her white translucent headscarf to her mouth.

"*Salaam,*" she said, smiling shyly.

"*Salaam.*" Dr. Hamilton replied, and the other ladies greeted her in unison.

"I see you're all hard at work," she commented edging over to the pattern table, "Is this suit for Nasrullah?" She fingered the chalked and tacked fabric, walked around the table, and fingered one of the other garments.

"Yes, Gulrez *Khanum*, and for those accompanying His Highness to London." Dr. Hamilton frowned, concerned that Gulrez would disengage the pattern from its tacking.

"I'd love to learn your sewing secrets. But you're too occupied."

"You're always welcome Gulrez *Khanum*," Dr. Hamilton said courteously. "We did intend to train you and the rest of the ladies of the Harem-Sarai, so I beg your forgiveness. Once this is over, I am sure there will be time for you and the rest of the ladies to learn."

The Queen's strident voice was heard calling for the lady-in-waiting, "Did you take tea and pastries for the *Englees* ladies?" She walked in and immediately her expression gave way to annoyance, "Gulrez, why are you here? Can't you see the *Englees* ladies are busy as bees? Time is of the essence and every minute counts before they leave for *Englistan*."

"Sorry Bibi Jan, I was curious to see Nasrullah's suit," Gulrez replied meekly.

This sudden jarring note instantly darkened the atmosphere in the room and the ladies were thankful at that moment for the arrival of the lady-in-waiting and the subordinate concubines, who brought in the tea.

The clinking of teacups and saucers brought a return to normality, and the Queen relented a little, "Well, when his suits are ready then you can see them, but don't make it a habit to intrude too frequently. Oh, and make sure Nasrullah is reminded that he's not welcome here," she added.

"*Albata* Bibi Jan, of course!" Gulrez's fearful face turned pale.

"The proof fitting for Nasrullah will be in your apartment," she said, "you will be able to see it then."

The Amir's ambitious desire to seek the freedom of his nation from Great Britain would have had a very bumpy start were it not for his English friends. The intricate planning for Nasrullah's voyage and the ladies' magical couturiere was designed to present the young Prince with elegance and appropriate preparation before the royal court of Windsor. They worked not for their own ends, but for what they perceived to be for the good of Afghanistan—to free the nation to prosper on the world stage, based on its own merits. The ladies may not have been able to comprehend the intricacies of world politics, but they fathomed the meaning of freedom—man's desire not to be chained and enslaved against his will in his homeland. Freedom is that which pours the sunlight of the human spirit and human dignity through its window. For the Amir, it was to see his nation break free like the sun rising out of the ocean.

CHAPTER TWELVE

❧❧❧

"This is what I notice and hear about you. Not all of you, but some of you," the Amir shouted, his eyes locked on the audience. "To my face, you swear to Allah that you will always be faithful to my rules and you grovel before me. You bow to me like trees in a storm. Yes, you bow six-fold, kiss my feet, and clutch your hearts, revealing your fake loyalty!" He stroked his neatly trimmed beard, "But, an hour afterword, behind my back, you're busily plotting against my life! Just bear in mind, do not get caught, or, in the name of Allah, life will be hell for you and your families."

Fear compressed everyone's chest like a vise. He paused for a long moment. Every man gathered in the Darbar believed that his removal was about to be ordered and that he would disappear forever. Without warning though, the Amir shifted the subject to Queen Victoria.

"If you have any message of goodwill to Her Majesty *Malika* Weektorya then stand up and say it aloud. I have a hearing deficiency and cannot hear you well."

He nodded at the elder from Qandahar who seemed to wish to deliver a message of benevolence to the Queen of England. The elder appeared to be in his mid-forties and as he stood to his feet heads swung in his direction. He wore a patch over his left eye, and the end of a weighty black turban partially concealed his face, tendrils of hair that escaped from his turban were pigmented with henna. The man was clad in an ankle-length Afghan tunic with a cloak wrapped around his tall muscular body and draped loosely over one shoulder.

"*Bismillah al Rahman al Rahim! Manana Ala-Hazrat!* Thank

you, Your Highness!" he drawled with a Southern Pashtu inflection, his voice was somewhat muffled under the flap of the turban. "May Allah keep you in good health to lead this nation successfully. You are the shadow of the Almighty, your word is his word, your rule is his rule, and you're the only sovereign that unites us all." He raised his hands heavenward, "Also, please allow me to say this, we in Qandahar sincerely pray for a successful outcome of *Shahzadah* Nasrullah Khan's visit with *Malika-e-Englistan* and we also pray for his safe return. My clan and the rest of the Qandahar's clans have no doubt he will bravely impose your will on her." He spoke fearlessly as though he was tickling a tiger, "My name is Khairo Khan, leader of the Alakozai clan from the Maiwand district of Qandahar. Fifteen years ago, the 6th day of *Asad*, 1259, was a day of mayhem I will never forget. Despite our nation's victory against *Englistan*, I lost four brothers and a twenty-year-old daughter. Many of you may have heard her name, Malalai, and her fiancé." His voice cracked with emotion, "*Ala-Hazrata,* Your Highness," he raised a forefinger in the air, "losing those I loved was worth saving the nation from the aggressors who are still determined to uproot our beloved Afghanistan for their own cause. On that day, I not only lost my face and an eye, as you all can see." He dropped the flap of his turban to show that half of his face had been hacked away and removed a patch to reveal his blind eye. A collective hum rose from the audience. His disfigured face was as dry and rigid as a mummy; the eye socket, a dark cave. His gaze shifted from left to right and then back to focus on the Amir and his sons, "I implore you *Ala-Hazrat* to erect a monument in the name of our heroine Malalai. She not only brought dignity and stature to our proud nation but inspired every Afghan in the Battle of Maiwand to win the war." He dabbed his good eye with the end of his turban. "If it wasn't for my daughter's courage, I believe we would not be celebrating the victory of Maiwand." He swathed his turban around his face and reattached his eye patch. "*Tashakur*, and may God save you and the people of Afghanistan." He respectfully bowed and sat down. From the audience the mutterings of "*Ameen!*" echoed throughout the hall.

Before the Amir could respond, both Nasrullah and Habibullah leaned toward their father and whispered to him. After a brief moment of silence, the Amir responded. "Although your assertion has no relevance to Shahzadah Nasrullah's meeting with *Malika* Weektorya, I can understand your pain. My heartfelt condolences to you and your family for the loss of the brave men and the young woman. I have instructed Shahzadah Habibullah to come up with a monument for your beloved daughter and those who lost their lives in the Battle of Maiwand." He reverently raised his hands and the audience followed suit. The Amir called upon the Mullah to lead a prayer.

The royal Mullah lifted his hands and recited, "May Allah, *subhanahu wa ta'ala*, grant them *Jannatul-Firdaus* and forgive their sins. May He make their graves a place of comfort and light. It is He that takes and it is He that gives, and He prescribes a certain destiny for every matter. *Ameen!*"

"*Ameen*," was a united chorus throughout the hall.

∾◦⟞◦∾◦⟞◦∾

January 1895 -- Afghan calendar month: *Dalwa* 1273
Kabul, Afghanistan

Throughout the centuries, Afghans had reached many treacherous crossroads - one of the most personal being the crossroad of fear and valor. When a man once chose valor and conquered fear, he was encouraged to see himself in a new light. The next time he faced fear, valor became an easier choice. This was how individuals developed bravery, becoming those whose stories are told and retold

106

over centuries. For bravery beyond imagination, Khairo received a personal commendation from Princes Nasrullah and Habibullah who met in a private session at the Arg Palace.

"It's an honor to remember the martyrs who heroically fought in the Battle of Maiwand," Prince Habibullah said placing a sympathetic hand on Khairo's arm, "My utmost respect to you and your family. My brother, Nasrullah, and I have two options for you to choose from. First, a fifty-meter-high minaret that would stand tall in remembrance of the martyred in Maiwand. Second, for the same reason, an avenue, the longest and widest ever built in Kabul." The Crown Prince's eyes were gentle as he looked at this man who had suffered so much. "Tell me which one you prefer?" he asked.

"Your Highness, Shahzadah *Muhtarem*, I am fine with either one, I'd rather let you and *Shahzadah* Nasrullah Khan make the final call. My only goal is to commemorate the fallen . . . that is all I hope for."

Prince Nasrullah shook Khairo's hand in a congratulatory manner, "Let's give it a few minutes, maybe you will decide which one you prefer." He spoke quietly, "Khairo Khan, my compliments to you. You truly stood courageously explaining your deep pain and sorrow in the *Darbar* Hall, it touched many people's hearts, and I felt sorry for what the evil *Englees-Ha* did to you, your brothers, and your beloved daughter."

Habibullah frowned, drew a deep breath, and released it. "Nasrullah, we need to stick to the subject and build something in remembrance of those who lost their lives." As always, his impatience with his brother emphasized the stammer, "We ca-cannot waste time badmouthing the *Englees-Ha* at a time like this. If father hears, he will sh-shut this plan up entirely." He held his chin high and crossed his arms. "Please, we must get this done. Father as-assigned me to fulfill this task and time is limited," he paced impatiently, "He will be asking for the final decision. There is a budget to be allocated and money to be spent. Let's not talk about the *Englees-Ha*."

Unlike Nasrullah, both the Crown Prince Habibullah and the Amir, in some respects, had been fiercely protective of Britain and Queen Victoria in recent years. Between them, they were a powerful mountain to lean on. The vast English subsidies and internal autonomy were what kept the Amir in power, and the Crown Prince was fully aware of the benefits of following his father's policy as the key to a prosperous reign in the future.

Nasrullah cast a baleful gaze at his brother, "Habibullah Khan, we cannot deny the devastation the *Englees-Ha shaitan-ha*, the English Satan's atrocities brought to our poor people. You and my father believe this should be forgotten overnight and instantly heal the deep wounds our people suffered for years. Let me assure you, the pain and the scars are way too deep." His face was cold and expressionless, almost as one who is in a trance. "The *Englees-Ha* play us against each other, Pashtun against Hazara, Tajik against Pashtun, Uzbek against Shiites, for their own agenda." A frosty silence settled on the room.

At last, Khairo spoke up, "Your Highnesses. *Grano Sardar Sahibano*, My dear lords, I implore you to move forward and help me choose one of the options that His Highness, Prince Habibullah Khan proposed," he said. "How about we name the new avenue?"

"That's a great choice Khairo Khan, a great choice!" Nasrullah exclaimed, the excitement returning to his voice.

"*Mubarak*, congratulations you've made a perfect selection, Khairo Sahib. You have everyone's blessing," Habibullah said as he shook hands with Khairo.

"But, there's one problem," Nasrullah interjected glancing at his brother. "This cannot be named only after Malalai as there are thousands who lost their lives and they cannot be forgotten." Both Prince Habibullah and Khairo concurred.

"Let us call it *Jadeh-Shaheed-Hai-Maiwand*, Avenue-of-Martyrs-of-Maiwand." Nasrullah proposed, his eyes alight.

"That's too long and a little awkward. How about *Jadeh-*

Maiwand, Avenue of Maiwand? Everyone will know what it stands for, " Khairo said.

"Perfect. *Tashakur,* Thank you! Let's call it that. I will sign the papers and move forward with the name *Jadeh-Maiwand,*" Habibullah smiled broadly. "Khairo Khan, I'll get in t-t-touch with you and sh-show you the plan for *Jadeh-Maiwand* in a few days. If you don't mind, I'd like to excuse myself, I have another task that my father assigned me. *Insha Allah,* God willing, we'll make this happen and you'll be the one to cut the ribbon in the name of your heroine daughter and those fallen in the Battle of Maiwand. *Khodah Hafez,* God be with you!" Habibullah rose to his feet, adjusted his scarlet jacket, straightened his Astrakhan hat, and left.

"My brother, Habibullah, shadows my father when dealing with the *Englees-Ha,*" Nasrullah said rubbing his stubble. "I feel the opposite. The satanic thinking of the *Englees-Ha* is intended to use us Afghans as their chess pawns. They play us against Russia and the Russian Grizzlies use us against them!" He clicked his fingers at the pageboy who was hovering nearby and called for tea.

"We are just like paid sentries guarding India against a Russian invasion!" He took off his gray Astrakhan hat and set it on the table next to him. "To the British, Afghanistan is a fortified wall; they give us money and arms to stand against the Grizzlies. I hate that. I simply hate that policy!" He paused, shook his head, and looked sharply at Khairo Khan. "But let me tell you something confidential, and I hope you will keep it between us, Khairo Khan," he relaxed his posture and lowered his voice, "Can I trust you?"

"Of course, by all means *Sardar Sahib*, Lord Sahib." Khairo replied. He leaned forward in his seat and clasped his hands on the table between them, "Your Highness can confide in me with confidence. I am a man of trust."

"I value your honesty," Nasrullah lowered his voice further. " Nothing will change while my father is alive, the same policy will be the hallmark of his reign until he dies."

The pageboy handed them their teacups and backed away at a gesture from Nasrullah. "My brother, Habibullah, the Crown Prince, will never deviate from my father's policy. And I'm afraid, one day, the Satan *Englees-Ha* will fool him and annex the country like fifteen years ago when brave Afghans like you stood and fought them to their last man." He gazed at Khairo over the rim of his porcelain teacup, "My father talks privately with Habibullah and teaches him how to lead and rule the country, but little or nothing to me." He grimaced. "I don't understand why my father is sending me to face that old woman, *Malika-e-Englistan* when I don't agree with their policy regarding Afghanistan." He shook his head and gesticulated with his right hand, "I am simply perplexed and don't understand why I was chosen to fulfill his diplomatic mission with *Englistan*." He dropped a couple of sugar cubes into his cup and stirred it slowly. "My father and Habibullah both know I hate *Englistan* but they still want me to take the long voyage to *Qasr-e*-Weenzor and see that old *kaftar*, hyena."

As he listened to Nasrullah's frustrations, the conversation rendered solace to Khairo, whose feelings of hatred toward the British for the tragic circumstances that disfigured him and killed his family at the Battle of Maiwand ran deep. The Prince's words were like the quiet, washing sound of an ocean and he gradually warmed up to Nasrullah.

"I'm pessimistic about the whole journey. I am certain the *machakhar*, *Malika-e-Englistan*, will never accept my father's plea to have representation in the court of Sia Jaimes, St. James's." He rapped the table irritably with his fingers, "She will never give us the freedom to run our own country independently, but I cannot oppose my father's wishes." He looked down at the cup and picked it up aimlessly, cradling it in his hand. "My father desired independence from the moment he was enthroned fifteen years ago," he said shaking his head with an expression of exasperation, "but I doubt it will ever happen." He sighed deeply, "We will be disdained internationally!" He rose to his feet and paced the room. "If that happens, I will have no choice but to retaliate against that woman's decision. Even if it costs me my life."

"Your Highness, *Shahzadah-e-Muhtarem*," Khairo said. He stood up and walked across to the Prince. "I thank you for taking me into your confidence, I was unable to express myself fully in the *Darbar* Hall. I know His Highness, Amir Sahib will not tolerate anyone badmouthing the *Englees-Ha*."

Nasrullah smiled, "Yes, that is true. However, my father sometimes badmouths the British or *Malika* Weektorya himself," he said.

"Well *Sardar* Sahib, I took a chance. Even if he ordered my execution, I was ready to face the consequences. He looked Nasrullah in the eye, "For the sake of my family's blood, I traveled a month from Qandahar to join the *Darbar* to talk openly to everyone who could feel my pain and sorrow. I wanted them to look at my condition and know the deep misery I'm going through. *Sardar* Sahib, I have lost the opportunity to raise my only daughter, or to plow our family farm, or tend our pomegranate orchards with my brothers. They are dead, and life is over for me too. But now, one thing will keep me going and bring me comfort," he reached out to Nasrullah and gripped his shoulder. "Your Highness, I found that you believe what I do. The Satan *Englees-Ha* should think twice before annexing our beloved land again or claim a single *belest*, hand-span, under their sphere of control." Khairo wrapped the end of his turban more tightly around his disfigured face. "*Pa-Khodai-ke*, in the name of Allah!" he swore in his lilted Pashtu, "as long as I am alive they will never set a foot inside Afghanistan again."

"You have nothing to worry about while we're in this together, Khairo Khan." A silence descended over the room as Nasrullah removed his tunic jacket and draped it over the crest rail of his chair.

"Can I ask you a question Shahzadah?"

"Of course."

"I hope it's not too much to ask," Khairo said, "but I am curious. Do you recall when I finished talking in the *Darbar* Hall?"

"Yes, I do remember clearly."

"Your Highness and Shahzadah Habibullah Khan whispered something in Amir Sahib's ear."

"Yes, we did."

"What did you discuss, if I may ask?" Khairo sat back in his chair and rested his hands on its arms.

"Khairo Khan, I believe it would be better if we left it there and did not discuss it, it was a confidential matter between my father, Habibullah, and me."

Khairo nodded, " I understand. But rest assured, I'll do anything to help our cause, as long as I have you and Allah on my side. *Insha Allah*, God Willing."

Already, a unique bond was beginning to develop between Khairo and Nasrullah. Khairo was taller than Nasrullah, broader, a formidable square-shouldered man, and about ten or eleven years (twenty+) older than him. This unexpected acquaintanceship with the Prince uplifted his morale and gave him renewed confidence. He left this first meeting energized and warmed towards life again. Later, Khairo, the Alakozai tribal elder who had experienced the horrible battle of Maiwand firsthand, would become Nasrullah's tutor in arms, instructing him in combat, wrestling, fist and dagger fighting, and more. These were skills that had been passed down to him through generations.

CHAPTER THIRTEEN

෨ඁඁඁ

It is far more important to prevent a dispute from escalating than quenching a fire that has become an inferno.

The Queen Sultana's agreement with Dr. Hamilton to allow the English ladies the use of her couture academy to tailor clothes for Nasrullah and his companions was two-fold. Queen Sultana recognized that a dispute with the Amir over this matter would spin out of control. She could not afford to jeopardize a mission of such importance to the sovereign. But, of equal importance to the Queen was Olivia Worth—the moon amongst the British stars. The Queen blossomed inwardly with the wonder of Olivia's presence. The granddaughter of a renowned fashion designer from Paris who was to design and make her dresses in Kabul—the world's most isolated city! This was a gift that soothed every discord regarding the tailoring in the Queen's sewing room, of the attire for Nasrullah and his companions.

When Olivia and Roma, accompanied by Lillias, visited Queen Sultana's apartment to show her the designs Olivia had sketched for the much-anticipated dresses, the Queen first invited them into her huge bed chamber. Queen Sultana sat at her dressing table and brushed her long black hair, "I'm sorry, ladies, for not being presentable, but I will be quick," she assured them.

Glancing around they noticed that the Queen's glamorous canopy bed occupied a separate section of the room.

On her marble dressing table was a huge jewelry coffer and next to it a stick of incense smoked idly. There were colorful ivory-topped jars filled with all sorts of scented oils and *attar*; flower-fruit, coconut, sesame, and the more delicate rosewater, and ice flowers.

"Please, open them," the Queen encouraged, when she noticed their interest—she waved a hand, "and smell." Whiffs of distinct, sweet aromas rose from each jar competing with the perfumed incense.

The walls were papered with a lavish pattern of roses and the whole suite was decorated with curtains and bedding in fabric bearing the same rich design. Pots of well-tended Indian ferns and miniature tropical plants added to the feeling of being inside a private garden. In one corner of her bed chamber, under a huge portrait, there were two sets of salon chairs and a chaise longue that the Queen used for her afternoon rest.

The Queen seated herself on the chaise longue, "Please sit down, ladies," she said. "Oilevia Jan, you come and sit beside me here."

The ladies could not take their eyes off the portrait. The Queen smiled, "That is my grandfather. It's the work of Daktar John Alfred Gray," she continued proudly. "He painted it from an image that . . . " She was lost for the word. "What's that box called that produces pictures?"

"Camera?" prompted Dr. Hamilton.

"Yes." She moved along to the topic of primary interest, "Oilevia Jan, I believe you're going to show me the sketches you made."

Olivia pulled her sketchbook from her leather bag and showed, one by one, the many dress designs she had sketched with the Queen in mind. One of them made the Queen gasp with pleasure. "Dazzling!" she exclaimed. The design showed a crimped collar, bows attached to the shoulder seams, a striped blue front with yellow pleats at the waist. A wide sash on the hips was fastened with a large round bead. There were three yellow stripes and two layers of lace at the hem of the skirt, while the sleeves showed four cascading layers of fabric. Once Olivia Worth had gained a sense of the Queen's preferences, a good combination of style and elegance, she and Roma took the Queen's measurements.

"We will be ready for a fitting in one week, Your Highness," Olivia said as they prepared to leave later.

January 1895 -- Afghan calendar month: *Dalwa* 1273 Kabul, Afghanistan

If Queen Victoria's Indian-born secretary, *Munshi* Abdul Karim Khan, who grew up in slums of India was presentable to the Queen and her court, why should anyone have a problem with him, Nasrullah argued. He was raised in an Afghan royal milieu, which in itself was proof of his ability to hold his own in any similar surroundings.

"What difference is there between a Weenzor Prince and me?" he demanded, clearly resenting any criticism of his normal patterns of behavior and resisting any pressure to change. For the English men and women at Arg Palace, Nasrullah's stubbornness and arrogance threw them into a state of incredulity. He would not bend at all in the face of seasoned knowledge or advice. The Afghan Prince seemed unable to comprehend that the social norms for upper-class Victorian men and women were governed by the dos and don'ts of etiquette. In Kabul, the Victorian notion of social avoidance held no place at all. It was acceptable and normal for an Afghan to gesture in a certain way in public, sit crossed-legged, eat with his hands, urinate crouched against a wall, or use dried clay to soak up the last drops of urine from his private parts. If Afghan society found no fault in such normal behavior, the Prince surmised, it should be equally acceptable wherever his travels took him. The Afghan Prince failed to see the possible repercussions if he was seen doing such things in public. And even such a minor faux pas such as addressing a member of the British Royalty by the wrong title or rank, or failing to know with whom he was conversing, particularly if there was no proper introduction, would not be dismissed lightly. To represent the court of his father and speak for Afghanistan, and to secure the same stature as other nations in the court of St. James's, involved portraying himself as a worthy envoy to the Royal Court of Queen Victoria.

"No rose is unaccompanied by thorns," the Amir said bluntly, using the well-known Afghan proverb, meaning no one is perfect. Prince Nasrullah is not a perfect human being, nor is *Malika* Weektorya, nor am I. We are all creations of *Allah* but not without faults. Nasrullah must show himself to be strong and courteous at all times, and I expect Daktar Laila Jan and her *Englees* friends to help Nasrullah, and those accompanying him, to undergo the proper training."

Embarrassment seemed inevitable. They had tried without any success to bring about the changes in behavior that were needed but failure lay like a cloak over Nasrullah's shoulders. Frank Martin witnessed the Prince's many blunders and mentally replayed them before Britain's Queen.

"Damn, I often see him digging deep inside his Bartlett pear-shaped nose. A habit he's had since I've known the jackass," Frank Martin muttered to his wife. "I told him once, 'your nose will drop off! Stop digging! I noticed waves of shame ran through him, but the next day it was back to square one."

"Just make sure he understands the inappropriateness of nose-picking in public. Heaven forbid if he does that in Windsor Palace," Charlotte Martin murmured disgustedly.

The burden of training the stubborn and arrogant Prince was as hard as building a wall of sand. But, despite the limited time, the English ladies had a lot of other duties to accomplish before the prince and his entourage set sail.

In addition to sewing the formal suits for the men, the English ladies also had the burden of training six of his accompanying entourage as well as Nasrullah - from table manners to handshakes, to every necessary demeanor to circumvent any embarrassment that the British tabloids and newspapers would be eager to publish.

At 8:30 am, the carriages snaked their way towards the secluded Bagh-e-Bala Palace where a meeting would take place between the English tutors and Prince Nasrullah and his six top courtiers. They brought little William and Prince Omar Jan to amuse themselves in the Palace.

The night before, the palace storytellers had entertained the youngsters with the tales of a carpet weaver who created magic carpets, and on the day of his death, he commanded his creation to spread themselves throughout the palace and find masters worthy of them to serve as they wish. While the boys were pursuing their mission to entertain themselves with the magic carpets, Nasrullah and his courtiers were to undergo their first day of practical instruction. To that end, Dr. Hamilton and Chief Engineer, Frank Martin had spent hours planning and preparing for this introduction to the English protocols. The Amir had requested his English friends to vigorously monitor the Afghans to ensure that no mistakes cropped up during their visit to England.

The large circular parlor where the group had gathered to wait for their students to arrive, overlooked Kabul's picturesque eastern plain. An endless sea of parallel grape orchards stretched toward the ashen foothills. Roma Hamilton stood by the window, gazing out at the grapevines as she sipped a steaming cup of tea. With the morning fog drifting like gauze through the naked amber stems of the grapevines it was a picture-perfect moment.

"This country is breathtaking. Delightful!" Olivia said as she walked over to join her. She was wearing a honey-yellow silk dress with chiffon trims around the neck and shoulders, adorned with sparkling crystals and metallic spangles set in floral motif patterns.

"I am so glad I came to witness this beauty for myself," Roma replied.

A massive chandelier hung suspended from the vertex of the onion-shaped dome, reflecting a fine gloss onto the mahogany table beneath which was surrounded by ten immaculately upholstered mahogany chairs. Around the main circular parlor were several archways, each connecting to an octagonal hallway. Doors on either side led to a bedroom—a total of six in all.

A clock in the hallway chimed ten o'clock but still, the Prince and his courtiers had failed to arrive. William and Prince Omar moved from one carpet to another where they sat crossed-legged and chanted their incantations in various singsong tones hoping they would fly magically.

"It's important to teach punctuality to the Afghans on this first day of training," Mrs. Martin said with an expression of annoyance. "An hour past and still no trace of them."

"Even the time in Kabul takes its time," Mr. Clemence commented with heavy irony, "Or you could say, anytime is Kabul time!" His voice drifted in from the hallway where he and Mrs. Clemence were examining Amir's exquisite tapestries which looked as though they could have been displayed in an art museum.

"This is not the first time he's been late," Frank Martin said. "The Prince sleeps as if he has all the time in the world." He peered through the window impatiently, "Well, the Amir authorized proper training to make him understand the reality of the upper echelons in Windsor Palace. That's exactly what we will have to do."

"It will be a huge insult if his habit of tardiness is carried through into Windsor," Mrs. Martin said, glancing at her reflection in the gilded mirror hung on the wall. "The boys have gone off somewhere, Frank, I had better check on them,"

Twenty-year-old Nasrullah stayed up late and slept in late and could barely mumble a greeting or match his shoes first thing in the morning. It was patent to all that changing this pattern would not be easy and it would be up to Frank Martin, as far as possible, to ensure he kept his appointments in England.

"There!" Dr. Hamilton exclaimed from her position at the window, "I see horses coming over the narrow pass." She sat back in the winged armchair and continued to sip her tea.

A few minutes later a white-turbaned footman stepped into the room, "His Highness, Prince Nasrullah Khan is here," he announced. He bowed deeply and backed out of the parlor.

CHAPTER FOURTEEN

❦❦❦

The marble fountain in Harem-Sarai was no longer spewing water from its orifices but was newly adorned like a birthday cake with glazed frostings and ornamented icicles. The Afghan winter had come down like a hammer with bleak skies and frigid temperatures blown in from off the Hindu-Kush freezing the blood to ice.

The Amir was visiting his domineering wife, Queen Sultana, in her apartment and, as usual, his arrival brought a feeling of discontent amongst the rest of the ladies and concubines; a choking and plague-laden cloud. Whenever the Amir favored any of the wives or concubines with a visit, jealousies erupted among the others. But none would ever dare to disrupt the private time with the chosen lady of the moment.

The Queen and the Amir sat cozily by the crackling fireplace sipping warm pink-tinged *qaymagh-chai*, tea served with clotted cream.

"I've invited Daktar Laila to join us," the Queen said, "she should be here any minute."

"Dear Bibi-Jan," the Amir said reproachfully, "I intended this to be just us two, why did you ask her to join us?"

"Agha-i-Gul!" the Queen said. She used his family title, which is something most Afghan heads of households have in common. "I felt this was quite important." She sipped the last of her *qaymagh-chai* and put her cup on the table. She took a deep breath, "There are a couple of issues that required all three of us to meet and today was a good opportunity."

Dr. Hamilton had a keen understanding of the contentious relationships amongst the members of Amir's household; especially between the Queen and Amir. The issues were mainly his dealings with other wives, concubines, and their sons. Lillias was fully aware she walked a fine line. It required great discernment to avoid getting drawn into situations that could erupt into a royal inferno destabilizing her relationship within the palace, or the country as a whole.

Covetousness, jealousy, and bitterness had taken root over many years within the Arg and would take a miracle to undo.

The lady-in-waiting opened the door upon hearing the knock. Dr. Hamilton removed her otter fur muff and Garrick coat in the hallway and handed them to her. She peered critically at her image in the gilded looking-glass on the wall and entered Queen's parlor where the Amir and Queen were ensconced.

"*Salaam* Daktar Laila Jan . . . *Khoda hamesha shoma ra byarad!* You're always welcome by the grace of Allah!" the Amir said.

The Queen sprang up from her armchair, hugged Lillias warmly, and in the customary manner, they kissed each other on either cheek three times.

The doctor curtsied, "*Salaam* Your Highnesses."

"Please make yourself comfortable Daktar Laila Jan," the Queen gestured to the floral upholstered ottoman chair near the royal couple. The lady-in-waiting refilled their cups with *qaymagh-chai* and handed a cup to Lillias who she inhaled the sweet smell of the rich flavored drink that was one of her special delights in the cold weather.

"I have brought us together," the Queen said, once the general mundane questions were asked and answered, "to speak about Nasrullah." Her brown eyes gazed into the Amir's in a way Lillias recognized as the Queen's tendency to soften her approach to any difficult discussion. "Aghai-Gul, why in the world are you rushing to send Nasrullah to see *Malika* Weektorya? Can't you wait for a few years until Prince Omar Jan is old enough to be sent instead?"

This was a personal conversation that the Amir did not want to discuss with Dr. Hamilton present. He always worried about any major confrontations with Queen Sultana as she was the only woman sufficiently strong-willed to subdue him, like an Argus, by the sound of her words.

"Sultana Jan," the Amir said, "I have always shared my pain and sorrow with you and I will do it now." He turned to Lillias Hamilton, "My apologies to you, Daktar Laila Jan, for involving you in this personal matter."

"I am obliged to you for considering me as an entrusted confidant and I assure you that nothing will be revealed outside this room," she replied.

The Amir nodded and turned to the Queen once more, "My dear Sultana Jan. I cannot pass up this opportunity that *Malika* Weektorya has graciously given me. You know the state of my health, I am frail, and cannot undertake this journey myself." He paused, "There is a second reason why the timing is urgent. The political situation in Afghanistan is fragile and could become dangerous. I hope you understand my position," he looked into the fire that blazed in the hearth and took another sip of his tea. "I cannot go, and there is no time to wait for Prince Omar Jan. Nasrullah must go!"

Generally, in presence of the Queen, the Amir was like a lion with no teeth, but this time he remained quietly firm.

"Agha-i-Gul," the Queen said, pressing him further, "I share your pain for the frail state of your health, I know it would be impossible for you to take the long voyage. But, instead, you are risking everything by sending Nasrullah—would it not be better to send Habibullah? You know he is more presentable, well-mannered, and thoughtful."

"I cannot answer more than what I've answered!" the Amir replied angrily.

The Queen's countenance darkened and she replied with vehemence, "Well, I'm afraid he'll embarrass us in *Englistan* and we'll be the main topic in every newspaper. Is that what you want?".

"It is done! I have made my decision, *Qasr-e*-Weenzor is already informed!" the Amir straightened up and refused to look in her direction.

The Queen recognized her defeat and changed tack, "Is there any chance that Omar Jan could accompany Nasrullah to *Englistan*?" she reached out and gave his shoulder an encouraging squeeze. The Amir was silent for a long while. He knew it pained his favorite Queen that her son, the true royal blood from the ruling Barakzai clan, was not of an age to make the journey. Her son was everything to her, yet, despite the risks, she was willing to allow the six-year-old Prince to have the experience.

"I don't see why not, Sultana *aziz*, dear!" he replied at length, softening, as always, to her wishes. "Let me discuss this in the court and make some arrangements." He stroked his beard thoughtfully, " I was heading to the *Darbar* Hall to discuss further arrangements for the visit, I will speak to them today."

With the aid of his cane, he stood up from the chair and the lady-in-waiting helped to tuck him into his leopard fur *chapan* and handed him his gloves. He bid adieu as she pushed his wheelchair to the awaiting carriage. Relief brought a smile to the Queen's lips as soon as the Amir left her apartment. She rolled her eyes heavenward, exhaled, and sagged against the side of the hearth.

"Our family feuds are always entertaining," she said, "I'm glad it stopped before you witnessed an obstreperous showdown. Please forgive me for involving you, Daktar Laila Jan. I was afraid to ask my husband and I knew if you were here he would listen more quietly."

January 1895 -- Afghan calendar month: Jadi 1273

Kabul, Afghanistan

Dr. Hamilton had never limited her medical service to Arg Palace, almost all her spare time was given to Kabul's citizens. It was said that Kabuli's would sometimes queue outside her tent in Bagh-I Babur overnight and that, with her servants' help, would often treat as many as seven-hundred-and-fifty patients in a day. Eventually, she was able to establish a small clinic in the city. It was no wonder, therefore that some members of the Amir's household believed she had been sent from heaven. English doctors were highly respected and perceived as the most precious human beings on earth.

The Queen herself was fiercely opposed to the local Hakims; she had become suspicious of their scheming and unscrupulous ways, and regarded them as "rats near strange bread".

"If you see them around the palace, shoot them," were the Queen's words of advice to her husband. She held a particularly obsessive grudge against the Palace Hakim, Jon Mohammad, who for years had encouraged her to eat certain seeds with supposed anti-aging properties, which he declared, would keep her young and beautiful forever. As time went by, and upon frequent examination of her face in the mirror, she realized the accumulated creases were the result of the natural phenomenon of aging. Obviously, the cunning Hakim's prescription had not born fruit. Over the years her anger over the deception she had subjected herself to, proliferated like a cancer until one day she spewed a torrent of curses at the Hakim: "By the Most High Almighty, by the Prophet, by the exalted Qur'an," she screamed at him, "May you be destroyed and your house burned to ashes!"

By contrast, the Amir, who held no personal grudge against the Hakim, had a different view. He saw him as a devout Muslim who, by the grace of Allah, might cure him. The Amir believed both the Hakim and the Doctor were indispensable—each had equal powers of healing. Although in his mind, the science was not quite clear, he tended to weigh both science and God equally.

"Daktar Laila Jan, there's a rumor that the Hakim will travel with Nasrullah to Landan, is it true?" the Queen asked in astonishment.

"Yes, Your Highness, His Highness said it would put him at ease if the Hakim joins the Prince. I respectfully asked His Highness if I could be the one to make the final decision on any medical issues and he assured me that I will be in charge."

"I am aghast! I don't understand why that devious self-made doctor, who claims he knows more than a medical doctor, yet can't even cure a *peshak*, cat, let alone a human being, is allowed to go to Landan! I would not dare to let him make the journey."

"His Highness' justification was that the Hakim may prescribe *Unani* medicines for those accompanying Prince Nasrullah to London."

"That's *khanda-awar*, absurd! My husband is losing his mind! He is not rational!" the Queen retorted furiously. "Daktar Laila Jan, I'm still talking to my husband regarding my son, Omar Jan, who will possibly accompany Nasrullah to Landan. If the decision is made for him to go, please look after him. I don't want that shameless Hakim to come close to my son."

"You have my word, Your Highness, I assure you, I'll be looking after him. But please would Your Highness kindly speak with the Hakim and tell him he is not permitted to have anything to do with Prince Omar Jan?" Lillias grimaced, "He once almost made me give up my job here and retreat to India on horseback in the middle of the night. This was when His Highness was severely ill and almost on his deathbed. The Hakim told everyone that I may have poisoned the Amir and if he died he would hold me liable."

Queen Sultana nodded grimly, "I heard the story and always wanted to hear your side. However, you better believe it, Daktar Laila Jan. That immoral Hakim will hear me loud and clear so that he will never cross the line with you or my son. You're both very dear to me."

CHAPTER FIFTEEN

❧◦❧◦❧◦

Prince Nasrullah swaggered into the parlor with his courtiers in tow. He was wearing black knee-high riding boots and khaki britches. He greeted all those present as he removed his leather gauntlets and his black Ottoman lambskin hat and handed them to the footman.

"I apologize for being late," he said, "I was hunting cranes. As you probably know it's the migration season from *Roosya* to *Hindustan* and they sometimes land around Kabul. I saw flocks of them by Kabul River today and could not resist following them upstream. I shot and shot ceaselessly. There's enough for everyone, please help yourselves. They are in the scullery."

Silence descended over the parlor as the Prince and his men took their seats. It was broken by sudden bursts of laughter with the arrival of William and Prince Omar Jan walking into the parlor each holding a wing of a lifeless crane. The dead bird's long neck bounced off the marble floor at every step. The Palace Chamberlain hastily took the bird and ushered them outside to find other amusements, seemingly, they had exhausted their efforts at making a palace carpet fly.

Dr. Hamilton drew everyone's attention back to business. "Good morning your Highness," she said diplomatically, "I'm glad you arrived safe and well. Shall we start with the training?"

The Prince ordered the scullery attendants to prepare a few of the birds for lunch and to bag some for the English ladies. "Please, Daktar *Sahiba* Hameeltoon, start as you wish."

Across from Prince Nasrullah, three Afghan Army officers and the Mayor of Kabul took their seats. Next to him, two high-ranking Afghan officers sat on either side.

"Your Highness, would you kindly introduce your men to our guests?" Dr. Hamilton asked.

Nasrullah nodded. "Please meet my esteemed cousin, *Qomandan-e-Ala* Akram Khan, whom you may know," he indicated briefly. "We grew up together and we're inseparable brothers."

"Tashakur, Shahzadah!" Akram Khan bowed his head briefly and pushed his thick glasses further up the bridge of his nose. He was of royal blood, a man in his early twenties, of medium height, with a neatly trimmed beard. His Afghan Army rank of *Qomandan-e-Ala* was equivalent to a General in the British Royal Army. Akram Khan was always immaculately turned out in the teal Ottoman-style Army uniform with a tasseled Fez hat. As Nasrullah's closest confidant, of a similar age, and raised in the same household, Akram Khan shared a special affinity with the Prince; they hunted, fished, and rode together. Akram flared up like a match when the Amir picked him first to join Nasrullah's entourage to England. His wide grin stretched his handlebar mustache almost to his earlobes.

"May I also introduce our distinguished Naieb-Salar *Sahib*, Hassein Khan?" Nasrullah gestured toward him with a nod. "His loyalty to my father began from their exiled days in Samarkand, before I was born. He's like my own flesh and blood."

"*Mamnoon-e-Shoma* Shahzadah," hissed Hassein Khan with a slight tilt of the head. He was comfortably settled on the chair, his fingers entwined over his round belly: he gave the impression of being an old soldier fatigued by a long retreat from battle. His Afghan Army rank of Naieb-Salar was the highest after the Amir and was equivalent to a British Field Marshal. Hassein Khan was a stout man in his mid-forties, of medium height; with an enormous appetite for lamb kebabs. He was said to be the kind of man who would not hesitate to slaughter a sheep a day. His habit after a full meal was to light up a *beedi*, thumb his onyx worry beads, and drink his green *chai*. From the very outset of his friendship with the Amir, he started climbing a ladder and waiting awhile on each rung before the Amir invited him to climb the next. His loyalty to the Amir was etched in stone long before the Amir was enthroned. As the years of turmoil and war went on, the Field Marshal fought valiantly alongside his longtime friend, Amir Abdul Rahman Khan. He had suffered a wound that contributed to his impotency and was no longer able to consummate his love for the two wives he had married in Samarkand.

"Everybody knows our Chief of Police, *Kotwal* Sahib Parwana Khan," Nasrullah continued with obvious admiration. "As long as he is our Kotwal, no one dares to break the law of the land."

Parwana Khan, Magistrate of Kabul, the Amir's *Jalad*, executioner, half-stood from his seat and raised a hand, palm up. A smile like a devious little flame appeared on his face suddenly, and almost involuntarily; he suppressed it and sat down again. His eyes were as hard and cold as frozen ponds. He was clad in a double breasted-jacked with four metal buttons flanked in front, a gold aiguillette tipped with brass hung from his left shoulder and, affixed to the right side of his jacket, were two medals of honor received for accomplishing high-profile executions—courtesy of the Amir. He was a masterful hangman, who carried out the Amir's particular brand of capital punishment designed to create an air of terror and panic in Kabul. No one knew why the Kotwal of Kabul was to accompany Nasrullah to England—the Amir kept most of his decisions to himself.

Nasrullah gestured across the mahogany table, "This is *Dagarwal*, Zalmai Khan, the Head of the Palace Guard. May Allah protect us all and may our journey be safe and free of mishaps. We count on Zalmai Khan to keep us safe and sound, *Insha Allah!* He has the enormous task of taking us safely to Landan and bringing us safely back home. Let's pray for his success and well-being." They all obediently lifted their hands in a brief attitude of prayer.

"*Tashakur, Shahzadah!*" Zalmai Khan set his hand on his heart and bowed slightly.

Colonel Zalmai Khan was the son of a well-respected army officer who had played a major role in Amir's grandfather's Army. He spoke English passably and his Afghan military rank of *Dagarwal* was equivalent to a Colonel in the Royal British Army. He was a good-looking man in his mid-thirties whose facial features, framed by luxuriant hair and sideburns, emitted lucent intelligence. He was tall, lithe, and lean and his voice had a natural ascendancy well-suited for a commanding army officer. His sturdy muscular physique and self-confidence, in addition to his straightforwardness and perspicacity, had awarded him the task of guarding the Amir and his household.

Nasrullah went on to introduce his chief of logistics, the scar-faced Major Akbar Khan, a bony man in his mid-thirties, and his assistant, Lieutenant Mahmoud Khan, a bit older than the Major, a man of medium-height with a noticeably bulbous nose. Both he and the Major wore brown military uniforms to which the Lieutenant had added shiny knee-high boots and a brown Chitrali hat. As Nasrullah introduced the Major, he bowed low and the medals pinned onto his faded jacket emitted a high-pitched clink like the sound of a cowbell. The organization of night stops, food preparation, essentials, supplies, and moving, on the journey to London and back, were under the command of Akbar Khan and Mahmoud Khan. Both the Major and the Lieutenant were birds of the same feather. They were men of dubious morality; a fact which could, if they were caught, swiftly send them to the gallows of Kabul and know the tautness of a noose around their necks. Their love for the colorless *Arak* with sixty percent alcohol content, which they distilled covertly, made them vulnerable to the death sentence. But, fearless as strong-winged eagles, they preferred to enjoy the present buzz rather than concern themselves with the possibility of public execution. Many inhabitants of the land believed it was not the right way for an Afghan to prove his bravery: nevertheless, when their supplies ran short, the Major and his lieutenant would load their mules with their homemade copper alembic, burlap sacks of raisins, and other ingredients, and head off to some remote and hidden spot to secretly ferment their *Arak*—away from the Amir's spies, and the inquisitive eyes their Jewish neighbors. Once the distillation process was complete, the seasoned booze-makers topped up their *kozas*, clay jars, with *Arak* and returned to Kabul. The jars were hidden down their wells to keep curious neighbors and snitches at bay. They did not need a crystal ball to tell them they would eventually be caught. Their game was as dicey as trying to catch a fish by hand. Besides making and consuming forbidden alcohol, the Major and the Lieutenant had a fondness for the occasional departure into opium or hashish. So far, they had managed to escape any official notice of their activities.

With the introductions over, Dr. Hamilton announced the beginning of the training, observing with her keen eye, a deep-seated need for change in every participant.

"I will start with an overview of every topic that we will cover in the time ahead. Because we are English born, every one of us learned English table manners since we were children," she said, flipping to the page in her notebook. "And because it is different from the Afghan style, we are here to help you to learn the way to eat, drink, and converse with an Englishman or woman while you are in England."

"The invitation to Windsor is only limited to His Highness," she nodded at Nasrullah, "and possibly two of his courtiers, but the rest of you will be working with some high-ranking British officers with whom you will be interacting daily. Therefore, I suggest you will all need these skills." She paused, "but first and foremost, this is very important, we must discuss punctuality for appointments!" She glanced at the Prince and Major Akbar Khan. "Please be aware, you will be notified of your appointments with the Windsor Royal Court early—possibly one to two weeks in advance. Mr. Martin will be keeping you abreast of all His Highness's appointments."

Frank Martin leaned back in his seat and grinned, "I have the hardest job of all," he joked, but despite the smile, he meant what he said. "Somebody had to do it, and that somebody turned out to be me," he pointed wryly at himself and glanced at Nasrullah. "I have discovered that holding His Highness to specific times is next to impossible."

Nasrullah looked sufficiently chastened and suddenly found a need to study the fine Maimana rug at his feet.

"I'll do my best to help you, Sahib Maarteen," he declared contritely. "There will be no need to worry."

"The next important thing is hygiene," she continued pacing restlessly while reading her notes, stopping now and then to assure herself that every Afghan was paying careful attention, "clean clothing, skin, hands, including nails, and clean white teeth, are a must. Bad breath must be carefully monitored. As your doctor, I can supply you with some mouthwash, Odol perhaps, or some pungent chewing herbs to help you. And I also have scented oil to apply after a bath."

"On social matters which will be covered extensively," she retrieved her glass that sat on the mantelpiece next to a carving of miniature ivory elephants and took a sip of water. On the wall above the fireplace, a portrait of Amir's father gazed down on this unusual gathering. "Never sit with your back to another without asking to be excused. And never carry a private conversation in presence of someone else." She straightened the bow in her hair and continued, "Please, gentlemen, stop me if you have any questions."

"Daktar Sahiba Hameeltoon," the Prince said with ill-controlled impatience, "These things you're teaching us, we practice the same in Afghanistan. Do you ever see me disrespecting my father or someone in his presence? Is it necessary to waste your time teaching us what we already know?"

"You are right, Your Highness, but I'm making sure I cover

everything His Highness, your father, instructed us to tell you. But may I move forward to explain the proper etiquette that must be employed when you are with Her Majesty, Queen Victoria if you don't mind?" She turned to the next page.

Nasrullah's resentment reverberated in Dr. Hamilton's ears, and she was careful not to escalate this, or any matter, with the Prince. There must be nothing that might provoke Nasrullah to rage or ill demeanor and involve the intervention of the Amir—the small British group was especially sensitive to any disruption which might cause a possible cancelation of Nasrullah's meeting with Queen Victoria. Lillias had always walked a fine line in Nasrullah's presence; recognizing his unpredictable persona, she was always on edge around him and used ecclesiastical diplomacy to appease this rebellious young man. A quiet signal from Mr. Martin caused her to change her mind.

"Would you like a few minutes break?" Lillias asked with a smile, "Let's do ten to fifteen minutes and then resume with the session."

The fifteen minutes break was long enough for the Afghans to light up their *beedis* and perk up outside the parlor. They stepped out on the vast terrace, their footsteps clicking sharply against the marble floor. There was silence at first as they leaned against the handrails, allowing the blast of cool air to refresh their faces and to feel the coziness of their bodies inside their warm woolen coats. On this crisp, wintry day, the sun shone brightly in a clear blue sky and the melting snow had a purity that elevated their spirits. Ahead of them, a new chapter was set to open and a new story to be written regarding their voyage to London. As they looked out from the high terrace across the rows of grapevines still naked from relentless winter freeze, there was the sure promise of spring, when buds would sprout again from every stem.

Qomandan-e-Ala, General, Akram Khan leaned against the iron guardrails and, viewing the Kabul landscape through a blur, removed his dirty spectacles, breathed on them, and wiped them with his silken kerchief. He had heavy circles under his eyes as though he has not slept for days. Extracting a beedi from his top pocket, he put the cigarette between his lips and lit it with a single strike of a match.

"*Shahzadah*," he said, as the scented smoke spewed from his mouth; he clamped the beedi between his fingers, "Do you feel the same as I do? Isn't this training a humiliation to us Afghans? Do we have a hygiene problem?"

"*Sardar*, Lord, Akram Jan," Nasrullah replied, "this so-called etiquette training boils my blood!" He exhaled a long breath and shook his head irritably. "Unfortunately, my hands are tied because of my father. There's nothing you or I can do as long as he approves these *Englees-Ha* to be in charge! They are in charge of everything!" He gesticulated with a wide sweep of his arm as he spoke, "they tell us how to run our country, how to visit their Queen, how to eat, how to greet, how to stay hygienically clean. I wonder what else they'll add to their list of demands? I hope they won't tell us how to pray to Allah, that would mean bloodshed!"

Naieb-Salar, Field Marshal, Hassein Khan asked the General for a *beedi*, "*Shahzadah* and General Akaram Khan, may I request you to keep something confidential?" he accepted a light from the General, shielded the flame against the cool breeze, and breathed out a plume of smoke.

"Of course!" Nasrullah said and both men nodded.

"When His Highness, Amir Sahib and I were exiled in Turkestan, before the days he became the Amir," he took another drag of the beedi, "We made a deal with the *Naieb-Ul-Hokoma-e-Roosya*, Russian Governor-General, Konstantin Von Kaufman. We asked him for resources and fighting men to cross the Oxus River with us and kick the *Englees-Ha* out of Afghanistan." An intense odor wafted from the smoldering cigarette, a bit like last week's fish. The British and Indians brought those cigarettes in from India for their own use, and as presents for their fellow countrymen, while offering the Afghans harmful cheap tobacco flakes wrapped in tendu leaves. The Field Marshal went on, "Before we bid farewell to the Czarist *Naieb-Ul-Hokoma*, he gave us five-thousand gold coins and made arrangements with the Turkoman and Uzbek tribal elders in Afghanistan to give us men to start a war with them." The smoke partially obscured his flabby face. "When we arrived in Mazar-i-Sharif, the fighting men joined us to start the war against the *Englees-Ha*." He shrugged, "Suddenly four *Englees* men with top hats and frock coats met us. They wanted to make a deal to recognize Amir Sahib as the ruler and promised us hefty subsidies in return. "Amir Sahib made an agreement with them on one condition—complete Afghan autonomy! But then, you know, they changed their mind."

The *Kotwal*, Magistrate, Parwana Khan joined the conversation as the Field Marshal continued, "Obviously, we did not get full autonomy. However, that's behind us." He extracted his onyx worry beads from his pocket and began thumbing them over, one by one, "Let's look forward and accomplish our goal in Landan and not allow ourselves to be offended with the training. We Afghans are sensitive and serious, but there is no room for being upset over training that could benefit us in the long run." He cast his gaze at Parwana Khan, "Am I right *Kotwal* Sahib?"

The rhythmic clicking of his worry beads covered a short silence from the *Kotwal*. Parwana Khan nodded with a smile that exposed his rust-colored teeth and returned the Field Marshal's look.

"Absolutely *Naieb-Salar* Sahib."

As expected, those in higher command, Prince Nasrullah and three high-ranking officers, separated themselves from the three other Afghan Army officers, Colonel Zalmai Khan, Major Akbar Khan, and Lieutenant Mahmoud Khan, who descended the three flights of stairs to the grapevine orchards. Colonel Zalmai stood taller than the Major and the lieutenant, and glanced down as he spoke to them.

"As I passed by the General and the Prince, I accidentally overheard their conversation." The Colonel's one distinctive feature besides his height was his cleft chin, but there was kindness in the Colonel's brown eyes and a quiet strength in his deportment. "General Akram Khan and *Shahzadah* Nasrullah Khan seem angry about the training we are receiving."

"What the hell, man, who cares how you eat? That's why God gave me hands to take a big gulp and eat. God never gave me a spoon, and a knife and fork!" Major Akbar Khan whipped a box of chewing tobacco from the pocket of his faded blue jacket and offered a couple of pinches of the greenish *naswar* to Lieutenant Mahmoud and Colonel Zalmai. Zalmai refused, "No thank you, I'm done with that." He lifted his enormous hand in a dismissive gesture, "I've tried it a few times and noticed my gums were getting diseased. I'm not going to start it again."

Akbar and Mahmoud tucked the fine dried tobacco grounds, mixed with tree ash and lime paste, under their tongues. The powdery alkaline substance dissolved gradually giving them a slight high and sense of ease.

"I agree with General Akram Khan. These *Mordagow*, pimp, *Englees-Ha* think we Afghans are from another planet and have no manners," Akbar said, squatting against the feeling of dizziness from the *naswar*.

Mahmoud could not care less about the training conversation that Zalmai had overheard, instead, he focused on Roma and Olivia Worth.

"Those two *Englees* girls, what are their names?" He scratched under his Chitrali cap trying to remember. "Never mind their names, they're not bad at all!" He shielded his eyes from the bright winter sun. "The taller one's sparkling blue eyes, hair, tiny waist, and breasts. Ah!" said Mahmoud with a lustful look. "And the other girl! *Ba khoda, mesl-e-paree-koh-e-qaff*, by God, just as a ferry from the Caucuses." He spat out his *naswar* and the green mess splattered grotesquely under the grapevine.

"You horny tomcat," Colonel Zalmai said, "don't get caught for making inappropriate comments like that. Roma is Daktar Laila's sister and *Khanum* Oilevia is Queen Sultana's favorite person. Do you know the consequences you would face? What if Amir Sahib finds out?" He shifted a warning glance from Lieutenant Mahmoud and back to Major Akbar, a bemused frown furrowing his brow. "Are your heads still upon your necks?" he continued, "Are your hands still upon your wrists? Are you still in one piece?"

"Yes." Says Major Akbar Khan.

"Well then, shut up before they're hacked," he whispered in the lieutenant's face, "that is if the Amir doesn't lock you up in hanging cages to rot, which is the least punishment you would face!" Inwardly he raged at Mahmoud's stupidity.

At that moment, Frank Martin called that the break was over; the Major and his Lieutenant spat out the last of their *naswar* and followed after Colonel Zalmai as he marched upstairs.

CHAPTER SIXTEEN

Shahzada Nasrullah wrote an enciphered note to Khairo and handed it to the palace footman for delivery. 'Meet me at Bala-Hisar', the letter read, 'and let no one know you are coming.'

On this late January night, the sky over Kabul was bright with stars—the massive zodiacal spread clung like snow crystals to the black heavens. It was a serene and bucolic setting with an icy wind that cut like a thousand razors as it mercilessly swooped down from the northern highlands. A distant chorus of dog barks echoed from the nearby hills.

Nasrullah urged his horse to a canter on the three-mile ride to Bala-Hisar. The fifth-century fortress lay at the southern end of *Koh-i-Sher-Darwaza*, known as the Lion Gate mountain. Khairo was already waiting in the shadows.

"Do you still want to hear what I whispered in my father's ear after you talked to the audience in the Darbar hall?" Nasrullah called, as the horses' hoofs thudded on the damp road towards Butkhak, approximately twenty miles east of Kabul.

"I would be glad to hear it, Your Highness," Khairo's voice was muffled by the covering of his turban." Curiosity alerted him like thirst. They slowed their horses to a trot.

"When you badmouthed *Englees-Ha* that day, the Amir was ready to send you to the *Siyah Chal*, the Black Pit, up there in Bala-Hisar. There are plenty of human remains there and I am sure few are close to death as I'm speaking to you right now. You would have rotted there without food or water. In this weather, you would have frozen solid. Failing that, he would have buried you alive—used whatever means

to get rid of you, but Habibullah and I asked him to spare your life."
Nasrullah revealed the truth to Khairo because he had shown himself
to be faithful, splitting his fidelity equally between his homeland and
Nasrullah himself.

"Your Highness, I owe you my life! It is with sincere gratitude I
ask the Almighty Allah that he may grant you success. I did nothing
deliberately to offend or insult your father except to reveal the
facts about the murderous *Englees-Ha* who killed my daughter and
brothers, but as I said to you before, I was ready to face death if he
chose to order my execution."

Prince Nasrullah slowed his horse to a walk, "Khairo Khan! I'm
grateful that your life was spared and you should be grateful because
I despise the *Englees-Ha* just as much as you do." As they quickened
their pace again, Khairo's thoughts followed the pounding of his
heart. His body swayed back and forth with the canter of his horse.

"Shahzadah! I pray to Allah for your well-being and good
intentions. I hope you make these bastards pay for my family's
blood." For a moment he held his woolen shawl wide open with both
hands and then wrapped himself snug and tight and grasped the reins
again.

"Khairo Khan," Nasrullah shouted back, "I must keep my
thoughts to myself because of my father who wants this deal with
Malika Weektorya to result in his favor." Again, he reined his horse
in hard and it pawed the ground, whinnied and snorted, and then
trotted on as Nasrullah eased his grip. "According to his advice, he
wants me as humble as a lamb when I see *Malika Weektorya*," he
continued, "but believe me, in my heart, I'm not as genuine with my
father as I should be." He gripped the rein of Khairo's horse and
stopped them both. He stared at Khairo, "I feel the trust between you
and I has been deepening, and that's why I'm open to revealing these
confidential family issues to you. You can count on me as long as you
don't betray me!"

"*Shahzadah*, you have my word." The Prince nodded and released his horse.

Khairo followed Nasrullah down a narrow path and across a wide stream and patted his horse's neck as it regained its footing. Behind them, they could hear the sound of cascading water as it battered against boulders and rocks and, in the distance, the barking of dogs spoke of the presence of villages.

"I get angry when my father and Habibullah praise the *Englees-Hai-e-shaitan*. Not long ago they signed the treaty of *Khat-e-Deourwand*, Durand Line, and divided Afghanistan almost in half. Those bastards have done nothing good for us but used us and divided us as people, they claimed half of the Pashtun land for themselves!" Prince Nasrullah raised himself on his stirrups and gently swayed with the rhythm of his horse as they made their slow way back to the main track. "*Ba Khoda*, by God, if I had had a say in this, it would not have been allowed to happen," he continued. "I'm hearing from many tribal elders that this was wrong on my father's part to have the filthy *Englees-Ha* annex our Pashtun land and name it Northwest Frontier, dividing brothers and cousins—dividing sons and fathers."

"I agree with those tribal elders," Khairo said dispiritedly, "It is the same in the city of Quetta, we have been divided from our family members there. Many Alokozai clansmen live there and many in Qandahar."

"I know for a fact many tribes are beginning to rise against the *Englees-Ha*. The Afridis are dispatching their men at the Khyber Pass and not allowing one British garrison to control the lifeline," the Prince added bitterly. "I cannot believe that *Mordagow,* pimp, Durand, convinced my father to break Afghanistan with that so-called *Khat-e-Deourwand*.

The treaty had been signed in Parachinar, Afghanistan, twenty-six months before, to delineate the tribal areas between British India and Afghanistan separating the Pashtun and Baluch tribes on each side of the one-thousand-five-hundred-mile long border. The architect was Sir Mortimer Durand who convinced Amir to sign the treaty.

"*Shahzadah*, there is nothing to worry about. They can build the bogus *Khat-e-Deourwand* with a steel wall and still nothing will stop us from coming and going to our land and people. It's only an imaginary line in their feeble brains," Khairo spoke quietly to pacify his friend. "Your Highness, what is Amir Sahib's position on this if I may ask?"

"Well, my father has a point too, but the notion is hard to digest," Nasrullah replied. "He constantly repeats it in every meeting of his royal court, so the people can be reminded of the hardship he's undergoing with the *Englees-Ha*." The clatter of their horses reverberated in the background. "He says *Englees-Ha* are superior and have a strong military and they give us subsidies to stay afloat. If he refused to sign the treaty they would have replaced him in two days with another Shah-Shuja who would abide by their demands and rules and we would have had another round of bloodshed for years to come." He drew his leopard-lined *Chapan* coat more tightly around himself and covered his neck with its fur.

"Well, Shahzadah," Khairo sighed deeply, "the bastards have us by the balls. Damned if you do, damned if you don't. But regardless, and I'm repeating myself to Your Highness. Nothing to worry about. That *Muzakhraf*, stupid, imaginary line doesn't mean anything to us Afghans," he gestured to the south with a wide sweep of his hand. "Generations will pass but no one can stop us from crossing their fictitious borderline. I have many cousins and in-laws on the other side and they're not worried either, and those Baluchis I know in Qandahar and Quetta feel the same." He looked up, "the Almighty above us," he raised his index finger towards the countless bright stars above, "will give us the helping hand to break the back of these *Englees-hai murdar*, filthy English.

Prince Nasrullah reined in and dismounted, "My apologies, Khairo

Khan, my bladder is ready to burst. In the winter, I always need to urinate often." He handed his horse's bridle to Khairo, removed his knee-long trench coat, and set it on his horse. "I have no idea why my father is so worried about what *Malika* Weektorya might say when I present her with his letter." He unbuckled and unbuttoned his britches and crouched next to an oak stump.

"Your Highness, if she wants popularity and support in Afghanistan she should give Amir Sahib his wish to run his foreign policy." His horse pawed restlessly and swayed its neck. "As my father told us the story, *Malika Weektorya* had bad experiences with your late Uncle, Sardar Sahib Wazir Akbar Khan, who decapitated the British General Pollack and suspended the head from the dome of Char-Chatta bazaar." He smirked, "For a month, it entertained the crowd." He paused, "I am told the Queen was also in deep distress when the bad news of the massacre of sixteen-thousand British in the Pass near *Khord* Kabul was dispatched to her as they were in retreating to Hindustan. That was exactly fifty-three years ago." He pointed in the direction of the Pass, "Right there, the Pass is less than an hour away. Most of them that were not massacred by Afghans froze to death," he continued, "only one was left alive to report the mayhem they endured." He tightened his grip on the reins as Nasrullah's horse shifted impatiently. "If I recall my father said he was a Daktar."

"Are you talking about Daktar Weellioom Baridoon, Doctor William Brydon?" Nasrullah asked, still crouching.

"That's right Your Highness, May Allah reward you, yes, his name was Daktar Baridoon. He reached safety in Jalalabad at the end of the long retreat from Kabul," Khairo went on, "wounded and exhausted, slumped over the saddle of his wounded horse."

"You certainly taught them a lesson at Maiwand!" Nasrullah rose to his feet and picked up a small piece of hard clay.

"That's etched in stone, *Sardar Sahib,* and will never fade from their memory," Khairo said, "even their little dog witnessed their screams when that little beast barked at me for decapitating them. Blood was splattering in all directions - my hands were submerged in their crimson blood." He straightened his voluminous turban, "Yes, that made them run with their tails between their legs."

"I can imagine the scene - them running for their lives!" Nasrullah replied as he dabbed his penis with the clay. "Knowing these *Englees-ha*, they'll do anything to shun my father." He tossed the urine-soaked clay over a bolder. "I'm pessimistic that the *Malika* will do anything." He stood up, buckled his britches, and shrugged into his coat.

"Do you have another option, if she says no?"

"Don't know, I haven't thought about it much. I'm sure there's an option for everything with those bastards. It depends what choice will be the best."

"I wish I could go with you."

"Do you want to?"

"Of course, Your Highness!" Khairo said, smiling. He covered his disfigured face.

"I would need to do some hard thinking if I wanted to take you to *Englistan* with me," Nasrullah said, "my men have already been chosen, but there may be another way . . . "

"I am sure Your Highness is looking forward to unencumbered travel to *Englistan*, but amongst the rest of those who are accompanying you, I could be marginalized and isolated because of my disfigurement. I would not get in the way."

"I can't promise, but let me try talking to Daktar Hameeltoon to see if she thinks your wounds are treatable in *Englistan*," he took his horse's reins from Khairo and looked him in the eye, " I don't want anyone to become suspicious as to why you will be accompanying me. It must not be for any other reason than recovering your features."

"May Allah reward you for your good intentions, Your Highness, I will be forever grateful."

As Nasrullah and Khairo rode back towards the Palace the black curtain of night enveloped them and the midnight wind was dry and as fresh as ice.

Khairo slipped into a deep reverie as he followed the Prince making their way between boulders, rocks, and over-flowing streams. There were times when he had felt as if the world was slowly fading before his eyes and the pain of the loss of Malalai and his brothers became unbearable. The entire Maiwand population had endured hardship and loss in the fifteen years following the battle, but this resilient nation had always pitted itself against mighty foes yet healed and strengthened itself to face the next challenge as a new cycle of life evolved. It was an all too familiar pattern of life for the Afghans and Khairo was just an infinitesimal example of the whole; he could bring himself back to a standing position, yet his tears flowed in such generous streams with longing for a hand to reach down. His virtue lay in the ability to climb hearing only his footfalls; yet still, he imagined, life would become brighter in the company of a friend like Prince Nasrullah Khan.

Facing the iron-fisted Amir in his *Darbar* hall in the audience of some five-hundred other tribal elders could have cost Khairo his life when he recounted the atrocious British acts he and thousands of others had witnessed. As a result of his bravery, Khairo's wish to accompany Nasrullah to England was soon to become a reality. On that night ride, however, the feelings of hopelessness perished, and his friendship with the young prince strengthened.

CHAPTER SEVENTEEN

The English ladies had meticulously planned a rehearsal in royal dining for the Afghans. Chairs were set on either side of the mahogany table in the Palace's dining hall with one at each end, comfortably spaced for the guests to dine and with sufficient room between each seating for those who would be serving. A place-setting eighteen inches across for each guest was set on a crisp white linen tablecloth.

"It is just like a silver service dinner at Windsor but on a smaller scale!" Roma said enthusiastically when they stood back to admire their work.

At this rehearsal, the guests of honor were made up of all the new British arrivals, Messrs. Clemence and Frank, the Afghans, and Prince Omar Jan. Mesdames Clemence and Martin were to pose as staff of the royal household and serve the meals. Each setting on the table consisted of a brass service plate; a finely pleated stiff napkin folded in the form of Bishop's miter; three forks on the left; spoons and knives on the right; four crystal glasses - one glass for each sufficed for the anti-bibulous settings on the Afghans' part. The service plate would be replaced by a dinner plate immediately after the appetizers were served. This was a complete setting for the three-course servings before dessert. Thereafter, dessert spoons and forks were to be brought in on the dessert plate.

For the new learners, the anxiety to grasp this manner of dining was like a blow to the head. Some were frowning darkly, some fidgeting, and some were glancing at each other. The table was glorious, decorated with flowers in the most magnificent style, Frank

Martin had manufactured a grand pair of candelabra in the Amir's *Mashin-Khana*, resembling the nine-branch at Windsor Palace. They were fitted with white wax candles and symmetrically placed at either end of the table along with assorted trays of fruit, apples, pears, pomegranates, oranges, and a large assortment of grapes. Everything was geometrically spaced and balanced. Dr. Hamilton and Chief Engineer Martin cordially ushered everyone to their seat, which was identified with a name card. Lillias and Frank both took their seats and called upon the rest to watch the dry run.

"The settings may not exactly resemble those in Windsor Palace, but will be close enough for you to understand what to expect," Dr. Hamilton explained. Raj the translator interpreted in his lilted Dari. Offering a bemused smile, Lillias started the drill. "The order for the menu is: *Bolani* or *Samosa* for an appetizer, soup for the first course, then fish; for the entree will be two cranes replacing the roast chickens previously planned, and lastly, salad."

"You all should be grateful to me for hunting the cranes - they are now part of the training," the Prince said, wiggling his eyebrows and chuckling.

"Of course, Your Highness." Dr. Hamilton smiled, sharing in everyone's amusement. "Before we move forward," she continued, "let me explain about the utensils and settings. You have the following: a service plate," she pointed at it. "It is used as an underplate for your first course. You'll possibly have two service plates changed, and this is a butter plate." She raised the utensils one by one, "This is a dinner fork, fish fork, salad fork, dinner knife, fish knife, salad knife, butter knife, soup spoon, or fruit spoon." The Afghans listened and watched attentively like snakes to a charmer's flute.

For centuries Afghans had eaten their food with their right hands from a plate shared with two or more people. It took skill to elevate a hand laden with rice and meat and fill their mouth with a stroke of their thumb while ensuring that not a single grain of rice fell.

Lillias took the crisp napkin, unfolded it, and placed it neatly on her lap. "Please do the same," she said and everyone followed suit. "Never start eating unless the hostess or the host starts first." She sat stiffly in her seat, "You hold the fork in your left hand, tines downward," she said, demonstrating on a piece of crane breast, "hold your knife in your right hand, an inch or two above the plate, then extend your index finger along the top of the blade," Lillias paused, "like this," and she cut it with dexterity. "Can everybody see my hands?" Some further away bobbed their heads for a better view, "Use your fork to spear and lift food to your mouth." She chewed in little spasms, her mouth closed.

"When you dine formally and food is offered," Frank Martin said, "take a little bite of everything, even it's something that you don't like," he glanced around the table. "Then, without raising an issue leave the rest of it on your plate."

"*Sahib Maarteen*," Nasrullah said, leaning forward on his chair. "You know we don't touch anything that's not halal, blessed the Islamic way." He furrowed his brow, "You've lived in Kabul long enough to understand this. Why make us do something that we won't do?"

"I understand Your Highness, we have to find a way around that and make it easy for you."

"The way around is already set." Nasrullah looked at Frank Martin intently. "My two royal chefs and four culinary assistants are to accompany me to Landan, they will cook exactly what I eat." The Prince drew his shoulders back and raised his chin high. "When I go to *Qasr-e-Weenzor* I don't have to eat or drink anything!" he declared stubbornly, "or maybe my chefs will prepare the food for me in *Qasr-e-Weenzor*. We just can't eat anything you eat."

"Your Highness." Lillias Hamilton concurred, "I understand your apprehension, it is something we had not thought about. Let's give Mr. Martin the chance to investigate how this can be resolved." She took a deep breath and glanced at Frank.

"I will make some inquiries with the office of British Viceroy in India and will get back to Your Highness soon," he promised.

Mesdames Clemence and Martin began to remove everyone's appetizer plate, while some were still working on their final bites. Seated next to Roma was the Prince's Head of the Palace Guard,, Colonel Zalmai Khan. The Colonel was anticipating the next course and trying to recall which utensils would be used. Roma pointed out the correct cutlery.

"Here's how you grip a knife and fork, Colonel," she demonstrated with a smile.

"Thank you," the Colonel flashed his gleaming white teeth.

Nasrullah's brows darkened and his eyes narrowed as envy hit him like a lack of oxygen.

Sitting at the far corner of the table, Lieutenant Mahmoud Khan also eyed Roma and Zalmai jealously—lust was gnawing at him. But any insubordination towards the Colonel would jeopardize his position as the Chief of Logistics and he had no choice but to observe and remain silent.

"Thank you again," Zalmai replied, his warm affectionate eyes met hers and unexpectedly caused Roma to tremble. "Like this?" he gripped the fork clumsily.

"I'll be happy to show you again if you like," she said. Her warm perfume reached his nostrils and he felt his heart beat faster as her gaze met his.

"I'm grateful to you Ms. Roma."

Nasrullah eyed Zalmai and Roma from the corner of his eye and he noticed her gaze straying toward Zalmai's broad shoulders and strong biceps. He could not tolerate this moment of flirtation any longer.

"Daktar *Sahiba*!" Nasrullah snapped, "Could you please continue with the training? Immediately!" He clenched his teeth in a grimace.

Lillias Hamilton immediately cast an eye at Roma and Zalmai, "Of course Your Highness." "Can I have everyone's attention, please? Since I am the presumed hostess and have already finished this course," she entwined her fingers and rested her elbows on the table, "My plate will be removed and yours will be removed at the same time, regardless of what's left." She rose to her feet and paced around the table. As Raj was translating, he was trying to stay abreast with the Doctor. "You must keep up with the hostess or else you may lose the opportunity to finish your favorite course.

Her focus turned briefly to William and Prince Omar Jan, "You seem to be doing well, little men!" She stood behind them and patted their heads.

"Daktar Hameeltoon," General Akram Khan pushed his thick-lensed glasses up the bridge of his nose with one hand and raised the other.

"If I could share this short story about *Malika* Weektorya." he paused waiting for permission.

"Yes General, please, by all means."

"Daktar Alfredo Gray once told us *Malika* Weektorya eats very fast and no one can keep up with her. Everyone's plate gets removed before having a bite or two to eat. Is that what you know too?"

"Well, General *Sahib*, what you heard from Doctor Gray is not for me to judge, I've never dined with Her Majesty. When you are in Windsor you will witness her eating habits for yourself."

"This is your first course," Lillias said, as the ladies set steamy bowls of spicy lamb soup before them. "Does anyone know which spoon to use for the soup?"

Nasrullah pointed to the dessert spoon and said, "That one!"

"Your Highness, you're close but not quite." She looked around. " Would anyone else like to try?"

Roma raised the spoon above her head drawing Mahmoud's gaze to focus on her bosom shaped like pale crescent moons above her bodice. The Prince also eyed her seductively, and for a moment a smile spread across his thinly bearded face like a crack spreading across a dam. Every so often both the Lieutenant and Prince Nasrullah would sneak a glance at Olivia who was seated safely between Thomas Clemence and Frank Martin.

"Thank you, Roma, could you please explain the difference between that and a dessert spoon?" her sister asked.

As Roma pointed out the difference between the two spoons several minds wandered and chose to contemplate her beauty and charm; her pink rouged cheeks, dark lashes, oiled eyelids, glossy lips, and the gentle swell of her breasts.

The signal was given to start their soup, and there followed a sudden chorus of slurping sounds - loud and audacious; the magistrate, Parwana Khan, was the loudest of all.

"Please stop! Please stop everyone! I want you to watch me," Dr. Hamilton called disapprovingly. "Firstly," She raised her index finger, "do not blow on your soup, let it cool off on its own. Step two," she raised her middle finger. "Do not slurp. The noise is not only distracting but unpleasant for other people at the table. I want you to hold the filled soup spoon low over your bowl for about thirty seconds to cool, and then proceed to eat without any sound. Now let us try it again."

This time resulted in a better outcome but was still a work in progress.

"Your second course is deep-fried trout," Lillias said glancing at Lieutenant Mahmoud Khan. "Lieutenant, can you please explain how you normally eat your fish?"

"Do you mean how we Afghans . . . " he cleared his throat, "eat our fish?" He sounded as though his vocals were raspy, dry, and cracked from dehydration.

"Yes please," Dr. Hamilton said.

Crossing and uncrossing his legs, the Lieutenant wriggled nervously like a captive fish, "We normally place the deep-fried fish . . . on a long flat Afghan bread." He gave another hacking cough, "Then we shake some hot pepper and salt and squeeze a lemon over it. Thereafter, we tear a hunk of bread and eat them together with the fish. Don't forget to remove the bones. That's it!" He touched his brown archery hat.

"Eat with your hands?"

"*Balay!* Yes!"

"Not when you are in London."

"Mr. Clemence, could you explain the manner of eating fish the English way?"

"I'll be glad to, Dr. Hamilton," Thomas Clemence said enthusiastically, "This is a fish knife . . . " suddenly, Nasrullah interjected.

"I'll be glad when this voyage is over," he said getting to his feet. He sauntered over to the colossal window facing the view of Kabul and the palace grapevines, with his hands in the pocket of his riding breeches. "So, I can continue to eat as I like to eat. Why is this so complicated? Why use different forks and different spoons for different foods? Why can't you *Englees-Ha* eat everything with one spoon and one fork? Why is it shameful to you if I eat with my hands?" A hush filled the parlor. Not even a single clink of cutlery could be heard. He slowly spun on his heel and faced the table. The two English ladies who had worked tirelessly until that moment remained fixed to the spot, plates in hand. "That's why Allah has given us hands to eat with," he continued, "why should we be forced to eat with spoons and forks?" Everyone in the dining hall squirmed with discomfort. "I don't understand. This is the culture we have practiced for centuries. Why should we change for you *Englees-Ha?*" Nasrullah demanded.

Off he goes, the idiot is irrational again, can't accept anything beyond his own way of upbringing, Frank Martin thought, rolling his eyes as he looked in Dr. Hamilton's direction. But Lillias Hamilton knew the Prince's thinking was not at fault. Before the arrival of the

East India Company, Afghanistan had remained isolated for centuries and few Europeans had crossed the border to travel inside the country. Thus, the incorrigible norms of everyday life from plowing, to weaving carpets, to ways of eating, were firmly entrenched in the culture. Lillias was also well aware that in Afghanistan, one must adapt to their ways and traditions to be accepted by them. There was no antipodal approach. But, now, she had hoped, there might be a breakthrough for the first time.

"Your Highness," Dr. Hamilton said humbly, "Your questions are legitimate – I quite understand your viewpoint. May I attempt to answer your questions?"

"*Khwahesh mekunam*, please, go ahead," he replied calmly. He was leaning against the window frame with one hand in his pocket.

"Thank you, Your Highness. Firstly, there is a reason why utensils are useful when hot foods are served. That way hands and mouths don't get burnt." Her eyes moved between the Prince and the others at the table. "Secondly, as your Highness perhaps remembers, when I arrived in Kabul I immediately attempted to master the skill of eating with my hands. I practiced with every meal in my private setting so no one could watch me, but I did watch how you, and others in the Royal household, ate your food. I saw the dexterity in your wrists, fingers, and joints . . . how masterful you all were at eating the way you do." She smiled, "Before coming here to serve His Highness I lived in India but I never saw one Indian eat the same way as an Afghan." Her smile widened as she switched the story to herself. "Your Highness, you've seen me eating in the palace gatherings lately, I eat like an Afghan. No doubt, I can press the rice and lamb to a perfect consistency in my hand and eat it just like anyone in this palace."

William and Omar bored with the long lecture, left the table. Mrs. Martin gestured to William to sit down again but to no avail.

Dr. Hamilton went on, "I did this because I respect the Afghan traditions and culture . . . and, of course, His Highness and the rest of the Royal household for accepting me as one of your own."

"Of course, Daktar Haameeltoon. My father is grateful to you for saving his life," Nasrullah said with an expression of genuine appreciation. He sat down on his father's swivel rocking chair and faced the table.

"I'm obliged, Your Highness, but could I explain why the use of utensils is needed."

"*Khwahesh mekunam.*" Nasrullah said with a slight nod.

"The use of various utensils is part of the wider culture of demeanor and standards."

Nasrullah narrowed his eyes uncomprehendingly.

"It may not be a problem if Your Highness uses the wrong fork or spoon, but it is essential to understand and exercise the rules of the game. Your Highness needs to act as if you belong with the rest . . . like those who don't know any other way of eating." She glanced at her English friends and said, "If any of you object to my assertion please tell me. So, Your Highness, I implore you not to stress yourself if you use any spoon or fork incorrectly. It is really not an issue at all! And frankly, I'm also sometimes confused as to which spoon I should use for which meal!" This confession resulted in a sudden burst of laughter and the atmosphere relaxed.

"These are not strict protocols, but just a Victorian advancement in the fashion of dining," she stood up, gave a lopsided grin, bowed her head, and said, "Thank you for listening, Your Highness."

"*Tashakur*, Daktar Hameeltoon, I'm much more at ease hearing this. I'll try to do my best when I'm in *Weenzor*," he replied.

CHAPTER EIGHTEEN

❧❧❧

"Your Highness, when you are in Landan keep an eye on the diamond attached to Victoria's crown."

"Is it the Koh-i-Noor . . . the biggest and brightest in the world?" Nasrullah asked intrigued, "my father seldom brings it up and when I ask him questions, he changes the subject. Tell me about it."

"Yes, Your Highness, that's the Kho-i-Noor . . . it is this big!" he clenched his fist. "Amir Sahib has a point," smiled Khairo. "He doesn't want people to rise against the *Englees-Ha* for stealing the diamond from us."

Nasrullah shot a sideways glance at Khairo as their horses cantered abreast. "What do you know about it? Tell me."

"Your Highness, before I reveal the story, I implore you to keep it to yourself. If Amir Sahib finds out, he could make me disappear with a snap of his fingers."

"You have my word. I never normally take a private ride with anyone without the approval of the court. You are the only one. I see the truth in your eyes. Don't worry . . . again, you have my word," Nasrullah winked.

"Humayoun, the second Mughal Emperor who ruled after his father, Babur, said this about the Koh-i-Noor," he threw a glance at Nasrullah then back at the road ahead. "'Such precious gems cannot be obtained by purchase; either they fall to one by the arbitrament of the flashing sword, which is an expression of Divine Will, or else they come through the grace of mighty monarchs.' So, Your Highness, I am making sure you know what the precious gem of Koh-i-Noor can do to empires and monarchs."

"C'mon Khairo Khan, tell me the story."

"Here's what my father told me in my youth," Khairo cleared his voice with a slight cough. "It weighed about eight *misqaal*, slightly over 37 grams, the largest and brightest *almas*, diamond, in the world."

"I already know that," Nasrullah retorted.

"I don't know how the Mughals first got the precious stone in their possession. No one knows the origin of the Koh-i-Noor, but it is clear how it left the Mughals' hands. It is written in the *Baburnama*, the autobiography of Babur, the founder of Mughul dynasty." The horses' tails swished from side to side as they rode. "His descendant, Shah Jahan who built the Taj Mahal had the magnificent stone set into his Peacock throne. Another Mughul descendant, in fact, the last one in the dynasty, Mohammad Shah Rangila, the colorful Mohammad Shah, was seventeen years old when he was chosen as the emperor." The steady rhythmic pounding of the horses' hooves formed a relaxing backdrop to their conversation. Khairo adjusted the covering to his disfigured face. "That Shah was a weak ruler, he loved to be entertained. For his morning pleasure, partridge and elephant fights were scheduled, in the evenings, jugglers, magicians, and mime artists performed for the Emperor who attended dressed in his bright tunics and pearl-embroidered shoes." The wind was dry and as fresh as ice against their faces. "He led an extravagant life: Delhi's poets, painters, scholars, theologians, mystics, musicians, and dancers, were among those that amused him. Finally, the longest-reigning Emperor was presiding over the declining power of the three-hundred-and-thirty-year-old dynasty." Nasrullah's horse snorted. "This was more than a hundred-and-fifty years ago. It was at that time that Nadir the Great, the mighty ruler of Persia defeated Mohammad Shah's army and advanced into Delhi."

"Well, what happened to the Koh-i-Noor?" Nasrullah interjected, glancing impatiently at Khairo Khan. Both men were silent for a moment listening to the distant barking of villagers' dogs.

"I'll get there Your Highness," Khairo said. "After Nadir lost nine-hundred of his soldiers in a bazaar brawl, he ordered a massacre. At the end of a single day's onslaught, thousands of Delhi's inhabitants lay dead. The generational Mughal Empire's hard-earned wealth was hauled away in a caravan of several hundred carts and camels." The long manes of their horses were swept up in the wind.

"Was the Koh-i-Noor also on a jewelry cart?" Nasrullah asked anxiously.

"No, Your Highness, Nadir took the possession of the peacock throne himself. He carried it across the Khyber Pass and then into Persia, where he was brutally killed by his own men. Then the first lady, Nadir Shah's wife handed the Koh-i-Noor to Nadir's entrusted bodyguard who was also his top general," Khairo reined in his horse and grinned at Nasrullah, "Can Your Highness guess who I'm talking about?"

Nasrullah fidgeted on his saddle, "No, tell me."

"That was Ahmad Shah Durani, our own great *Baba*, also known as Ahmad Shah Abdali, the founder of Afghanistan." He chuckled proudly and continued. "So, the Koh-i-Noor was now in our hands and stayed within the Durani family for a couple of generations until about ninety years ago when his grandson, Shah Shuja, was jailed by his rivals. His harem of seven wives and concubines escaped to British India for their safety." They dismounted and walked together for a few minutes, while Khairo finished his story. "In Lahore, a one-eyed and scar-faced Sikh Maharajah, Ranjit Singh, invited Shah Shujah to his Palace. There, Shah Shuja was separated from his harem, put under house arrest, and told to hand over the precious diamond. His harem was accommodated in another mansion with no access between them. Food and water rations for the disgraced Amir were reduced or randomly cut off." Khairo walked his horse to the stream bank close to the road and Nasrullah followed him. "The *haramzadah*, bastard, slowly increased the pressure on Shah Shuja and eventually caged him. He caved in and gave Ranjit Singh the diamond when his eldest son, Timur Shah, was tortured in front of him."

"Truly a bastard!" Nasrullah frowned.

"Yes Your Highness," chuckled Khairo, "That midget bastard also had a love of his own lethal homemade wine," He chuckled again, "he called it firewater . . . it was made with grape juice, orange seeds, and crushed gems."

"What happened to the Koh-i-Noor after that?" Nasrullah asked, preventing Khairo from straying off the subject. "Did he give it to the *Malkika* Weektorya?"

"No Your Highness," as Khairo shook his head loosening the flap of his turban—he wrapped it again around his face. " He proudly wore the diamond on his arm for the next ten years until he died. It was then donated to some tenth-century Hindu Temple in Jagannath, Puri."

Nasrullah laughed boisterously. "So, all of a sudden in his old age, he's as religious as a lizard on a rock and connects to his God with the stolen diamond!" he exclaimed through his laughter, "And, he's dying of crushed gem juice."

"From here on Your Highness, it gets much more interesting," Khairo said, chuckling with Nasrullah. "So, when Ranjit Singh died the *Englees-ha* wanted the diamond for themselves. They're like foxes, gray before they're good." He got back into his saddle. Immediately Nasrullah heard the British wanted the diamond, his blood boiled—a fire burned in all his branches and twigs. "Bastards!" he shook his head. "*Kho! Bogo! Baz chee shod?* Well! go on! What happened next?" he demanded.

"So then, the Satan *Englees-Ha* instigated a war between Sikh factions which engulfed Punjab province to a point of submission.

Once they muddied the waters, the East India Company annexed the Kingdom of Punjab. They officially ceded the Koh-i-Noor to Queen Victoria and Ranjit Singh's other assets to the Company."

"Their wickedness is like a ball of snow, when once set to roll, it must increase," Nasrullah commented. He remounted but allowed his horse to graze. "By Allah!" He raised his forefinger heavenward, "I'll make them pay when I see the *Malika*." Agitation and fury flowed from him like lava, "This was the same as the force used against *Haramzadah* Ranjit Singh." He stewed angrily then turned his horse towards the road. "Let's get out of here." As the horses began to move at a trot, he explored another thought, "But the great Nadir's wife handed the diamond to us Afghans. She handed it to us because of Ahmad Shah Durani's honorable long service and his record of excellence to her husband." He shook his head, "His top general! He was highly entrusted by Nadir, but neither Ranjit Singh, who had a heart like a snake, nor the *Englees-Ha* who're merciless as bailiffs, deserved the diamond."

"But lastly they made it look as if it was a gift from Ranjit Singh's family to *Malika* Weektorya and a treaty was signed."

In Article three of the treaty, it was written: 'The gem called the Koh-i-Noor, which was taken from Shah Shuja by Maharajah Ranjit Singh, shall be surrendered by the Maharajah of Lahore to the Queen of England.'

About fifty-four years before, in presence of the Board of Administration for the affairs of the province of Punjab, Ranjit Singh's ten-year-old son was compelled to hand over the precious diamond.

As he listened to the full story of the Koh-i-Noor, Nasrullah's eyes glowed with malevolence. The young prince had not yet looked into the magic mirror to reveal the truth about himself. This was where the answer as to how to resolve inner conflicts resided. He was riddled with self-doubt and in need of confidence to face the Queen of England, not only to bring his father's request, but now to claim the precious gem he deemed Afghan property. Property which was bestowed to Nader's entrusted General, the founding father of the Afghan nation. He did not fully understand the mission his soul had been questioning, and it was unknown if the revelation he was seeking would appear any time before he arrived in Windsor. Nasrullah's future seemed to be an obscure mirror. He who tried to look into it would see nothing but a dim outline of a bewildered and unpredictable face.

It was before midnight and the darkness was almost absolute, but the heavenly skies were scattered with luminous stars. Nasrullah and Khairo had called it a night and were heading back towards the city center when they heard the steady thunder of approaching galloping hooves. Nasrullah reached for his Nagant revolver and Khairo pulled a long-curved knife from his saddlebag.

"*Khabardar*, Be aware, we are from the Arg Palace," came a familiar voice. Other voices repeated questions in quick succession.

The familiar voice asked for the call sign, "What is the name of the night?".

"Don't shoot! There's no need for me to identify the name of the night. This is Prince Nasrullah, son of the Amir, and my companion with me is Khairo Khan," he yelled.

Silhouetted against the pitch dark, armed guardsmen approached.

"Why are you here?" Nasrullah asked, aghast.

"Your Highness, this is Zalmai, Head of the Palace Guard," he heaved on the reins to stop his horse and raised a hand to halt the mounted squad behind him. "Your Highness, you know that anytime you leave the Palace, it's our duty to give you security protection."

"Go back immediately. There is no need for you to give me protection, and by the way, come here . . . close."

The colonel tugged the reins and moved closer to Nasrullah. "*Amer Konaid Shahzadah*, What are your orders, Prince," the Colonel asked.

"Never tell anyone I left the Palace this late or who accompanied me. Understood?" Nasrullah spoke quietly but with authority. He bellowed then, "Now! Gallop back!"

"But Shahzadah Sahib, His Highness Prince Habibullah Khan, and General Akram Khan are behind us. They will be here at any moment!"

Already, the sound of approaching horses could be heard and Nasrullah felt himself sweating despite the cold.

"Why are you out so late?" Habibullah called out reproachfully once he had taken in the scene before him. "Can't you see you are in danger out here? Are you insane to roam in this area with no security protection?"

"We're armed and fully protected," Nasrullah replied waving his revolver. "And so far there hasn't been any danger. We are capable of defending ourselves. Nothing to worry about." He covered his anger with the lightness of his response.

"You think a revolver would stop a gang of five or ten armed men?" Prince Habibullah continued irritably, "You are going to *Englistan* and if a misfortune were to happen tonight, then what?"

"You're knifed by anxiety, brother," Nasrullah replied sarcastically, "And that will shorten your life considerably."

The Crown Prince turned his attention to the second rider who had remained silent and recognized Khairo from the way he used the flap of his turban to swathe his disfigured face.

"And why is he with you?" he demanded.

"Why not?" Nasrullah said condescendingly. He paused for a moment, "I'm planning for Khairo to accompany me to Landan."

"Why?" Habibullah asked in astonishment. He dismounted and walked across to Nasrullah, "He's neither a courtier nor holding a position of importance to accompany you to *Englistan*," he said, keeping his voice low. "You're a fool to believe our father is going to approve of him going."

"Don't you worry about that," Nasrullah's retort was sardonic, "I intend to talk to father and Daktar Hameeltoon."

"Do as you wish," he mounted his horse. "We're heading back." Habibullah beckoned the guard squad to follow him.

After the long night with Khairo, Prince Nasrullah turned his horse toward home. As he approached the Bostan-Sarai Palace he became aware that the flickering *chiragh-Ha*, oil-lamps, emitted light from every window in the parlor.

"It must be another *nautch* dancing event for father," he muttered to himself. He dismounted and handed the reins to a waiting groom. He trudged up the three flights of stairs to the marble balcony drawn by the sound of music - the melodious *ghazal*, the rhythmic thudding of feet, and tinkling bells.

The Amir surreptitiously arranged these rare occasions as he was reluctant to attract attention in the Palace. The dances were performed for men, as elements of eroticism played an integral part of the presentation. There would be the suggestive use of the dancer's bosom, some display of legs when spreading the long skirts, and a provocative locking of the eyes with the audience. Knowing Queen Sultana's jealous behavior, the Amir did his utmost to keep such things from her in the certainty that she would protest and disrupt the costly event.

Nasrullah followed the two *mashaulchis*, torch-bearers, through the dark corridor. As they flung open the double doors into the vaulted parlor, he was met with a cloud of scented tobacco smoke from the *nargilas,* and the enchanting swirl of Indian music. Two Indian dancers danced synchronously, and the brass bells laced to their ankles resonated throughout like marbles rattling in a tin.

The renowned dancers, Sundar and Alla Bundi, who had traveled from India at the invitation of the Amir were the best in their country. The Amir had a variety of young dancers who received excellent pay for their performances, but these two could not be compared to any he had invited before. He had looked forward to this for months and was completely focused on their every move and would not be impressed with any intrusion to divert his attention away from the dancers.

Over the years, the Amir had transformed Afghanistan into a more conservative society by elevating Shariah law over customary law. Thus, the law forbidding Afghan women from dancing to a male audience was circumvented by allowing Indian women to perform. These girls performed *nautch* dancing for pleasure only, whereas Indian classical dance, including the ritual dances in the confinement of the Hindu shrines, was to uplift the shrines' deities.

Sundar was dressed in a purple saree exuding a redolent Nepalis *attar* fragrance and she had adorned her blue-black hair with *dhatura* flowers. Her eyelids were darkened, and a little cinque-spotted mole rested at the corner of her left eye; her full lips titillated the senses, inviting kisses, and she swayed as though drawn to Nasrullah who still stood, entranced for a moment, in the doorway. Throughout the vast parlor, multiple *mashaulchis* holding oil lamps illuminated the charms of the dancers' every move. The oil lamps picked out the scarlet hues of the knotted carpets, the trays of sweetmeats, ceramic tea kettles, and cups, and the brass *nargilas*.

Alla Bundi was similarly attired and made-up. The mellifluous *ghazal* accompanied her gestures as she slid her hands sensuously over her petite body, moving her fingertips to and from her lips. The henna on her fingertips caught the light, as did the rare bracelets of Kashmiri enamel on her wrists.

The Amir gestured to Nasrullah to take the vacant seat next to him. On his left, Prince Habibullah and his nephew, General Akram Khan were snugly seated on carpet-covered *toshaks* and leaning on embroidered bolster pillows. A few cushions down. Amir's executioner, Parwana Khan, watched the dancers intently, although his two lines of vision to the dancers were not parallel. Next to the Amir's executioner was *Naieb-Salar*, Marshal, Mohammad Hassein Khan, happily thumbing his onyx worry beads and sipping tea as if the dancers were performing for him alone.

Across from them, five musicians sat crossed-legged on cushions with their instruments: *sarangi, tabla, manjeera, harmonium, dholak* and *ghazal*.

Nasrullah leaned back against a bolster pillow.

"Where have you been tonight?" the Amir, asked sharply, his full gray brows knit together in a frown.

"With an acquaintance from Maiwand," the color heightened in Nasrullah's face.

"Who?"

"You know him," both were watching the dancers' movements, their heads almost touching as they spoke. "Malalai's father, that faceless Khairo, the elder of Maiwand who lost his family in the battle."

The music stopped to give the dancers a moment to change for their next performance.

The Amir turned to Nasrullah. In the corona of an oil lamp, his face looked agitated and predatory. "How dare you meet with him without my approval?" he spat pounding his right fist into the bolster pillow.

"Whoever reported to you must have said the wrong thing," Nasrullah said quietly. "Father," he looked him in the eye, "I will tell you everything in detail."

"What Habibullah told me was concerning, I want to hear your side of the story!" His attention was suddenly diverted by the return of the dancers, but his eyes still glared in anger.

The dancers returned wearing *ghargras*, long skirts, to perform the roles of peacocks trying to attract peahens. Alla Bundi, fair as lily and beautiful as fire, had a large gold hoop pierced through her nose that encircled her cheek with graceful pendant pearls dangling provocatively above her upper lip. It was joined to her ear by a gold chain studded with miniature precious stones. She took the lead as both dancers hopped to the beat of the music and spread their long, peacock-colored skirts creating breezy pirouettes representing the outspread feathers of the peacocks. In nature, Peahens choose their mates based on their color, quality of feathers, and size. Much the same, the quality of *nautch* dance is based on the quality of the *ghagra*, the grace of the dancer, and the extent to which she could increase her proportion by spreading her *ghagra*.

Alla Bundi and Sundar suggestively displayed the roundness of their breasts, and spread their long skirts to reveal their legs while glancing provocatively at the Amir, his two sons, and nephew.

"Father," Nasrullah ignored them and leaned forward, "I've suggested to Khairo Khan that he join me on my journey to *Englistan*."

"Son, you must be out of your mind!" the Amir snapped quietly, but irritably. He tilted his chin and stroked his full beard, "His hatred towards the British runs deep . . . it is like a ripe fruit. Losing a daughter and brothers in the battle of Maiwand will never be easy for him to forget. I fear he would ruin our mission with the Queen." His eyes were glued to the dancers. "Why do you want him to go?"

"Dear father," Nasrullah glanced at him for a split second, "I believe his face is treatable in *Englistan*, I am going to discuss with Daktar Laila Hameeltoon."

"I don't think his face is treatable."

"There is a possibility that some medical treatment in *Englistan* could fix his face," he repeated. The music and the dancers were in full swing. "If it is treated, he and his entire Alakozai clan, as well as the rest of Qandahar, will respect us."

"His face is gone and incurable, son."

"Father, again, I'll discuss this with Daktar Hameeltoon. But concerning his obedience, rest assured, you have my word, he will be submissive and respectful of every *Englees* during his stay in *Englistaan*." They looked back at the dancers: "His pain needs to heal," Nasrullah said raising his voice to be heard above the music, "He stood as a hero and fought bravely. His daughter's name is proudly spoken in every village in Afghanistan and will be remembered for generations to come. If this treatment can be done, it will not only make us look good but make God happy."

The Amir nodded his consent. "But let me be clear, if he causes any disturbance we'll be doomed and never be able to entice *Malika* Weektorya to give us what we want."

"I promise that it will be fine, by the Grace of *Allah*. He's a very humble man and supports your interest in every way he can. *Baley*, *Padar Jan*, I must thank you for allowing him to join me on my trip."

The dancers had moved on to imitate a kite and the person who flies it. To the Amir's ears, the dance was sweeter than the sweetest chime of magical bells by Sundar and Alla Bundi and would be ingrained in his memory until he died. The musical instruments enchanted the air like the south wind, like a warm night, or like swelling sails beneath the stars. The music was balm to the drowsy ear as the heavy horsehair-bow of the *Sarangi* was drawn across its strings combined with the gentle thrumming of the Tabla. And as the player's fingertips fluttered over the drum's surfaces and increased the tempo to create a flurry of ringing tones and fluid thumps, it became an arithmetic of sounds, forming complex rhythms simultaneously thrilling and mesmerizing.

Alla Bundi depicted the graceful ascent of the kite, its tussle, the moment when the thread entangles with another, and the slow descent after the string is cut. Dancing to a slower tempo, Sundar represented the kite flier, emphasizing grace, elegance, and poise. Their gestures, energy, and emotions were integral to every move. They both came close to the Amir, his sons, and nephew, one teasing the Amir, and the other Prince Habibullah, by slowly advancing in a manner suggesting an imminent kiss, yet quickly retreating at the last moment.

CHAPTER NINETEEN

❧❧❧

As novices in the etiquette of fine dining, Nasrullah and his entourage needed to master the craft before arriving in England. They were quick to realize that having their meals with others would bring them into a relationship with their English hosts. Learning this new skill not only presented them as men of the world and worthy of their position, but it created a societal stepping-stone. Nasrullah had been allowed the opportunity to portray himself as a Prince of nobility and royalty in a nation that was a guardian of the Indian subcontinent where English wealth was generated. Good manners were seen to be the fruit of a noble mind and would, partially, form Nasrullah's entry ticket into British society. To be accepted as an advocate of his father amongst the Victorian nobility and royalty, he would need to know how they thought and how their society was structured. As the time for his voyage drew closer, it became obvious that the Prince was not going to absorb every facet of the British aristocracy, and neither did he want to. But, at the very least, it might be possible for him to master the skills of dining and table manners; to avoid blowing his nose into a beautifully starched dinner napkin or emitting a hearty belch.

If Nasrullah had been fluent in the English language, it might have afforded him some immediate stature; but that was an unrealistic expectation for the young Prince to have achieved in the remaining time. It was obvious Prince Nasrullah lacked the finesse, tact, and wit, to carry on a conversation with dignitaries, while his misogynistic mindset promised to be a disaster in the royal court. To the English contingent of trainers, the prospect of achieving his mission in Windsor

Palace looked bleaker by the day.

They were now ready for the main entree. The Palace servants carried in two enormous trays laden with roasted cranes. Mesdames Clemence and Martin had assisted the chefs in roasting the large birds in the English fashion. Their legs had been trussed towards the back, wings were cut-off at the body joints, necks bent about upper vertebrae, and bills tucked into breasts. Indeed, the glowing colors of the roasted birds spoke to their freshness and the conspicuous flavor to come. The sight and aroma brought a gentle nudge to their hunger for this hearty feast. The erect roasted birds surprised little William and Prince Omar Jan and their giggles rose to a pitch.

"This is my recipe, *Demoiselle* Crane *au Poivre* rubbed with cracked peppercorns and roasted in clay oven, topped with its sauce," Mrs. Clemence declared proudly.

"It looks juicy and crispy! You truly dispense happiness, *Khanum* Cleemess," Nasrullah said appreciatively. By the other exclamations of surprise, it was probably the first time any of the Afghans had eaten roasted crane in that fashion. Mesdames Clemence and Martin cut slices of the roasted cranes for the guests of honor who were comfortably seated and waiting, napkins on laps.

"Please bear in mind, at the formal dinner, no part of the roasted crane or any entree is eaten with your fingers!" Lillias said. She picked up a piece of the roasted bird from her plate with her fork to demonstrate, "However, at an informal dinner, you can pick up the bones after you cut off most of the meat. But never pick up the carcass."

"And why not the body?" the General asked, as he set his utensils down on his plate and dabbed his greasy mustache with the napkin.

"Because of its size," Lillias Hamilton explained. "It would be clumsy and draw attention and you don't want that."

"These rules are truly laughable," the General mumbled glancing at Nasrullah.

"I understand that it's irritating using a knife and fork for this sort of thing," Lillias said, "but you've no choice but to use them while you are there." She looked brightly at everyone, "Are you ready to start? If so, please go ahead."

Holding the utensils uncertainly, there could be heard a tapping, ticking, and screeching of knives and forks against china plates. Crane bones and meat flew onto the tablecloth, and jerking hands knocked down crystal glasses. They were as jumpy as goats. Lieutenant Mahmoud Khan and Parwana Khan were seemingly in need of bibs and to be spoon-fed; blobs of greasy sauce dripped onto their jackets as they tried to bring the forks to their mouths. *Naieb-Salar*, Field Marshal Hassein Khan's enormous appetite was not sufficed by a plate or two of roasted crane, he could have devoured the entire bird in minutes. His rugged fists covered the handles of the utensils entirely revealing very little beyond. He was nervous and his flabby face quivered like forest leaves in a breeze. His spectacles occasionally slid down on his sweat-beaded nose and he repeatedly pushed them back. Hesitant as to whether to eat with hands or cutlery, he dropped the knife and fork onto his plate, reached for the food with his fingers, hesitated, and then picked them up again. It was like a free show.

"Marshal Sahib, please stop!" Dr. Hamilton smiled charmingly, raising a hand, "I want Messrs. Martin and Clemence to demonstrate, please watch them carefully." Everybody stopped and there was a sudden silence as everyone watched with undivided attention. So, the practice sessions continued with varied success among the participants.

"When you arrive in Windsor, the Chief Engineer said, "you will be briefed on what to expect and how to interact with the Queen. I'm certain General Akram Khan will be companying His Highness, Prince Nasrullah, on all occasions and the rest of you occasionally," Frank Martin pulled his pocket watch from his waistcoat and checked the time. He continued. "Guests are not to speak to the Queen unless spoken to by her first, and then they can raise their questions." Martin brightened perceptibly and engaged everyone with a smile, "I have some good news!" he said looking directly at the Prince, "I received a wireless message late last night from the office of British Envoy in Calcutta, India. Let me read it to you."

"TO MR. FRANK MARTIN JAN 9, 1895

CHIEF ENGINEER TO AMIR OF AFGHANISTAN. H.M.'S INDIAN SECRETARY, MUNSHI ABDUL KARIM KHAN, CONVEYS HIS ASSURANCE THAT WINDSOR PALACE IS COMMITTED TO PREPARE H.H. PRINCE NASRULLAH KHAN'S CULINARY IN THE ISLAMIC WAY. A SEPARATE SCULLERY WITH FOUR INDIAN CHEFS WILL BE AT HIS SERVICE."

"That's great news!" Nasrullah said, his eyes danced with pleasure and he grinned widely, "I knew we would be given halal meat if we asked. That is thrilling!" He raised his hands heavenward. "Allah would have been extremely displeased with us if we ate non-kosher meat that is prohibited by his Almighty himself."

"Ameen!" everyone agreed in unison.

"Your Highness, we still have to resolve the culinary issues onboard the troopship from Bombay to Portsmouth and back to India. There is no way of providing fresh meat on a three-week voyage for an entourage of a hundred people plus." Frank Martin said.

"Well, if you British colonized the world, I am sure you can find a way you provide halal food," Prince Nasrullah replied arrogantly.

Anger flared for a moment in Frank Martin's eyes as he met Dr. Hamilton's gaze. *The idiot's inability to rationalize is sometimes beyond belief,* he thought.

෯෯෯෯෯

January 1895 -- Afghan calendar month: *Dalwa* 1273
Kabul, Afghanistan

A letter arrived addressed to the Amir, from the Viceroy of India, Alexander Bruce. It was written in a fine secretarial hand on two sides of watermarked bifolium, embossed with the Viceregal royal arms in gold. It read:

> *"November 25, 1894*
>
> *His Highness, Amir of Afghanistan, Abdul Rahman Khan, Light of the Nation and religion.*
>
> *Your Highnes*
>
> *Her Majesty the Queen will be glad to receive His Highness, Prince Nasrullah Khan upon his arrival in Windsor Palace.*
>
> *I had the honor, in course of evaluation which Her Majesty granted me to place before Your Highness certain facts relating to His Highness, Prince Nasrullah Khan's voyage to England. The following is the confirmation for the itinerary from Peshawar to Portsmouth:*
>
> *Embarkation: (On board Royal Victorian) Peshawar Cantonment Train Station, April 20th, 1895 at 12:00 noon.*
>
> *Arrival: Port of Karachi, April 23rd, 1895 at 8:30 morning.*
>
> *Embarkation: (Onboard troopship HMS Victory) Port of Karachi, April 24th, 1895 at 12:00 noon, onboard HMS-Victory.*
>
> *Arrival: Port of Bombay, April 26th, 1895 at 9:35 morning.*

*Embarkation: (Onboard Troopship Clive via Canal Suez)
Port of Bombay, April 29th, 1895 at 2:20 afternoon.*

Arrival: Portsmouth, May 23rd, 1895 at 9:00 morning.

*The Royal Victorian Train and HMS Victory are
exclusively reserved for His Highness Prince Nasrullah Khan
and His Highness' entourage. It will be my honor to receive
the names and titles of those accompanying His Highness to
England.*

*Your Highness' concern regarding the cholera epidemic
is well taken. I have ordered extra precautions imposing
quarantine at all times, proper hygienic applications of the
troopship Clive, and onboard instructions for the prevention
of the disease. Severe monitoring will be applied during stops
for coal loading in the ports of Aden, Alexandria, and Malta.
In addition to Your Highness' personal Doctor, Miss Lillias
Ana Hamilton who will be accompanying His Highness
and under her constant monitoring, I have also ordered Dr.
Mathew Connelly to be of service during the voyage.*

*I have also deputed my esteemed secretaries of Indian
Government, Colonel Adelbert Talbot and Sir. Gerald
Fitzgerald to wait upon His Highness and make necessary
arrangements during the voyage and in England.*

*I would be honored to receive a reply should Your Highness
have any questions.*

Yours Sincerely,
Victor Alexander Bruce
Governor-General of India"

The letter was stitched at the gutter margin into a simple folder
together with three Persian letters, one of which is almost certainly a
translation of the Viceroy's letter.

CHAPTER TWENTY

❧❧❧

January 1895 -- Afghan calendar month: *Dalwa* 1273
Frogmore House, Windsor, UK

When Queen Victoria agreed to invite Nasrullah to England, Munshi Abdul Karim could not disguise his ebullient anticipation of the arrival of this Prince and fellow Muslim. He felt a keen desire to aid Nasrullah in his endeavor to fulfill his father's dream of representing his nation in the Court of St James—a dream of accreditation in the royal court of the Sovereign of the United Kingdom. A dream of rubbing shoulders with ambassadors, marshals of the Diplomatic Corps, and high commissioners from the United Kingdom. A grandiose dream of prestigious advancement that would pan out amongst other Muslim nations of the world.

On this dark and turbulent night, Munshi Abdul Karim gazed through the window of Frogmore House as the incessant rain gushing over roofs and terraces dousing the flames of some of the outside lamps. Earlier, violent gusts of wind had scattered leaves over the pathways leading to King George IV Gate at Windsor Palace, and the sprawling lawn connecting the private lake and Prince Albert's mausoleum.

Nasrullah's arrival in England was fast approaching and Abdul Karim had had no personal interaction with Arg Palace and was unable to reach out to Nasrullah personally to offer his help without the knowledge of the Queen or the royal household. Queen Victoria and Amir Abdul Rahman communicated officially via British Governor-General in Calcutta but Munshi Abdul Karim was not able to get in touch with Kabul through those channels. He planned to influence Queen Victoria's decision in the Amir's favor while sharing a few insights about the Queen with Nasrullah in advance of his arrival in Windsor.

He sat on his fine upholstered *toshak* in his private suite in Frogmore House, a seventeen-century mansion within a stone's throw of Windsor Castle. The Queen had graciously approved his residence in Frogmore so that she could ride her pony-carriage to meet with Abdul Karim at her convenience. As he unwrapped his white silk turban, his Indian associates, Mohammad Buksh, and longtime friend Rafiuddin Ahmed, joined him. Rafiuddin was a Muslim barrister, journalist, politician, and Queen Victoria's personal representative to Sultan Abdul Hamid of the Ottoman Empire. He was a tall man who wore round-framed spectacles. His raven hair was brushed behind his ears under a neatly wrapped flowery turban; his native dress was generally completed by a long black embroidered cape draped over his shoulders. Mohammad Buksh was a servant at Windsor Palace who had also been chosen and sent from India, along with Abdul Karim, to attend the Queen at her Jubilee ceremony some years before. Buksh was stout with a wispy, well-groomed beard.

"Unwrapping your turban means you're going to bed," Rafiuddin commented in his strong Indian accent. He smiled, exposing two gold teeth that flashed as they caught the light from the massive gasolier hanging from the finely ornamented ceiling medallion.

"Not sleeping yet, just relieving my head of the weight. I am glad you dropped by Rafiuddin Sahib. I've been deep in thought about Prince Nasrullah Khan." He gestured to Buksh to bring tea to prevent him from eavesdropping on their conversation. "Listen, *Baboo*, what I am about to say needs to be confidential," Munshi said quietly. "Do you know why Nasrullah is coming to see the Queen?"

"No, for a twenty-year-old boy, let me guess. Maybe for amusement? To watch circus clowns, or a Punch and Judy show?" Rafiuddin grinned and shook his head from side to side as if it was attached to an oscillating spring.

"None of those, *Baboo*, the Queen made the offer to invite Amir Abdul Rahman first, but he's ill and cannot travel," he crossed his legs and rocked to and fro. "So, then the Amir advocated his son, Prince Nasrullah, to come in his place," he continued in the same quiet tone. "Her Majesty has agreed to receive Prince Nasrullah in the Amir's place . . . *Baboo*, I need your help."

"Of course, what's there for me to do, Abdul *Jee?*"

"Moulvi Sab," Abdul Karim called him by his title, "you know many Muslim leaders in the world . . . "

"*Jee Han Aziz!* Yes, dear!" Rafiuddin replied in his native Urdu language. Oscillating his head again.

"Do you know a way for us to establish a personal introduction with the Amir or his son in Kabul?"

"I don't understand why you want to contact them when Nasrullah is already coming here?"

"Let me explain why," Munshi cleared his voice with a cough. "I have noticed Her Majesty is not very happy about Prince Nasrullah coming to London. She shows signs of tension when his name is brought up by either Betty or some courtier in the Palace. She speaks of him as 'that young immature boy' or 'I don't know how to deal with a juvenile'. I also understand that her court advisers are telling her to deny Amir Abdul Rahman's request for his country to obtain independence." Munshi Abdul Karim fingered his trim beard. "I have tried on a few occasions to ask the Queen whether she will grant him that privilege but she avoids answering. The last time I was told not to ask her this question again," he continued to mutter quietly. "I want to help the Amir to achieve his goal and run his country himself. He's capable of keeping Afghanistan under his control and I'm sure he can deal with the outside world on his own."

"Munshi *Jee*," Raffiudin said quietly, "you have a point!" He stared at him intently, "If the Amir is given independence, India will endeavor to follow suit and that could be the start of Indian autonomy as well!"

"Her Majesty's advisers are well aware of that and they have already reckoned that India will erode if Afghanistan is given autonomy," he shook his head and gestured with finger and thumb as if twisting a knob, "Indian independence is not going to happen anytime soon."

"Well," Raffiudin said, raising his chin determinedly, "we need to think of a plan for Prince Nasrullah."

"I'll attempt to speak to the Queen one more time and see if she listens," Abdul Karim replied with renewed confidence, "I can only approach her when she's happy and chirpy."

"Why don't we both approach her?"

Mohammad Buksh walked into the suite holding a silver tray laden with a porcelain teapot and cups, placed it on the floor between Abdul Karim and Rafiuddin, and filled their cups.

"Have you seen my new portrait?" Abdul Karim asked, promptly diverting the conversation. He gestured towards the image in which he was portrayed in a bust-length portrait wearing traditional Indian clothing and a turban.

"That is truly a masterpiece!" Rafiuddin exclaimed in astonishment. "Who is the artist?"

"Her Majesty asked her daughter Vicky, Empress Frederick, to have Von Angeli, the famous Austrian portrait painter paint it. He made me sit for hours," he complained, sighing deeply. "He was telling me to sit this way or that way, don't move, don't look out of the window. It was tiring and boring!" He shook his head bitterly, "He scrapped two half-done canvases because he told me I wasn't posing naturally," he rolled his eyes, "I put up with him because Her

Majesty wanted an outstanding portrait of me in case I would take it in my head to run away and hide somewhere. What is a portrait for?" he demanded, glancing first at Rafiuddin and then at Buksh. "Would either of you care about having a painting done of yourselves?"

"You need to treasure that, you will not regret it when it's passed on to your descendants," Rafiuddin picked up his teacup and pensively swirled the liquid around.

"Moulvi Sab, this gets interesting," grinned Munshi. "At first Her Majesty was not too happy with the painting. She said Von Angeli painted the color of my complexion too dark, but he did another portrait, a copy of this," he gestured towards the portrait, "Twice as big!" He stretched his arms wide, "and it is now displayed in her parlor."

The Arabesque longcase clock standing against the wall chimed the exact hour before the Queen's hearty afternoon tea was to be served.

"Buksh, it's time to get ready to serve Her Majesty," Munshi Abdul Karim said authoritatively.

"*Dschii haan, Bohat Acha.* Yes, very well," he shuffled out and closed the tall double doors behind him.

Rafiuddin Ahmed and Munshi Abdul Karim's relationship was one of extraordinary benevolence—they were twin souls bound all the more tightly together because of the foreign setting in which they found themselves. They had been drawn into the closest association with the Royal British monarchy that no other Muslim had had the privilege to attain. But now they were intent on pursuing a fine line by which the rug could be pulled from under their feet.

"I understand the issue now," Rafiuddin declared, as their subject of conversation reverted to Nasrullah's visit, "I would like to help a Muslim country succeed and stand on its own feet." He stood up to leave, tucking his long black robe around him, "I need a few days to think how I can help you. I will get back to you Abdul *Jee.*"

❦❧❦❧❦

February 1895 -- Afghan calendar month:
Dalwa 1273, Kabul, Afghanistan

The line of royal carriages made their way towards the banks of the Kabul River where Amir's *Mashin-Khana*, factory, emerged from the gorge between the Asema-Ye and Shir-Darwaza mountains. From a distance, its two tall smokestacks spewed black smoke skyward as if the wisps were swaying snakes hypnotized by the sound of the charmer's flute.

It was the eighth anniversary of the *Mashin-Khana*, the Amir's signature achievement, where ammunition, muzzle, and breech-loading field guns, Martini-Henry rifles, and boots for his military personnel were manufactured. In this multi-production factory, cartridges for the Martini and Snider Enfield rifles were loaded at the rate of seven thousand a day. The *Mashin-Khana* contained a complete tannery, sawmills, steam hammers, lathes, and machines for making a variety of articles from breech-loading cannons, to soap and candles. In addition, secretly, a brandy distillery was tucked away in a secluded area of the *Mashin-Khana*, producing eight-hundred bottles a day for export to India.

In celebration of the *Mashin-Khana's* eight-year milestone, the frail Amir who could not attend, sent his two sons to represent him in an official capacity. They were to boost employee morale and learn about its production and history. Engineer Frank Martin was also to advise Nasrullah on the purchase of new machinery while they were in England.

The well-guarded carriages, flanked by mounted lancers, passed through the gate. On the arched brickwork above the entrance, banners were displayed that had attracted many Kabulis to catch a glimpse of the event from outside. "*Khosh Amaded Shahzadah*

Habibullah Wa Shahzadah Nasrullah!", welcome Prince Habibullah and Prince Nasrullah, and *"Zenda-Baad Amir Sahib!"* long-live Amir Sahib.

The cavalcade consisted of the Royal *Sardars*, Lords, courtiers, and the Royal bodyguard of lancers. In the lead was Prince Habibullah accompanied by three *Sardars* and his personal Chamberlain.

Crown Prince Habibullah, stepped down from the first carriage. In the following carriages, were Prince Nasrullah; his cousin, General Akram Khan; *Naieb-Salar*, Marshal Hassein Khan; and Amir's executioner, *Kotwal* of Kabul, Parwana Khan, all of them taller than Prince Habibullah.

Habibullah, Nasrullah, and Akram were dressed in Khaki britches, jackets, and knee-high boots, looking as though they were off for a hunt. Nasrullah and Habibullah sported their Astrakhan Karakul hats, while General Akram matched the rest of his attire with his khaki felt hat and a white silk cravat, and would have passed easily as British. His smudged eyeglasses had gone opaque in the morning sunshine.

Engineer Frank Martin who presided over the *Mashin-Khana* had carefully informed the three-and-half-thousand employees about today's celebration. Every department was warned of the possibility of a random inspection to avoid any mishaps. He had held meeting after meeting to ensure that conditions would be in perfect order before the arrival of the Princes.

"They are here!" he called and holding his bowler hat firmly on his head as he hastily descended the flight of stairs from the balcony to greet the princes and their guests. The factory employees strode quickly into the factory courtyard as Frank Martin greeted the entourage cordially. His Afghan workers bent forward, held each guest's hand with two of their own, tilted their heads, and respectfully set their hands on their hearts.

"Your Highnesses and honored guests," Frank Martin said,

throwing his shoulders back ceremoniously, he bowed his head. "Welcome to the *Mashin-Khana*! And congratulations on the eighth anniversary of this magnificent achievement."

He ushered them through a dark corridor to a hall where a few employees were holding gaslights, "Please follow me." On the opposite wall of the vaulted hall, hung a large oil painting of Amir, "This splendid portrait of His Highness is the exemplary work of Doctor Alfred Gray who was his physician. By profession, he was not only a medical doctor but a renowned artist, traveler, and writer. As most of you know he left us two years ago after five years in Kabul and Doctor Hamilton was gracious enough to take up his demanding position."

Doctor Gray did a few other portraits of the Amir, one hung in Queen Sultana's bed chamber and one in *Bagh-e-Bala* Palace. By sketching and painting the Amir's portrait, Doctor Gray probably ministered to him with every stroke of his brush.

Frank Martin introduced the next portrait. "Here is the French electrical engineer, Mathias Jerome, the founder of this *Mashin-Khana*." Jerome's portrait showed a middle-aged man with a receding hairline, a lumpy nose with gaping nostrils, and a face too small for such a huge head. "He laid the foundation here before he left, but didn't last long," Frank grinned, flashing his gleaming teeth.

Ten years before, the Amir was in Rawalpindi to meet with the British Viceroy, where he met the savvy electrical engineer Mathias Jerome. He astonished the Amir by attaching his portable engine to a dynamo, which revolved, lighting a flashlight: the Amir chuckled with delight, mesmerized to witness such outstanding technology. When he was informed that Mathias Jerome had a great deal of general experience in mechanical engineering, he asked him to establish the manufacture of arms and ammunition in Kabul. Jerome was delighted to land such a high-paying job, but shortly after he arrived in Kabul, he looked out of his window one morning and saw two men hanged

KHALIL NOURI

on the gallows and two women having their throats cut. The striking display proved too excessive for the gallant Frenchman. On being sent to Europe to procure machinery, he decided not to see such Afghan medieval exhibitions anymore. The machinery was forthcoming, but not the Frenchman.

As they were about to move away from Jerome's portrait, Frank Martin turned the attention of the princes and the royal noblemen to yet another portrait, "This is Sir Salter Pyne who built up the *Mashin-Khana* after Jerome and brought it to fruition," he gestured towards Pyne's portrait, which reflected him as a sleek man in his mid-thirties, with a well-trimmed drooping mustache. The portrait showed him wearing an upturned collar, a white shirt with a fine cravat, and a top hat. "He trained the people here to make the products that you will see shortly," Frank Martin said, "Without him, I don't think this place would be what it's now."

Sir Salter Pyne had narrowly escaped death when he was attacked while riding to the post office in Kabul. The thrust of a soldier's bayonet missed Mr. Pyne's chest when his horse veered away from the attacker. Mr. Salter Pyne was shocked beyond measure when he heard that not only the soldier but his entire family, some forty in all, had been executed as a result. Naturally, he objected to this atrocious act.

"Why was it necessary to wipe out the entire family for one person's fault, Your Highness?" he asked in disbelief.

"You know not," said the Amir, "that if I had punished only the soldier, every one of his relations would have had a blood feud against you. The only way of saving you to build the *Mashin-Khana* was to kill the lot. You do not understand Afghanistan!" The engineer's life had to be protected by the most stringent precautions after that because of his vital importance in bringing the *Mashin-Khana* into full production.

The next portrait was Frank Martin's. For his image, he had chosen to wear Afghan clothing and a well-wrapped turban. The thousands of workers under Frank recognized his empathy and respect towards them and knew him to be a man of virtue and kindness; they worked hard to learn his trade and to mutually gain his trust and respect. He had implored the Amir to stop the recent execution of ten factory employees, but to no avail. Like Jerome and Sir Salter Pyne, Frank Martin could also have given up and left at that point, abandoning his workers but, instead, he moved forward and dedicated himself to the betterment of those who valued him. His happiness had become mixed with anxiety, something he hoped he could hide from others but it lay just beneath the surface. While this nagging apprehension was foreign to him, he chose to simply focus day by day on the task at hand; to help his fellow factory workers to succeed and become invaluable to Afghanistan. This was where he found solace and completion—in teaching his men to produce parts, to manufacture shoes and soap, to assemble guns and so much more. Often, the work was tedious, but the result was all the inspiration he needed. There was a joy in hearing the occasional call in unison, "*Zendah-Bad Fraunk Maarteen Sahib*, Long live Sir Frank Martin," when he entered the hum and clatter of the factory floor.

CHAPTER TWENTY-ONE

⋖⊙⌒⊙⌒⊙⌒

March 1895 -- Afghan calendar month: *Hamal* 1274, Kabul, Afghanistan

The cold days were less intense; the damp air was abating and new energy was rising, the air was pure and brisk and there was a sense of expectation in Kabul for the blue skies to sing the arrival of summer. Spring sunlight flooded the streets of the city like good news. The clouds disappeared, the sky was the most immaculate azure blue, and an unexpected and unfamiliar spirit of joy and love seemed to be everywhere—it was in the air like a triumph and a prophecy. Every year at this time, the Afghans witnessed its arrival when the Northern mountain tops became embroidered with gold. The melt caused the river to snake ferociously between its stony walls and new vivid green lines appeared like streaks of lush paint between its rockeries.

The Hamilton sisters and Frank Martin were strolling through Kabul to procure souvenirs. The scintillating sun forced them to shield their eyes to observe their surroundings and the city bustle. They arrived at the entrance of *Pul-e-Yak-Paisagee*, the only toll bridge that connected Kabul's foot traffic, commerce, and bazaars. Close to the entrance, a man with a bloated stomach sat crossed-legged on a *charpaie*, straw-cot, collecting the toll-charge of a copper coin, one *Paisa*—about one-eighth of an English penny. As Frank and the Hamilton sisters tossed their tolls to him, the man clutched his turban, sprang to his feet, and, with remarkable alacrity, chased a culprit who had attempted to run across the bridge. He clutched him by the scruff of his neck and brought him back to the entrance, "No *Paisa?* No *Paisa?*" He yelled furiously, "Then swim across!"

"I've seen men swim the frigid river for not having the toll," Frank said, throwing the unfortunate individual his fare. The man lifted his hands to praise Allah for Frank's benevolence, bowed multiple times, and clutched his heart.

"Thank you, thank you, Allah be praised!"

Despite the Hamilton sisters' attempt at disguise in full-sleeved *dolaq*, Afghan dress, and embroidered head-scarves concealing their blond hair, and Frank wearing full Afghan garb and a silk turban, most Afghans still recognized the English foreigners from Amir's Palace. No one dared cause any mishap or mischief to endanger the protected Britishers, lest they face punishment on the gallows of the bazaars.

Frank and the Hamilton sisters queued to walk the five-foot-wide bridge, which possessed no guardrails and carried heavy pedestrian traffic. Lillias and Roma glanced nervously at the river that raged ferociously beneath. Broken branches and other debris swirled in the flow and, as some impacted the wooden columns, the rickety structure rocked like a cradle. The footbridge was crammed with traffic from both directions, men carrying *tabangs* on their heads, carts, laden animals, haulers, and porters. There were incessant cries of "*khabardar!* beware!" Walking gingerly the two women arrived at the toll on the opposite bank of the river with some relief and were instantly surrounded by beggars who swarmed them like bees. Roma's attention was drawn to one, a child no older than six. Flies crawled over his head, some feasting on open sores, and his skeletal legs wobbled under the strain of a tumefied stomach. He stretched his cupped hand to Roma and she rummaged into her small valise and planted a few *Paisas* in his grimy hand.

They broke away from the beggars and continued into the city.

KHALIL NOURI

Lopsided poles supported stretched awnings that held together like a vast tent over a long line of little shops. Lillias, Roma, and Frank Martin strolled on past open shop fronts displaying bulging sacks of rice, colorful spices, and fruits. They were caught up in a river of sound; the chattering of buyers, the bellowing of vendors, warnings shouted by laden carriers, "*khabar-dar!*"; screaming children, and wailing babies.

Frank discussed Nasrullah's trip while Roma and Lillias glanced into shops for items of interest.

"It was brought up in the *Darbar* Hall," he said as they passed butcheries where freshly cut meat hung from steel hooks and stray dogs waited hopefully for scraps. "Planning for the voyage to London is in the final stages. There have been some additions and removals from Nasrullah's entourage."

A few beggars sat crossed-legged in the dirt of an alleyway soliciting for *bakhshish*. Roma bestowed some money and covered her mouth with her headscarf as the smell of rot in the bazaar intensified.

"Roma," Dr. Hamilton exclaimed sharply, "If you do that we will be surrounded by beggars again."

Roma smiled sweetly," Sorry, Lillias."

"I'm relieved the training of the Afghans has come to an end!" Lillias Hamilton said, "Actually I am delighted!"

"Well done," Frank, said absently as he picked up a sixteenth-century sword and glanced at the Qur'anic etched calligraphy on its blade.

"And soon their formal attire will be completed," she added with a sigh of relief.

"Another milestone around the corner," Roma agreed.

"I'm deeply grateful to you and all our English friends for helping in that marathon effort," Dr. Hamilton added. "I don't know what we would have done without you..."

"Is the Amir going to pay us for all the work we did?" Frank asked

183

with a hint of a smile.

"Actually, he has already agreed to," Lillias replied, "he gave me his word."

They were assailed by another group of beggars. "Disguising ourselves as local Afghans does not work," Roma laughed as she heard the word, "*Farangee!*" for the dozenth time. "Somehow they recognize that we are foreigners."

"Well, we are the only blue-eyed and fair-skinned shoppers here," Lillias said with a smile.

"We were wrong if we thought only a few men were going to England with Nasrullah," Frank commented as he began to haggle with a shopkeeper for a curved seventeenth-century dagger. "Apparently, this belonged to one of the Great Nadir's men," he said, impressed. By the merchant's smirk, the two women could tell that his broken Dari was awful. "First it was twelve high-ranking dignitaries then the Amir cut that to six. Now they even want to drag a group of bearded Mullahs into the mix." He shook his head in frustration. "I don't get it. What's the point of sending those religious fanatics?" he asked, glancing at Dr. Hamilton as though she would have the answer. "So now, all together, they plan to send more than a hundred people!" He agreed with the price, handed the shopkeeper the money, and concealed the dagger under his vest. Then, straightening his silken turban, he clasped his hands behind his back.

Proprietors strove to sell them merchandise holding out bolts of colorful fabric to tempt the women and pointing to an array of weapons and coins in the hope of drawing Frank's attention.

"Is the Amir out of his mind?" Lillias asked flabbergasted, "Why send those Mullahs? Isn't that idiot Hakim enough?" She stared at Martin, her irritation showing, "So now we have the Mullahs as well?"

"Their function will be Nasrullah's religious observance." Martin replied, "And the Amir has also given his approval for Prince Omar's introduction to Queen Victoria."

She stopped walking, met his gaze, and whispered in astonishment, "This is madness! I heard the same from Queen Sultana but I fancy she will be disappointed. That little boy is not officially invited and I doubt he would be received at Windsor." She snapped at a persistent beggar, "*Boro! Ney!* Go away! No!" She turned to Frank, "All they need is few people, not the entire Royal Afghan court! And not the obtuse and ignorant Mullahs, nor the platoon of lancers." She exploded again at the beggars, "*Boro!* Go!"

"I am sure the changes of plan are infuriating, Lillias," Roma said calmly, "but you do not have a choice but to accept Amir's plan, do you?"

Lillias took a deep breath, "I don't, but Nasrullah's visit is an official visit. It's not like a family gathering where little Prince Omar Jan sweetly shakes hands with Queen Victoria. We can't prevent him from going on the voyage but we must make sure he is not presented to the Queen."

"I wonder if the Afghans understand what is meant by an official invitation in British terms?" Frank said uncertainly. "There is always tension between Queen Sultana and the Amir over Prince Omar Jan's recognition as Crown Prince and they feel that he should at least be presented as the future Amir of Afghanistan."

"That's typical Arg Palace brouhaha!" the Doctor replied cynically. A necklace of sapphire, emerald, and ruby displayed in a shop diverted her attention from the Palace intrigues and she bent forward to take a closer look.

"Salaam!" the gray-bearded proprietor appeared from the shadows of his shop rolling an opium ball between his fingers.

"*Salaam!*" Dr. Hamilton replied straightening her headscarf so that it covered some strands of hair that had trailed across her face. "Could you kindly hand me the necklace?" She took it from the proprietor and examined it intently while continuing the conversation with Frank, "I must tell you something, but you will need to keep to yourselves." She ran the necklace through her hands. "Do I have your word?"

Both Roma and Frank nodded obediently.

"The Amir and Queen Sultana make terrible decisions fairly regularly, especially lately. She is a demanding wife and has a long list of things she expects him to do. When he can't, or won't, meet her demands there are awful arguments." Lillias spread the necklace across the wooden counter and examined the stones one by one, to make sure they were genuine. "Then the Amir goes off in a vengeful rage and kills some of his subjects," she picked up the necklace again and scrutinized every piece several times before she was satisfied. "He confessed to me that the Queen's pressure causes him to go into a rage and consequently he makes wrong decisions."

"Well, it's their first voyage and to them, it seems like a trip to another planet. They are excited, anxious, and sometimes out of control, God only knows what is actually going on behind the scenes in the Arg," Frank Martin said.

"This is beautiful Roma!" Lillias suspended the gleaming gemstones against her sister's neck, "It looks wonderful on you."

The proprietor offered a mirror, "Here, please see yourself," he said. The image was streaked and wavy but Roma was already sold.

"How much is it?" she asked anxiously.

"One-thousand-rupia!" the proprietor replied unblinkingly from eye sockets deep as those of a death's head.

Their jaws dropped when they heard the outrageous price! "No! You quadrupled the price because we are *Farangee?*" Roma replied in astonishment, "that's my entire expense for one year!"

"How about nine-hundred-and-fifty Rupia?" asked the proprietor.

They walked away without bargaining further. Roma was deeply disappointed to let the magnificent necklace go but she was determined not to be paltered by a crooked proprietor.

"Back to the issue of the Mullahs," Dr. Hamilton said as they continued to saunter through the hubbub of the bazaar, "tell me again, Frank, why are they going to England? I don't feel you have given me the whole story."

"I don't know for sure," he replied, "but I gather taking a few of those Mullahs to visit the Muslim leaders in England is intended to test whether England has a genuine sympathy towards its Muslim subjects." He shrugged, "The aim seems to be that it will make the Mullah's more sympathetic to Queen Victoria."

"Complete hogwash!" Dr. Hamilton replied forcefully. "It makes little or no sense!' She touched a dazzlingly embroidered Qandahari dress and turned enthusiastically, "Roma! Could you see yourself in this?" she stretched the dress across her sister's shoulders, "You would look wonderful in it!"

Roma smiled with delight and her blue eyes shone with joy, "It is lovely, Lillias!"

They haggled with the proprietor for a few minutes until both Roma and the shopkeeper were satisfied with the price.

"Queen Victoria seems pleased to receive Nasrullah to Windsor," Frank Martin said. "She believes it's a sign of goodwill not only between herself and the Amir but between Britain and the Muslim world. But, I also heard from another source in India, that she would prefer he did not approach a British-born man, Henry Quilliam, a Muslim convert, who goes by the name of Abdullah Quilliam. He is popular in Liverpool where he resides, but he rigorously recruits people into the Islamic religion." Frank Martin removed his clumsily wrapped woolen cloak, stretched both arms wide, and flung it round himself.

"Abdullah Quilliam?" Dr. Hamilton said thoughtfully. "That name rings the bell. If I am not mistaken, the Amir mentioned something to Nasrullah about donating money to him."

"This journey is going to be an unprecedented event for the

Afghans, especially as Nasrullah will be arriving in England in time for Eid."

"What's Eid?" Roma asked.

"The Muslim festival commemorating the sacrifice by Abraham of a sheep in the place of his son, Isaac." Dr. Hamilton said, "They wear their best clothing for the celebration and children receive gifts from their elders—a bit like Easter."

"These are the same Mullahs who continually preach Jihad or Holy War against us," Frank Martin said in frustration. "To them, Christians are infidels and English devils, no matter how you toss the dice."

It took Rafiuddin two days to get back to Munshi Abdul Karim regarding the plan to help Nasrullah. Rafiuddin's past diplomatic experience with the Ottoman Empire and his exposure to a network of powerful people in the world was an excellent opportunity to promote such a proposal. Like Munshi, Rafiuddin had a desire to see a Muslim country like Afghanistan free from British dominance but his real dream was to see his native India, attain independence. The lavish lifestyle of the British lords, earls, dukes, and duchesses was propped up by the wealth from England's colonies, India in particular, where the common people remained hungry and destitute.

The glossy Brougham drawn by two sleek horses arrived at Frogmore. Rafiuddin stepped down and greeted Munshi with open arms. "Here is what I've come up with," he declared, grinning widely, causing his gold-plated front teeth to catch the light of the afternoon sun. "His Highness Emir of Bahrain, *Sheikh Isa Al Khalifa*, is a longtime friend who might help. The plan is to send him a sealed letter to deliver to Amir Abdul Rahman," he continued. "And in a good faith, a couple of Arab bred horses for his two sons. That will establish close contact and will put the Amir at ease to count on us," he pummeled Munshi's arm gleefully, "What do you think, *Baboo?*" Their footsteps crunched against the fine gravel as they walked toward the mansion.

"Is the Khalifa of Bahrain anti-British?" Munshi asked as he led the way into the suite.

"Yes, and for that reason, he'll help us wholeheartedly," Rafiuddin continued, "I must confess that I bolstered that thought in coming up with the plan."

"No doubt Moulvi Sahab, you've done well. However, now, I have to find a way to put it into action," Munshi said thoughtfully. "I could send him a wireless telegram immediately to expect the sealed letter via a merchant ship to Manama. He should receive the letter in a week. I'll appoint an emissary and give him all the details."

"My plan of action was to write the confidential letter to Manama on your behalf."

"You would have to make sure the letter is not intercepted, else we're doomed. We would completely lose Her Majesty's trust!" He raised his hands and lifts his head in prayer, "I pray to you, Almighty, for our success."

"Don't worry, *Baboo Jee*, you make sure to work with Her Majesty for a good outcome, while I work through with Sheikh Isa Al Khalifa to contact the Amir."

"*Insha Allah*, God willing," Munshi replied. Rafiuddin left him deep in thought plucking absent-mindedly at his beard.

CHAPTER TWENTY-TWO

∾෨෬∾෨෬∾෨෬

Exactly at noon, a thunderous blast ripped throughout the gorge, across from the *Mashin-Khana*, causing the windows of the workshop to rattle like hundreds of glass bells. No one showed any concern. They were as careless as children at play.

Prince Habibullah pulled his watch-chain from his waistcoat pocket and flipped it open,

"I have a perfect watch," he declared proudly, "it's exactly noon."

From the window in the Mashin-Khana, the cannon's position could be seen where it sat on a flat hill adjacent to the Sher-Darwaza mountain. The sixty-four-pounder Rifled Muzzle Loading gun had been manufactured in the workshop. It was, almost certainly, the only cannon in Afghanistan that fired blank, without a cannonball, and for the many inhabitants who had no watch or clock, it afforded them a single time fixture every day. Timepieces were scarce but, for the most part, unnecessary; the minutes ticked off and the days passed, while the preciousness of time was largely unrecognized in that part of the world. The daily blasting of the cannon was always great entertainment for the children. They waited for the event and cheered with delight when fire, then smoke, burst forth from the cannon's mouth; they delighted in the roar and the anticipated trembling of the ground under their feet.

Once the cannon was fired, total silence permeated the *Mashin-Khana*; it was the signal for a break. Machines ceased humming, and the noise of hammers, chisels, and files ceased.

Frank Martin escorted the Princes and royal noblemen through the main armories, from the drop forging, blacksmithing, polishing, and foundry, to the gun-rifling department. He halted the party at that point to give a demonstration of how it was done.

"Your Highnesses, *Sardars*. This is an Afghan invention and a proud moment for His Highness, Amir Sahib, and for us all, and I am eager to apply for a patent in England," Martin said. He ordered the demonstration to begin. The lead mechanic was a tall, middle-aged man with a beard that followed the line of his chin. He was wearing an oil-stained overall and the end-flaps of his black turban hung to the small of his back.

"This rectangular, heavy wooden frame is a tool to hold a hollowed stock of steel," he explained. "In the center of the frame is this long screw with a worm of the same number of turns." He raised the long screw above his narrow shoulders and set it back on the rectangular frame, "that makes the rifle cut. It is positioned so: " He located the screw and worm into the smooth barrel. "Those are the exact number of turns required in the rifling," he paused for a moment. "It's then actuated by this long handle that applies great force," the mechanic nodded at his helpers who are stood by to rotate it. "After that, the shaft is taken to the drilling tool consisting of a powerful spring. That fits snug tight with this file," he compressed the spring into the muzzle of the gun, and a groove was cut as the men slowly and laboriously worked the screw to and fro. The factory workers regarded this tool as the masterpiece of human innovation and they named it *Mashin-e-Amir-Sahib*. Amir Sahib's machine.

Since the inception of the *Mashin-Khana*, small choices had been made and put into action daily to improve the environment of their workplace. It had become a place for technological dreams, innovations, and high achievements. The men performed honest work from the heart, it afforded a sense of dignity and they were reminded with pride and loyalty that they were Afghans.

Frank Martin showed the visitors the three framed poster-sized copies of the Civil-Military Gazette that hung on the wall.

"Your Highnesses and *Sardars*, this was an interview with the Gazette," Frank Martin said pointing to the first one. "And these are the translations in Dari and Pashtu so the factory workers can understand." He gestured to those on the right. "Our workers' worthiness and notability was recognized by the Amir's former dentist, Dr. O'Meara, who gave a rare interview to the renowned English journalist, Rudyard Kipling. It was published in the Colonial British Civil and Military Gazette in Lahore on twenty-seventh October eighteen-eighty-seven," Frank read it aloud:

"Rudyard Kipling: 'Did you see the gun-factories by any chance?'"

"Dr. O'Meara: 'Well, I took up an English Martini-Henri carbine, and when I was in Kabul was shown and offered, for one-third of my weapon's price, a Kabul-made article which, to look at, seemed just as good as mine. Of course, it had been hand-rifled, and I don't think it could have shot absolutely true, but still, it was surprisingly well-made for a thing made by hand.'" Frank Martin paused, "Gentlemen, it gets interesting from here," he continued to read. "'If they can get English machinery into the workshops, I should think that they could make really first-class rifles. The Kabuli workmen are very clever and very quick to take a hint. I had a man out of the Amir's workshops put under me, in order that I might give him some rough knowledge of my profession; and he was very quick at picking up things.'"

"Frank turned to Prince Nasrullah, "Your Highness, while we are in England we must source the right machinery for this workshop."

Nasrullah nodded in agreement, "Of course, Eengeeneer Sahib Maarteen," he replied clasping his hands behind his back, "*Insha Allah*, we'll procure the best machinery."

Martin continued the tour showing his guests of honor the manufacturing of cartridges, Martini-Henri guns, muzzle, and breech-loading Enfield guns, and, ultimately, the manufacture of soap, candles, boots, gunpowder, fuses, swords, furniture, carriages, jewelry, and almost everything required for war and peace.

This celebration of the Mashin-Khana brought new zest to the workers - a sense of hope and warmth that would move mountains, charm demons, and accomplish great victories. Prince Habibullah turned to face Martin, "You've done well, Eeneeneer Sahib Maarteen," he said warmly, placing a hand on the Engineer's shoulder. "Have you heard of this saying? he asked. "'Successful minds work like a gimlet, to a single point.'" He smiled as his words were greeted with rapturous applause, "Indeed," he said to Frank Martin, "you have a successful mind."

"Thank Your Highness!" the Chief Engineer replied as he graciously doffed his bowler hat and escorted them out.

❧⟡❧⟡❧

"Lillias, can you keep something confidential?" Martin asked in an undertone.

"Of course Frank. I would never betray you. I told you something confidential about the Amir, so you can tell me what is on your mind," she glanced at him reassuringly. "You can trust me."

"One of our agents in Kabul who contacts me on regular basis has been asking whether the Amir and Munshi Abdul Karim are in cahoots," he pursed his lips and looked down.

"Is this agent the one in the clandestine network set up by Governor-General, Lord Bruce?"

"Yes."

"What was your reply?"

"I told him he was barking up the wrong tree and that I have no information whatsoever, but he has come back to me again and again," he stopped pacing. "He's a paranoid freak and a misfit, and he is constantly in search of information as to what is going on inside the Palace walls."

"How often do you see him and where?"

"I can't go in details, but he's a British agent disguised in a filthy Afghan outfit. You cannot even tell the difference between him and a regular destitute Kabuli."

"He must be good at what he's doing or else, he would be caught in a heartbeat in this forbidden city." Dr. Hamilton said thoughtfully, "is that the same British Colonel, who has set himself up as a Hakim—fluent in Dari and Pashtu?"

"Yes!" he nodded. "But you never heard it from me and please do not let the Amir discover it or he will see us as accomplices to this spy operation," he pursed his lips and rubbed his cleft chin.

"Don't worry, I heard that from an Indian woman who was the mistress of a British officer in Lahore. He betrayed her. She asked me whether he was a British spy in Kabul and if I knew him. Connecting the dots, I believe I could find out more from that woman." She frowned, "But, honestly, I don't think I should interfere in British government business. After all, I'm privately employed and have no desire to be part of this," she declared, matter-of-factly.

"I feel the same, Lillias," he raised his hands, palms up, "I just want this man to disappear and stop bothering me."

"Well, just remember Frank, he has a job to do and there's nothing you or I can do to stop him." She looked up at him, "But you can control one thing."

"What's that?"

"Just don't give him any information!" she waved her index finger in refusal. "You don't know anything."

Queen Victoria's courtiers and the Royal family were fiercely opposed to the Queen's association with Munshi Abdul Karim. Most recognized the hold he had over the Queen and that he won her full support and attention. He was always alongside, even in matters of British national security, or on issues concerning members of the Royal household. Queen Victoria's close advisers repeatedly advised her not to reveal secret information in presence of Munshi, for fear he would inform leaders of British colonial powers resentful of British domination of their home countries. But, Queen Victoria had a blind spot where Munshi Abdul Karim was concerned and refused to hear any criticism.

The covert clique between the Amir of Afghanistan, the Ruler of Bahrain, Munshi Abdul Karim, and Rafiuddin Ahmed would have been regarded with deep suspicion and alarm by the British government if the connection were discovered before Nasrullah's departure.

CHAPTER TWENTY-THREE

୭୦୦୭୦୦୭୦

March 1895 -- Afghan calendar month:
Hamal 1274, Kabul, Afghanistan

Unexpectedly, a sealed letter and two magnificent horses arrived at
Arg Palace. The four bearers introduced themselves as representatives
of the ruler of Bahrain. The letter read as follows:

> *Windsor*
> *Sept. 8. 1894*
>
> *H.H. Amir of Afghanistan,*
> *Zia-ul-Millat-Wa-Ud Din, Light of the nation and*
> *religion.*
>
> *Your Highness,*
>
> *As a friend and brother, my heart overflowed with joy*
> *when Her Majesty, Queen Victoria and the Empress of*
> *India, graciously announced the arrival of Shahzadah*
> *Nasrullah Khan to Windsor Palace.*
>
> *With a depth of feeling which is fully known to the*
> *heart of none but a devotee of The Almighty and his*
> *messenger, Hazrat Rasul-Ullah, I pray Your Highness*
> *to accept my offer of help, for your benevolence, to be*
> *of service advising Shahzadah Nasrullah in matters of*
> *Her Majesty's Royal Court.*

In addition, as a token of good faith and friendship, His Highness, the Sultan of Bahrain, Isa Ibn Ali Al Khalifa, whose emissaries traveled across the Persian plateaus to hand you this confidential letter. He is conveying his utmost respect and gratitude and humbly presenting two splendid Arab Horses as gifts to your beloved sons, Princes, Habibullah and Nasrullah.

Your Gracious, Amir Sahib, if I may also introduce my dearest friend Moulvi Sir Rafiuddin Ahmed to His Highness, Shahzadah Nasrullah Khan. He conveys his high regards and utmost respect to you and the Shahzadah.

Please expect us to be of service upon the arrival of His Highness Shahzadah Nasrullah Khan.

May Allah grant you his Grace, through life, and at the last a Crown of Immortal Glory.

Your Highness' Sincere and Grateful Servant,

Munshi Abdul Karim
Indian secretary to Queen Victoria

The letter was beautifully hand-written on paper with a three-quarter-inch black border and the envelope, with a half-inch black border, and was sealed with black sealing wax. It was also specified "confidential" by the Indian Secretary to Queen Victoria.

The Amir raised his eyebrows wondering immediately about the clandestine delivery. Why had the letter not been delivered by the Indian government under British rule, rather than through a small fiefdom in the Persian Gulf? And, why the two horses? Nevertheless, the Amir sent sealed letters in reply, thanking the Sultan of Bahrain for the magnificent horses, and to Munshi for his kindness in offering to help Nasrullah upon his arrival in England.

He immediately summoned Princes Nasrullah and Habibullah to Bostan-Sarai. "Sons, this could be good news!" he said as they entered the drawing-room. "I smell subterfuge by Munshi Abdul Karim," he continued quietly. "Keep this a secret and never talk about the letter to anyone. No one must know Abdul Karim has contacted us without going through the British Governor-General in Calcutta. Daktar Laila or any *Englees* especially must not hear of this!"

"If Munshi desires to help us then it's good news," Crown Prince Habibullah said.

"Rest assured father! We will make sure no one knows about this," Nasrullah replied.

"Padlock your lips," the Amir said. "We must find out more about Munshi's ambition and relationship with the *Malika-e-Englistaan*."

❦

The Hamilton sisters and Frank Martin strolled through the famous onion-domed Char-Chatta bazaar.

"Did you know this bazaar was burned to ashes by British General George Pollock in eighteen-forty-two?" Martin asked.

"No!" both Dr. Hamilton and Roma replied in unison.

"It was renovated by the Amir's Grandfather, Amir Dost Mohammad Khan," Martin said, glancing up at one of the four high domed ceilings. "It was burned down in retribution against the Afghans for displaying General William Macnaghten's head up there," Roma looked up, somewhat shocked by that revelation. "Also, for the brutal massacre of General Elphinstone and his army of sixteen thousand men. The design is impressive, don't you think?"

"*Salaam!*" They turned to see Lieutenant Colonel Zalmai's familiar face. "I had difficulty recognizing you. You blend in well with the Afghans, wearing our local dress."

"*Salaam,*" Frank Martin replied with a smile as he shook hands.

"Good day to you all," Zalmai put his hand to his chest and bowed politely. He was dressed in a long copper-colored tunic, with a white *Perahan-Tunban*, and white turban; a curved dagger hung from his cummerbund. On the middle finger of his left hand, he wore a single ring of gold set with a large gleaming sapphire. His gaze met Roma's, her blue eyes lit up and she returned his smile.

"Thank you for all your help in teaching me English ways of dining, Roma Jan. I have been practicing ever since you showed me," he adjusted his tunic lapel awkwardly. "You look almost like an Afghan girl," he smiled.

Lillias observed the look that passed between Zalmai and her sister and drew his attention elsewhere.

"Beautiful ring Colonel. I've never seen you wearing jewelry before," she said.

"True, *Daktar Laila Jan*, I only wear jewelry in private settings. My grandfather is a fourth-generation jeweler so I can pick and choose whatever I wear," he smiled.

"I know your father was also an entrusted officer in the Amir's grandfather's army, but I didn't know about your family's jewelry business," Lillias said.

"Yes, he brings most of the jewelry back from India and Arabia and Amir Sahib's family and the royal courtiers buy them."

"Perhaps it is fortunate that we met with you today," Dr. Hamilton smiled, "Your knowledge of jewelry might help Roma. She fell in love with a necklace she saw here today, but the proprietor down the street would not reduce his outrageous price."

"If I may suggest something," the Colonel said, his brown eyes sparkling, "never buy anything without an entrusted Afghan guide." He smiled, "this ring," he lifted his finger and the ring gleamed in the afternoon sunshine, "would cost you four times as much as it is worth if you bought it, but I could get it at the right price."

"Then perhaps you could help me to buy that necklace, Colonel?"

Roma asked with a smile.

"Of course, Roma Jan, please call me by my name, Zalmai, let's drop the formalities."

"I'd appreciate your help, Zalmai," she replied. "I adored the design and gemstones, but that proprietor…" She shook her head.

"Thank you, Zalmai," Lillias said. "Roma, would you like to go and let Zalmai bargain that necklace for you?"

"Yes please."

"I have few things to discuss with Mr. Martin, you will find us in that tea house when you get back," Lillias said, pointing to a shopfront where steaming brass samovars were displayed.

"I would love a hot cup of tea, would you, Frank?"

"I am all for it," he agreed obligingly.

The pure-bred Arab horses, one black as a raven and the other white as snow were immediately named *Almas-e-Sya*, Black-Diamond, and, *Baarfi*, Snowy. Mr. Clemence gave them each a lump of sugar and let them loose in the pen. The acclaimed stamina of these dashing chisel-headed, large-eyed creatures, was exhibited in the speed and freedom of their movements. In the Palace stables, there were more than a thousand horses of a few different breeds, but these newcomers with long, arched necks and high tail carriages attracted as much attention as if a circus had arrived.

The Amir, the Princes, the British men and women, little William, and Prince Omar Jan, watched with joy and laughter as the two horses rejoiced in their strength, manes and tails streaming as they galloped into the wind that blew down from the northern ranges. The two comrades had been constant companions from the day they were foals. Their appearances emitted energy, intelligence, courage, and nobility.

Nasrullah's covetous nature impeded his claim on a particular horse. He turned sullen, "I want the white," he said. "No, the black!" He kicked a post of the pen, "I've made up my mind—the white." Finally, after multiple times back and forth, he hesitantly settled on Baarfi.

Knowing the young prince, Thomas Clemence discerned the need to take on the difficult task of educating Nasrullah to form peace with Baarfi, to respect him, to become his companion but never to master the magnificent beast; only then would he become a loyal defender, and would take him into the craters of hell at one beckoning.

Frank Martin lifted the thick, oil-stained flap that covered the door of the teahouse and ushered Lillias in before him.

The turbaned equivalent of the Maitre d' shouted a welcome, "*Khosh Ameded!*" and escorted them to a corner of the room. The clamorous noise and air that had remained unventilated for weeks hit them immediately. The table and chairs were not only in poor condition, they also rattled and wobbled on the uneven brick floor.

"Please," Frank asked, "can you get something to straighten . . . ?" he demonstrated the need. A few pebbles were brought in and jammed under the short legs.

"*Khoob?* Good?" the Maitre d' asked.

"*Khoob!* Good!" Frank replied.

"*Chai?* Tea?"

"*Doo chai enja byar!* Bring two teas here!" the Maitre d' bellowed like a bull calf.

Ordering eats was only done by yelling above the noise. The waiter took the order, shouted at the chef, and the chef howled at the server when it was ready. The noise never stopped but grew in volume during the lunch hour peak. Sometimes the system led to confusion if the order was forgotten or taken to the wrong customer; in which case, the noise level became deafening.

Close to the entrance, a man was sitting crossed-legged against the dented and bent brass samovars. He was the cashier but also poured hot water from the samovars into the cracked porcelain teapots. The black smokestacks from the samovars protruded through the mud-covered roof spewing steam into the sky. inside the teahouse, the steam was intermingled with the stifling and acidic smells of footwear and armpits forming a late winter Afghan cocktail in immediate need of airing. Both the English Doctor and the Engineer quickly acclimatized in that setting like fish to water.

"*Che dega khwahesh dared?* What else would you like to have?" the Maitre d' asked. A dirty red napkin, which he shared with other customers, was flung over his shoulder. The waiter brought two flowery porcelain teapots, two green porcelain cups without handles, a saucer filled with hard deformed pea-size candies, and set them on the table, which still wobbled.

"*Tashakur,* Thank you, *bas chai tanha*, only tea is enough," Frank replied in his broken Dari.

"Amir thinks Nasrullah and his entourage will be housed in Buckingham Palace like the Shah of Iran. What was his name?"

Franks looked at her thoughtfully, "It was something like Naser Shah… I do remember that he was a renowned womanizer."

Lillias smiled and gripped the cup at the rim between thumb and forefinger lifting it deftly to her lips.

"Naser-Udin Shah, that's right. He stayed in Buckingham Palace years ago," she replied, looking at Frank Martin over the rim of her cup.

"Have you tried the teapot soup they make here?" Martin asked. "My workers order it for lunch and they have let me try it a few times. It is really delicious."

"No, what is it?"

"A lamb soup," he replied. " They cook it overnight in the same teapots," he gave a wide grin and pointed to the teapot on the table. "They leave it in the charcoal embers and by morning it's succulent, tender and delicious . . . the meat just falls off the bone!"

"Let's try it," she said enthusiastically

Frank raised his hand and beckoned the Maitre d' who walked quickly to their table.

"*Befarmayed, che mail dared?* Please, what would you like to have?" the red napkin still sat over his shoulder.

"*Doo Shorwa-e-Chainakee byar*, bring two teapot soups," Frank Martin said.

The Maitre d' bellowed the order across the crowded room.

"There's another thing Amir is nervous about regarding Nasrullah's trip," Dr. Hamilton said.

"And, what's that?"

"He's concerned that Nasrullah may catch cholera during the trip to Portsmouth. There are reports about the troopships being checked, cleansed, and disinfected before arrival at any port and even during the voyage . . . particularly those bound for Portsmouth. They are only admitting people under strict quarantine."

The Maitre d' brought the teapots filled with soup, some freshly baked Afghan bread, green onions, sliced tomatoes, and green chili peppers and set them with empty ceramic bowls on the table.

A Kabul-made water container with a tap stood by the entrance for customers to wash their hands. Martin made his way between the tables, retrieved the rough bar of soap, and rinsed his hands. He politely refused the Maitre d's red towel and, using his kerchief, dried his hands as he made his way back to the table.

Taking the lids off their teapots they inhaled the steamy rich smell. Lillias opened her small valise.

"Frank, I have another spoon if you want, I brought it for Roma."

"I'm fine thank you, I'll eat the Afghan way. I believe it when they tell me food tastes better eating with your hands." Frank tore chunks of bread and mixed them into his soup, pressed the soaked bread and lamb together and thrust it into his mouth. "Didn't you say in the training that you can eat with your hands like the locals?"

Lillias laughed and went to wash her hands.

"This is delicious," she said after her first mouthful, "What did you call it?"

"It's called *chainakee* . . . *chainak* means teapot."

The astonished Maitre d' stared at the two foreigners savoring every mouthful like native Afghans.

"If Amir is concerned about cholera infection, he should ask the Governor-General in India to keep the troopship reserved for him constantly cleansed, disinfected, and quarantined."

"I doubt whether the British government would bear the expense of keeping one troopship quarantined," she protested, "not when it is generally in use transporting troops back and forth between India and England. Trust me they will not keep a ship idle only for Amir's son. The Amir is aware of the two major cholera epidemics recently, but I'm not sure if he knows troopships can be infected with cholera when they are in use." The soup blossomed its special fragrance from her bowl and every mouthful was a gentle massage to her soul. "Leaving it overnight on the charcoal is obviously what does the job," she added, randomly changing the subject from the cholera epidemic.

"It certainly does," he replied with a smile.

Lillias returned to Nasrullah's voyage, "I've no doubt the British are disinfecting every troopship bound for England."

The Maitre d' stopped to check on Frank and Lillias, "*Khoob?*" he asked.

"*Khoob!*" Frank replied, "*Tashakur.*"

"I hear most of the ships going through Suez don't dock to load coal or take on board any necessities," Frank said, eating with obvious enjoyment. "Reportedly, the epidemic is high in and around Egypt," he paused for a moment. "Not long ago a telegraph was dispatched from

Alexandria, stating that at Aden, of seventy-eight cases of cholera, fifty had ended fatally and most troopships stop to load coal there."

"That's a bit high, but I'm sure it will be quarantined if they do load coal," Lillias used her kerchief to dab her lips.

"Did you read what Rudyard Kipling wrote in the Calcutta gazette recently?"

She shook her head.

"The crowded troopships and the cholera-stricken camps are a bad mix when heading to Portsmouth. Don't you think Amir has reason to be concerned for his beloved son?"

"I concur with Kipling, but the troopship that we will board won't be crowded. . . although it might have been crowded in previous voyages. A little over a week of quarantine would rid it of any infection." She finished her soup and followed Frank to the water container to wash her hands. "That's partly why Amir wants me to accompany his son to monitor his health and his food and drink consumption around the clock. Here I am, going on a voyage with Nasrullah, accompanied by an Indian doctor who will also be taking care of him, even though the Amir is not impressed. He's just like the local Hakim," she said. "But that could change and be replaced by a British doctor." She wiped her hands with her kerchief as she sat down, "Fortunately, Queen Sultana wants me to bring another woman physician from England. I have thought of asking my longtime friend, Doctor Kate Dally if she is up to the task."

"Roma and Zalmai may be outside waiting. Are you ready to leave?" Frank asked.

"Yes, I'm ready. Thank you for introducing me to the delicious teapot soup, it was wonderful. We must do it again."

CHAPTER TWENTY-FOUR

❦❦❦

January 1895 -- Afghan calendar month:
Dalwa 1273, Kabul, Afghanistan

Princes Habibullah and Nasrullah ordered the Palace grooms to saddle and bridle Almas-e-Sya and Baarfi. Immaculate Afghan carpet paddings were placed under the saddles of the two horses, and small bags of sugar were put into their leather pouches. Thomas Clemence and Frank Martin were to accompany the Princes on the day's ride to advise them about their new Arab mounts.

The mounted platoon of security protection was in tow a mile behind, as Nasrullah and Habibullah clapped the reins and spurred the horses, they galloped effortlessly eastward to a nearby mountain gorge with towering sheer cliffs. The two horses' manes and swishing tails fluttered like banners and the pounding of their steady hooves echoed like machine-gun fire in a well. Mud splattered in all directions. Both, Baarfi and Almas-e-Sya, were strong young stallions in their prime, and their gait was even and definite. With the pleasant thrust of the breeze from the Hindu-Kush mountains against their faces and the reverberating pulses of the hooves beneath them—it was a sensation of power, unlike anything the Princes had experienced before. Eventually, the horses' tails dropped a bit and their pace changed, and every other accompanying horse followed suit. They approached the canyon at a steady canter, then reined in their horses and dropped from their saddles to let them quench their thirst at a flowing stream that cascaded down from high glaciers. The horses, like their riders, were short of breath and glazed in a shimmering luster of perspiration.

"Your Highnesses," Clemence said, "I am amazed! Where did these magnificent beasts come from?" He sauntered to the stream to let his horse drink, "There was no order or request on my desk for their purchase," he said as he turned to face the two young men, "it baffles me how they got here."

"*Aghai* Cleemess, is it hard to find beauties like these?" Nasrullah asked cagily as he rubbed Baarfi's neck, feeling the rhythmic pulses as the horse swallowed water.

"No, Your Highness, they're easily found in Arabia, Iran, and elsewhere, I'm just curious because most of our horses are crossbreeds of Russian and Afghan," he glanced down as his horse dipped its head into the stream. "As Your Highness knows, I keep a full record of every horse that His Highness, your father, has in Afghanistan, in fact, thousands." Clemence took his mahogany pipe from his safari jacket and clenched it between his teeth; he struck a match and puffed until the smoke obscured his debonair mustache and goatee. "I have ten record keepers working twelve hours a day in my office in Beymaroo to keep track of the horses," he declared, glancing at the red glow in the bowl of his pipe with satisfaction.

"I don't understand why you're telling me all this, *Aghai* Cleemess."

"Your Highness, I need to register the new horses and keep their records clean. That way if something happens to either of them, the records are often of great help."

"What is there for us to do?" Nasrullah blurted out.

"I need their information, date of birth, breed, sources of purchase, and all related information." The smell of Clemence's exotic English tobacco drifted past everyone's nostrils.

"No harm done asking the questions, *Aghai* Cleemess," Prince Habibullah cut in. "To be honest, neither my brother." nor I have any information about the horses." He avoided eye contact with the vet by stroking Baarfi's velvety white coat. Frank noted the telltale nervous stammer.

"Let me give you the little information I know," Frank Martin cut in. "Just a few days ago, four armed men wearing Arab clothing came by the *Machin-Khana* asking the way to the Arg Palace, two of them were riding these horses." He looked pointedly from Nasrullah to Habibullah, "They couldn't speak Dari or English, only Arabic." He sat down on a rock next to the stream, bent to fill his water bottle, and slung it over his shoulder. "Luckily an employee working for me knew a little Arabic and gave them directions to the Palace."

Listening to Frank Martin's account, both Habibullah's and Nasrullah's eyes narrowed as they tried to decide how best to play the game in the light of Martin's story. Habibullah realized he had no choice but to keep up the pretense that he knew nothing. He could not betray his father's secret, neither could he gain much by lying, except to lose the trust of their British friends. He was walking a very fine line; saying the wrong thing at this critical moment could lead to the exposure of the collaboration between the Sultan of Bahrain, Rafiuddin, and Munshi Abdul Karim Khan, at Windsor Palace.

"We don't exactly know where these horses came from," he said hesitantly. "I think someone gifted them to my father?" He shrugged. "Perhaps you should ask him," he said evasively.

But Nasrullah bolstered his thoughts differently, "Eengeeneer *Sahib* Maarteen and *Aghai* Cleemess," he said, holding the rein in one hand and rubbing his stubble with the other. "Is there any reason you could explain to us why we shouldn't be given horses?" His Astrakhan Karakul hat tilted forward and he adjusted it with one hand. Baarfi whinnied and tossed his head.

Clemence removed the pipe from his mouth, "Your Highness, I don't fully understand your question?"

"Fine, let me say it another way." Nasrullah's thin eyebrows peaked in anger, "Why are you interrogating us about where these horses came from?" he rubbed the back of his neck. "Why are we being scrutinized for having horses? Is this now another restriction for us to have horses?"

Clemence blew a cloud of smoke, "Your Highness has misunderstood the reason for my questions," he replied matter-of-factly; his tone was congenial. "What I'm trying to express is that all the horses in the Afghan army go through the normal protocol. This was established by me and my predecessor to keep important information about them. It's just like we humans, we all have identities and records of our physical descriptions, backgrounds and so forth . . . "

Habibullah interjected, "My apologies for stopping you, *Aghai* Cleemess." his smile was conciliatory. "Let me find out the information you need about the horses and submit it to you. That will include the date of birth, their names, and so forth." He clasped Thomas Clemence's upper arm in a friendly manner, "I am sure my father will have the information you need." Almas-e-Sya tugged at the reins and snorted impatiently. "I would like to seek your advice as to how to take care of these beauties," Habibullah gently rubbed Almas-e-Sya's chest; the horse lowered his head and moved towards him.

Even at this young age, Habibullah was the master of diplomacy. His attitude and manner produced the emotional waters in which people around him swam cordially. He was the sort of person who held back on the negative and expressed the positive—in short, a peacemaker.

"Of course, Your Highness," Thomas Clemence said. "I'll complete the records for the new additions to our Arg stables and monitor their state of health frequently."

Still sitting on the rock, Frank Martin nodded in agreement. "By all means, let us move forward," he stood up, uncapped his water bottle, and took a mouthful of fresh glacier water.

〜ⓐ〜ⓐ〜ⓐ〜

Was the proprietor pursuing a personal vendetta in setting a high price for the necklace because Roma was English? Perhaps he, like most Afghans, saw the British as demons and villains and held an obsessive grudge against them for causing the everlasting quagmire and bloodshed in his homeland. He was mindful of the consequences if he mistreated an English guest of the Amir. Some lines could not be crossed without anticipating severe punishment, if not death; but attempting to sell a necklace at an inflated price was a subtler message of contempt.

There was no fixed price for an item in Kabul's bazaars and haggling was the accepted method of purchase. However, it had the disadvantage of creating an air of suspicion between buyer and seller. There were always two prices: a foreigner price and a local price. When it came to a local price, an Afghan was the only one who knew how to deal with an Afghan and that pertained to any item in the market—from cattle exchange, merchandise of all sorts, and to dowries.

"I'm glad I ran into you today, Roma Jan," Zalmai's expressive brown eyes met hers with the warmth of an embrace, "I'll do whatever I can to bring the price of the necklace down for you."

"It is such a wonderful chance meeting, Zalmai," she replied, "I am happy to see you, and of course I would be delighted if you could be of help," she looked up at him and smiled. The roar of the cannon from across the city alerted everyone to the time.

"If I may ask, what price was he asking for it?" he queried, as he paced with almost scissor-like precision beside her. Zalmai carried himself well and even his gestures demonstrated an inherent elegance.

"One thousand Rupia and then a counter-offer of nine-hundred-and-fifty," Roma answered.

"That's outrageous for a necklace in Kabul. Unless it was studded with diamonds, but that would be rare."

"No, nothing like that, but it was delicately made and beautiful," she gave him a little more information and described how it was displayed in the jeweler's shop. As they make their way through the bustling throng, Zalmai took the lead and Roma was now in tow.

"I've been busy training the lancers and guards to accompany the Prince to England," he said.

"I presume you will guard us all on our way?" overhead, pigeons were circling and cooing and Roma could make out the blue of their wings against the warm blue of the sky.

"Of course, I will be responsible for your safety," he shot her a quirky smile. "Roma Jan, I'd like to negotiate the price with the proprietor alone. I don't want him to know you are with me at first, or else he will not reduce the price. Can you show me which shop it is?"

She complied inaudibly and gestured towards the building with an awning that extended out into the narrow alley. Again, she became aware of the putrid smell that hung over the narrow street.

"I know the owner, he sometimes trades jewelry with my grandfather." He shook his head, "If you had told me you wanted a necklace, I could have you one made in my grandfather's shop," there was mischief in the way his lips pursed in a smile, "Stay here, Miss Roma, and I will beckon you when the deal is done."

Around her was the hustle and bustle of chattering buyers and vendors who sat crossed-legged in their shops and booths; donkeys and mules ambled by; women in burkas and head scarfs of diverse colors, some carrying brass *lotahs* on their heads, others with infants in their arms. There was the tapping and hammering of coppersmiths, the clucking of caged chickens, and the cries of beggars. Roma found a secluded spot away from the bazaar's hubbub, from which she could see the alleyway, and patiently waited for Zalmai to signal her.

They spoke as if they had known each other since their youth. The proprietor's gregarious and ingratiating demeanor was in sharp contrast to that which he had displayed to his prospective English

211

customers earlier. He ordered tea from the samovar nearby and offered Colonel Zalmai Khan a lopsided stool to sit on. After the inevitable lengthy pleasantries were exchanged; inquiries after the wellbeing of their families and mutual friends, the proprietor moved on to probe the reason for Zalmai's presence.

"How gracious of you to visit me, Zalmai Jan-e-*Aziz*. What brought you here?" His deep-set eyes had a haunted look and his heavily-turbaned cranium twitched weirdly in the semi-gloom. He lit up his turquoise-colored *nargilah* and the odorous smoke filled the shop. The samovar boy brought the tray of tea and set it on a threadbare carpet that could have passed as an ancient shroud.

"I would like to buy that necklace from you," he gestured towards the display.

"Zalmai Jan, I'm honored to hand it to you at no charge. I've known your father and your family all my life. Both our families' indulgent demeanor towards each other goes way back . . . generations! I can't take your money." He stood up, wrapped the necklace in a silken cloth, and handed it to him, "Please take it, I insist!"

His sanctimonious act was something most Afghans were known for. In some instances, sincerity would be obvious, at other times vague, shallow, or fake. It was necessary to sense the motive of the benefactor. But, in this case, the generosity could open doors for future help, Zalmai held a powerful position as Colonel in Amir's army; his father was a well-known army officer in the Amir's grandfather's army, and his grandfather a popular jeweler. Zalmai therefore was a person to cultivate. He could cause the proprietor's business to flourish.

"You are a very generous and kind man," Zalmai said to the proprietor. "Here's one-hundred-and-fifty Rupia," he attempted to hand him the money.

"No! I refuse. Please don't do this, you are embarrassing me!"

"Please take the money, else I will not come again," Zalmai said, placing the money on the cracked glass counter. He glanced up the alley and beckoned Roma.

"Let me introduce you to Miss Hamilton Jan," the Colonel said with a sweep of his hand. "She is sister to Amir Sahib's Daktar and likes the necklace." He handed her the wrapped parcel and gave a half-smile.

"Thank you!" she said. Her eyes flashed with joy and a smile danced on her lips.

"I know her!" the proprietor's jaw dropped and he looked at Roma with a jaundiced eye. "She was here with another woman and man—all *farangees*! Zalmai Jan, *worora*, I wish you hadn't done that." He shook his head and looked at the floor in humiliation.

"Don't be upset, she's our guest, and we Afghans are hospitable people. Show your generosity and kindness and Allah will reward you for your good intentions."

"Zalmai Jan, for the sake of our families," he replied, pointing first at himself and then at the Colonel, "I'm going to disregard this. Maybe it is Allah's will, and let us say it is the Almighty's desire for me to hand her this as a courtesy. But I cannot forgive when Joorj Palak, George Pollack, set ablaze this very same Char-Chatta Bazaar, forty years ago, killing my grandfather and burning down his business." His eyes welled up with indignation at the British for their atrocious acts. "Since then, we've struggled to feed our families!" He cast his gaze at Roma, "My sincere apologies for my disgruntled feelings."

"Brother," Zalmai replied gently, "remember it as though it was a bad dream. Discard the past nightmare that we all went through."

Zalmai and Roma left feeling sympathy for the proprietor and sincere gratitude for his generosity.

"How much do I owe you Zalmai?" Roma asked, her voice bubbly with pleasure. She rummaged inside her embroidered reticule and took out some Indian Rupees.

"Nothing."

"What do you mean?" she asked in astonishment. "Did he give

you the necklace?"

"It doesn't matter, it's yours now," he replied with a smile. "Next time, please take my advice when buying anything. I don't want anyone to cheat you."

"Do you mind if look at it?" she asked

"Not at all."

Roma stopped walking and unwrapped the necklace. "It is so beautiful!" she said in awe tracing her fingers over the beautiful stones and the softly glittering chain. She held it up to the sunlight. The chain was made of interlocking sections of gold and silver, each shimmering charmingly, and the stones too were magnificent; the verdant emerald, the scarlet ruby, and the azure sapphire. "This will attract many envious souls when I wear it in London. Thank you, Zalmai, I wasn't expecting you to pay for it," she said softly. She lifted her headscarf and chignon away from her neck, "Would you please help me to fasten it?"

His fingers rubbed across the nape of her neck as he scuffled with the latch. His touch made her stomach flutter and she turned to look at him over her shoulder. "Thank you for your *baksheesh*," she smiled. "It means so much to me."

"Please don't mention it Roma Jan. This is nothing. I'd be happy to make you a necklace myself," he whispered as his fingertips drifted along the length of the chain and trailed her neck.

"It feels very gratifying," for a moment she couldn't recall what she had meant to say, only that she wanted this new relationship to continue. "We must get back," she said suddenly, "my sister and Frank Martin are waiting for us at the teahouse."

They hurried back to the central Char-Chatta bazaar; their arms, now and then, brushed together as they walked. Zalmai was struck by a sense of agitation and even jealousy when the bazaar's proprietors and bystanders looked curiously at Roma. For any young couple, strolling or co-mingling in Kabul was not taken lightly, and Zalmai already knew he was swimming against a raging current of tradition and religious doctrine.

CHAPTER TWENTY-FIVE

❦

March 1895 -- Afghan calendar month: *Hamal* 1274, Kabul, Afghanistan

As Queen Sultana had banished Nasrullah from her apartment, Lillias, Roma, and Olivia arranged to meet him and Queen Sultana in Gulrez's apartment for the first fittings.

The concubine's excitement rose like a hot dry wind at the thought of hosting the three English ladies in her home, but she was as frantic as a mouse in a trap to hear that the Queen would be joining them. She spent hours preparing culinary delights kneading and rolling dough to make stuffed leek bread, fried wheat grains, deep-fried pastries known as elephant's-ear, and *khajoor*, and *qaimaq-chai*, cardamom tea with rich cream. She dusted and cleaned her apartment and dressed in a cotton undergarment, her new one-piece dress and a light cotton scarf she had made for the upcoming *Nowruz* festivity. Skipping from one foot to another as she worked, Gulrez hummed and sang songs that women of the Wakhan corridor had sung for generations.

Luck had shone on her face when she transitioned from the nomadic life of pitching yurts, and milking yaks, to becoming a concubine to the Amir. The two sons she had brought into the world were both vital to the Amir's future missions, but still, there had been no marriage agreement between the Amir and Gulrez. She held no primary or high stature like the legitimate wives of the Amir, whom he had married thereafter. She was treated by them as any other concubine in the

Harem-Sarai—as a slave—a low-caste woman separated from them by their distinction of royal hereditary, rank, and wealth.

Competition intensified when other concubines, younger than Gulrez, had limitless opportunities to indulge Amir's sexual desires, and produced children. Gulrez was only superior to the other ladies of the Harem-Sarai for one sole reason: her two sons, the heirs to the crown. But life for Gulrez had never been rosy since giving birth to Habibullah and Nasrullah; and in the same way as moths gnaw garments, envy consumed her, as it consumed all the ladies in the Harem-Sarai.

On this rainy Spring day, the English sisters and Olivia lifted the hems of their long and voluminous skirts with one hand and held their parasols with the other. As they entered the marble-floored hallway through the mahogany door they were met by the tantalizing smell of shortening, garlic, and onion.

"*Salaam!*" Gulrez greeted them with a wide smile that caused her cheekbones to rise and her eyes to narrow to two slits. "*Khesh-Amedee.*" You are welcome." She spoke with a distinctive Wakhi accent and Saira, the interpreter, translated for her. "Please come in." Gulrez set their parasols by the door and ushered them into her apartment. Carpet-covered mattresses were neatly set against the four walls of the medium-sized room. On the front wall, hung a ceramic plate with a calligraphic verse of the Qur'an. Above the plate, a silken-covered Qur'an was placed on a small unpainted shelf.

"Please make yourselves comfortable."

The ladies removed their bonnets and sat close to one another on a mattress.

"I'm very happy for you to come here to help Nasrullah with his fitting," Gulrez said, "I apologize about Queen Sultana's fury at me the other day," she talked with a gentle malevolence, "It's always hell with her. Her harsh words dishearten me very much."

"I understand, *Khanum* Gulrez," Dr. Hamilton said. "As you

know it's very hard for me to get involved in the personal matters of the household. I don't want to make Amir Sahib upset and tell me I'm crossing the line." She smiled and diverted the tale-telling to the subject of Nasrullah's fitting, "*Khanum* Gulrez, could you please send for Nasrullah, so that his fitting can be done?"

"Immediately Daktar Sahiba," Gulrez said, a thoughtful frown joining her thin eyebrows together, "But, Nasrullah is not here yet."

Dr. Hamilton took her watch from her dress pocket and flipped it open, "The Prince is late as usual."

"Yes," his mother replied rubbing her arms in anguish. "He's young and irresponsible, he sleeps long hours and is always forgetful about his appointments." She covered her mouth with her gauze scarf in embarrassment, "I'll send for him immediately, Daktar Sahiba." She pursed her thin lips, "I will also bring you some pastries I made this morning."

Before Gulrez was able to hurry from the room, Lillias said sternly: "*Khanum* Gulrez, please let Prince Nasrullah know that I have to make my routine visit to monitor Amir Sahib's health and I've little time left. Also, if I may ask you to convey this to him, his departure for London is coming soon, and the fitting must be done now."

"The Prince's time crawls by like last year's flies," Olivia said cynically to the amusement of the others.

"I have sent a page to call Nasrullah," Gulrez said setting the tray on the floor. She offered her guests pastries and stuffed leek bread, and poured the cream tea into green ceramic cups. She could not take her eyes off their dresses that, to her, looked like dazzling silver clouds with their beautiful sleeves fluttering like wings. She moved closer and fingered the fabrics. "Was this expensive?" she asked. "How much did you give for it?"

"I would say it was reasonable," Olivia replied with a smile, "my grandfather designed it."

"Can your grandfather make me one?" she asked in her child-like way. Gulrez had no concept of who Olivia was, but even if she did it would not have made any difference.

"He passed away not long ago."

She lifted her hands devotedly, "May the Almighty forgive all his sins!" she said. "Please enjoy the *bolanee*, leek bread."

Gulrez took Roma's hand in her own and gently pushed back the lace cuff to examine her skin, "I wonder why my skin is not fair like yours? No matter what I do, or how much I scrub, it doesn't change. You all smell like roses," she went on, "What soap do you use?"

"I'll give you a bar of English soap, and if you like it, I'll bring you more from England," Lillias set her teacup on its saucer and tore a piece off the elephant's-ear pastry on her plate. The crushed pistachios and cardamom on the crispy sugary dough was delectable. "Very tasty, Gulrez," she said with a warm smile.

"Thank you Daktar Sahiba, you are verysweet. May Allah reward your wishes!" Gulrez glanced once more at Roma and Olivia, "You are very beautiful *Nam-e-Khoda*, in the name of God." She stood up with the swish of her long dress and covered her chestnut hair with her scarf. "One moment please!" she exclaimed before dashing to the other room, "I have to rid the evil eye that may be upon you beautiful *Khanum-ha*, ladies."

"Where did she disappear to so abruptly?" Roma asked, confused.

"Mysterious!" Olivia commented with the semblance of a smile.

Gulrez returned with a brass charcoal brazier in one hand and a plate of something in the other and set them down by the ladies, "May this protect you from the evil eye." The Hamilton sisters and Olivia gazed at each other incredulously.

"What is on the plate?" Dr. Hamilton asked.

"*Espand,* wild rue seeds," Gulrez replied.

"Oh, please rid us from the evil eye!" Roma said somewhat sarcastically. Gulrez tossed the seeds into the red-hot charcoal where they crackled and popped and emitted a fragrant cloud of smoke. "So that chases away the evil?" she asked innocently.

Gulrez nodded, picked up the brazier and swirled it around, and chanted a short rhyme. "This is *espand*, it banishes the evil eye; The blessing of King Naqshband; Eye of nothing, Eye of relatives, Eye of friends, Eye of enemies, Who ever is bad should burn in this glowing fire." The smoke encircled them with its flowery aroma.

The queens and concubines of the Harem-Sarai believed the magical power of *espand* was a supernatural protector against negativity and bad luck, and the ritual was employed anytime there was a suspicion that an evil eye rested upon them.

Moments later, Queen Sultana swept into Gulrez's apartment with her lady-in-waiting in tow carrying Nasrullah's uniforms and the Queen's dress. Lillias, Roma, and Olivia immediately rose to their feet and curtsied.

"*Salaam* ladies," the Queen smiled. She sniffed and turned to Gulrez, "I smell *espand*, did you try to shoo off the evil eye for the ladies?" she demanded with a sardonic gleam in her eyes. "Were you trying to destroy the devil?" she set her alligator-skin reticule on the floor and continued, "Not in this life, my dear." Fear instantly clutched at Gulrez's heart as if a tigress was about to tear her apart.

The Queen turned to the English ladies, "I was told you are all here to do a fitting of Nasrallah's suits?" With swishes of her long dress and the clinking of the chatelaines, the lady-in-waiting crossed the room and handed Roma and Olivia the garments.

"Daktar Laila Jan!" the Queen said. "As you and I privately discussed, my husband gave his approval for Prince Omar Jan to join you and Nasrullah on the trip to Landan," she piously raised her hands in prayer for her son's safe return. "Is there any reason his attire was not done first?"

"Your Highness! I'd refer your question to Roma and Olivia who are more acquainted with the timeline of Prince Omar's clothing." Roma looked at Olivia who quickly responded. "

Your Highness," she briefly closed her eyes and calculated what remained to be done. "We'll have his suits ready by tomorrow. It's a promise."

"Gulrez!" the Queen turned on her fiercely with a flash of anger. "Did you ask Daktar Hameeltoon to start Nasrullah's attire first?" She swept her bulging eyes up and down Gulrez's body.

"No Bibi Jan!" A dash of wild color rose in her face. "You would have paid dearly if it wasn't for them," she gestured with a sweep of her hand towards the ladies. She looked down her nose at the cowering woman, "Why do you always compete with me? Why? Let me tell the ladies who you really are!" she continued aggressively, "You are one lucky woman!" She pointed her finger at her, "When my husband's second wife, another idiot, could not conceive, she presented you to him as a concubine, you were lucky to give birth to sons!" She asked the ladies to take their seats and continued her furious rant. "If I was the first wife you and your sons would never have existed!" Her voice shook with passion.

Gulrez's eyes were misted with tears.

"Let me remind you again," the Queen said, her lips twisted with scorn, "don't ever think you are above me, or your sons are above my son." With a note of determination in her voice, she stated proudly, "My son is on his way to Landan too!"

Gulrez clung to her scarf and covered her mouth, tears trickled down her cheeks and her bruised heart pounded.

Queen Sultana constantly poured fuel onto the spark of fear in Gulrez's belly. She used words, fashioned them into a saber, which she sunk into Gulrez's soul with her cold but bewitching almond-shaped black eyes.

At that moment, Nasrullah stomped into the room and gave his cursory Salaams.

"*Wahwah!* Look who is here!" the Queen commented sarcastically. "Is your beauty sleep finally complete? Making Daktar Hameeltoon,

Roma Jan, and Oilevia Jan wait for you is not the way to show how much you care for them!"

"I am very sorry for being late," he said automatically, rubbing the sleep from his puffy eyes.

With not a flicker of a smile on her face, she said: "Are you being sent to see the Queen in *Qasr*-e-Weenzor? How embarrassing would it be if you sleep through when you are supposed to be seeing her?"

"I don't think so, Bibi Jan. That will not happen," He sat down beside his mother and immediately noticed she was weeping quietly and dabbing her eyes with her scarf.

"Why are you crying? What happened, *Modar* Jan?" Nasrullah asked, with genuine concern.

"Stop interrogating! Let them do a fitting of your damned suits, they don't have all day!" Queen Sultana ordered. "*Khoda Hafez*, Goodbye!" And she and the lady-in-waiting were about to leave the apartment, she turned, "Daktar Laila Jan, Roma Jan, and Oilevia Jan, I am hesitant to have my fitting done here. When you have a chance, please come by my apartment and I promise a quick fitting on my part." She stared haughtily at Nasrullah, "Don't talk behind my back when I shut this door. If you're brave enough, say it to my face!" The slamming of the door behind her resounded like a six-gun salute.

"Modar Jan, do you know what your problem is when she always abuses you?" Nasrullah asked quietly.

"No son, I wish I knew," Gulrez replied.

"You are not equal to her. You're a concubine, a slave and she's a legitimate wife of my father." He looked into her reddened and swollen eyes, "I want to discuss this with Habibullah, we both need to convince our father to legally marry you," he gently touched her hand. "Then you will be equal to her."

Sadly, that would never be the answer. The Queen's pride was partly based on being a descendant from royal blood, but her diamond-flush beauty and regal carriage, as slender and tall as the Eiffel Tower, set her above all the woman in the Harem-Sarai—none could be her equal. She was stylish, well-spoken, and possessed a sharp mind. Even if Nasrullah and Habibullah could convince their ailing and bedridden father to marry Gulrez, it would be to no avail.

The Hamilton sisters and Olivia spent ages in Gulrez's apartment waiting for Nasrullah to begin his fittings but, instead, they had been, as usual, subjected to the royal household's palaver.

"Your Highness," Dr. Hamilton said to Nasrulah, "I must leave now to see Amir Sahib. I trust Roma and Olivia will be able to do all that is necessary?"

"*Hatman*, absolutely, Daktar *Sahiba*," Nasrullah answered, "I can see they are skilled in their work," he grinned broadly and turned his gaze to the two young women.

"Ladies," Lillias said, "Will you manage on your own?"

"*Bien sûr, docteur, j'ai le Plaisir,*" Olivia replied, "*Bonne journée, docteur.*"

Although Lillias's primary focus was Amir's health and far less on what the Prince would wear in London, she was the prime liaison between the Amir's family and her English friends. If she had not spearheaded this effort, Nasrullah's journey would almost certainly have ground to a standstill. Her generous and charitable nature never exceeded her ability to give of herself wherever she was needed. She had gained popularity amongst the local population in Kabul for her offer of medical service to all and made public announcements in advance for when she would be available in the bazaars. Many would queue the day before to be seen by her.

"Your Highness," Roma said enthusiastically, "Olivia suggested this cut for you," she unfolded the vest and held it out for him to admire. "She sketched it from her Grandfather's catalog," she handed him the neatly tacked single-breasted evening waistcoat.

"*Votre Altesse, C'est beau,*" Olivia said fingering the richly floral scrolled fabric. Saira, the interpreter faced a new difficulty in attempting to translate French into Dari.

"It will have a lapel and collar and a wide opening in the front," Roma said as she draped the fitting across his shoulders, "and the off-white floral will have a white silk lining. Please put it on, Your Highness, so we can see whether it fits."

Olivia pinned the seams and chalk-marked the excess around the seam lines, drawing the fabric in and smoothing the wrinkles. Her waist was contoured to hourglass perfection by the floral bodice she was wearing. Two beautiful ladies swirled back and forth looking at his vest as though they were painting a canvas in concert.

"One more waistcoat, then the suits, and that will do for now," Roma said. "Your Highness, you will stand out amongst the best dressed at Windsor Palace."

"Of course, Roma Jan. I look forward to the audience at the Royal Court." His eyes caught hers, and Roma saw his expression change and she experienced a prickling up and down her spine. For a moment the room was quiet apart from Olivia's footsteps moving to and fro. When he spoke, his voice was sharp, accusing, "Roma Jan, when you were in the Char-Chatta bazaar the other day, did you buy anything of interest?" he demanded.

" Just a necklace, Your Highness."

"I hope you bought it for a fair price," he said, arching his brows.

"Did you see me, Your Highness?" Roma asked, lifting her chin a little defiantly.

"Not personally, informants made me aware." Olivia, sensing the rise in tension, helped Nasrullah remove the fitted vest and put on the evening coat. "I am just making sure you are given protection when you roam outside the palace."

"Your Highness, thank you for your concern and trying to protect me, but I was not alone," Roma replied politely.

Olivia pinned and chalked the coat on Nasrullah, "*S'il vous plaît*, please, lift your arm," she said pleasantly.

"Who were you with?"

"My sister and Frank Martin."

The evening coat was of fine black and navy milled cloth, while the liner was a smooth, double-breasted cut with a long waist and short full skirt. There were black pantaloons of the same fabric. Olivia and Roma excused themselves while the Prince put on the pantaloons and returned to the room when he signaled to say he was ready. They both slowly moved around him to assess the fit and make corrections, delicately stretching, pulling, and applying weight until the fabric hung to perfection; chalking where it pulled or puckered, and rearranging the darts.

The Prince had never experienced a woman's touch during a fitting, nor, for that matter, at any time. Roma and Olivia's floral fragrances wafted around him making him feel as if he was in a botanical greenhouse. Roma's colorful oil-tinted nails glowed like gemstones and her long, flowing, barley-colored hair swayed from side to side with every move she made. Olivia's bewitching eyes were made to captivate any heart. Her red cheeks contrasted with her pale skin, which was far lovelier than a rose, covered by morning dew.

"Your Highness, we'll do the second fitting and then the final stitching. I am sure you will be pleased with the result," Roma said, attempting to cover the sting she felt from Nasrullah's insinuations.

"We'll be embarking from Kabul in the first week of April, and it is now the first week of March," Nasrullah said matter-of-factly, "Do you expect to be finished in time?" Without waiting for an answer, he again looked directly at Roma, "Roma Jan," he stroked his thin mustache, "my informant saw you with Colonel Zalmai Khan in the bazaar." His chin jutted forward defining his jawline sharply. He flashed a quick smile like someone with a fever.

"That's correct, Your Highness, he ran into us there and helped me to bargain for a necklace I wanted."

"Of course, Roma Jan," Nasrullah said with a sneer. "I can easily differentiate between bargaining for a necklace and you allowing him to latch it." His face became stern, "Let me give you my thoughts. We in Afghanistan do not mingle with unmarried men or women," he looked down on her stiffly. "Maybe you are not at fault because it would be acceptable in *Englistan*, but Colonel Zalmai Khan knows well that he violated our norms and culture!" He glanced at Olivia who was folding the clothes in readiness for the next fitting. "Especially when you are a guest in our country, our men must honor and not take advantage of you in any way." He adjusted his karakul hat, "If my father found out, that idiot's punishment would be severe and quick."

Roma turned cold at the veiled threat. "No, Your Highness, of course he has not taken advantage of me. He offered his help and my sister was fine with it."

"If he, or anyone, harasses you or takes advantage of you, let me know. I promise he will regret his mistake."

"Your Highness, I have not experienced any harassment from anybody," she replied quietly, but her heart wrenched with fear. "I believe Colonel Zamai's intentions were perfectly innocent."

"Afghan men are unlike English men. Always remember that," he replied shortly.

March 1895 -- Afghan calendar month: *Hamal* 1274
Kabul, Afghanistan

At exactly nine o'clock, the lapis lazuli clock chimed and the golden bird sang, "cuckoo" in Queen Sultana's sewing room. The English ladies were already hard at work on the final touches of the clothing. Mrs. Clemence melodically hummed *The Soldiers Of The Queen*, against the parakeets' incessant noise. The Queen's lady-in-waiting rustled to and fro across the room pouring tea and handing plates of freshly baked cookies and profiteroles for the couturiers.

Mrs. Clemence delicately removed the basting stitches and started the binding and facing, paddling the Singer machine, which whirred smoothly as she expertly guided the fabric. She was pleased to join the rest of the English ladies and Frank Martin on the journey back to England but leaving her husband behind worried her. "I'll miss him," she muttered with a sigh. Setting a damp gauze on Nasrullah's tunic, she lifted the blazing coal iron from its marble slab and pressed the tunic firmly, partially obscuring her face in a cloud of steam as the iron sizzled.

Roma Hamilton leaned forward on her elbows against the sewing table as she attached twelve shoulder boards for epaulets on six full regimental tunic jackets. She thanked the lady-in-waiting automatically as she poured her a cup of spiced tea.

Occasionally, as Olivia whip-stitched buttonholes, her thimble captured a beam of morning sunshine and flashed. She looked up from working on one of the Queen's dresses, stretched her arms and neck, and briefly massaged her hands and wrists to get the blood flow circulating again.

"*Belle matinée mes chers amis.*" she commented. She inspected Charlotte Martin's work, turning Nasrullah's suits inside out to see the quality of sewing, "Lovely work, Charlotte." Near the sewing tables, three full-size mannequins made by Frank Martin at Olivia's request, stood erect and draped with garments.

Prince Omar and William Martin appeared from the parlor to show off their spinning whirligigs. Their attention quickly shifted to the trays of cookies and profiteroles.

"Ah! I am glad you're here Prince Omar. I was about to send for you to try your final fitting," Mrs. Martin said, arms outspread. "Are you excited to join William on the long voyage to England?"

"Of course. I've never been on a ship and or seen the ocean before."

"Most people in your country haven't had that experience, you will be among the first," she said handing him his two suits. "Try them on and see how they fit."

He returned shortly and Mrs. Martin ushered him to the tall pivoting looking glass. He looked very English. The smocked ice-blue coutil jacket was double-breasted, with small shawl lapels. Its collar and cuffs were edged with Anglaise lace. Mrs. Martin buckled the leather belt around his waist.

"Everything fits you like a duck's foot in the mud," she said, "you look wonderful!" She smoothed the fit with a stroke of her hand and stood behind him with her hands on his shoulders staring into the mirror good-naturedly.

"How do I look *Bibi Jan*?" the little Prince asked as the Queen walked in.

She spun him around. "You look absolutely fabulous!" she said in delight. "Thank you *Khanum* Cleemess and everyone, for all you have done for my son." The second suit was of Reseda Cashmere with two wide rows of pleats at the hem, a straight, finely pleated vest, and a pleated back with a cashmere scarf. It had a large pleated collar, and the cuffs were edged with finely tailored white lace.

"He looks like a Londoner now," William said.

"Another fabulous design," the Queen remarked in astonishment.

"Am I done?" Prince Omar pleaded, "We're off to the stables for pony riding."

"Yes, you are done," Mrs. Martin laughed. "Be careful, both of you!"

The Queen was examining the dress on the mannequin, "Oilevia Jan, this is gorgeous, I can't even thank you enough."

Olivia ran her fingers through her shoulder-length hair. "Your Highness, we used the foulards silk for your summer outfit, you will be able to wear it until late autumn."

"It looks marvelous," the Queen said as she fingered the soft twilled fabric.

"*Merci*," Olivia said with a smile. "You see, the dress does not crease," she lifted the skirt to fully display the violet and white pattern of the material. The lower portion of the skirt was gracefully scalloped, attached with wavy bands of creamy taffeta, and trimmed with one row of black stitching and a second of violet. It formed an undulated edge, set over a loosely pleated flounce, and secured under the stitched bands.

"Your grandfather bequeathed you his magnificent talent, Oilevia Jan, I am sure he must have been very proud of you."

"Yes, Your Highness, I miss him a lot. *que son âme repose en paix.*"

"I adore the cut of the bodice!" Delight rang warm in the Queen's voice.

"I am happy you like it, Your Highness." We thought you might wear the bodice with this pleated blouse. You see we combined the silk band garniture of the upper bodice, high and the back and low in the front with a shield effect over the chest to produce the fashionable straight effect."

The Queen's eyes sparkled, "I'm so thrilled and fortunate to have you here, Oilevia Jan."

"I believe this *convient à une reine* like you well. I am sure you will love the dress, Your Highness, let me show you." Olivia lead the way to the gown on the next mannequin, delighting the Queen with detailed explanations of fabric and form.

"*Votre Altesse*, Your Highness," Olivia said, "the credit goes to everyone here. I could not have done this without help from Roma, Mrs. Clemence, and my dear friend, Charlotte Martin. They all, also, have done a *phénomènes* job with the Prince's suits," Olivia declared as she pointed to another mannequin standing under the clock. "I'll leave it to Roma and others to explain."

The Queen was not eager to hear anything about Nasrullah's clothing but she glanced politely at the blue coat with its gold epaulets signifying Nasrullah's high stature in rank. The jacket was flanked with a row of silver buttons on each breast and resembled the sort worn by the Fleet Admiral of the Royal Navy.

"Your Highness," Mrs. Clemence pointed out, "He will wear a golden aiguillette on his other special tunic jacket." She pointed to where it lay on the sewing table, "It's of the best quality British Melton wool, with a luxurious lining of Korain material.

"Well done ladies," the Queen smiled. "You have done wonderful work! I'm embarrassed to wear these clothes," she declared, lifting her long skirt, "which I now see are thirty years out of fashion," she looked at them with a grin. "You've spoiled me! I want Daktar Laila Jan to also bring me some clothes from Landan when she returns." She looked around at the group of ladies, "As a token of our appreciation, my husband and I have decided to give a gift of three hundred pounds to each one of you." The announcement came as a complete surprise and Mrs. Martin and Charlotte Clemence glanced at one another with delight. As the average salary in England was less than ten pounds a week, the sewing and training they had undertaken constituted more than half a year's salary.

"Thank you. Your Highness, we are very grateful for your generous offer!" Roma Hamilton said on behalf of them all.

CHAPTER TWENTY-SIX

❧◦❧◦❧

Shafts of afternoon sunshine streaked in through the floor-to-ceiling windows of the Amir's huge private chamber highlighting the colors of the Afghan rugs scattered across the highly varnished wooden floor.

Habibullah and Nasrullah summoned the nurses into the Amir's chamber to tend to him while they quietly discussed Nasrullah's plan of marrying their ailing father to their mother. They ensconced themselves by the windows in the warmth of the sun where tea, sweetmeats, and fruit were set for them to enjoy. As his sons sunk their voices to a whisper, the Amir slept soundly and his snores grew impressively in volume, like notes from an organ pipe.

The marriage of the Amir to Gulrez had been the topic of discussion for some time. Disputes were difficult to avoid as it hardly appeared right to discuss such things, and it required wit and wisdom to avoid contradicting one another outright. With Nasrullah's conceited persona and Habibullah's pragmatism, a conclusion would inevitably be difficult to reach. Both Nasrullah and Habibullah had their legitimate viewpoints, but, it seemed, the decision was no longer up to Amir and Gulrez but their sons to arrange the marriage of their parents.

"You heard what Daktar Hameeltoon said, he's ill and frail, and I should agree with you to marry them?" Habibullah asked while he loaded his plate with vibrant red pomegranate seeds.

"How else can we stop Bibi Sultana's harassment towards our mother?" Nasrullah asked.

"What makes you think she will stop abusing her?" Habibullah's expression was fixed, as if for a camera.

"The purpose of their marriage is to raise the stature of our mother from a concubine to a queen." Nasrullah lifted his teacup and saucer and glanced irritably at his brother.

"Think about what you just said, brother!" Habibullah set his plate carefully on the cast iron table so as not to wake his father. "You are optimistic if you think this will stop Bibi Jan from harassing our mother. You need to think in reality. You can't conceptualize something impossible to fix."

"Once they're married, it will be up to you and me to defend our mother against her," Nasrullah said fingering the stubble on his jawline.

"Nasrullah, you're dreaming, the Queen is from the huge Barakzai clan, her siblings and extended bloodline will twirl around us defending her. You and I are alone with a mother who has no power whatsoever. As long as our father is alive nothing can change."

Nasrullah knew his brother was right on that point. Queen Sultana's grandfather, Amir Dost Mohammad Khan, married twenty-five wives and produced twenty-seven sons, and twenty-five daughters; he also had an unknown number of concubines. Any attempt to defend their concubine mother against Queen Sultana would leave them overwhelmingly outnumbered. Despite the imbalance of family power, Nasrullah remained persistent. "It must still be written in stone that our mother is a legitimate wife of our father," he persisted, "I will not feel at ease leaving for *Englistan* before this happens."

"Well, brother, I can't go along with this," Habibullah replied vehemently, "I will let you be at the center of ridicule for this nonsensical ambition!" He picked up a handful of roasted pinenuts and began to crack them between his teeth. "This is not the right time to attempt to stop Queen Sultana from harassing our mother."

"When is the right time, Habibullah?"

"You know better, everything will change once father leaves the earth. I'm the crown Prince, and once I assume power I will have her quietened then. Now is not the right time."

"I believe it must be now, I cannot see my poor mother taking so much abuse! Be informed, I will convince father."

March 1895 -- Afghan calendar month: *Hamal* 1274, Kabul, Afghanistan

The Amir's health was deteriorating steadily. The two Indian-born nurses, aides to Dr. Hamilton, tended him around the clock. As they walked to and fro in Amir's private chamber in Bostan-Sarai Palace, their voluminous uniforms fluttered like sails on masts. Their stylish sleeves, puffed at the shoulders, were in sharp contrast to their white overly-starched floor-length pinafores. They resembled nuns of some Roman basilica, yet veiled, with red-cross emblems inches above their red Hindu *bindis* marks. Dr. Hamilton relied on them to administer the Amir's medicines, to groom his beard and hair; clean and wipe with soapy rags the grain of his crumpled skin; under the arms; to incline his body forward and scrub the back; lay him down, wash each leg at a time, probe free the groin and scour the privates; in between the toes; clip the nails, toes, and fingers. All this was done meticulously, following his wish, as correct bodily hygiene proceeds from due reverence to *Allah*. That was the Amir's quest for an agreement between the divine and his deep soul.

Dr. Hamilton entered the Amir's private chamber and curtsied, "*Salaam*, Your Highness. How do you feel today?" the two nurses stood abreast behind her.

"Sorry Daktar Laila Jan," he cupped his ear, "*Che?*, What? *Che-Gooftee?* What did you say?" he asked weakly. "I am not hearing well at the moment."

"How do you feel today?" the doctor repeated loudly, but she received no answer.

"He's been very quiet today. He had a bad dream, shouted something, and woke up in apprehension," one of the nurses said.

"Do you know what he said in his dream?"

"We could not understand the Dari words but he repeated the name Weektorya, Weektorya many times."

Lillias had noticed that the Amir had become cold in his demeanor, humorless, he sulked more often, and seldom laughed. Many people had become nervous in his presence. His strong persona was fading precipitously, and he was having moments in which his mental acuity showed signs of fading. All these symptoms could have been due to anxiety regarding Nasrullah's trip and the uncertainty of the outcome of his meeting with Queen Victoria.

"How is his heart rate?"

"I haven't checked in the past two hours, Doctor *Jee*."

"I thought you both had been given the sort of training in nursing to know these things are important," she said sternly. "And my instruction was that you must check his heart, lungs, and blood pressure constantly."

"We have Doctor Sahib, but he fell asleep two hours ago and we could not check."

"How was his heart two hours ago?"

"Irregular, over a hundred beats per minute."

"As you are aware, I have ordered that no one but Princes' Habibullah and Nasrullah, should visit him," she looked them both in the eye. "Has anyone else been?"

"Yes, the Kabul Magistrate," the nurse replied awkwardly, "the man with crossed-eyes."

" Parwana Khan! Did you tell him that I had imposed visiting restrictions?"

She nodded, "But he dismissed our request and Amir Sahib said he could come in."

Whenever the Amir deemed it necessary for an execution to take place, Parwana Khan was called to receive his instructions; he had been in and out of his private chambers frequently of late. Dr. Hamilton was becoming convinced his symptoms were connected with his mood. He would summon Parwana Khan and order execution after execution of those of his subjects whom he believed had committed crimes—especially those enemies who threatened his power.

"Yes, he has been having some bad dreams lately, and I believe it has to do with Nasrullah's journey to see Queen Victoria," the Doctor said. She pulled a varnished flat mahogany box from her medical valise, "You understand of course, that I will not be here for a while," she opened the box and took out her stethoscope, "I will be going to England with the Prince for several months, and you will be working temporarily under an Indian doctor from Calcutta."

"Very well Doctor *Jee*."

"You have to make sure everything is done well and on time." She asked for complete silence as she placed the funnel-shaped chest piece on Amir's back and then his chest. "Please breath in, Your Highness. Breath out." Lillias listened carefully and then put the stethoscope aside and placed her ear directly on his chest, in that way, she could hear the cardiac and pulmonary sounds more clearly. "Your heartbeat is a bit irregular, Your Highness."

"What do you think, Daktar Laila Jan?"

"I'm afraid anxiety and stress are taking their toll on Your Highness," she said, "isn't it time for you to relinquish some of your responsibilities to others?" A flicker of irritation and impatience showed in Amir's eyes.

Dr. Hamilton straightened up, "As Your Highness's physician, I'm ready to make that decision if you can't, to save your life, as I did when I saw you first." She understood him well enough to know that he would be likely to recover faster if she offered him the emotional support and attention he needed.

"I accept your advice, Daktar Laila Jan. It is time for Habibullah and Nasrullah to help me," he replied wearily. "My life will never be any better than this." He could feel the degeneration of his body and the inevitability of death. "I'm becoming useless; life is becoming harder for me by the day. I can't even trust my own judgment anymore." He pointed a forefinger toward the heavens. "I'll ask *Allah* for an easy death, but before I die, my wish is to see Nasrullah upon his return from *Englistan*. I wish him success."

At that moment, footsteps were heard from the Palace foyer and Nasrullah and Habibullah entered the Amir's private chamber. They had just returned from hunting, and they were both wearing gray lambskin hats; Habibullah with jodhpur breeches, twill jacket, and paddock boots, while Nasrullah was clad in a pair of khaki French Baroque pantaloons, a safari jacket, and knee-high boots.

"How is my father today?" Nasrullah asked. Habibullah stood alongside his brother, his hands hanging loosely at his sides.

"His speech has slowed and he has trouble hearing," Dr. Hamilton whispered. "He appears to be quite anxious and has had bad dreams lately calling the name Queen Victoria, but his mind is active."

"Habibullah," the Amir called drowsily, "Daktar Laila Jan has suggested that I should ask someone to help me in my daily responsibilities. I have no choice but to depend on you. Go, lead the *darbar* events for me. You will have to make final decisions on my behalf," he struggled for breath, "in the matters of the country . . . I trust your judgment, my son."

"I'll help in every way I can Father," Habibullah said.

"Daktar Hameeltoon," Nasrullah said, trying his best to remain polite, "Please give us privacy. About a quarter an hour. I have some family matters to discuss with my father and brother."

"Of course, Your Highness," Lillias Hamilton replied as gestured for the nurses to leave too. "Please summon us if His Highness needs help and if I may ask you both a favor?"

"Of course, Daktar Hameeltoon."

"Please keep everything as calm as possible, whatever the discussion, keep a mellow tone. Please."

"We will be careful, Daktar Sahiba."

"*Padar*, Father," Nasrullah sat next to his father's bed and leaned towards him, "Habibullah and I are here to ask for your help."

"Nasrullah," Habibullah said matter-of-factly, "speak for yourself. I am not in this."

"What can I do to help you, my son?" the Amir asked.

"Our mother is going through so much with Bibi Jan Sultana Jan."

"Why?" the Amir asked irritably, "She lives in the palace, has a set salary, has servants. What else could she ask for?"

"You have seen the pain she has gone through over the years and she is still suffering greatly. It needs to stop. It is very hard for us . . . for me, to see her harassed and abused."

"Son, let me teach you something about women," his voice wheezed with the effort of speaking. "They all gossip, quarrel, fight and show jealously towards each other, no matter what you do. That is their nature."

"To stop this agony she's going through, we . . ." he glanced at his brother, who shook his head and pointed a finger back at him. "I want you to officially marry her."

"Son, how could you think like that?" Amir replied breathing with difficulty. "I'm frail and weak . . . what you're asking of me is absurd!"

"Every time I see my mother sobbing because her feelings are hurt," Nasrullah cracked his knuckles nervously; sweat beaded his forehead, "my heart aches for her. I am at a point of blowing up at your dominant wife if you are unwilling to intervene!" he blurted.

"Be careful of badmouthing her!" Amir's frail face reddened and his grayish eyebrows knit together. "She's worse than me for not having rule over her own spirit. She will walk all over you like a carpet." He raised a finger at Nasrullah without lifting his hand from the bed.

"She sees herself as the primary power who subdues you also," Nasrullah curled his lips.

"Nasrullah," Habibullah warned quietly, from where he was ensconced in a chair, sipping tea and listening to their conversation. "Remember what Dakar Laila said about father's health? Don't raise his anxiety!"

"I thought you said you are not in this, Habibullah, so let me discuss this with Father!" Nasrullah shifted his gaze back to his bedridden father. "Father, if you want my mother's happiness and mine, so I can face *Malika* Weektorya with valor, then marry my mother." The Amir rolled his eyes wearily. He was beginning to wonder whether Nasrullah's mission to England could be affected by this ongoing household melee.

"We could keep it confidential, no reception, no gathering, no feasting, no entertaining . . . it can just take place in the presence of a Royal Mullah who will approve the signed marriage paper." He lifted his hands devoutly, "You will please Allah for doing this."

The Amir listened attentively but was still confused and weak, "Son! This is humiliating. I'm probably on my deathbed. My subjects will laugh at me for marrying at this age and in this condition!"

"That's what exactly I said," Habibullah agreed, "Father will be the center of ridicule." He raised his teacup to his mouth, "But you ignore what Father and I tell you."

"Off you go again, brother!" Nasrullah looked Habibullah straight in the eyes, "Stay away, please!" He turned back to his father. "Humiliation is when our mother is bullied! Why did you never think about marrying her in the first place, when you knew you had only two sons?" He was aggrieved by his father's lack of empathy. "*Padar Jan*, dear Father," breathed Nasrullah, "if you want to see me sail happily to *Qasr-e*-Weenzor then marry my mother."

Suddenly the fight went out of the Amir and he lay back on his pillows exhausted. "Fine, let's make this quick and keep it confidential, send for your mother and the Mullah and let us put this behind us. We need to move forward with important issues rather than this nonsensical marriage. But I have to warn you, Bibi Sultana will never stop, and she will now be armed with this untimely marriage to grill me with. Her form of punishment is tormenting."

The Amir had to accept his son's demand. His plan to send Nasrullah to see Queen Victoria took precedence over resolving the ongoing family feud. He was obsessed with the need for Queen Victoria's acceptance of his request and no issue must be allowed to distort that mission. Nasrullah instinctively knew his father's weak point and successfully used it to undermine the will of this stubborn man who seldom bent to anyone's demand and rule.

March 1895 -- Afghan calendar month: *Hamal* 1274, Kabul, Afghanistan

Nasrullah spearheaded the wedding of his parents in a quiet, religious setting. Habibullah agreed to participate in persuading the Royal Mullah to deviate from the accepted elaborate marriage ceremony, in which everyone became a witness, to a small and limited one, and to proceed with the union swiftly. Within an hour, Nasrullah had secretly summoned the Mullah to a closed-door session and informed him of his wish. To lure the Mullah into tying the knot, he was showered with cash, a fancy meal, and sets of newly tailored *Perahan-Tunban* outfits.

"Mullah Sahib," Nasrullah said, conveying in the meaningful way he looked into the man's eyes, an understanding of quid pro quo, "please accept these small tokens for your help in marrying our parents."

"This matter must not be revealed to anyone," Habibullah added, "do you understand?"

"You have nothing to worry about, *Shahzadah*." The Mullah lifted his hands sanctimoniously, "Snitching is the devil's work. May Allah deliver me from the devil. But *Shahzadah*," he bowed his head in Prince Nazrullah's direction, "who will be the witness for your mother?" The full-bearded Mullah sat crossed-legged on a carpet-covered mattress, thumbing his prayer beads and rocking to and fro. "In a normal marriage ceremony, the presence of bride's and groom's fathers, or male guardians and their guests, are essential to witness and approve the wedding."

"Mullah Sahib, can we bend the rules?" Nasrullah asked quizzically.

"What do you have in mind, *Shahzadah*?" The beads clicked rhythmically through his fingers.

"I'll be the witness for my mother and *Shahzadah* Habibullah for my father."

The Mullah laughed like a hyena. "I have never wed a couple whose guardians were their children."

The first sign of ridicule, Habibullah thought.

"Would that be an issue, *Mullah Sahib*?" Nasrullah asked, and added, direct and to the point. "Perhaps you are looking for more of an inducement?"

Shame flooded the Mullah's face, "No, *Shahzadah*. But it would have been better if a brother or cousin related to your mother was brought as a witness." He shifted the flap of his turban over his shoulder.

"I wish it was that easy, *Mullah Sahib*," Nasrullah replied, "but my mother's blood relatives live in Wakhan Valley. It would take months to cross the passes before they got here and we have no time to wait. This has to be done before I leave for Landan."

Habibullah again nodded in silent agreement.

"As you know, *Shahzadah*," the Mullah interjected again, "the wedding paper will bear the names of the witnesses and their relationship to the bride and groom." He stroked his curly, black beard. "But do not concern yourselves, we will finalize this in any event." He gave an easy nod, "But, *Shahzadah*, I have another question that perhaps you could help me with."

"What's that?"

"What is the amount for the dowry?"

"*Mullah Sahib*, let us keep this simple. You know a dowry is not a problem when my mother is on the royal payroll."

"Well, we have to make it legitimate under Islamic law, and write down some reasonable amount in order to sign and seal the marriage certificate." The beads clicked over, one by one. An agreement was underway.

Nasrullah, Habibullah, and the Mullah arrived at Bostan-Sarai where the Amir and Gulrez were impatiently waiting for the Mullah to begin the ceremony. Vaulting the three flights of the marble staircase to Amir's parlor, they entered his room, hands on their chests, bowed incessantly, and greeted the frail Amir who was seated in his wingback chair,

"This should not take more than ten minutes," he said authoritatively, gazing sternly at them.

Gulrez was in a separate room away from the Mullah's eyes. As he was not an immediate family member he was not permitted to see her and so, to hear her confession to the marriage, he would communicate from outside the door.

The Mullah read the *Nikah nameh*, marriage certificate vows to the groom, perhaps one of a very small number of grooms to be married, to all intents and purposes, on his deathbed, to repeat after him.

"I, Abdul Rahman, pledge, in honesty and sincerity, to be for you a faithful and helpful husband."

He repeated the reading to the Bride and she responded from the other side of the door, "I, Gulrez, offer you myself in marriage and, in accordance with the instructions of the Holy Qur'an and the Holy Prophet, peace and blessing be upon him, I pledge, in honesty and with sincerity, to be for you an obedient and faithful wife."

The certificate was signed by the witnesses and the Mullah took his seal and ink from his waistcoat pocket and placed his mark on the document. As one, they lifted their hands before the Almighty to seek his blessing and acceptance of the marriage.

"*Mubarak!*" Nasrullah and Habibullah smilingly congratulated their father and mother.

But the Amir did not approve the marriage without expecting to receive something in return. He had agreed with Nasrullah for only one reason; that he would send his son to Windsor Palace in a positive frame of mind to convince Queen Victoria of the need for the independence of his homeland. Nasrullah, similarly, expected nothing beyond modest gratitude for raising his mother's status. And the Mullah expected nothing more than some cash, a full belly, and a few new sets of clothes. But once word of their marriage spread like wildfire; Queen Sultana's anger would impact the Amir like a malignant tumor.

Inevitably, the knot-tying rumors spread. Gossips scattered this delicious titbit of news amongst the ladies of the Harem-Sarai and beyond the walls of the Arg Palace. Although the source for the account would probably never be revealed, someone, almost certainly, would be used as a scapegoat and surreptitiously punished to quieten the spread of gossip and ridicule. Most resented this untimely and amusing marriage between the feeble Amir and his concubine which was becoming the main topic of conversation in the Char-Chatta bazaar. They spoke in hushed voices for fear of eavesdroppers from Amir's secret police.

Queen Sultana fumed. She was as mad as a wounded serpent and showed menace in every way possible.

"Are you out of your mind?" she demanded of the Amir. "Who marries on his deathbed?" She was breathing heavily and the expression in her eyes showed the measure of her contempt, "You have hardly any teeth left in your skull and still you crave marriage!" She gesticulated violently. "You are the center of ridicule everywhere!"

The Amir had been feeling a bit better. His demeanor was calm and he was in full control. Summoning the Chamberlain for his afternoon tea, he tap-tapped with his cane to the marble balcony to soak some early spring sun.

The Queen followed him determined to continue her tirade. "Marrying that low cast concubine is a betrayal against your bloodline and mine!" she said bitterly. "You have turned against those who wed us. Rest assured, Abdul Rahman," only when she was furious, did she call him by name, "I will not be idle!"

"Just do not send your lady-in-waiting to push Gulrez to her death off the roof," the Amir retorted; he glanced at her meaningfully, eyebrows raised.

"What makes you think I would do that?" she asked defensively.

"I have spies who saw your lady-in-waiting and the concubine from Herat on the roof minutes before her death. Just don't get us in trouble with Nasrullah and Habibullah. Killing their mother will defeat my mission to *Englistan*." He took a sip of his tea.

"In the report, you said Feroza's death was an accident!"

"Yes, I had no choice but to declare it an accident."

"Are accusing me of a conspiracy?"

"No," the Amir replied running his fingers through his stringy beard. "But if the same thing happens to Gulrez it will cause a huge fire between you, Habibullah, Nasrullah, and myself." He wrinkled his brow. "Do not even think of doing such a thing or you will regret it. Keep quiet and get over it. There is no harm done in marrying my sons' mother. And remember, you are known as the first lady and no one dares to challenge you. Let's keep it that way."

"Abdul Rahman, I will not easily forgive you for marrying that Wakhani woman. Shame on you for not marrying me before you met her! You are of royal blood, nephew to my father! You went ahead and fell for these Yak herders and lowlifes."

"Sorry, I was exiled in Russia," he returned, refusing to be ruffled by her accusations. "It was not my fault that I did not marry you first."

"Just bear this in mind," she retorted. "Even if you are no longer the *Padshah*, King, nothing will change. That outsider, Gulrez, has not gained anything. She is the same donkey except with a better saddle."

"Here is my advice. Your son, Omar, will be accompanying Nasrullah to London, so be merciful and let them have a safe voyage."

CHAPTER TWENTY-SEVEN

᷈᷈᷈

April 1895 -- Afghan calendar month: *Hamal* 1274
Osborn House, East Cowes, Isle of Wight, UK

In his youth, Abdul Karim had wished his life were like a dream. A dream so magical, so unbelievable that he would ask a wish and it would be granted immediately, and he would fly away on his magic carpet into the realm of infinite possibilities. This fairy-tale dream found a place in reality when Queen Victoria revealed her special affection for her Indian-born attendant. No other royal servant was afforded such support, or given such personal protection, as Abdul Karim. The Queen not only granted him high stature as her Indian secretary but also bestowed on him an honor, the CIE (Companion of the Order of the Indian Empire). In addition, the Munshi was provided Frogmore Cottage in Windsor, Arthur Cottage in Osborn House, East Cowes in the Isle of Wight, and 'Karim Cottage' in Balmoral Castle, Aberdeen Shire, Scotland. He was as blessed as one of the meek who shall inherit the earth.

"We'll do a semi *fête champêtre* at the beach tomorrow," announced Queen Victoria who, with little Looty on her lap, was comfortably seated on a tufted mohair sofa in the Durbar Room. Her favorite nightcap, a single Scotch malt whisky and claret, was on the table next to her. "If the weather permits, of course," she said to Beatrice who was sitting next to her, "Betty darling, wouldn't it be marvelous to start Spring with breakfast and lunch in the cool breeze off the Bay tomorrow?"

"It would be lovely, mother," Beatrice replied with a smile.

"My precious baby," she reached out to touch her. "Those blissful days at Osborn with your father linger in my memory. Are we clear about tomorrow?" she asked turning to the chamberlain.

"Yes, Your Majesty."

"I would like my favorite curry dishes for lunch." She sipped her whisky and extended her order to Abdul Karim who stood behind her sofa. "Munshi, please instruct the Indian chefs to prepare them for me."

Munshi bowed obediently. "The pheasant and halibut, Ma'am?"

Queen Victoria visited Osborn House on Isle of Wight every Spring and loved the botanical gardens tended by her late husband, Prince Albert. The spring blossom of the cherry, wisteria, azalea and much more, on this secluded royal estate was mesmerizing. The climate was similar to the Mediterranean and warmer than at Windsor. The Queen delighted in the aroma; the magnificent array of tulips in the Wall Garden; the wonderful assortment of plants in the gargantuan greenhouse; the fabulous clusters of soft pink, magenta, and white blossom on the ancient apple trees, and the colorful magnolias. The setting filled her with pleasure and solace as she remembered her beloved husband.

"Munshi *Jee!* Munshi Dear!" the Empress of India attempted a few Hindustani words occasionally, "I need to have some discussions with you and Sir Rafiuddin regarding the Prince of Afghanistan. Remind me of his name."

"Prince Nasrullah, Your Majesty," Karim replied.

She nodded, straightened her voluminous black dress, and flinched, clutching at her leg. She had been diagnosed with gout, which was becoming increasingly severe, and she was often tormented by the pain of a million red-hot needles penetrating her leg and ankle joints.

"I've summoned Lord Falmouth tomorrow afternoon. He will join us at the beach. There is a lot to be discussed in preparation for that young Afghan Prince." She thought for a moment, "Nosroolah arrives in Portsmouth next month. Not too far away." The Queen dismissed the Chamberlain and footmen except for Karim and her ladies-in-waiting.

Beatrice rose to her feet and sauntered around the Durbar room marveling at the Indian artworks. Abdul Karim's tales of the Taj Mahal had inspired the Queen to hire Indian and English architects to decorate the room in recognition of her new title as Empress of India. John Lockwood Kipling, father of Rudyard Kipling, one was of those chosen to bring the project to fruition. The effects of mixed Mughal and Hindu decorations were overwhelming. Even the andirons and door handles were richly and intricately detailed to resemble the artistry of India.

"Munshi," the Queen asked, "did you confirm that Sir Rafiuddin would be here tomorrow?"

"*Acha*, Your Majesty, he has been informed and I have had confirmation," Abdul Karim said. " With your permission Your Majesty, I have some questions." He wobbled his head from side to side as if his neck was a coil, a somewhat disconcerting mannerism of the Indian people the Queen had become accustomed to.

"*Ab ei Munshi kya hai?* What is it now Munshi?" the Queen replied in her broken Urdu.

"Your Majesty, I believe Amir Abdul Rahman is a capable leader able to lead his country in matters of foreign affairs. He has demonstrated a firm grip on the country."

"Carry on," the Queen interjected.

"He's much stronger than his predecessors like Shah Shujah who was enthroned by General Pollock and Elphinstone. Forgive me for saying this, but they all failed in their mission to secure Afghanistan's future." He linked his hands before his chest in an almost prayerful gesture. "Instead of pouring out England's resources to ensure Afghanistan's security against Czarist Russia, would it not be best for Your Majesty to allow Afghanistan's representation in the Court of St. James's? He shifted his weight to his other leg, "If Abdul Rahman fails, Your Majesty can always say, we gave you a chance and it didn't work." He touched his neatly swathed silk turban and dropped his hands to his sides.

"Well, Munshi *Jee*, if Abdul Rahman failed and Russia invaded Afghanistan, we would be likely to lose India. How would one reverse that?" She pursed her lips deepening the creases on her face, "And at what cost?"

"Your Majesty, he would be firm and strong against the Russians, as long as he has England's support."

"Munshi *Jee*, during my reign as the Queen, I've encountered multiple contentious moments with the Afghans. The first and second disastrous wars we fought with them are not easily forgotten." She lifted Looty to eye level, smiled at him, and settled him down again. "I remember Abdul Rahman's grandfather, Dost Mohammad. We exiled that stubborn man to India and enthroned Shah Shuja. Thereafter, hell broke loose in the country so I ordered Dost Mohammad to lead the country—his son, Akbar, was another thorn in our eyes." She patted the dog absentmindedly, "Their internal skirmishes, and blood feuds between brothers and cousins made us reluctant to hand them their autonomy. They are like children in need of constant adult supervision!" She took a sip of her whisky and set the glass back on the marble tabletop. "I can guarantee you there are squabbles inside Abdul Rahman's household, even now." She gestured calmly, "What I'm really worried about is if I grant Abdul Rahman his wish and he dies—then what?" Looking up at Munshi she said, "How could we trust his two young boys to run the country given what we have experienced in the past?"

Munshi listened intently but could offer no logical reason to change her mind.

"I hear Abdul Rahman is seriously ill and his two boys have not shown whether they would want to support our policy or not. It is a difficult chance to take, Munshi *Jee*." She chuckled, "I am sure you have heard the saying, 'You can only rent an Afghan, but you can't buy one'?" Munshi smiled politely. "If Russia offered them more than they are getting from us, they would abandon us in a flash."

"Your Majesty," Munshi agreed, "I understand your logic wholeheartedly, however, I know for a fact, Afghanistan has changed drastically under His Highness Amir Abdul Rahman. Sir Rafiuddin and I agree on one thing, Abdul Rahman has set such a firm foundation for Afghanistan that the country could be run by his sons for another hundred years."

"Munshi *Jee*, once Afghanistan's autonomy is granted and out of our jurisdiction, it will be very hard to convince Abdul Rahman to make his decisions based on our desires." She clutched her leg again and then moved the flap on her widow's cap behind her neck, "It is late and I'm a bit worn out, but I'll say this and call it a night."

"Of course, whatever Your Majesty desires."

"Munshi, I've always listened to you and asked you questions on many issues. I'll seek your assistance in matters of Afghanistan if I have a need." She gestured him to sit on the leather-tufted chair across from her, "But for now, I want you to keep advising me on matters of India and will leave the delicate decisions of Afghanistan's future in the hands of my other capable advisers." She continued with an air of confidentiality, "Munshi . . ."

"*Jee han ap ke azmat*, Yes Your Majesty?" He bowed slightly, pressing his hands together.

"Let me say this. In the early days of our busy foreign affairs, my Prime Minister and foreign policy expert, Lord Palmerston taught me a lesson." She glanced at the grandfather clock with its swaying pendulum ticking away the seconds. "He always reminded me not to trust anyone except our own English advisers to dictate England's foreign policy." She met his eyes meaningfully, "I would not be comfortable with Abdul Rahman dealing with Germany, Russia, or Ottoman Turkey, without our presence and advice. I would not sleep a wink not knowing what was decided behind our backs. India is too precious for us to lose. I cannot allow my beloved India slip out of my hand."

"I fully understand Your Majesty's position."

"I would have to seek Lord Rosebery's or Lord Salisbury's advice before I would consider handing Afghanistan's foreign policy to Amir Abdul Rahman."

Abdul Karim tilted his head to the side, "Would Your Majesty still approve of His Excellency, Lord Rosebery's presence in Osborn Bay tomorrow?" he asked pointedly. Rosebery had, as an advisor to the Queen, been afforded almost carte blanche on all matters of England's foreign policy. "Is Your Majesty aware of the latest rumor about him?"

She gave a brief nod, "Thank you for the reminder, Munshi, it has been an ugly scandal! Reluctantly, I am obliged to change my mind. I can no longer seek his advice on matters of Afghanistan." Lord Rosebery, twice England's Foreign Minister, and outgoing Prime Minister, was a brilliant man in matters of foreign policy and Afghanistan. There had always been speculation that Rosebery was a homosexual but, as his intimate friend had recently died of injuries during a shooting party, rumors of suicide or murder abounded. Despite a verdict of accidental death, it was speculated that there may have been a threat to expose the Prime Minister that lead to the shooting.

"To answer your question, no, I don't think it is a good idea for Lord Rosebery to join us, I would rather have Lord Salisbury, who will soon replace him."

With the help of her cane and her lady-in-waiting, the Queen rose from the sofa and walked across the room. She gazed up marveling at the huge peacock design over the mantelpiece. It was lit with the defused glow of gasoliers.

"Isn't it majestic, my love?" she said as Beatrice came to meet her

"Of course, Mother. It is truly an Iconic work of art. I am so proud of my sister, Louise. She is quite a sculptor and artist."

"Yes, my precious Betty, she is very talented." She's held up her gas lamp and gazed a moment longer at the huge sculpture on the wall. Then with her lady-in-waiting, and Looty in tow, she made her slow way towards her bedchamber.

The Queen awoke to birdsong. Glancing through the windows of her room, her mood brightened with the beauty of the morning. It was a mild early Spring day at Osborn House and the gardens were lush with clusters of daffodils, trilliums, crocuses, and colorful wall-flowers. Her eyes were transfixed by a tree and the reverie transported her back in time. *That beautiful Picea pinsapo tree, I was thirty years old when my beloved Albert gave me the shovel to plant it. Exactly forty-six years ago.*

It had been a year since Queen Victoria was last on her private beach. She was greeted by the familiar calmness of its setting where the cool air and the slow tidal waves seemed to be in harmony with each other. The waves were neither those that lapped the beach like an overflowing bathtub nor the ferocious kind which met the beach with force. They moved lazily but died within a few feet. A salty fragrance was borne on the breeze from Osborne Bay where small sailboats drifted around the Isle of Wight like birds on the wing. Seabirds cried and circled lazily in the sky.

The royal waiters, waitresses, and footmen were hard at work preparing Queen's breakfast. In the semicircular alcove where she usually enjoyed private family time during summer days. A table for eight was meticulously laid with double white starched cloths, engraved flatware with British-crown emblems, and each piece of silver and glassware precisely positioned.

Her breakfast menu consisted of porridge, an asparagus parmesan omelet, grilled chicken, assorted juices, coffee and tea. Victoria was always convivial when food was served and she often overindulged. The Queen was served by three footmen dressed in black double-breasted coats, waistcoats, black tie, and striped black and gray trousers. Although this morning's breakfast was served in an informal setting, the Queen had allowed Munshi Abdul Karim and Rafiuddin to join her at the table.

"Before Lord Falmouth and Lord Salisbury join us this afternoon, I need to find out more about Nosroollah. What do you know of him?" She scooped a spoonful of porridge and blew on it lightly to cool it down.

"Your Majesty, we do not know him personally, of course, only that he is in his early twenties," Munshi replied.

"I hear he's a barmy young man, sometimes uncontrollable, who may place us between the Devil and the deep blue sea," the Queen said, picking up the white starched napkin from her lap to dab her lips.

Sir Rafiuddin dropped two sugar cubes into his porcelain teacup and stirred it thoughtfully. "Your Majesty, His Highness, Amir Abdul Rahman Khan is a clever man and, should he need to, knows well how to exert a tight grip on his family members and countrymen." He set the spoon down on the saucer, "I give Your Majesty my sacred honor that Nasrullah will be cordial while he's in England." Although Rafiuddin meant well, his reassuring words about Prince Nasrullah, were anything but prophetic.

The servant removed Queen's plate and poured her coffee. Queen Victoria raised her eyebrows, "I have heard he requires a lot of reassurance and flattery and often has the need to prove that he measures up to his more sensible older brother, the Crown prince. I am never sure of their names, is Habiboollah the elder brother?"

"Yes, Your Majesty," Munshi replied. "Your Majesty, may I say this about Nasrullah."

"By all means Munshi, as always, I'd be delighted to hear your advice."

"Thank you, Your Majesty," he cleared his throat and politely covered his mouth. "Nasrullah may be insecure at his young age, but that can easily be dealt with. Some of the Prince's entourage are part of his close family circle and they know him very well. He will have advisers to give him the right way to interact with Your Majesty, and with the Royal household."

"We are all fully aware of the reason Abdul Rahman is sending his son," Queen Victoria replied. "As you and I discussed last night, Munshi, I will be leaving Afghanistan's foreign policy in the hands of my brilliant Major General, Lord Falmouth, and our Foreign Secretary and soon to be British Prime Minister, Lord Salisbury. And, of course, our esteemed Governor-General in India, Lord Bruce." She lifted her coffee cup, "If they advise me against granting the Amir his wish, I hope Prince Nosroollah will accept the decision, else it will be at his own peril."

"Your Majesty, I assure you that, if necessary, Sir Rafiuddin and I would be prepared to ensure Prince Nasrullah Khan understands and agrees with whatever decision is made."

"Splendid!"

"When General Roberts marched to Qandahar after the Second Anglo-Afghan War, Your Majesty, my father was with him and he met the Amir in person. He told me that the Amir learned things and solved problems quickly. I am sure he can also be counted on to help to resolve any issues."

"Munshi *Jee*, the Amir and I have one thing in common, we are both struggling with gout, this evil demon attacking our toes and feet! However, if Nosroollah refuses to accept the outcome, we're thousands of miles apart and powerless to discuss the matter in person. But I am hoping for a good outcome. As the world's colonial power, we have much bigger problems to solve than Afghanistan, but just at this moment Afghanistan is the top of our list."

Munshi's gaze briefly met Rafiuddin's, his eyebrow arched. *This is not going to be easy.*

CHAPTER TWENTY-EIGHT

~~~oc~~oc~~oc~

The news of the Hakim's sex potion reached *Naieb-Salar,* Field
Marshal Hassein Khan's ears. This was the most trusted man in the
Amir's court, who had fought alongside him for years while they were
still in exile in Russian-occupied, Samarkand. Hassein Khan was
married to two Uzbek wives, who had given birth to several children
in the early part of their union. But, while he was on the battlefield,
Hassein suffered two bullet wounds and, for a while, lost the sensation
in the lower part of his body. While he recovered the ability to walk
and was able to function in his daily duties, the emotional turmoil had
resulted in impotency. His penile impairment was a private matter
and only the Amir was aware of his friend's condition. He had tried
to persuade Hassein Khan to allow Dr. Alfred John Gray to evaluate
his problem but he refused. Later, when Dr. Hamilton took over Dr.
Gray's position, the Amir suggested he see her, but again, it fell on
the Field Marshal's deaf ears. However, finally, out of desperation, he
approached Parwana Khan and confessed his problem.

"That Hakim, Delnawaz, is the talk of the town," the executioner,
Parwana Khan said as they were walking together after leaving the
afternoon prayer, his non-parallel eyes scanned the marble steps of
the mosque to ensure there were no eavesdroppers to their private
conversation. "An acquaintance also enquired about him in the Char-
Chatta Bazaar the other day, and someone else I know, but cannot
reveal his name, said his erection lasted hours after taking the potion
given to him by Delnawaz."

"Do you think it is worth going?" Hassein Khan replied hopefully, "It would be good to put a smile on my face again before we head off to *Englistan.*" He unwound his onyx worry beads from his wrist and began thumbing them one by one. "Why is he suddenly so popular? Has anyone questioned his credentials?" He raised his hands in perplexity leaving his worry beads dangling.

"Naieb-Salar Sahib, sometimes small-time Punjabi swindlers make their way to Kabul and use their charms to deceive people. I don't know any more about this Hakim Delnawas, but why not go and see him and we can judge him in person?"

The Field Marshal nodded, "It is worth a try," he admitted, "living like this is humiliating! But we will have to go secretly, no one must see either of us in such a place!"

On the following day, Pawana Khan and Hassein cloaked themselves in shawls and cantered through the narrow alleyways between the three-story high mud huts, dismounted in the area close to the Hakim's place of practice, and tied up their horses.

Continuing through two more narrow alleys, they found themselves at his metal-spiked double doors, skillfully hand-carved with a lopsided, steel handle on each. Above the door frame, a sign was written in *nastaliq* Dari, "*Tababet-e-Hakim Delnawaz, Doo-Paisa-Barai-Yak-Zendagi Khosh*", which, translated, meant "Medica of Hakim Delnawaz, Two *Paisa* For a Happy Life". There were several people ahead of them in the queue, but a little extra money greased the palm of the Hakim and saw them welcomed in before the others.

Set on the low table in the room where he mixed his potions was a brass mortar and pestle, a hand scale, and two lighted candles in their wooden holders. Hakim Delnawaz peered over the frame of his round glasses and touched his forehead with four fingers to reveal the callous from years of vigorous praying. He nodded at Parwana Khan and the Field Marshal, Hassein Khan with an ingratiating smile.

"*Befarmayed*," he said and indicated that they should sit on the faded, soiled, and malodorous cushion opposite. His neatly duck-tailed gray beard and tight black turban gave the impression of one as upright as the rightly-guided *Avicenna, Ibn-e-Sina*. On the wall behind him hung rows of wooden cabinets, all slightly askew, filled with dusty amorphous objects - bottles, containers, and pots of every description.

The Hakim sprang from his filthy cushion and handed each of them an item wrapped in a golden leaf. "*Ein Ra Bokhor baz khob meyshee*, Eat this and you'll be cured!" he assured them.

The opulence of the wrapping was impressive as it glistened against the candlelight. Both men unwrapped this treasure only to discover crystallized gooseberries.

"Is this the sex potion?" asked Naieb-Salar Hassein Khan incredulously. He was sitting crossed-legged with his hands laced round his rotund belly.

"Yes, but there's also the *Arak*, brew, you can take a sip for another two *Paisa*."

Hassein took a tentative sip of the malodorous Arak that was noxious enough to make him pinch his nose and gasp for air.

Parwana Khan wrapped his shawl more tightly around his face. "How is it prepared?" he asked.

"I would be obliged to announce my ancestral recipe passed down through twelve generations," the Hakim crossed his legs and proudly continued. "It's mixed with markhor testicles, *kaftar* uterus, finely ground deer hoofs or antler horns, pigeon or partridge brain, squirrel or rabbit kidney, Indian macaque navels, six-year-old chicken eggs, a small *Koza* filled with river foam, and brown lamb's intestines. All these are mixed and pounded to paste and dried in crystalline form, which is what you just drank."

Hassein and Parwana Khan glanced at one another.

"What if it doesn't work?"

"*Bey gham bash, Sahib*. No need to worry, Sir." Delnawaz replied confidently. "I have had no complaints from anyone who came and tried my potion, and they repeatedly return to queue at my door. I guarantee it's the best in all Kabul!" He continued to expand enthusiastically on the marketability of the elixir recipe and signaled to his aide, "Fetch me the large wooden bowl." The aide set it close by him and removed the white gauze cover. Glancing forward for a better view, the men could see the grape leaves lining the bowl beneath the dark, evil-smelling paste. The Hakim swept a sanctimonious glance heavenward then fell on his face in an attitude of prayer. Continuing in this attitude of piety, he read some appropriate verses from the Qu'ran then laid the holy book aside, brought the bowl close to his mouth, and blew in a circular motion, "Chuff! Chuff! Chuff," those throaty mutterings unintentionally showering the potion with his saliva.

In the land where, predominately, the illiteracy rate was high, the cause of sickness was often attributed to demons, gins, and the wrath of *Allah*, who, therefore, must be appeased lest the illness exacerbates, or death lurks at the patient's door. In Kabul's *chaikhanas*, bazaars, and places of gathering, others such as Hakim Delnawaz, soother of heart, also dispensed their aphrodisiacs to men who lacked sexual prowess. This would be where the *Hakims*' quackery stepped in to rescue the bedridden and medically dysfunctional. These are the so-called "wise men" or "self-made physicians", the practitioners of herbal remedies, especially Greek and Islamic medication. They masterfully instilled into the patient's mind that the proper remedy for a blissful cure was to consume the blessed water of Zamzam, which may have been drawn from local wells or springs, but certainly had not come from Mecca; or to consume their specially made herbal medicines, exquisite sherbets of *Rooh-Afza*, Dari for the elixir of the soul, and even prescribed amulets containing Qur'anic verses to be worn on clothing or braids. Throughout history, some Hakims earned the respect of their communities and reflected sound stature and dignity, but not those who through deceit had mastered their tricks of charlatanism.

A few days later, when it became obvious that the Hakim's potion was proven beyond doubt to be worthless, Hassein Khan, at the executioner's insistence, reported the incident to the Amir.

"Bring me that *padarlanat!*" The potion maker was summoned trembling to Arg Palace where the Amir roundly cursed his father and heard his confession of quackery. As the proper punishment and lesson for other Hakims of his kind, the Amir ordered his incarceration: but first, he was publicly humiliated, mounted on a donkey in reverse position, and paraded throughout the bazaars of Kabul.

CHAPTER TWENTY-NINE

∽◊∽◊∽◊∽

Wednesday, April 6, 1895 - Afghan calendar month:
Hamal 17, 1274.
Kabul, Afghanistan

Sumptuous C-Spring barouches and landaus rolled into the Arg Palace grounds carrying courtiers and their families to bid farewell to Prince Nasrullah. The palace's facade and premises were festooned with Amir's plain black flags. This was the very first Afghan flag bearing no emblem of any kind—nothing to symbolize or identify the country on the world stage.

To the surprise of the guests, on this eve of Nasrullah's departure, the Amir's royal guards were no longer clad in ragtag, tattered uniforms. They turned out well-groomed, wearing white helmets with silver stars, and scarlet tunics covered with glittering brass cuirasses shaped in crescent moons with emblems of *Allah-Hu-Akbar*, God is Great, etched on them. Bayoneted matchlocks were proudly slung over their shoulders; even the mounted lancers on well-groomed horses trotted in somewhat better formation than before.

Amir recognized his Head of the Security, Colonel Zalmai Khan, and the chief veterinarian, Thomas Clemence, for their sedulous work in enhancing the guard of honor and the horses that were to accompany Nasrullah on his voyage to England. Through sweat and hard work, Mr. Clemence had given his utmost in training the mounted lancers and their horses to move rhythmically and in harmony.

The young Colonel was clad in a heavily braided dark blue hussar jacket, and black pantaloons with a double white stripe. A scabbarded saber hung at his side. He was commanding his guardsmen to move with precision from one formation to another. The lancers displayed the prowess of their horses through a show of standardized marches—walking, trotting, loping, and cantering. The men were all Durani Pashtuns and Uzbeks, handpicked for their special features: strong, tall, broad-shouldered, and handsome. There had been a true transformation of Amir's guard of honor for this occasion.

The frail Amir was seated in his wheelchair under a well-guarded pavilion with a banner displayed above it written in Dari, 'May *Shahzadah* Have a Safe Trip with The Grace of *Allah*.' He faced the crowd on the sprawling lush green lawn, his sweat-beaded brow glittering in the warm afternoon sun. Shielding his eyes, he saw Princes Nasrullah and Habibullah approaching to pay their respects. Both wore princely outfits with sashes across their chests, and golden epaulets on their black tunics. They bowed and kissed their father's hand respectfully in a gesture expected of all Afghan children to their elders, and as they stood, adjusted their karakul hats.

There was a tremendous atmosphere of gaiety. Tribal elders, religious leaders, courtiers, and members of the royal household cried out happily in celebration of this historic milestone as their young prince prepared to meet the most powerful monarch in the world. Multiple musicians from famous *Kocha-e-Kharabat,* the Mecca of Afghan music, had been hired on this celebratory occasion to perform and pervade the evening with joy and happiness. They sat crossed-legged on a carpet-covered-dais, readying themselves to perform. They were gaily dressed for the occasion in embroidered vests and flowing white Afghan costumes. As they tuned their string instruments of *rubab, tanboor, sarinda,* and *gheechak*, twisting and turning the pegs, they sounded like multiple cats in agony.

The English contingent was elegantly turned out: the men in top hats, frock coats, and cravats; the women clad in colorful dresses and flowery and feathered bonnets. Roma and Olivia carried parasols. They were all seated side by side next to a tinkling water fountain, across from the Amir's pavilion canopy. As a gesture of gratitude on this occasion, the Amir permitted them to drink their choice of beverages in celebration of their accomplishments and as a joyous farewell to his son. They openly, but moderately, sipped glasses of wine and goblets of whisky, while Thomas Clemence drank leisurely from a gleaming flask of brandy he carried in the pocket of his frock coat.

Dr. Hamilton was, as always, keeping a close eye on the Amir's health, aware that his energy seemed to be ebbing away. Gout had turned the inflamed flesh on his legs into a slough of broken skin and, lately, he had suffered high fevers and had had trouble breathing. She consoled him sympathetically. "You have my promise, Your Highness, that the nurses and my assistant will take good care of you while I am away. They will ensure you receive the same medical routine you are accustomed to."

"My first hope is to see Nasrullah return safely," the Amir replied wheezily, lifting one hand heavenward, "I pray to the Almighty, "I will live to see my beloved son again. My second hope is that *Malika* Weektorya grants me autonomy."

"Your Highness, I'm hoping your wish will come true."

The Amir leaned forward and raised his voice above the music. "Daktar Laila Jan, we need another Daktar like you. Please don't forget, upon your return from *Englistan* to bring an assistant lady Daktar with you. My life isn't getting better and I need another female Daktar to help you to help me."

"By all means, Your Highness," she bent the brim of her straw-bonnet to deflect the sun and brought her ear closer to hear him.

"*Tashakur*, Daktar Laila Jan. And of course, you know I must have a lady Daktar for the ladies of the Harem-Sarai," he continued. "I forbid any Hakim to examine them. The one before Jon Mohammad, told me he was a *mahram* and an entrusted man to examine the ladies. I believed him and gave my permission." He shook his head regretfully, "The women were cloaked from head to toe as if they were shrouded in burial cloths, but still, the *haram-zadah*, the illegitimate son of a woman, touched them indecently! His punishment was severe. I ordered that his member be severed and tossed for the stray dogs to eat. He finally rotted in the deep well of Bala-Hisar without food or drink." His fingers tapped his bottom lip—an agitated gesture, "I cannot trust those vulpine Hakims."

"Do not concern yourself, Your Highness." She untied the ribbon under her chin and readjusted her bonnet. "Frankly, Your Highness, I see the need for a second doctor to help me here. I'd be delighted to bring along someone with a solid medical background to treat Your Highness and the ladies of the Harem-Sarai."

"I knew I could count on you Daktar Laila Jan. *Tashakur* for your understanding."

The gathering on the palace lawns was joyful. The music played, there was chattering and feasting, the hustle and bustle of pageboys, servants, and guards, and children scampered about getting in everyone's way.

"Your Highness, may I ask for your help?" Dr. Hamilton asked hesitantly.

"Of course, Dakar Laila Jan. I'd be obliged to listen."

She brought her chair closer to him. Since the Amir found most of the Hakims untrustworthy and had mentioned the deceitfulness of the one who indecently touched the women of Harem-Sarai, it seemed the perfect moment for the Doctor to raise the issue of Hakim Jon Mohammad. Opportunities to discuss these delicate matters with the Amir were rare and she did not want this moment to slip by.

"Since we leave tomorrow, may I ask whether Your Highness has spoken to Jon Mohammad regarding medical decisions on the voyage to England and back?"

"I've passed the word out through my Chamberlain to let him know you will be in charge, but I would be happy to tell him to his face in your presence if that is what you want."

"I'd be obliged if Your Highness did that so he can fully understand what's expected of him."

"Of course, Daktar Laila Jan. I trust Jon Mohammad and elevated him to the highest position as Royal Hakim. I know he will obey me one way or another."

"Indeed, Your Highness's words weigh more highly than anyone else's."

"Daktar Laila Jan, my nerves pulsate through my veins today," he touched his head. "I hope you'd be kind enough to give me some of that *Sharbat-e-Asaab*, Nerve-Juice."

She rummaged through her leather medical bag and pulled out two small bottles of nerve tonic. One was a mixture of lithium salts and cocaine, and the other was opium-ether, he liked both.

"Which one would Your Highness prefer today?"

He pointed to the opium-ether, "We will talk about the Hakim as soon as my pain disappears. I don't want to resolve the issue by using a noose around his neck."

Lillias obediently gave him a dose of the opium-ether and the Amir slumped into his wheelchair, set his elbows on the arms of the chair, hands under his chin, and fell into a reverie. Shortly afterward, Lillias sensed the return of tranquility to his mind and body as the pain was brought under control. It was like the calming of an ocean after a storm. His lips parted and his droopy eyes became transfixed on the musicians and the guests.

Further down, a sequestered marquee tent was pitched for the royal ladies of the Harem-Sarai and their close female relatives to participate in this farewell gathering for Nasrullah. The gray-bearded watchmen monitored both entrances at all times. Outside the tent, a *Qalandar*,

Gypsy girl of fifteen or sixteen years of age walked a tightrope as naturally as a spider on its web. Children focused enthralled as they watched her performance. Moments later, while her teammate held it vertical, she shimmied up a twenty-foot pole as if it was a ladder; another mate built up the tension on a drum as she gyrated herself in a cantilevered position or rotated around the pole in a centrifugal spin. Every year the Amir invited a group of amusing peripatetics, jugglers, acrobats, magicians, and impersonators from India to perform their shows at the Arg Palace. This year, the entertainment had been timed to coincide with the eve of Nasrullah's departure for England.

A little distance away, monkeys imitated feuding lovers, policemen, and soldiers, and rode tiny bicycles with precise balance. In another intricate demonstration of balance, a boy of around thirteen, first with a tumbler of water, and next with a pole and plate on his forehead, contorted himself to different positions while holding the plate on the pole in perfect equilibrium

For the children, this entertainment was where their lives were shaped to dream. It was a lesson in encouragement for what can be accomplished when consistent practice was met with passion and perseverance.

Suddenly, a delighted round of applause and excited shrieks emanated from every quarter. More than a hundred-and-fifty sheep, twenty-eight calves, and five-hundred chickens had been slaughtered and prepared for this night's occasion. Long *distarkhwans*, white cloths, were being spread out on carpet-covered areas for the guests. The delicious aroma of allspice from the lamb kabobs wafted from multiple pits as hundreds of skewers sizzled on the glowing charcoal. In one dexterous pull, the royal chefs slid the mouthwatering kabobs from twenty skewers, sprayed them with extra spices, and nestled the meat into long clay-baked loaves of bread. These were heaped onto huge copper trays and served to the guests.

Multiple culinary units had also been set up on the lawns. Fires blazed under the cauldrons preparing assorted rice dishes and stews of all kinds. As the day wore on, some guests lapsed into a crapulous state, dozing off crossed-legged until the next round arrived. It was the greatest gathering and feast since the Amir was enthroned fifteen years before.

"Go fetch the snake charmer," Nasrullah told the page boy. As a young boy, all Nasrullah wanted to learn was magic, puppeteering, tightrope walking, backward arching, and hand-standing. He also greatly enjoyed watching brutal camel, dog, cock, and pheasant fights. Part of him was still attracted to those pastimes. Years had rolled in one against another; everything had its proper time and purpose. That is, until now, when he was expected to shoulder the huge responsibility of representing his father before England's Queen; he was still unable to comprehend the finite nature of every increment of life's journey. Before long, Prince Nasrullah would have to face dignitaries; highly experienced men and women that he would meet in an official capacity, and be expected to give them his full and undivided attention. Nasrullah had shown keen interest in England's amusements. He had heard of many entertaining shows, prize fights, and the famous pleasure gardens. The time ahead would prove whether he would be consumed with his own pleasures, or rise to the call of Afghanistan's expectation of him.

Clad in a *pagri* turban, a soiled, sweaty loincloth, and bejeweled with earrings and necklaces of all colors and kinds, the snake charmer, like an itinerant beggar, sat crossed-legged on the palace lawn with three straw baskets about him. His willowy body arched backward before springing into an upright position.

"Stay calm!" he warned everyone, in the Urdu tongue. "Stay calm and watch closely."

King cobra, the very sound of its name seizes the heart and ignites the mind. The spectators gradually encircled the area as he removed the lid from one of the baskets and blew his *pungi*. As the enticing, haunting whine of the bean flute filled the air, it attracted spectators from every corner of the Palace. They saw the King Cobra's head, swaying as it rose gradually above the rim of the basket. It slowly erected its body, which measured about four inches in circumference, until it stood a meter high and flared its hood as wide as eight fingers, shredding the air with its fork tongue at lightning speed. The charmer blew his flute until his cheeks inflated like navel oranges, and gestured briefly to his *shagerd,* apprentice, to open the lids of the other two baskets. Now, three hypnotized King Cobras swayed in unison to the movement of the *pungi,* and then, while the crowd watched in awe, the charmer stopped blowing, leaned forward, and kissed the deadly creature on the head.

"*Wah! Wah!*" Nasrullah glowed with delight. It was like seeing Eid money handed to a needy child.

As the sun set behind the majestic Hindu-Kush Mountains, the sky turned blood red. A round of applause for the performers reverberated throughout the Palace gardens, The English ladies, little William and Prince Omar Jan had watched the *Qalandars* gleefully. Happiness had enveloped them all and they stood by the private marquee chattering happily, thrilled about their journey back to England on the following day.

"I miss the stout, and the fish and chips. We will eat and drink the minute we dock in Portsmouth," Charlotte Martin declared with a giggle, "Or, perhaps, the minute we board the ship in Bombay!"

"I'm glad my sister is accompanying me to England." Roma's blue eyes sparkled as she scanned the crowd and spotted Zalmai. He was about a hundred yards away, monitoring the formation of the guards under the willow trees, handsome in his full military uniform.

She glanced every few minutes in that direction hoping to at least attract his attention or, perhaps, to steal a moment to speak with him. With that expectation, Roma had chosen a honey-yellow gown she made herself that brought out the hints of gold in her hair. She caught his attention and their eyes locked. Zalmai made his way across the lawn to meet her and Roma thrilled to the warmth of his smile.

Zalmai was noticeably distressed by the lack of privacy. Meeting her in the open, visible to all, was complicated and even dangerous if it was brought to the attention of the Amir or his sons.

"Can we walk behind the tent?" Zalmai asked uneasily, "it is inappropriate for us to be seen together."

Roma tried to control her nervousness at being noticed as they walked to the back of the tent, but the intensity of their feelings for one another flowed through them like a tidal wave.

"Here is something I promised you," Zalmai said, and taking her hand, he placed in it a small parcel wrapped in green silken cloth. She held the delicate chain with its pendant up and the almond-sized green stone flashed as it caught the light from the torches.

"It is beautiful, Zalmai," she breathed softly. "What is this stone?"

"It's emerald from the mountains of Badakhshan," he smiled, "a token of my mother."

"It is the most bewitching stone I've ever seen," She looked up at him, feeling as she met his eyes, a stab of pleasure that was unfamiliar in its intensity.

"My father helped me make it. We spent hours discussing the design before we agreed to start the work," he seemed suddenly shy and almost humbled in her presence." He took a step closer seeking answers in her face. Roma's heart thudded so wildly that she was sure he could hear it.

Zalmai, lifted her chin between his thumb and forefinger, his brown eyes looking deeply into hers.

Suddenly, from behind them, an aggressive voice intruded.

"*Salaam!*" Zalmai stepped back in alarm. Nasrullah stood watching them, his muscles were tensed but the expression on his angular face mocked the couple before him. "*Khelwat kardee*, Colonel? Were you seeking privacy?" His voice dripped with sarcasm.

"*Bebakhshed, Shahzadah!* My apologies, Prince, Miss Hamilton had a question about the trip." Zalmai's heart thudded in his ribcage.

Nasrullah interrupted. "Miss Roma Jan, would you kindly give us privacy? I would like to have a conversation with the Colonel."

Roma's face clouded with anxiety. She started to move away, the necklace hidden in her palm, her gaze shifting desperately from Nasrullah to Zalmai.

"You have crossed the line, Zalmai Khan! Did you forget that we Afghans never betray our guests and seduce their women? Remember the code of Pashtunwali? Did it not it say that we must honor guests, and show hospitality?" His questions were tossed at Zalmai contemptuously. The young prince was unaware that he was revealing his duplicity. His deep-seated hatred of the British stood in direct contrast to treating them as guests of honor. And his condemnation of a love affair between a young Afghan Colonel and a British woman only served to demonstrate his jealousy. "Beware of Jealousy," the Prophet said, "For verily it destroys good deeds the way fire destroys wood."

"Breaching our code of hospitality is subject to death!" Nasrullah ground out. His hypocrisy and self-interest opened Zalmai's eyes in a flash, as though a light had been switched on, but he had no choice but to submit.

"I concur, Shahzadah, Prince."

Without warning, Nasrullah slapped Zalmai Khan viciously with an open hand, Zalmai staggered to the left, clutching his face as his eyes welled up. The blow left a livid red imprint on his cheek, and blood trickled from a small cut below the eye where Nasrullah's gold ring had caught him.

"For now, luck is on your side. You are needed for this trip to England so my father will spare your life." Nasrullah's nostrils flared and he raised his chin arrogantly, "If you prefer to live, never get close to her again."

The Colonel was badly shaken. He wiped the blood off his face with his handkerchief feeling at that moment, that although the imprint of Nasrullah's hand would fade, the sting would remain in his memory forever.

CHAPTER THIRTY

❦❦❦

The Queen alone stood between Munshi and the rest of the royal household. Almost without exception, everyone else in Windsor Palace kept an eagle-eye on him. The Queen's favor rested on her Indian teacher, in appointing him as her Indian secretary and adviser, he had been elevated well beyond his station. Jealousy against him had heightened when he was knighted by the Queen who then authorized his portrait to be painted by several of the world's most renowned artists. Munshi traveled with her throughout Europe and had the best seats reserved for him at banquets and operas. Indeed, he was widely perceived to be even closer to the Queen than her children.

On the other hand, Rafiuddin, despite his position as the Queen's representative in Ottoman Turkey, had lost credibility for working closely with William Henry Quilliam, a native Englishman from Liverpool who had converted to Islam eight years before and adopted the name, Abdullah. Rafiuddin Ahmad's ambitious plan was to expand Islam throughout Europe and England. Queen Victoria was furious from the moment Rafiuddin joined forces with Abdullah Quilliam to help his cause.

"Sir Rafi," the Queen said, turning her attention to him as she set her cup down on the table. "Have you seen Henry Quilliam lately?"

"On occasions, Your Majesty, we see each other whenever I'm in Liverpool or he's in London." He straightened the embroidered lapel of his long black velvet coat.

"I presume he is still active in recruiting people to Islam and spreading the gospel of the Mohammedan?"

"I am not aware, Your Majesty, but I do know his pamphlet, Faith of Islam, and his weekly Islamic record, The Crescent, are both published widely in England." Rafiuddin had turned a bit pale, uncertain as to where this line of questioning was going.

"In fact," the Queen replied sternly, "it is published internationally and circulated worldwide. Did you know that as the editor, he is very highly paid by Muslim sympathizers around the world to publish those papers?" Her eyes were narrowed." Mr. Quilliam has been instrumental in organizing a massive Islamic following." The Queen glanced out across the bay and then turned back to Rafiuddin. "Will you be introducing Nosroollah to Henry Quilliam?"

"I've no plans to do so, your Majesty," Rafiuddin said, nervously tilting his white silk turban to one side. "But I believe the Amir of Afghanistan and Nasrullah must be aware of Mr. Quilliam since he's been recognized by Sultan of Turkey."

"Yes, indeed he has given his allegiance to the Ottoman Caliph," the Queen replied shortly.

"May I add one thing, Your Majesty?" Munshi asked.

"Of course, you may."

"I concur with *Moulvi Sab* Rafiuddin," Munshi said, "There's no doubt the Amir already knows about Abdullah Quilliam and would have instructed his son to pay him a visit."

"Well, just bear in mind, that you should avoid any undue attention if Nosroollah does meet Henry Quilliam. It would harm Britain and the monarchy, and it could trigger disturbances in India and the Arab world, destabilizing our colonies. I hope I'm clear."

"Yes, Your Majesty, we understand your position on this and we will conduct ourselves accordingly," Rafiuddin agreed.

"I will bring this issue up with Lords Falmouth, Bruce, and Salisbury this afternoon. The Crown will keenly protect our interest in the colonies and maintain our superiority in the world. Henry Quilliam's endeavor will not be allowed to weaken us."

The seagulls wheeled overhead and the cool breeze sent little waves curling and lapping at the length of the Royal beach. Munshi and Rafiuddin courteously requested that they might be dismissed. Facing Queen Victoria, they both shuffled backward, palms together, bowing and touching their foreheads in the manner of *Taslim*. Their plan to help Nasrullah seemed to be at a dead end.

"Lead the way, Munshi Sab," Rafiuddin bowed casually gesturing to Munshi that he be first on the walkway from the alcove. "She's the Cock of the Walk," Rafiuddin said as they strolled together along the sandy beach. "Convincing her to approve Amir's request is impossible. Just impossible." He shook his head, "I thought you and I could reason with her and persuade her that the Amir was worthy of receiving independence for his country, but we failed."

"Her Majesty and I had a lengthy conversation in the *Darbar* room last night," Munshi replied moodily, "She was like a brick wall. She will never bend rules where British interests are concerned.

Both Munshi and Rafiuddin realized that Queen Victoria's fifty-eight years on the throne gave her enormous experience. That period had been marked by a great expansion of the British Empire, and she had become a national icon for strict standards of personal morality. During the span of her reign, she had been served by thirty-three prime ministers who strengthened her belief that the preservation of the monarchy and the superiority of Great Britain, the largest empire and global power on the world stage, were her prime priorities. She was stubborn; born to grasp, to win, and to defend what she believed in, to show her true loyalty and reliability to those under her protection and nurture—the people of England and its colonies. In return, their beloved sovereign, their Queen, received the loyalty of her people.

"Yes, we came a cropper!" Munshi replied pessimistically.

"Had the Amir come instead of sending his young and inexperienced son, the outcome might have been different."

The seagulls swooped and ascended against the backdrop of the coastal skies.

"I wish this had been planned well in advance. One of us could have gone to Kabul to work with the Amir, but it is too late now," Rafiuddin mourned.

"Moulvi Sab, I don't think that would have worked either."

"Why?"

"We were not alone in recognizing Afghan autonomy would be a recipe for Indian autonomy, which is why the Queen is set against it, she is perfectly aware of the outcome."

He nodded. "I know. You are right of course, Munshi Sab."

"Let's not waste time in the vain hope Her Majesty will side with the Amir," Munshi said. "We must do whatever we can to expand Muslim influence in England. Quilliam must be told to contact Prince Nasrullah directly when he arrives, but we must not be seen to be involved. Any contact with Abdullah Quilliam now would be reckless."

Rafiuddin shielded the morning sun from his eyes. "I think we would be better off contacting my good friend, His Highness, Sheikh of Bahrain, to inform Amir Abdul Rahman and Nasrullah to meet with Quilliam. There will be nothing to link us to him. What do you think Munshi Sab?"

"Perfect! Please inform him immediately to send a wire to Kabul before Nasrullah leaves." Munshi fell silent as he thought deeply, "Rafi Sab," he said at length, "now it's known that the Queen won't budge on the issue of Kabul's request, perhaps the Amir should instruct Nasrullah not leave London until the Queen grants him autonomy."

"Blackmail!" Rafiuddin breathed, "That's a thought, do you think the Amir would go to those lengths to get what he wants?"

"Blackmail is a strong word, Moulvi Sab, I would call it persuasion."

"I'll send a message tonight. But we must both be very cautious, we can't afford to be intercepted by the Queen's intelligence officers."

Meanwhile, the Amir had been briefed regarding Abdullah

Quilliam, and English newspaper reports were already suggesting that during the visit to England of the Muslim Prince, a meeting with Quilliam in Liverpool was likely to take place.

Shortly after lunch, Lords Falmouth, Salisbury, and Bruce met with the Queen in Osborn Bay. They gathered on the waterfront terrace under a royal pavilion tent. The Union Jack and Royal Standard flapped on nearby masts. Visible from that distance, little yachts moved silently on the briny water like blown leaves. Along the waterfront, the golden sands formed a continuous thick ribbon between the slow rippling waves and the vegetation.

"Lord Salisbury, I discussed with Munshi some important issues about Afghanistan last night, but we'd rather have your view as to what policy we should adopt in that country. Could you kindly give us your thoughts?" the Queen asked. Sitting next to her on the gilded sofa, was her Lady-in-waiting, Countess of Errol. Her presence ensured that constant help was on hand if needed for the elderly Queen. Victoria straightened her silken headscarf as the Indian servants with richly colored uniforms and turbans served tea and refreshments for her and the dignitaries.

British Prime Minister Robert Gascoyne-Cecil, 3rd Marquess of Salisbury was in his mid-sixties. He was of medium height, stocky, with a full beard and walrus mustache that covered his mouth.

Queen Victoria had chosen not to include Munshi Abdul Karim or Rafiuddin at this formal assembly recognizing that having her British and Indian advisers together could cause unnecessary debate and disagreement. She was in the delicate position of having to weigh up their views without causing friction between the two sides, specifically where British foreign policy in matters of India and Afghanistan were discussed. But, she generally endeavored to hear and accept the views and decisions of the Lords rather than her Indian advisers.

"Your Majesty," Lord Salisbury said, his sharp eyes peering at the Queen from under bushy brows. "We have had years of trouble with

Afghanistan that none of us would like to repeat." Any movement of his mouth was almost invisible under his mustache. "As Your Majesty is well aware it is a wild and lawless country and every man, woman, and child is obsessed with hatred against Britain after the wars. I have no other words, Your Majesty, except to say we should avoid shedding any more blood in that troubled land. War and bloodshed are embedded in every Afghan's veins." His balding head was beginning to catch the glare of the mid-afternoon sun. He cleared his voice politely, "To answer Your Majesty's question with regards to choosing the right policy for Afghanistan, I believe we're in good standing with the current ruler, the Iron Amir, and it would be wise to maintain that without compromising our position," he took a mouthful of gin and dabbed his wet mustache with the napkin.

"Indeed Lord Salisbury," the Queen agreed, "hard lessons were learned on both disastrous occasions." She shook her head regretfully. "I must say the ambush on General Elphinstone's army in the mountain pass towards Jalalabad cannot be forgotten. The General made the wrong decision when he withdrew the troops and their families from Kabul in the middle of a freezing winter. Naturally, the Afghans took advantage and attacked our retreating force. They gained confidence and humiliated us. I do wish he had called for backup from India rather than fleeing without a viable strategy."

The Queen turned to face Lord Bruce, the Governor-General of India, "What are your thoughts about Afghanistan Lord Bruce?"

Victor Alexander Bruce, 9th Earl of Elgin, Viceroy of India, was the son of James Bruce, 8th Earl of Elgin who had been the Viceroy to India three decades before. Victor Alexander Bruce was a staunch colonial officer and a man of luminescent wit, who had recently entered his fifth decade. He was famously quoted as saying: "India is the pivot of our Empire. If the Empire loses any other part of its Dominion we can survive, but if we lose India, the sun of our Empire will have set."

"I fully agree with the Prime Minister," he said, "As you know, I am a firm believer that Afghanistan's independence would erode Britain's colonial power over India." Lord Bruce was a stout but handsome man whose face was framed by well-groomed hair and side-whiskers. He proudly wore the three orders attached to his chest. "Things have returned to calm in Afghanistan under the Amir, Your Majesty, he knows how to keep his subjects in check." In the distance, a vessel's horn blared out once over the Bay, and two more short blasts followed. "We've found the right man for the job. He is resolute, firm, and never accepts no for an answer." He reached forward to set his glass of whisky on the gilded table across from him. "Of course, we've provided the Amir with the weaponry and power to deal with his countrymen." He leaned back in his chair. "As I have said before if India is allowed to fall the effect on our Empire will be devastating and permanent." Lords Salisbury and Falmouth nodded in agreement. "We need to have faith in Abdul Rahman's leadership, Your Majesty." His expression softened as he fingered his auburn beard and shifted his blue eyes from Lord Salisbury to Lord Falmouth and then back to the Queen. "The question remains though, how do we answer the request for Afghanistan's full autonomy?"

"From your summaries of the situation, we need to keep the Amir on our side without necessarily giving him what his son will be requesting of us," Queen Victoria replied. "In other words, how do we say no to his son?"

"I believe we have to say no, bluntly, to his son when he asks," Lord Falmouth replied.

The British occupation of Afghanistan had taken place in the early Victorian era in a bizarre manner. The superpower neither sought to colonize the country, nor conquer it, but rather installed a sovereign sympathetic to British interests, one who agreed to permit Britain's control over Afghan foreign policy and prevented Russia from invading Afghanistan. The present Amir, in contrast to his predecessors who agreed to accede to those conditions, wanted the full autonomy of his nation back in his own hands.

"That's precisely the way to handle it." Lord Salisbury concurred.

"What happens if we lose the Amir?" the Queen asked.

"Your Majesty," Lord Bruce replied confidently, "the Amir needs us more than we need him. Just two years ago, he dared to question us regarding the demarcation of the Durand Line, yet he fully accepted all the terms and conditions we proposed to the Afghans in Parachinar. I have full confidence he will ultimately accept our decision." His eyes gleamed with satisfaction. "This is all part of the Great Game."

The "Great Game" was the term given by the Queen's military advisers to the power struggle in Central Asia between the two major world Empires, Britain and Russia. It was initially coined to refer to the rivalry between the British lion and the Russian bear by a young British officer with the 6th Bengal Native Light Cavalry, in the early Victorian period. He assisted with British reconnaissance and map-making in the region and was deeply involved in the "Game" along the frontier of British India. He wrote to a friend: " . . . A great game, a noble game."

"Lord Bruce, you picked Colonel Adelbert Talbot and Sir Gerald Fitzgerald to accompany Prince Nosroolah on his voyage to Portsmouth." She added in a confidential undertone, "I hear Colonel Talbot is one of our best officers in the British Directorate of Military Intelligence, who will report every matter of importance regarding the Afghans during the voyage. I gather Talbot is well versed in both Afghan languages?"

"Yes, Your Majesty!" Lord Bruce assured her. He leaned forward, elbows on his knees so that he could keep his voice low. "Talbot is the right pick for the job and he always amazes us with his courage and dedication. He works alone scouting from Peshawar to Kabul, to Kandahar, to Herat. Anywhere, inside Afghanistan for only one purpose—to collect intelligence for a possible later strike. And yes,

Colonel Talbot is flawless in both Afghan languages and is, therefore, a highly valuable asset. Above all, he blends into the population without anyone noticing that he's English. Only one thing worries me about him."

"And, what's that Lord Bruce?" the Queen asked.

"His blue eyes, Your Majesty. But, he gets away with that, portraying himself as a descendant of Alexander the Great."

The Queen smiled and turned to Lord Falmouth, "Lord Falmouth, will you be receiving the Prince upon his arrival in Portsmouth?" she asked.

Major General Evelyn Edward Thomas Boscawen, 7th Viscount Falmouth, was a stout man in his sixties. Although he was of medium height and wore the tallest of top hats he still seemed short beside the towering figure of Lord Bruce. Having removed his hat before entering into the Queen's presence, his bald pate was starting to turn a little pink in the sun. Lord Falmouth fought in the Anglo-Egyptian War in 1882 and had been recognized with numerous orders from Queen Victoria. He recently had been commissioned into the Coldstream Guards.

"Yes, Your Majesty," Lord Falmouth replied. "I have organized a welcoming ceremony for the Afghan Prince from the moment he descends the gangplank," he straightened the angle of his bow tie. "A twenty-one-gun salute will be given in his honor and he will then be taken to view the annual parade of the British troops."

"Thank you, Lord Falmouth, for your well-planned efforts. Our preparations for the best hospitality and pageantry for the Prince may please his father, if not our decision to refuse his hope of Afghan representation." She asked her lady-in-waiting to fetch Looty if his grooming was complete.

"You may be certain, Your Majesty, that the Afghan Prince will receive excellent attention."

"I'm sure it will be a memorable time for the Prince," the Queen agreed. "Lord Falmouth," she raised her brows. "Where will the Prince and his entourage be accommodated? Is it to be Buckingham Palace, as Munshi suggested, or do you have somewhere else in mind?"

Lord Falmouth hesitated and Lord Salisbury Interjected, "If you have no objection, Your Majesty, and Your Excellency Lord Falmouth, regarding the Prince's accommodation may I suggest the following?" Lord Bruce's reluctance to approve Nasrullah's stay in Buckingham Palace was instantly noticeable by the Queen and the others.

"Of course, Lord Salisbury. Please give us your thoughts," the Queen said glancing at Falmouth for his approval.

"By all means, please speak, Your Excellency," Lord Falmouth consented with a brief gesture.

The Countess of Errol brought Looty and set him on Queen's lap. As she rubbed the little Pekingese's newly groomed lion-like mane, the silver bells around his neck tinkled.

"This little lad has been my companion through difficult times and the joy he brings me is without measure," Queen said lifting him to where he was level with her eyes. "Please carry on Lord Bruce," she said, setting the dog down on her lap, "My apologies for the interruption."

"Not at all, Your Majesty, Looty deserves attention as much as we do," Lord Bruce smiled charmingly. "I have doubts that the young Afghan Prince and his entourage will be interested in the limitations and full security of Buckingham Palace," he said.

The Countess of Errol suddenly leaned towards the Queen and whispered something in her ear.

"Oh yes, thank you for reminding me, Countess. When The Shah of Iran was here - I don't recollect his name?"

"*Naser-Udin Shah*, Your Majesty," Lord Salisbury said.

"Thank you, Lord Salisbury, yes. He was housed in Buckingham Palace about twenty-two years ago. Dreadful man! The Duke of Cambridge told me the Shah drank straight from teapot's spout!

He completely ignored the cutlery and simply ate with his hands! Above all, he was discourteous!" the Queen declared with a look of repugnance. "I immediately canceled my reception the Shah leaving the Duke and his close courtiers to dine with him. I remember he told me afterward, 'no one could have behaved better or been more dignified whilst at dinner,'" she rolled her eyes. "It was also reported that sheep were slaughtered and skinned in the Palace gardens and the kitchens prepared an entire sheep nightly for the Shah to eat in his room!" The Lords laughed. They had heard most of these stories several times since the visit but they still found it amusing. "Since the Shah was invited by Prime Minister Gladstone," the Queen continued, "I asked the Parliament to pay for the cleaning of the filthy, greasy carpets and to have the rooms redecorated. I hope to goodness we are not going to go through the same ordeal with this young Afghan prince?" She flinched as a sharp stab of pain shot through her leg and fell silent for a moment waiting for it to subside. "He may not like our food, but it would be disgusting to see puddles of blood in Buckingham Palace's grounds!" Turning slightly, she looked out over the bay and watched a flock of pale gray and white terns diving to catch fish. "It must be almost time for their migration to begin," she mused. Briefly, everyone followed her eyes and paused to watch the Kamikaze-style plunge of the birds into the sea. Queen Victoria soon returned to the more important topic of conversation. "Lord Salisbury, where else could the Afghan Prince be housed while he is here?"

"Your Majesty, if I could interject," Lord Bruce said. "The word has already been conveyed that Prince Nasrullah will be staying in Buckingham Palace. It would be difficult to change that so late in the day." He turned his tall frame towards her as he spoke.

"With Your Majesty's permission may I answer the Governor-General?" the Prime Minister asked.

"Please, Lord Salisbury."

"Lord Bruce, I am sure there will be no damage done if we change our minds. This young Prince probably wouldn't be able to tell the difference between a hotel and a palace anyway," Lord Salisbury said frowning darkly.

"It's not simply a question of accommodation, Mr. Prime Minister, it's a matter of diplomacy. Our obligation is to keep the Amir happy, to ensure peace is maintained between the nations. Should we care more about a few greasy carpets in Buckingham Palace than keeping the peace?"

"Your Majesty, I think I may have a solution agreeable to both the Prime Minister and the Governor-General," Major General Falmouth interjected.

"Please explain, Lord Falmouth!" the Queen said.

"Thank you, Your Majesty," he sat back and rested his hands on his cane. "Perhaps the Prince could be accommodated somewhere that has no ties with the palaces, but would be acceptable to all?" He stroked his droopy mustache pensively.

"Where do you have in mind, Lord Falmouth?" the Queen asked.

"How about Dorchester House in Mayfair? I could arrange everything. Prince Nasrullah and his retinue could all be housed there, and it would be less costly to clean than the Buckingham Palace."

"Yes, thank you, Lord Falmouth. That sounds splendid," Queen Victoria said, looking to the others for approval.

"Dorchester House is spacious enough to house them all and its architecture is impressive. I would say it is an excellent solution," Lord Salisbury agreed.

"Hyde Park is right across the street," Lord Falmouth added, "which will allow them the freedom to take a stroll if they so wish. It will restrict them far less than Buckingham Palace."

"Indeed Lord Falmouth," the Queen added thoughtfully. "The Prince may enjoy a tour of Crystal Palace, which is within walking distance of Dorchester House. In fact, Dorchester House is within close reach of all the amusements. Perhaps we should present him with the new portable camera obscura, or even one of Mr. Thomas Edison's Kinetoscopes with an ample supply of Mr. Eastman's reels of film? It would be wonderful for the Amir to have a visual record of his son's visit!"

H.H. Shaikh Hamad bin Isa Al Khalifa King of Bahrain
Riffa Palace, Kingdom of Bahrain

Your Highness,

I write this letter to Your Highness in advance of H.H. Prince Nasrullah's departure from Kabul to London.
Munshi Abdul Karim Khan and I implore Your Highness's assistance to reach out to H.H. Amir Abdul Rahman Khan and H.H. Prince Nasrullah Khan and letting H.H. Nasrullah Khan know to meet with Abdullah Quilliam in Liverpool. Also, it would be of importance not leave London for Kabul unless the Queen agrees to grant H.H. Prince Nasrullah Khan his demand for Afghanistan's foreign policy.
For Your Highness's Information, due to firm Windsor protocol, we have no means to contact H.H. the Amir and H.H. Nasrullah Khan to relay this information.
May Allah be Your Highness's savior.

Sincerely Yours,
Moulvi Rafiuddin Ahmed
London, GB

This was clearly an act of collusion on Rafiuddin and Abdul Karim's part; a dishonest and even treasonous plot hatched up between two of Queen Victoria's most trusted men. Their habitude was inextricably linked to their upbringing, as a betrayal of the Crown in favor of their own cultural and religious background was given higher precedence than the trust placed in them by the most powerful sovereign in the world. The Queen had not only bestowed on Munshi and Rafiuddin everything and more, than they needed, but had given them far higher privilege and stature than most Englishmen could have hoped for. Karim was her teacher, political adviser, and, perhaps most importantly, trusted friend. Munshi's intelligence and his knowledge of Indian culture and politics allowed him to advise the Queen on all matters of the Indian subcontinent.

The Queen believed that Britain brought economic development, the rule of law, and liberties to her colonies. She often told Munshi that colonialism stressed the primacy of human lives, universal values, and shared responsibilities.

"It constitutes a civilizing mission that leads to improvements in living conditions for most people on the Indian subcontinent," she declared repeatedly, "No other colonial power in the history has done more to promote the free movement of goods, capital, and labor than our British Empire." And imposing Western norms of law, order, and governance around the world also appealed to Victoria's matriarchal role over the colonies.

By contrast, both Munshi Abdul Karim and Sir Rafiuiddin took a different view, one they kept to themselves. They questioned why the country of their forefathers was colonized and taxed to produce wealth for the Empire? Why should their Indian brothers shed their blood in support of British wars against other British colonies for the Queen and her empire? Why were India's resources such as precious stones, metals, and other riches, shipped to England to run their industry and economy? If Britain could transform itself from a backward, undemocratic state into a modern industrial power, why could India, or any of Britain's other colonies, not do the same?

The East India Company, the international trade, and opium trafficking business, with headquarters in England, collected taxes in India, and then brilliantly used a fraction of those earnings to finance the purchase of Indian goods for use in England. The Company incurred no costs, it never spent from its pocket at all. Goods were purchased from every level of Indian society, from peasants to goldsmiths, with money that had been taken from them as tax revenue. Secretly Rafiuddin believed and stated that India was governed for the benefit of Great Britain.

The movement to liberate India had already started. The opponents of the empire, like Rafiuddin Ahmad, demanded that equality and liberty be applied to them as well. Afghanistan was seen as the key to eroding the British Empire and bringing about its fall in India. The eyes of Rafiuddin and Munshi Abdul Karim were upon Nasrullah to begin the process without leaving any trace for British intelligence.

Lately, Queen Victoria had withdrawn from social life and even, to a degree, from family. Not everyone could grasp the reasons without knowing the intricacies of her life. Her son, the Crown Prince Bertie's shortcomings were obvious, but chastising the fifty-four-year-old Prince for his numerous affairs and for spending time in brothels was difficult. Apart from what Bertie was doing to degrade the royal family, there were yet other issues within the royal household that were deeply depressing.

Also troubling, was the rise of Islam in Britain. Henry/Abdullah Quilliam's influence was beginning to be felt among all levels of society, but the particular focus was on converting the destitute populace to Islam and money was pouring in for that purpose from every sympathizing Arab Sheik.

"So, I gather from the intelligence you have received, Lords Salisbury and Bruce, that the Amir plans to donate a huge sum of money to Henry Quilliam through Nosroollah?" the Queen commented icily.

"From the report I have received, Your Majesty, the Afghan Prince will be bringing a huge sum of money with him. Some of it appears to be designated for the purchase of machinery and essentials for the Amir's workshop which is presided over by engineer, Mr. Frank Martin." Lord Bruce replied. "Frank Martin is to accompany him on his journey and show him a few industries in England. But from the intelligence I received from Calcutta last month, a large portion of the money will find its way to Henry Quilliam."

"Can we stop the Prince from donating to Quilliam?" Lord Salisbury asked.

"Your Excellency, there are no laws preventing a charitable donation." Lord Bruce replied. "And, by the by, stopping the Afghan Prince would be unwise, Quilliam will receive his donations one way or another." His eyes met the Prime Minister's, "Even if we blocked every donation to Mr. Quilliam, we would face a huge blow-back from the Muslim world. Indeed, it is a gloomy situation, but I guarantee that any attempt to stop Quilliam would be treacherous for us in the long run."

"The name Henry Quilliam never crossed my mind when I approved Nosroollah's invitation," the Queen said in exasperation. "I was neither advised nor did I factor in, the part Quilliam might play in this visit."

"After all, Your Majesty," Lord Falmouth said, "our English subsidies to the Amir also find a way in the hands of opponents who are detrimental not only to our policies but to the British Empire."

Lord Bruce added, "I must say, unfortunately, we can't stop Quilliam from recruiting people to Islam, but as the Good Book says, Madam, 'Refrain from these men and let them alone, for if this work be of men it will come to naught.'"

CHAPTER THIRTY-ONE

Despite the torches flickering everywhere on the Palace premises, pockets of light scarcely illuminated the courtyard where the Amir and Nasrullah were engaged in earnest discussion, the tips of their karakul hats almost touching.

"Son!" Amir's anxious demeanor signaled he was about to convey something of importance. "You'll be on your way tomorrow," His brow furrowed with anxiety. "Don't embarrass me there, I'm counting on you to act wisely and maturely!" he reiterated. "Do not go in there thinking you can fight with a fist and, in the end, fall with no more ammunition in your arsenal. Remember, this is a serious matter. You will be shouldering a huge task, the future of our country is in your hands!" Nasrullah listened intently to his father. "If you ever stall and cannot understand what game to play, seek counsel from your advisers. *Qomandan-e-Ala,* Akram Khan and *Naieb-Salar Sahib*, Hassein Khan. They are the ones to help you." The night was filled with cheerful shouts, music, and applause, but father and son were oblivious to the noise. "I'm not expecting you to approach the *Malika* with timidity," the Amir continued, "but to respectfully and cordially demand the rights of our homeland." His brow creased again, "*Malika* Weektorya is not naive when it comes to matters concerning Afghanistan, she has dealt with your great-grandfather, and great-uncles Sher Ali Khan and Sardar Sahib Wazir Akbar Khan. Both Anglo-Afghan wars happened during her reign."

"You'll be proud of me *Padar* Jan! Your stature will not be diminished, you must have trust in me," Nasrullah answered confidently.

"I'm confident, by the grace of Allah, that you will be back with success." The Amir laced his fingers and rested his hands on top of his bulging belly, "My letter, and our many gifts should be enough to show her our good faith."

"*Padar* Jan, I still don't have faith in *Englees-Ha*," Nasrullah said, revealing the uncertainty that lay just beneath his confident facade. "I am doubting they will deal honestly with us." He leaned back in his chair and dropped his chin on his chest.

"Just leave it to the gracious Allah," Amir declared as he lifted his forefinger to the heavens. "Son, you do your part and Allah will reward you for our good intentions. I am hoping that one day our nation will stand on its own feet and be independent of *Farangees*." He stroked his beard, "I'll pray for your safe return my son."

They were interrupted by courtiers, *Naieb-Salar* Mohammad Hassein Khan, *Qomandan-e-Ala* Akram Khan, and Parwana Khan, all of whom would be leaving with Nasrullah early the following morning, requesting dismissal for the night.

Both, *Naieb-Salar* Hassein and *Qomandan-e-Ala* Akram readied themselves for a heel-clicking salute as they prepared to pay their respects to the Amir. They stood erect and their posture was correct, chins up, chests out, shoulders back, and, supposedly, stomachs in. But it was not the case with *Naieb-Salar* Hassein, as his belly stuck out like a watermelon. They synchronously lifted their right hands, palms down, fingertips touching temples in a salute and an audible click of their heels as they held the dangling sabers attached to their belts. Their right hands dropped down at once, middle fingers parallel to the seams of their dark-brown trousers. As they saluted, *Qomandan-e-Ala* Akram Khan's thick spectacles slid to the tip of his nose and he hastily pushed them back.

Nasrullah glanced at Habibullah, his brief sarcastic smile was tantamount to a wink or a nudge in the ribs.

"Looking good *Naieb-Salar Sahib*, and *Qomandan Sahib*, you'll make us proud in *Englistaan!*" the Amir said with the delicacy of a lilac bud but as sharp as a cut-throat razor.

"Nasrullah," the Amir said, "only you, *Qomandan-e-Ala* Akram Khan, or *Colonel* Zalmai Khan, are to inspect the guard of honor in Qasr-e-Weenzor." He indicated to the chamberlain to hand him his water goblet. "I don't want us to look like fools and be ridiculed." He met *Naieb-Salar* Hassein's embarrassed glance, "My dear friend, Hassein Khan," the Amir said soothingly. He took a sip of water from his goblet, "You never left me during the worst days of my life when I was exiled in Samarkand, we've made it through the vicissitudes of life together, but time has arrived for us to pass the baton to these young men to carry our responsibilities. These drills of salutation are not for you, or me, anymore."

Naieb-Salar Hassein Khan grew still and gazed absently down at his highly polished boots. "Yes, Your Highness, that time has passed for us. I thank you for allowing me to accompany *Shahzadah* Nasrullah Khan to *Egnlistaan*." He lifted his rugged hand in a brief salute and asked, "Permission to be dismissed, Your Highness."

"You all can be dismissed except for *Kotwal Sahib*, Parwana Khan," the Amir replied. He ordered his chamberlain to fetch Doctor Hamilton and Hakim Jon Mohammad for a private meeting.

As everybody retreated, he waved his entrusted Mayor of Kabul to a seat, "I'm sending you with Nasrullah for only one reason," the Amir scanned the surrounding area, to ensure no one was eavesdropping. "Keep an eye on everyone. Just as I have given you full authority in your daily responsibilities as the *Kotwal*, Chief of Police, the same purview will fall on you during the voyage. Nasrullah is first in the line of authority, then *Qomandan-e-Ala* Akram Khan, then *Naieb-Salar* Hassein Khan. But you will be the adviser to all those I named. For the rest, you have the highest supremacy, even if you deem right to toss a culprit into the sea."

"*Alahazrat-e-Muazam*, Your Highness." Parwana Khan said. "You

are the shadow of Allah, your order is the order of the Almighty."
He clapped a hand to his chest." *Pa dowarlo stergo*, with utmost
attention!" he said in Pashtu, and raised his hands to his eyebrows
symbolically assuring the Amir or his intention to fulfill the order to
the utmost.

As usual, the Hakim was wearing a long black robe, a tightly
wrapped turban, and curly-pointed shoes. As he bowed and mumbled
a salaam, the Amir pointed to the seat next to Parwana Khan.

"Sit there!" he ordered. The Hakim's heart thudded with dread as
he glanced from the Amir to his executioner.

Within minutes, Dr. Hamilton arrived and, holding her long
rustling silk dress, curtsied to the Amir.

"Your Highness."

She nodded cordially to Parwana Khan and the Hakim.

The Hakim set his hand on his chest, gave a brief nod, and laced
his long fingers.

The Amir softly tapped the arm of the chair signaling Lillias to sit,
"*Befarmayed*, please, Daktar Laila Jan."

The jubilant sounds of the crowd faded into the background.
Despite the happiness of this special occasion, the Amir's attitude
was solid, resolute, blunt, and demanding. His gaze flitted over the
Hakim and said sharply, "Hakim Jon Mohammad, I appointed you
as the royal Hakim because I saw a glimpse of worthiness in you!"
He glared. "I had hoped that you would not follow in the footsteps of
your predecessors . . . remember the one tossed in the *Sia-Chal*, black-
well, in Bala-Hisar? The vultures left his bones?"

The Hakim shrank down in his robe, as he felt the cold touch of
death shrivel his very being. His eyes focused on the points of his
shoes.

"Do you recall the other *ahmaq*, idiot, who mislead people with
his fake sex potion?"

"Yes, Your Highness," he whispered submissively.

"Let me ask you something. Do you object if Daktar Laila Jan makes medical decisions for me and the rest of the royal household?" he snapped.

"*Alahazrat-e-Muazam*, Your Highness," His crinkled face showed deathly pale in the uncertain light from the torches. "As Your Highness's Hakim, should I not also have a say in the status of your health?"

"Stop your stupid arrogance! Do you imagine you are the best *tabib*, physician, in the whole wide world? How foolish can you be to imagine yourself above a Daktar?" he gestured towards Dr. Hamilton. "She was able to help me recover so quickly from my deathbed when she came here! Your so-called *tababat*, medical practice, prescribed every herb in the world and none cured me!" the Amir shouted. "Let me make this clear, your service as a Palace Hakim will be revoked followed by a severe punishment if you ever compare yourself to Daktar Laila Jan." He turned towards Parwana Khan, "*Kotwal Sahib*," he said, "you are a witness to this, Hakim Jon Mohammad is no longer accompanying you and the rest to *Englistan* tomorrow."

Parwana Khan nodded, "At Your Highness's *farman*, edict," he replied.

The Amir turned back to the Hakim, " Hakim Jon Mohammad," he said calmly, "you will remain at Arg Palace for the time being and prescribe and provide the *Unani* herbs, but one step out of line, and you will face the same fate as your predecessor, is it understood?"

"Yes, Your Highness," the Hakim replied meekly. Silence drifted among them like night fog, each one engaged with his thoughts.

The Amir stared at him intently. "Whatever you packed for the journey you can go and unpack right now, and remember my words. *Kotwal* Parwana Khan is my witness."

"Your Highness's order is Allah's order," Parwana Khan replied. There was a malicious glint in his eye and a twisted smile on his face as his gaze rested on the unfortunate Hakim.

CHAPTER THIRTY-TWO

❧✿❧✿❧

Thursday, April 8, 1895 -- Afghan calendar month:
Hamal 19, 1274

Kabul, Afghanistan

It was early morning when the travelers gathered to depart for England. The unsettled state of the weather had diminished Nasrullah's wanderlust. Heavy thunder and rain had kept most of the aspirant travelers awake the previous night and now the sky was gloomy and overcast. Just an hour before they were due to leave, a vicious hail storm hit Kabul, stripping the blossom from almost every fruit tree. It lasted only a few minutes but whitened the ground with golf-ball-sized hailstones, which thawed almost immediately. Despite the gray skies and chilly weather, Kabul's inhabitants were eager to bid their prince farewell outside the Palace gate.

Two cavalries of royal guards, Uzbeks, and Durani-Pashtuns, were to escort Nasrullah and his entourage through the one-hundred-eighty-mile rugged terrain across the Khyber Pass to Peshawar. In ten days they were expected to board the British Government's chartered train to Karachi.

At the palace gate, Colonel Zalmai Khan ensured that his armed guards were fully equipped with their Martini-Henry rifles and the essentials to ensure a safe journey across the mountains. The men were dressed in baggy corduroy trousers, knee-high boots, and tunics with crimson and white trimmings. On their heads, the Uzbeks wore gray felt jockey caps strapped under their chins. The Durani-Pashtuns had their heads well-wrapped in black turbans with the flaps wrapped around their faces. Two logistical companies with required essentials had left two days earlier to set up tents and prepare food for the night stops.

On this inclement Spring morning, everyone prepared to mount their horses. Their toes were numb and their teeth chattered. Everyone from the royal household had come to say farewell to their loved ones. The British ladies bade farewell to the ladies of the Harem-Sarai, kissing each other's cheeks three times. Sobs from the Harem ladies broke to the surface like bubbles of air from a percolating spring.

The charming couple, Thomas and Elizabeth Clemence who had stood by each other for years bade adieu to one another once more. Veterinarian Thomas was the only British national in the Amir's employ to stay behind.

Thomas Clemence removed his pipe from his mouth, "I wish you a safe trip home, Elizabeth."

"I'll miss you, Thomas," Mrs. Clemence replied and kissed him on the lips. Suddenly, in a moment of passionate sweetness, Thomas embraced and kissed his wife intertwining their souls in a way that perpetuated the eternal bond between them.

Observing this passionate display, the shocked Harem-Sarai ladies froze as if caught in a still photo, never having seen such an intimate spousal interaction publicly. Any sign of public affection was culturally inappropriate in Afghanistan and the ladies soaked it up like blotting paper; that moment would be ingrained in their minds for as long as they lived.

A young Mullah holding a Qur'an above his head ensured that every member of Nasrullah's entourage passed underneath and so be blessed with safe travel. One by one they passed beneath the sacred book and many brushed away a tear.

Nasrullah approached his father's wheelchair, bowed down, and touched his feet.

"I will see you, Father," he said, "with the grace of Allah."

The Amir blessed his son, asked him to draw close, and kissed his cheek, "*Insha Allah*, son, I pray for your safe return and a successful outcome in *Englistan*. Remember, be very cordial and humble to *Malika* Weektorya."

"I promise to hand you the gift you have longed for," Nasrullah replied, "*Khoda Hafez,* Father."

The brothers embraced and held each other at arm's length, "Be well, brother!" Habibullah said. He looked him directly in the eyes, "I truly wish you success in your trip. Our hopes are on you." His face lit up with an engaging smile.

"*Insha Allah*, Brother." Nasrullah planted a kiss on his cheek. "Count on me. I promise not to return home empty-handed." He turned to go, "I'll surprise you with how *Malika* Weektorya will be convinced to hand us full independence!"

Habibullah's lips parted in astonishment at hearing Nasrullah's temerity, "I've nothing else to say, but to pray."

Nasrullah tapped him on the shoulder, "*Khoda Hafez*, be well, brother!" He took Baarfi's reins from the groom and vaulted onto his horse. The horse's bright white mane stood upright, its whispy ends twisted gaily and he lifted his tail gracefully, like a flag. The immaculate beast with its balanced equine head looked more than ready to carry Nasrullah across the mountains and deserts.

Elizabeth Clemence, Charlotte Martin, Olivia Worth, and Roma Hamilton approached the Amir to bid their farewell. They lowered their eyes and curtsied with well-rehearsed submissiveness.

"I shall return to serve Your Highness and the royal household," Dr. Hamilton assured him sincerely. "The Indian doctor and nurses will look after Your Highness with great attentiveness while I'm away."

"I have full confidence in you Daktar Laila Jan. I wish you a safe trip."

Roma Hamilton and Olivia mounted their mares. Roma was wearing a classic safari dress, fashionable and conspicuously voguish; a Khaki skirt and blouse, with knee-high leather boots. A mosquito screen draped from her cloth pith helmet, and a pair of binoculars hung from her neck. Olivia wore a similar outfit to Roma's but hers was teal in color. Lillias and other ladies were sensibly turned out in uniform warm twill traveling attire; ankle-length skirts and jackets with puffy shoulders, durable shoes, and stout gloves; Lillias sported a chic bonnet for the occasion and the others wore caps set at a jaunty angle. Off they trotted as the weeping women of the Harem threw water behind their horses from all manner of receptacles, as they wished them safe travels.

"May your journey be free of mishaps my son, my beloved Nasrullah," Gulrez cried out, dabbing her tearful eyes with her headscarf. She tossed water from a pewter mug in the wake of Nasrullah's horse, accidentally splashing him and Baarfi at the same time.

"May God curse you!" Queen Sultana snapped, her eyes narrowed with contempt. "Can't you even throw water properly?"

The Queen was wearing a voluminous dress in a shade of violet so dark that it almost appeared to be black. To offset the impression that she was in mourning, stunning emeralds dangled from her ears, a string of black pearls hung over her bosom, and a precious agate brooch was pinned beneath the ruff at her neck. To complete the effect, she held a crocheted black parasol.

"You are stuck in your benighted world of superstition!" She gestured with an arrogant sweep of her hand, "But of course, having an obtuse mind like yours, you would wet the horse and rider together!"

The Queen stepped out behind the horse General Akram Khan was riding with her son, Prince Omar, "Flow as smooth as water with a safe return. Good luck my beloved son. May you be in Allah's protection." At that moment of separation, the Queen's agony was palpable. Tears ran down her face as she watched her son leave. She gestured to the hired *Saqow*, the water carrier carrying a *mashk*, a fifteen-gallon goat-skin water bag on his back, to splash the ground behind the horses.

"*Bakhair bya yee*, may you return with no harm," the Amir shouted, struggling up from his wheelchair. He leaned on his cane squinting to bring into focus the blurry image of Nasrullah and his horse. Then he waved at young Prince Omar, reverently lifting his hands. "*Allah* lives in the heavens and rain is his tears," he cried out. "Splash more of the Almighty's tears behind the *Mosaferereen*, itinerants, who will be missed. With the grace of *Allah* may you return safely." His voice was beginning to weaken with the effort and he sat down again. "Look after my sons! he called out as Dr. Hamilton and Frank Martin passed. "May Allah be with you all!" With a circular motion of his head, he intoned more verses from the Qur'an. At that moment, with his frail health, he was unsure if he would see any of them again knowing dying was as natural as living.

"Splash more water," he said almost to himself, "it will bring them health, purity, heavenly good, and power. Stay well, my sons."

Outside the gate, hundreds of Kabulis and courtiers lined the route, waving their hands and shouting cheerfully and offering incessant prayers for Nasrullah's safe return.

Some miles further on, the dirt road that stretched out ahead of Nasrullah and his entourage narrowed. On both sides of the muddy road, hundreds of common people queued to extend their blessings to Nasrullah. Guns roared out from the adjacent hills in quick succession like a summer thunderstorm; a salute on the departure of their Prince. The members of Nasrullah's entourage snaked through the cheering crowd along the road to Jalalabad. Marshal Hassein Khan, General Akram Khan, the Amir's executioner, the Royal Mullah, the secretary, the Chief of Logistics, and others rode proudly behind Nasrullah, waving, bowing, with a hand on their hearts.

The single rutted narrow road snaked down the towering, scree-sloped mountains to a wide lush valley adjoining British India's frontier. From the high pass, looking down on the road below, it resembled a gray ribbon over the highlands until, eventually, it vanished into the horizon where the earth met the vast sky.

Along the mountainous climb, they followed the tumbling Kabul River. At one point, it dropped into a waterfall of some fifty feet, and fish swimming upstream, scaled the cliff face against the misty torrent, making their journey into the mountainous streams and tributaries to spawn. As they thrust forward along the river road, the Amir's escort guards, under the command of Lieutenant Colonel Zalmai Khan, were constantly vigilant, scanning behind boulders and rocks in case of a surprise ambush on the Prince, his entourage, and accompanying guests. They were armed with matchlocks and Armstrong machine guns and trained in Morse code. Every seven miles, they received transmissions via reflected flashes of a mirror from the reconnaissance party ahead of them confirming the caravan was safe to move forward.

As they neared the mountain pass gorge, everyone was called to dismount. Then one by one, they walked their horses along a narrow a rutted path with the mountain on one side and a sheer drop of hundreds of feet on the other. Incoming caravans halted about three miles ahead waiting for the trail to clear and ensure no person or beast fell to their death. The terrain was utterly inhospitable, both animals and travelers were prone to attacks of acrophobia on that route, fearing the abrupt finality of death. Faced with that precarious path, the English ladies murmured prayers that their lives, and the lives of the others, might be spared such a calamitous end.

The history associated with this mountain pass when more than sixteen-thousand British soldiers were brutally massacred, during the first Anglo-Afghan war fifty-three years before, still haunted the British members of the party. William Brydon, a doctor, was the only survivor to reach Jalalabad to report the gruesome news to his fellow men. Nasrullah delighted in repeating the story to Frank, who did not need to be reminded. "Thousands perished except for a dying doctor," Nasrullah declared happily, "Daktar Bareedoon."

"England always remembers the unnecessary loss of lives," was Frank Martin's sober reply, "It was a lesson that we British learned the hard way."

Nasrullah encouraged Baarfi forward by a gentle movement of the reins as he walked the Arab beast behind him on the treacherous path. "By the grace of *Allah*," Nasrullah assured him, "times are much different from when Eleephantstone passed through here." His words were accompanied by the crunching of pebbles under the hooves of their horses. "You *Englees-Ha* should thank my father for stopping the hostility towards you all. Now you can travel freely around the country without any violence. *Insha-Allah*, we'll have a safe journey."

"Of course," Frank replied dismissively.

They had reached the end of the three-mile mountainous corridor. Sighs of relief were heard as each person arrived safely on the other side.

"Thank God there were no fatalities," Olivia said as she gulped water from her canteen.

They passed the multiple *Kochi*, nomad, caravans, and other travelers who had been halted for Nasrullah's convoy to clear the narrow passage. The *Kochi* caravans included a mix of sturdy humped, shaggy-haired camels carrying hefty loads. Afghan nomads were masters in improving the appearance of their transportation animals and adorned their beasts with bridles of bright crimson, cyan, charcoal, and ashen beads, some were festooned with bells and various ornamental objects. Each *Kochi* family owned at least one camel, and their children thrashed the camels with knotted branches, shrieking loudly to keep the grunting and spitting creatures on the rutted path. Wooden carriers akin to crates and padded with sheepskins hung suspended on either side of the camels' humps and little children were cozily tucked inside them. Their small bobbing heads swayed from side to side with every step the camels took. These ships of the desert would have been like galleons adrift had they not been strung to one another and led by a herder. One beast, emitting a low gurgling sound, displayed his soft palate filled with air which protruded from the side of his mouth like a foot-long pink balloon. Foam bubbled and dripped from his mouth, informing the lady camels, I'm hot to trot. Another ship of the desert urinated on his tail, spraying his pee by using his tail like a fan to attract a mate with his urine's female-attracting pheromones.

The buzz of activity in a nearby *caravanserai* drew Nasrullah's immediate attention. A vast crowd was clustered like a swarm of bees at the entrance to a compound. It was a huge square structure with high walls of stone and a tall semi-circular tower erected at each of its corners. It resembled a fort from the Bactrian days and provided overnight accommodation and protection for travelers and their animals. From the cheering and whooping, it sounded as though something akin to a gladiator fight was taking place.

Nasrullah halted his caravan in a crisscross of caravans from all directions. Clouds of dust arose as people made their way towards the *caravanserai*.

"What's the hubbub about?" he asked a bystander holding the reins of his lead camel. The grubby *Kochi* was clad in flowing tattered robes and the rims of his eyes were blackened with *kohl*. The henna-stained tendrils of his hair hung from under his stained black turban.

"*Salamoona Shahzadah Sahib* Nasrullah Khana. May Allah bring you back safely from *Englistan*," He spoke rapidly, "There's an event .

. . a camel fight!" He clutched the reins of his camel as the sturdy beast tugged impatiently. "*Shahzadah* Nasrullah Khan, your enjoyment of such an event is known to all. Go and be entertained!"

Curious onlookers had begun to gather around Nasrullah and immediately his security guards moved in to protect him.

"Let the man come forward," he ordered. The mere thought of a camel fight caused his heart to soar.

"How did you know I enjoyed such entertainment?" Nasrullah asked.

"*Grana Shahzadah*! Beloved Shahzadah!" the *Kochi* replied in the Pashtu tongue. "Such news travels quickly, *Masjet-Pa-Masjet*, Mosque-to-Mosque, *karawan-pa-karawan*, caravan-to-caravan, they are all intertwined like spiders' webs throughout the country." All Narullah's boredom for this stage of the journey was dispelled in an instant at the thought of amusement.

"You will enjoy watching this fight, *Shahzadah* Nasrullah *Khana*," the man assured him. "The mating season is about to end and it will be ferocious!" He flashed a smile revealing many gaps between teeth. "The males are far more aggressive than any other time. I would be divested if one of my female camels was there. It will be a bloodbath between the males. You'll remember the *jang-e-shotor*, camel fight, for as long as you live."

Nasrullah needed no further persuasion. He beckoned to the rest of the caravan, "Let's join them," he shouted, "this will be entertaining!"

Frank Martin, riding double with his son, William, rode across and faced Nasrullah. "Your Highness, we have no time for this, we must move on as quickly as possible."

"Maarteen Sahib! A brief camel fight won't hurt . . . let's make this a memorable trip."

"Let's watch the fight," shrilled Prince Omar Jan, riding double with his cousin, General Akram Khan. The General gently tugged his hand to silence him.

Little William turned his head and pleaded, "Please, Father, let's watch the fight."

Dr. Hamilton had moved her horse to where she was within earshot and caught the drift of the conversation. "Your Highness," she said, removing her bonnet, "We have a train to catch in Peshawar, a steamer in Karachi, then a troopship in Bombay, everything is carefully scheduled, time is of the essence."

"I promise, it won't be long," Nasrullah replied airily. He led the entourage to the *caravanserai*, where the roaring and cheering increased in volume. The air smelt like dung. Herds of bleating sheep and goats were grazing alongside the rutted path leading to the compound. Lieutenant Colonel Zalmai Khan and his security guards pushed ahead of the entourage to clear the way for Nasrullah and his companions to view the contest. The massive gate attached with heavy chains and festooned with metal spikes swung wide open and clouds of dust rose from under the hooves as the Prince and his entourage clattered under the pointed blue-tiled arch into the courtyard, the mounted lancers and security guards flanked alongside. A brittle silence descended upon the crowded *caravanserai* and people scattered before the powerful horses. Everyone's head turned towards the Prince except for the two ornately decorated and fiercely tussling beasts. Names were painted on each camel, "*Wahshee*, Wild" and "*Badmash*, Hooligan". Each was trying to pin the other's head to the ground, while their turbaned handlers ran around them, both wishing for a glorifying outcome for his camel. As Nasrullah's guards cordoned off the area, spectators were shoved back under covered walkways resembling monastic cloisters, behind which were the stables and storage rooms. Other spectators stood on the staircases leading to the upper floor with similar ringed walkways leading off into sleeping quarters for travelers. There too, tightly packed against the rickety birch-wood handrails that could fail against their lateral force, plunging them headlong onto spectators below, astounded onlookers watched the sudden invasion of the event. As one camel subdued the another, the level of cheering and yelling was muted to a less enthusiastic murmur of assent. Fear of Amir Abdul Rahman's despotic regime chilled the spectators like the shadow of a dark cloud.

From the very outset of the camel fight, the beasts' pantings and groanings did not cease, and, their aggressiveness was heightened in direct proportionality to their levels of testosterone. Winning bids had already been set, varying from an animal to a sack of grain; anything of reasonable value.

Wahshee tried nipping at *Badmash's* legs and *Badmash* retaliated using his whole weight to push back *Wahshee*. *Wahshee* staggered, lost his balance, and lay motionless on the hard earth, almost invisible through the clouds of dust. Suddenly, regaining his strength, *Wahshee* struggled back to his feet and, face-to-face with *Badmash*, the two animals sized each other up. Both shook their massive heads, saliva spurting in all directions. Streaks of the spittle splattered the handlers and those standing nearby. The beasts threw themselves head-to-head. *Wahshee* went for his foe's feet in an attempt to topple him. The crowd murmured as suddenly the camel's long necks interlocked like pretzels. There were a few jubilant cheers and Nasrullah followed suit. The handlers dragged on their ropes attempting to separate the camels before one was killed, but it was too late to stop the giant beasts. The two men fought to avoid getting between them knowing their ability to move surprisingly swiftly, especially when their necks were locked in a double helix. *Badmash* bit into *Wahshee's* neck with massive force inflicting very serious wounds. In the next move, *Badmash* tripped *Wahshee* and threw him off balance causing him to fall again. He fell on top *Wahshee* breaking his right leg before whacking him to death with cushion-like feet, equivalent to the sturdiest boxing gloves ever used in a prizefight. *Wahshee* no longer moved. Multiple handlers whacked the winning beast and removed him from the scene. The game came to an end with the roaring cries of *Wahshee* in pain, and, immediately, a ritual Islamic slaughter was carried out in the lawful halal manner.

"*Bismillah!* In the name of God!" A swift, deep incision with a curved sharp knife on *Wahshee's* throat severed the windpipe and arteries. Blood spurted out like a dark red spring. Three butchers set about cutting up the carcass with muttered prayers and called it sacrificial meat.

Wahshee's handler cried out to the destitute, "Oh people! Form a line and wait for your sacrificial meat. This was a demonstration of submission to Allah the Almighty. May he accept our good intentions to distribute this amongst you." In an impressively short time, the meat was divided amongst those who might not consume meat again for another year

As Nasrullah and his entourage left, Frank Martin led the way, "Your Highness," he rebuked the Prince in a quiet voice, "this was unnecessary time lost that will impact our arrival at the border."

Nasrullah failed to recognize the thievery of time that could not be regained. This reckless trait would ultimately result in severe consequences. Failing to observe the importance of time would prove to be an added hindrance to achieving the goal his father expected of him.

CHAPTER THIRTY-THREE

❧❧❧

Thursday, April 14, 1895 -- Afghan calendar month:
Hamal 25, 1274
Somewhere in Eastern Afghanistan.

AS Nasrullah's caravan passed through narrow gorges and towering mountains, villages come into sight. Picturesque mud-colored buildings lined the green valleys, and the afternoon sun cast shadows on their smooth dung-plastered walls. The distinct odor of burning dung from hearths and kilns drifted in the warm breeze.

On occasions, Colonel Zalmai Khan galloped the length of the column, from the beginning to end, ensuring that nothing was out of the ordinary. He convivially asked members of the entourage and the English ladies if they were experiencing a difficult trip so far. As he passed by Roma he met her eye, nodded, and covertly handed her a note. The scabbed cut on his face was clearly visible.

"Only for your eyes," he murmured and urged his horse to a trot. As he left her side Roma unfolded the scrap of paper. *Hope to see you at the stop tonight*, she read and immediately crumpled it in her palm.

"Anything *Passionnante*?" Olivia asked with a smile, having witnessed the brief interchange.

"Nothing of importance," Roma responded vaguely.

"L'amour est dans l'air, love's in the air." She brushed away the persistent flies that seemed to latch onto their faces for hours on end.

"At the moment just friendship, Olivia."

"Ahhh! L'amour. It begins with friendship," she smiled. "*Bel homme*, handsome, any woman would fall for him."

"He's a kind man and caring."

"*Oui, ma chere*," says Olivia. "Why a cut on his face? Did he fight someone?"

"Something happened the other day. I still need to find out."

Amir's hangman, Parwana Khan, had his hawkish eye on the Colonel like a cat watching a mouse.

"I was given the task to ensure you are fully engaged in protecting everyone safely," he said with just a hint of menace in his tone. The tassel on his Astrakhan hat swayed like a pendulum as he rode alongside Colonel Zalmai Khan.

"No need to worry, *Kotwal Sahib*, I'll perform my duties virtuously and with due caution. I assure you, I will do my best to keep everyone safe on this journey," Zalmai Khan answered with an aloof expression and wondered how he would manage to avoid him throughout the journey. But Parwana Khan had no intention of disappearing.

Zalmai gazed at the village they were passing where turbaned men sat crossed-legged on *kilims* sipping tea on the decks of crowded teahouses.

"Just remember, Zalmai Khan, everybody's life is in your hands . . . but yours is in mine." Parwana Khan flashed a cunning smile and galloped to the front of the caravan to join Nasrullah.

Across from the teahouses, at a small bazaar; goods, grains, and animals were being bartered. Under a weeping willow tree close to the road, men stood shoulder to shoulder on a huge straw mat cheering a pair of quails as the bobbing birds frantically fought each other. Their heads were lowered and the plumage around their outstretched necks stood erect as they parried warily. The quails eyed each other menacingly circling cautiously around one another then both rushed headlong at one another and sprang into the air. The air erupted with the collision of stiffened feathers as each quail attempted to thrust the other to the ground. Nasrullah stopped to take a closer look at the action bringing the caravan to a halt behind him. The quails, in the meantime, were fighting furiously, plucking each other to their last feathers.

As the locals became aware of Nasrullah's presence, their heads turned toward the Prince, bowing and raising their hands and seeking the Almighty to grant him long life and safe return. Once again, Nasrullah was like a child in an amusement park until Frank Martin and Lillias Hamilton stepped in and urged him back on the road.

The caravan train stretched some two-and-half miles. They had traveled forty-eight miles and had taken over six hours from the previous night's stop. The continuous clatter of the horses' hooves and the impact on their bodies from the rough ride over the rutted track had left the riders exhausted and feeling like soldiers who just retreated from a battle. The weariness and exhaustion also showed from the horses' slumped gait, necks drooping and swaying wearily from side to side. After six days of traveling, the caravan was nearing the city of Jalalabad and, finally, British India's frontier, the Khyber Pass.

In preparation for the caravan's night stops, the two companies of men, the cooks, and helpers traveled ahead of one another to set up the camps in two different overnight areas. Mules and camels, laden with tents, carpets, bedding, food, samovars, pots, pans, hookahs, chessboards, straw-woven cages of squawking chickens—in short, all the odds and ends needed for the camp.

From the crest of a hill, about two miles from *Surkhroad*, the Red River, they spotted the rising smoke and the pitched canvases scattered under groves of red willow and evergreen trees. Many of the road-ravaged travelers emitted sighs of relief.

"There's our night stop!" Frank Martin said tapping William's shoulder.

William beamed with delight and shrieked the news to Prince Omar, who was still riding with his cousin, General Akram Khan.

A feeling of contentment ran through Roma and she scanned the encampment from a distance, wondering where the rendezvous with Zalmai would take place. A huge sugarcane plantation skirted the north of the encampment like a verdant green sash and she contemplated the possibility of hiding there.

Lillias constantly advised both men and women to eat and drink to sustain themselves as they endured the harsh conditions while they were traveling. "Avoid dehydration and drink plenty of water," she said. "You cannot afford to get sick. The caravan will not wait for you to recover!"

The ladies, however, consumed minimal drink and food to avoid having to relieve themselves too often; their urinary leash dictated how far they could go before their bladders demanded respite and their long dresses and undergarments were a hindrance.

To urinate while on the move, the Afghan men would discreetly squat behind a bolder or a tree to relieve themselves, but the English ladies had a different solution.

"Time to pee," muttered Roma.

"Likewise," Olivia agreed.

They quietly bore off to the side of the rutted trail allowing the rest of the caravan to move forward.

"Will you keep a secret, Olivia?" Roma reached into her saddlebag to find her bourdaloue.

"*Bien sûr.*" Olivia replied, as she followed suit and retrieved the same ergonomically designed porcelain pee vessel from her belongings.

"I need your help," Roma said as she tucked the vessel firmly into place between her legs.

"Something to do with Zalmai, am I right?"

"Yes," she admitted, "I can't hide anything from you!" she laughed. "have a rendezvous with him, he wants to meet me tonight," she glanced at her friend to judge her response to this confession. She relieved herself, removed the bourdaloue, and tossed the urine away. "Could you cover for me if anyone asks for me while I'm away?"

"Count on me, Roma, *ma chérie*. I'll do my best to look out for you." She smiled as she put her bourdaloue back in the saddlebag. "But *mon chéri*," she warned, "be on the lookout for the Prince and that *méchant* crossed-eye one."

"I will, I am terrified when they are around! I cannot thank you enough for helping me."

"So, you said it was friendship, but you would not risk so much if that was so!" Olivia said, "I think you have fallen in love with Zalmai."

"I don't know," she mounted her horse and rode ahead of Olivia. "This is the first time that I have experienced such a deep feeling of contentment with a man. It's as if space and time stand still when he's around." She half-turned her body in the saddle to look back at Olivia, "I feel safe around him."

"*Très bien*," Olivia flashed a gentle smile, "Maybe you have found your knight in shining armor."

At the camp that night, Lillias, Roma, Olivia, and the Martins' sat on their folding Curule chairs around the campfire. The night brought an enchanting silence broken only by the crackling from the fire pit, gurgling from the two large brass samovars nearby, and the more distant rushing of the *Sorkhroad* River as it tumbled against boulders and rocks on its downward journey.

"I'm not convinced that the Afghans will remember their table manners," Doctor Hamilton said worriedly, her hands clasped around a steaming mug of tea. She was tired and bleary-eyed. "Perhaps we should make more effort to practice before we get to England. Tomorrow's breakfast . . . "

"I've noticed something about Afghans," Frank Martin interjected.

"When a factory worker is trained, others push themselves to learn by impersonating," he crossed one leg over the other, knees apart. "The Afghan learns by mimicry, but with a couple of caveats—one," he raised his forefinger, "they never understand how something functions. Two: they are fearless as lions and never worry about the consequences." He took a sip of his tea, "Training at the factory using machinery is dangerous with that mentality, and could result in a severed finger, or even a limb. But training using utensils is safe and nothing to worry about. Let us focus on training one or two and the rest will follow."

Charlotte Martin nodded and smiled, "The flock will follow the lead ewe," she said. William was cozily tucked up on her lap and beginning to fall asleep.

"We cannot let this go without constant practice," Dr. Hamilton reiterated drowsily, "I don't want any embarrassment at Windsor Palace."

Frank Martin removed his dust-covered safari pith helmet and set it on his knee. " He lifted his mug to the turbaned page for a refill. "We have three weeks on board the troopship to practice with them. Also, why not let Nasrullah and General Akram Khan lead the way? The rest may not even be part of Windsor's dining hall event."

"Frank, I love your idea," Lillias said. "Let's keep it simple and have the two of them practice." The wood fire was blazing cheerily casting red reflections on her dusty face and clothing, "I'm leading the kitchen crew tomorrow to prepare spinach omelet, roast chicken, porridge, toast, and jam for breakfast. We can put them both to a test then."

The pageboys moved around the little group warming up everyone's mug with freshly brewed tea. Some carried trays of sweetmeats to offer everyone. As Roma stretched out her mug for a refill, the pageboy poured her tea with one hand, and with the other, he covertly handed her a note. Roma unfolded the small piece of paper and it read,

Hope to see you near the sugarcane at midnight.

Roma's exhausted face changed slightly, her eyelids fluttered and her gaze moved to the crackling fire. She tightened the palm of her hand around the note, and her quiet smile was like a knife mark on fresh dough.

Roma, Olivia, and Lillias were sharing the same tent. They slipped into their nightgowns, loosened and brushed their hair, and put on their satin nightcaps.

"Good night Roma, good night, Olivia," Lillias called sleepily. She blew out the oil lamp and tucked herself up in the blanket. Roma and Olivia replied with their goodnight calls, but both lay wide awake.

Roma had her Elgin pocket-watch next to her. Once she was sure that Lillias was sound asleep, she opened the gold-plated case and squinted to see the time, but it was pitch dark in the tent. *What if night patrol questions me strolling this late at night? What if Nasrullah finds out?* Every nerve in her body was as taut as a steel spring, but the thought of seeing Zalmai winged her hope. She slowly climbed off the *charpaie*, making sure the cot did not rattle or squeak, opened the tent flap, and stepped outside. She could just make out the time now, it was a quarter to twelve. She was trembling with fear and excitement. Olivia joined her at the entrance of the tent and Roma gently took her hand.

"I'll look out for you, have no concern," Olivia whispered.

Roma stepped out, raised the hem of her gown, and tiptoed towards the sugarcane. Silhouetted hands waved, then beckoned.

"Zalmai!" she called softly. A sharp breeze had begun to whip up causing waves to pass across the sugarcane field and the sound was soothing, almost reassuring.

"Roma!" he took her hand and drew her into the cane field after him. Knowing they were concealed from the watchful eyes of Amir's executioner and informants, they turned to face one another.

Zalmai was holding a twig of orange blossoms, "For you," he said. She inhaled the almost intoxicating perfume of the flowers.

"Thank you!" Roma was euphoric but nervous. "Are we safe here?"

"I have coached a few of my patrolling men. They are trustworthy, no one will bother us." His calmness, anchored in his quiet self-confidence, gave Roma comfort, and she began to relax. They rested quietly in each other's arms for a long moment and then Roma tilted her face to his.

"What did Nasrullah do to you on the farewell night at Arg Palace?" she asked. Her eyes appraised and touching the small welt on his face.

"Nothing serious, just a rebuke," Zalmai replied.

"Just for being with me?" Roma knew the question sounded naïve, she had not forgotten Nasrullah's menacing tone when he questioned her during his fitting.

"I was warned not to roam too close to you ladies."

"Is it a crime?"

"It depends who in Amir's family adjudicates the so-called infraction." He leaned towards her, resting his face against her hair. In his mind, he replayed the threat and the abuse, as he had many times since that night. He lost sleep and had not found it easy to rest or eat in the days that followed knowing he was not irreplaceable and that his superiors would not hesitate to take his life by the cruelest of means if they thought that death was warranted. Zalmai also had no desire to cause animosity between the Amir's family and the British in his employ, especially Roma's adored sister, Dr. Hamilton.

"I was worried about you, Zalmai, but I knew, if I had stayed, it would have made things worse. Whatever happened, it's behind us. Let's look forward," she said reassuringly. Her mouth twitched in a tiny smile. She placed the palm of her hand on his chest, "I think your resolute calmness with Nasrullah served you well," she tucked a tendril of her hair behind her ear. "Stay that way. Don't let him destroy our hopes."

Her long hair had escaped from under her nightcap and was caught in a sudden gust of wind. It was well past midnight, and a strong breeze from the North swept across the unripe sugarcane. The clouds had started to mount and lightning streaked behind the mountains. Roma watched the threatening sky with indecisive eyes.

"We'll be drenched to the skin," she said nervously, "Is there shelter close by?"

"Come with me." He held her hand and they scurried towards the hillside behind the sugarcane. The lightning was almost on top of them, and the wind filled Roma's nightgown and Zalami's *Perahan-Tunban* like sails. They ducked under a natural rock shelter just as the sky opened and the downpour began. It was pitch dark in the shelter and Zalmai struck his tinder box and lit a few dry leaves that had blown in; within moments he had a stick burning.

He looked around in surprise, and ruffled a hand over his dark hair, "It must be a farmer's shelter." A blackened kettle sat on a rocky fire pit. A straw mat was laid out next to the pit with a small heap of wood, and a tin container of tea leaves. The two black stained vertical walls resembled the inside of a locomotive firebox. Sugarcane peels and *tufala*, the chewed-up remains, were strewn on the sandy floor. The smell was a mixture of smoke and hay.

Zalmai spread his woolen shawl over the straw mat and gestured to Roma to sit. Within no time, he had a small fire going.

"We are quite well hidden," he said as he bent down and blew the fire to get it going properly. "You must be sore from riding so long," he commented as he sat down beside her.

"Somewhat..." Roma's heart was pounding at Zalmai's nearness, and, at first, she crossed her arms over her chest protectively. The wavering fire crackled into life, throwing enormous shadows against the walls. She removed her nightcap and set it aside allowing her long hair, as smooth and shining as a hornbill's wing, to fall over her shoulders.

The downpour stopped. Stretching their open palms towards the flames, they could both feel their spirits rise. Smoke drifted out towards the moist, drizzly sky.

Despite their drowsiness and fatigue, there was a sense of relief and comfort now that they were together at last. Trust was growing between them, friendship, and more than friendship—that which soon bestowed the gift of heaven and the delight of great souls. Their eyes met and Roma instinctively moved closer, sinking into his arms and pressing her mouth to his neck. He wrapped his arms around her petite body, hands sliding up her back. She had no desire to move or speak. In Zalmai's arms, she felt free from every negative thought and simply consumed with the delight of his closeness.

"Our journey to London will be wonderful," he said at last, "just knowing you are near." His fingers laced with hers.

"It will be a memorable trip with you," she replied, tucking herself in the crook of his arm, "but I hope the Prince's envious nature won't come between us!"

"Jealousy is forbidden in Islam, and if he's a good Muslim he should avoid any reprehensible behavior." He pulled a stick from the pile and stirred the glowing coals until flames sprang into life. The glow illuminated his face trapping tiny shards of light in his deep brown eyes. Zalmai turned to Roma seeing how her cheeks flamed from the fire glow. Firelight touched her forehead, played over her lips, and teased new highlights into her hair; it painted her as both mysterious and alluring against the wet night sky behind her and melted every sinew in Zalmai's body. Still, with his eyes upon her, he sat down at her side drawing her close once more.

"If I hadn't traveled to see my sister in Afghanistan, we would never have met," she said smiling up at him.

"I had my eyes on you the first moment I saw you," he murmured. "But when it was announced later that you would be one of those who would train us, happiness grew like a beam of light to my soul.

I could not stop thinking about you." His yearning look gave Roma joy, as though the young bud of hope that had imprinted itself on her heart was about to flower into something amazing. Their lips were tantalizingly close when they heard rapidly approaching footfalls from the direction of the sugarcane field and hurriedly drew apart. Two of Colonel Zalmai Khan's subordinates appeared, panting. The teal turban of one of them had unraveled and was trailing behind him. Each saluted with a click of heels.

"*Dagarwal Sahib!* Colonel Sir! Parwana Khan!" His voice was shaking with fury and his face was ashen. "He was on his horse asking where you were. I told him you are patrolling the perimeter. He said he will come around and look for you."

Zalmai sprang to his feet, "Roma Jan, I'll have one of the guards to usher you back to your tent." He cloaked her in his woolen shawl and turned to the guard, "Quickly, do that and keep out of danger. You," he gestured to the guard and then to Roma, "never saw us together," he said authoritatively. He told the other guard to stay put and accompany him.

"*Baley Sahib!* Yes Sir!" Another loud click of heels and a salute.

Colonel Zalmai Khan gently held Roma's shoulder and touched her face. "You'll be fine Roma Jan. Go and get some sleep and be safe."

Parwana Khan, *Jalad*, the executioner, made his way around the camp perimeter to where Zalmai and his guard stood alert and waiting. For security purposes, it was their duty to question anyone who approached the camp's perimeter. When the pounding of approaching hooves was heard, Zalmai yanked his Lefaucheux pinfire revolver from the holster, cocked the hammer, and locked the cylinder in place, pointing it in the direction of the incoming rider. The guard aimed his Enfield.

"*Woderezja! Sok-Eey?* Stop! Who are you?" Zalmai demanded in Pashtu.

"*Zeh Yem* Parwana Khan, *Kotwal!* Chief of Police!"

"What's the night's security code?"

"*Kaftar*, pigeon!"

Zalmai uncocked the revolver and slid it back into the holster.

There was a brief exchange of pleasantries.

"Zalmai Khan, well done for checking and clearing me, which is exactly what I would expect of a security chief. The Police Chief dismounted and tied the reins of his horse to a tree. The fire was still casting light around the shelter, "You have chosen a very private place to patrol," he commented. He removed his soaked *chapan* and *pakol* hat and hung them on the peg against one of the black-stained walls but kept his leather whip in his hand.

"Kotwal Sahib, quiet and private places are hideouts where security breaches could occur," Zalmai said adding more logs to the fire pit. "A wet and rainy night like tonight, this shelter would serve well for culprits to breach security. This was one of the lessons I learned from my father when acted as chief of security for Amir Dost Mohammad Khan."

Parwana Khan noted the hot coals and accumulated ash. "This has been burning for a while," he said suspiciously, "were you alone all this time?"

"Where?"

"Here!" said the executioner. He was sitting crossed-legged on the straw mat.

A chill struck Zalmai when he noticed next to Amir's Chief of Police lay Roma's nightcap. "No, Kotwal Sahib!" he replied, "I have had subordinates in and out of here reporting on the status of security around the camp. Like this man," he gestured towards the guard who stood just outside with the Enfield slung over his shoulder. " Why are you up so late, *Kotwal* Sahib?" Zalmai asked with concern in his tone.

"I have my reasons."

"Kotwal Sahib, it is my duty to patrol and keep you safe," Zalmai said with a sharp stab of fear. He cleared his throat and threw the stick he had been holding into the pit. He forced himself not to start pacing knowing that if the Amir's executioner discovered Roma had been here, he would definitely act against him and do it right now, without any further questions asked. All he needed was evidence and that evidence was lying right next to Parwana Khan. The Colonel's dread was almost palpable, as he glanced at soft white satin and lace cap. So far, the executioner had not given it a second glance. The room was dark and the object was unfamiliar. If he had noticed, it might have passed as a gun cleaning cloth? To divert his attention, the Colonel stooped down to the blackened kettle as the water came to boil.

"Would you like some tea?"

"Yes, that would be welcome."

Zalmai tossed a few tea leaves into the kettle and allowed it to brew. It exuded the sweet floral fragrance of teahouses in Darjeeling. He poured it into a handleless cup for the head executioner, casually retrieved Roma's nightcap, and with a feeling of intense relief, slipped it into his pocket.

"Handkerchief? Do you have a cold?"

"Just the cool night air, Kotwal Sahib," he lied, relieved that the executioner was not able to see him clearly enough to perceive the guilt that must surely be reflected in his eyes. "It's the Spring weather," he took the cap from his pocket and blew his nose, "it always has this effect on me." He snorted once or twice and put the cap back in his pocket.

"Bear in mind, your responsibility to provide security for the Prince and everyone else," the Chief of Police reminded him with condescension. "You need to stay healthy. You are under scrutiny and I'll be monitoring your full efforts."

"Of course, *Kotwal* Sahib, this will pass. I am aware of my responsibilities."

Parwana Khan drained his cup and walked toward his horse. At the last moment, he turned.

"Come here!" he ordered. The Colonel stepped towards him and the head executioner clamped Zalmai's arm in an iron grip, leaned close to his face, and hissed, "Just make sure I don't catch you with the *Englees* girl. Or else, you will suffer the consequences." Zalmai recoiled inwardly under the threat and the putrid odor of Parwana Khan's breath. The executioner mounted his horse and trotted away into the dawn.

CHAPTER THIRTY-FOUR

At the most westerly edge of the Khyber Pass, at the border town of Landi-Kotal, Lieutenant Leigh of the British Army's Sixtieth Rifles was patiently waiting with his government-issued carrier pigeons to deliver the news of Prince Nasrullah's arrival.

Colonel Adelbert Talbot, an officer in the British Directorate of Military intelligence, was handpicked to escort Nasrullah and his entourage to England. A man in his late forties, Talbot was blue-eyed and wore round spectacles, he sported a clipped mustache and parted his hair in the middle. While wearing a military uniform, he was the archetypal British official; the son of a decorated Royal Navy intelligence officer who had followed his father into the field of intelligence. In his undercover capacity, the Colonel blended in well with the average local Afghans, being fluent in both Afghan languages and well-attuned to the Afghan culture.

Sir Gerald Fitzgerald, was also handpicked to escort Nasrullah to England, worked under Lord Bruce, the British Viceroy to India. As a British diplomat who had just entered his fifth decade, he had many years of foreign service experience under his belt, mainly in Turkey and Egypt. On casual occasions, Sir Gerald could be found wearing a plain coat of blue cloth, with a black velvet collar, and waistcoat. His convex gilt button bore a monogram of V.R. within a Garter surmounted by a Crown. When he removed his top hat, he revealed a gleaming bald pate that was offset by a well-groomed horseshoe mustache.

"Colonel Talbot," Sir Fitzgerald asked impatiently, "do we have any information yet about the arrival of the Afghan Prince?"

"No Sir!" With unblinking blue eyes, Lieutenant Talbot stared at him over his round-framed spectacles that had slipped to the tip of his nose. There was a note of irritation in his voice, "So far, no certain news has arrived. You'll be the first to know, Sir!" the Colonel spoke with a distinctive Yorkshire accent. The two men were seated on either side of a desk in the spacious office of the British cantonment of Peshawar.

Sir Fitzgerald folded his arms, his unlit pipe in one hand. "If the pigeons don't make it back here and the Prince suddenly shows up either before or after his scheduled arrival to board the train in Peshawar, what recourse do we have?" He paused, exasperation had brought the blood to his face. "The Prince was expected to be in Peshawar on April sixth, then it was the eleventh. We sent food, and essentials from Bombay to Peshawar, and everything spoilt. We threw that away and sent for a second shipment before his next arrival date, and once more we have had to discard everything. And, now, another shipment for April seventeenth?" His normally upright posture had slumped slightly under the frustration of the delays. He struck a safety match and lit his pipe causing a cloud of smoke to permeate the office. "It's already becoming too expensive to escort this young man to England and he's not even here yet!" His voice was so husky as to almost be inaudible. Wisps of silver-gray smoke curled and drifted away from his mouth and the pipe.

Talbot nodded, "I agree, Sir Fitzgerald. It was silly to invite this juvenile to Windsor, in the first place," he said tapping the arm of the chair with his long fingers. "Our squadron of the 13th D.C.O. Bengal Lancers have been waiting to receive the Prince at Torkham on the Afghan border since April 7th," he continued. "A grand reception for the entourage, but a major inconvenience for the men involved. And I simply cannot imagine why these shipments of food and supplies were sent, and then tossed to the jackals and locals." He leaped to his feet and began pacing the office. "Our men in logistics have no clue to the conditions we face in this area."

"Colonel," a cloud of smoke momentarily obscured Fitzgerald's face, "This isn't a logistical issue, but an information-gathering or intelligence issue. "I wonder if Lieutenant Leigh is savvy enough with the pigeons? Or could it be that the Hindu-Kush hawks devour them before they arrive to give us the report?" Smoke flared from his nostrils like a dragon in a cartoon.

"Sir, my subordinates in Landi-Kotal and Peshawar are well-trained officers of Army intelligence. I know that for a fact because I trained them. And, I personally know Lieutenant Leigh is one of the best officers in the force." Colonel Talbot removed his spectacles and began to wipe them with his kerchief. "Pigeons have an amazing sense of direction and a deep connection to their owners," he checked his spectacles, put them on, and leaned against the wall under a portrait of Queen Victoria crossing his arms, "I have yet to see creatures more loyal than pigeons. No matter how far from home base they are, or what threats they face, the birds stationed in our cantonments in India, by their almost flawless instinct, fly back to their keepers. They are worthy carriers in war, as well as in peace."

Lieutenant Liam Russell on the receiving end shouted in excitement. "There she is!" The British Colonel and diplomat ran out to where Russell was standing. He passed his binoculars to Talbot. A small dark body was soaring across the gray foggy skies of the Khyber Pass, its white wings just visible against the sullen sky.

After its thirty-seven-mile flight from Landi-Kotal to British Army cantonment in Peshawar, Lieutenant Russell ushered the pigeon into the nesting box and gently brought it out again.

Colonel Talbot gestured towards the pigeon with his swagger stick, "I believe this is pigeon CV-409, the one given to the British navy by Queen Victoria, am I correct Lieutenant Russell?"

Russell nodded, "Correct, Sir." He was holding the pigeon gently with his right hand, and its legs with the left, as he carefully removed the metal capsule containing the message. He handed the note to the Colonel, "*Two messengers of H.H. Prince Nasrullah Khan arrived in Landi-Kotal. Prince and the caravan are in Jalalabad. Will be in Peshawar Saturday noon.*"

"I don't understand." Sir Fitzgerald said uncertainly. "What makes them think they'll make it to Peshawar in two days if they haven't left Jalalabad yet? It takes three days from Jalalabad to Peshawar."

"Must be his flying carpet," Colonel Talbot replied facetiously and chuckled. "I think we should head out to Landi-Kotal to escort the Prince to Peshawar's train station. Time is of the essence."

Not much later, wearing a rain poncho over his handsome hussar uniform, Colonel Talbot led the security cavalry towards the Pass.

∽⊙∾⊙∾⊙∾

Thursday, April 18, 1895 -- Afghan calendar month: Hamal 29, 1274.

Landi-Kotal, India

Despite Prince Nasrullah's late arrival at Landi-Kotal, Colonel Talbot and Sir Fitzgerald were determined to carry out their diplomatic duties in welcoming him into the British military cantonment. The six-hundred plus men comprised of a battalion from the Sixtieth rifles, including Punjab infantrymen, and a platoon of Fifth Gurkha rifles made their way through the jagged mountain gorges to the outpost of Landi-Kotal

"Why is the Prince so provocatively slow?" Colonel Talbot demanded, an exasperated expression on his face. Has there been any news of his whereabouts? When will he be here?"

"Sir," beamed the British Major of Landi-Kotal. "We just received a note from the Major of the squadron of the 13th D.C.O. Bengals

Lancers at the Afghan border town of Torkham. The Afghan Prince was honorably received by the Lancers and you can expect him here within a day. And Sir," the Major added, "Two men representing the Prince are here. They brought a note from the Prince."

"Call them in!" Sir Fitzgerald said with a bemused expression, wondering why the Prince would have sent representatives in advance. He removed his wet poncho, stroked his receding hair and horseshoe mustache, and clenched his unlit pipe between his teeth.

Raj, the short, stout, carroty-whiskered translator lead the way into the tent with Major Akbar and Lieutenant Mahmoud close behind. Both men wore silver-mounted swords and cummerbunds. The swords were encrusted with gold and silver decorations. Their studded gems and floral motifs bore far more significance than their use as weapons, and such talismans were believed to be a powerful form of defense. Fine artistic calligraphy with Qur'anic passages and prayers were etched on the full length of the blade as an expression of piety and belief in the protection of the Almighty.

"Heelloo!" Raj greeted as he shuffled in, head bowed and palms pressed together; he was wearing a creamy *kurta churidar* and a brightly colored *pagri* turban. "This is Lieutenant Mahmoud Khan," he said brightly, in his singsong voice.

Mahmoud placed the palm of his hand on his heart and greeted Colonel Talbot and Sir Fitzgerald. "*Salaam Agha-hai Muhtarem!* Hello Respectable Sirs!" He took a drag of his *Beedi* as if it was a *chillum* packed with hashish.

"And this is Major Akbar Khan," Raj continued. "They're here to inform you of His Highness Prince Nasrullah Khan's arrival."

Colonel Talbot returned the greeting in Pashtu. "*Sheh Raghlast*, welcome." He flashed a smile revealing two gold-tipped crowns. Colonel Talbot and Sir Gerald Fitzgerald extended their hands to greet the two Afghans and ushered them to their seats.

"People tell me your patience is running out regarding the late

322

arrival of Shahzadah." Lieutenant Mahmoud Khan said.

"A set time schedule was sent to the Prince to board the troopship in Bombay. He needs to be there on time," Fitzgerald managed to crack a smile.

"*Insah Allah!* God Willing, the Shahzadah will be arriving soon," Lieutenant Mahmoud Khan replied pursing his lips as he inhaled his cigarette. "He is the Prince and the son of our *Padshah*, King, his wish is *Allah's* wish, and his demand is Allah's demand. He's free to come or go anywhere, at any time." He turned to Major Akbar Khan, "isn't that right, *Grana* Major Sahib?"

"Absolutely," he agreed lifting a hand heavenward, "May *Allah* spare our Shahzadah's life." He crossed his ankles, displaying as he did so, his boots covered in dried mud. "You can't rush him. Do you believe he has wings to fly?" His smile broadens ruefully. Discolored lower teeth attested to his love of *naswar*, which had caused his gums to rot. "I hope I'm clear to you *Angrez-ha*, British," his eyes suddenly bulged like marbles.

"Splendid, it should be fine if he's here tomorrow," Sir Fitzgerald said diplomatically, "otherwise, changes will have to be made to his itinerary, which will affect his schedule for the rest of the journey." His unease was clear to Talbot alone. "Of course, he's the Prince and the Amir's son, and the ship would probably wait for him to board because it's chartered.," he went on. "It would not wait for anyone else, even the viceroy! The next one will be the Prince's choice." He nodded and smiled. A shaft of afternoon sunlight penetrated the tent adding a shine to his balding head.

As an experienced diplomat, Sir Gerald was known for his attentive listening skills and ability to mend relationships during tough times. He was an outstanding example of the upper-class code of the Victorian Age; always mindful of his duty as a nobleman to act morally and honorably.

The large tent was pitched over red wooden poles that contrasted pleasantly with the faded canvas. In the corner, a dining area with a table for twelve was superbly decorated with grand candelabras, flowers, assorted fruits, and crystal glasses. It was prepared for British officers and delegations who, from time to time crossed into Afghanistan to meet with the Amir.

"Are you ready to receive His Highness tomorrow?" Major Akbar Khan asked almost gargling over the *Naswar* packed into his mouth.

"I beg your pardon?" Sir Fitzgerald croaked.

Akbar bustled out of the tent, spat out his green spittle, and dashed back in. "They told us not to trust a single *Angrez*, English. I want to ensure there won't be any surprises before His Highness arrives tomorrow." He lounged back in the chair, re-adjusted his silver buttoned corduroy waistcoat, and straightened his ornamental sword.

"And, if I may ask, who exactly told you we the British not to be trusted?" Colonel Talbot demanded.

"There's a saying in Afghanistan, *Dozd-Sar-e-khod par darad*, a thief has a feather attached to his head. What he has done many times makes the culprit stands out." Akbar pushed the flap of his turban back and rubbed his scarred face. "Should I remind you of how you *Angrez-Ha* toppled and exiled our beloved Amir Dost Mohammad Khan and installed your yes-man, Shah Shujah?" he snorted, "An incompetent donkey?" He regarded Sir Fitzgerald and Colonel Talbot slyly, "Was he admired and loved by you *Angrez-Ha* because he was wearing the Koh-i-Noor diamond as a bracelet? The same diamond that belonged to us Afghans and shone so brightly that you couldn't resist attaching it on your Queen's crown?" He looked pointedly at Raj to translate exactly what he said.

"Mr. Akbar, *da ghalat da*, that's wrong," Colonel Talbot replied politely in Pashtu, "*Hess cha da khabara na manai*, no one believes that story. It will not help us to argue when our present business is to escort the Prince and his entourage to England," he looked across at the two men. "*Wobakhsha*, sorry, for my bluntness. I hope we are not going to waste our time talking about issues that will neither benefit the Amir, nor the Prince, nor Her Majesty!" He sprang to his feet and sauntered over to the bar table. Pouring a scotch from the crystal decanter for himself and Sir Fitzgerald, he turned to the Afghans, "Would you gentlemen like some whisky? It will relieve your exhaustion after the long ride from Kabul." He handed Fitzgerald the amber liquid. "I've taken that tiresome journey many times to and from Kabul," He pulled a silver flask from his pocket. "I always carry this when traveling." He strolled back to the bar table, "You both deserve a little relaxation time."

Colonel Talbot was perfectly aware that Islam forbade the consumption of alcohol. But some drank secretly and he had no hesitation in testing their amenability.

"*Sharab?* Booze?" Lieutenant Mahmoud Khan asked, animated.

"Yes," Talbot replied. "*Da der khwand laree*, it tastes very good."

"I've never tried Hu'iski before, I would like to try some." Lieutenant Mahmoud glanced at Major Akbar Khan, nodded and raised his brows signaling him to follow suit.

"I will drink too, but only on one condition," the Afghan Major said cautiously.

"And what might that condition be?" Talbot asked, his blue eyes meeting Akbar's brown.

"That this will not be revealed to anyone." The scar on his face widened as he grinned, "Can this stay private between us?"

"Of course," Colonel Talbot replied, "But how do you hide from *Allah?*"

"It's between myself and *Allah*, but no one else. If I drink *sharab* I'll answer in *akherat*, the judgment day, and to no one else."

"Gentlemen!" Colonel Talbot raised a brow, "Are you sure you want to do this, doesn't Islam forbid Alcohol?"

"Just like you and everyone else we're not perfect humans. We're sinful in countless wrongdoings," the Major said, but his voice cracked a little. "Adding another sin," he gestured toward the whisky decanter, "makes no difference. We're not strangers to *sharab* but we always ask the Almighty forgiveness for our sins, and the Great *Allah*, undoubtedly grants us his compassion." He paused, "You didn't know the Lieutenant and I drink *sharab*? I go to Kabul's *Yahoodi Mahala*, Jewish quarter every so often, my *Yahoodi* friends make good *sharab* and sell me a bottle or two every so often. God always forgives me for my sinful act, and he'll do the same now. Pour me a glass."

Colonel Talbot handed them glasses and lifted his in a toast, "May the Prince's trip be of success and a safe one. And, long live Queen Victoria and the Amir." Talbot and Fitzgerald clinked their glasses.

"May Allah return him home safely," Major Akbar Khan said. "Again! Will you give me your word not to reveal this to anyone?"

"You have my word. It will stay in this tent."

Both Afghans slumped onto a chesterfield couch, crystal glasses of whisky clasped in their hands, hoping, as always, that the answer rested at the bottom of the glass, and the next and the next. As first-time whisky drinkers, they despised the taste but adored the feeling the amber liquid gave them.

"*More Shaaraabb Khwahesh mekunam!* More Hu'iski, please!" the Afghan Major pleaded in slurred Dari.

Colonel Talbot emptied the decanter into their glasses. Few words were exchanged between them and anything Maj. Akbar and Lieut. Mahmoud spewed out was becoming increasingly garbled and senseless. Unlike Colonel Talbot and Sir Fitzgerald, the two Afghan men had a low tolerance and high sensitivity for strong drink, and at this point lifted their hands and swayed their heads with less coordination than concussed boxers who just lost the fight in some tavern.

"Dinner is ready!" announced the Indian-born waiter.

"Gentlemen!" Colonel Talbot said. "Let's eat! You must be starving."

"*O'Baaacha! Bekhez!* H-h-h-heeey, boy! Get up!" Slurred Major Akbar Khan, jabbing a finger into Lieutenant Mahmoud Khan's chest. He cleared his throat as he slowly rose to his feet only to fall back on the couch at his first attempt. They finally managed to stand and stagger to the dinner table, gripping one another for support.

Ensuring the two Afghans in Landi-Kotal were treated with superb attention, the British sought to demonstrate by their hospitality, that they sought peaceful interaction with the two men. The Indian waiters clad in teal British military outfits and turbans pulled out their chairs to seat them. Neither Mahmoud nor Akbar had ever experienced this level of hospitality before, but their tipsiness left them unimpressed. The table was set with assorted Afghan, Indian and European entrées.

"*Kooffftttaa Paallloowww!* Meatbaaaall Pilaaaafff!" Lieutenant Mahmoud said happily, swallowing back the saliva that threatened to ooze from his mouth. He drained the last of his whisky. The glass tinkled sharply against the utensils as he set it down on the table. Leaning back in his seat, he placed his elbows on the arms of the chair and rested his face on his hand. "*Akbara! Tarjuman ta pushtana woka, dodai halal da?* Akbar! Ask the translator if the food is kosher."

Major Akbar's head swayed in slow motion like the repetitive movement of a praying mantis but he referred the question to Raj who was sitting next to him.

"*Agha Jan!*" the translator had tucked his serviette into his tightly buttoned *kurta* collar. He placed a hand before his mouth to direct his whispered reply to Major Akbar, "The food is prepared by Muslim cooks. It's kosher. Just don't eat the English food!" He raised his glass and drank a sip of water.

Major Akbar scooped up *a* large helping of *koofta* pilaf, his hand swaying like a cradle as he brazenly loaded his plate.

"Major Akbar Khan!" Colonel Talbot exclaimed, "did I overhear you asking if the food is kosher?" he placed his knife and fork on his plate, picked up his napkin, and dabbed his mouth.

"*Aghai* Tallboot," slurred Maj. Akbar Khan. "We only eat *halal* meat. *Jai Tashweesh nest*, don't be concerned." His eyes were bloodshot and his eyelids drooped as he stared vacantly at his porcelain willow-patterned plate filled with the pilaf.

"Mr. Akbar Khan, why are you concerned about halal meat and not alcohol? Don't you think it's a bit of hypocrisy on your part? Why this mucky, abhorrent bamboozle, this devilish serpent game? Does the Prince also drink like you?" Colonel Talbot demanded. Tensions rose sharply and the silence stretched like taut wires across the table.

"*Aghai* Tallboot, I'm not going to…"

"My apologies for interjecting," Sir Gerald Fitzgerald said calmly. "You must be excited about boarding the train in Peshawar and the ferry ship in Karachi for the first time?" He quickly cooled off a situation that had threatened to escalate out of control. There was a brief silence, like an indrawn breath, and then the clatter of utensils as the meal resumed.

"Yes! *Aghai* Fessjarwoold," Major Mahmoud Khan nodded contritely. "I am looking forward to the trip."

After years of bloodshed between Afghans and the British, Fitzgerald was eager to promote peace and mend fences with the Afghans and was particularly cautious about provoking the two Afghans regarding religion, culture, or their women, but still, Fitzgerald attempted a personal approach, "Do you both have children?"

"I have three grownup sons and two young girls," Mahmoud Khan replied, his eyelids almost shut. He was struggling to remember how to hold his knife and fork. He compromised, tore the meat with his hands, and spiked it with the fork.

"God bless them!" Sir. Fitzgerald said. Glancing at Akbar he asked, "How about you Major Akbar Khan?"

"I have t-t-two sons and one daughter from my first w-w-wife, three boys from my s-s-second, and two daughters from my y-y-youngest wife. We all reside happily together."

Fitzgerald was cognizant of the fact the two Afghans would not want to inflame the issue with an angry response for fear of attracting further attention to their drunken state.

"Akbar!" Lieut. Mahmoud Khan said in a slurred stage whisper directed at the Afghan Major's ear, "Remember not to eat with your hands, use utensils as we were told." He was still not sure whether to hold the fork with the right hand or left, himself. "We must have some self-control - don't exacerbate the problem or else, tomorrow, when the Shahzadah arrives, he'll order our execution right here, in Khyber-Pass, f-f-for drinking *Sharab*."

Major Akbar Khan's hand coordination was gradually slowing down. Holding the utensils loosely as he ate, his mood changed and he grew visibly anxious as he tried to cut the egg-size *koofta*. He muttered angrily under his breath. Suddenly the spring-loaded meatball catapulted off his knife and fell in a perfect trajectory across the table into Colonel Talbot's whisky glass, splattering his face and military uniform.

"Are you new with utensils, Major Akbar Khan?" Colonel Talbot questioned laughing. He dabbed his face and uniform with the white starched napkin. "But I must say, you show superb talent in golfing, perhaps you could participate in the British Open when you're in London and compete against the champion, John Ball?" The entire tent erupted into laughter at that, even the attendants and servants giggled behind their hands. The Afghan Major's and Lieutenant's bewildered faces showed expressions of uncertainty as to whether to laugh uproariously like the rest, or apologize. Instead, they felt they were being humiliated, and this was seen as a mockery of their characters. Talbot's joke exacerbated their nervous self-consciousness. It was now clear that the two Afghans bruised easily and were becoming as skittish as horses bewildered by lightning.

"*Shoma A-A-Angrez-Hai Mordagow!* You pimp B-B-Brits!" the Afghan Major retorted drunkenly. He pounded his fist on the table causing his whisky glass to tip over and spill. "A-A-Are you criticizing me with y-y-your laughter ju-ju-just because am not used to your da-dam-damn fo-fo-fork 'n knife?" He brandished the offending utensils. "*Koosmodar-ha*, Motherfuckers!" He slurred, each word and syllable blurring together until it became a single *padarlanatkharkoosha*.

"My dear friends!" Sir Fitzgerald interjected as the attendants cleared the table, "allow me to give you a word of advice." He filled his mahogany pipe methodically, "You were sent here in an official capacity to inform us of the Prince's arrival." Clenching his pipe between his teeth, he lit a match and moved the flame in circles over the bowl. After a few steady puffs, he went on, "How if we keep it in that official capacity and not turn this into a circus?" he nodded with a smile.

The translator tries to find the word for circus in Dari and says, "*Bazeecha*."

After a few periodic puffs to keep the pipe alight, the British diplomat continued, "Gentlemen, I'm truly sorry if we upset you. Please forgive us for our uncalled-for laughter. It was just a very funny scene but we didn't mean to humiliate you. How about if we keep this issue quiet between us? He drew a hand over his receding hair, "Don't you think this will be troublesome for you and us?" A thin wisp of smoke trailed up from his pipe. Let's not exacerbate this to a point that our government in India and yours in Kabul will have to deal with."

As Raj interpreted, Mahmoud and Akbar's gazes flitted around the tent without settling on any object or person for long. Then they looked at each other, their hearts leaping in their rib cages. "*Ba-Ba-Baash! Saber-Kon! Wai-Wai-Wait!* Restrain, patience! *Khwahesh mekunam nakun!* We can resolve this in a friendly manner. Let's forget what happened tonight," Lieutenant Mahmoud Khan said fearfully. A perfect way to bring the two under their rule, using whisky as their leash.

꧁ೀ꧂

In preparation for Nasrullah's arrival in Landi-Kotal, both Sir Gerald Fitzgerald and Colonel Adelbert Talbot assessed the rehearsal of the Fourth Gurkhas marching band. As the final procession was about to end, the sounds of bugles, bagpipes, trombones, tubas, and drums echoed back at them from the mountains. The platoon of thirty-two men each contributed his full share to the volume of sound, the like of which had rarely been heard in the Khyber Pass before.

Both, Colonel Talbot and Sir Fitzgerald applauded the men for their proficiency. "Truly impressive work!" Colonel Talbot said as he shook hands with the stout middle-aged bandmaster. Both saluted respectfully. "I'm sure the Afghan Prince will be impressed." He glanced at Akbar and then Mahmoud as they were also observing the marching band, "What do you think of their performance?" he asked in Pashtu. "I believe we will give the Prince an honorable reception."

"I'm certain it will be memorable," Mahmoud responded with a tremor in his voice.

"You look despondent," Sir Fitzgerald said. "Is everything alright?" Looking over at Akbar, he added, "Neither of you seem to be in good spirits. I hope the alcohol last night didn't contribute to your melancholy, is there anything we can do to make you feel better? The Prince will be arriving soon and you both need to greet him with an ebullient welcome."

"Can you keep last night's Hu'iski drinking incident a secret?" whispered Major Akbar Khan, uneasiness creeping into his voice.

"Major Akbar Khan," he puffed at his pipe, "you can count on Colonel Talbot and myself to keep this confidential, but how will you convince Raj?" he removed his pipe from his mouth and gestured with it toward the interpreter," and more than ten other Indian servants not to speak about it?" He clenched the pipe between his teeth once more and allowed the smoke to drift. "Unfortunately, I can assure both of you," studying the Afghan Major and then the Lieutenant, "that the entire encampment knows about last night."

"It's a topic of conversation and amusement among everyone here," Colonel Talbot cut in, "It won't be easy to contain it now." His blue eyes drilled into Akbar Khan's and Mahmoud's worried faces and panic made them prone to believe the worst was to come. On one hand, they felt as helpless as turtles on their backs, while on the other, they felt the tautness of the leash around their necks.

Dominance and control were Talbot's forte, and the two Afghans had fallen into his trap. They had just unwittingly joined his intelligence network and their job would be to eavesdrop and pass on information to Talbot regarding Prince Nasrullah's plans and state of mind. Fear and intimidation were useful tools in the Colonel's hands. Akbar and Mahmoud, sent to relay Nasrullah's time of arrival in Landi Kotal, found themselves caught up in Talbot's intelligence web with no other option but to abide by his rules. They were teetering on the edge of a cliff, as Talbot knew full well the Amir's response to his subjects exploiting the *haram* alcohol. They would face severe punishment, if not death. Lieutenant Mahmoud Khan spat his thickened saliva and it splotched on the arid ground.

"*Khodai de khwar nakee!* May God not ruin you!" the Lieutenant said. He praised Colonel Talbot and Sir Fitzgerald piously and obsequiously in Pashtu lifting his hands to the heavens. "You are both chieftains of this encampment. No one can disdain your word. You have vigor and weight to refrain anyone from spreading the story of our Hu'iski consumption." Both British men stood silent. Colonel Talbot tapped his swagger stick against his knee-high boot. Sir Fitzgerald with his hands on his waist and his pipe between his teeth puffed little clouds of smoke.

"You, *Aghai* Tallboot," Mahmoud continued, "invited us to drink Hu'iski with you." He pointed his finger heavenward. "*Allah* was our witness that we were forced to drink the *haram Sharab*. You made us believe it was like pomegranate water!"

"Perhaps you should remember your words when I poured the whisky for you," Talbot replied, still tapping the swagger stick. "'We're sinful in countless wrongdoings. Adding another sin makes no difference. Remember?"

"This is the usual British trap to leash us Afghans like their dogs. This has been their trick for years," Maj. Akbar said bitterly. "When is this going to stop?

"*Bas!* Stop!" Colonel Talbot interjected, "I'll make a deal with you." He took off his round spectacles and wiped them with his kerchief. "We will make sure this matter is kept secret if you do the same for us." Hope arose and their panic and anxiety dwindled slightly; Mahmoud still trembled. His eyes shut and slowly opened in the direction of Talbot's newly cleaned spectacles.

"May the Almighty Allah be your safeguard," he breathed, clamping Colonel Talbot's hand in his. He knelt as if to kiss it, "Of course, we will keep your secrets private!" he grinned widely, flashing his greenish *naswar*-stained teeth. Throwing a glance back at Major Akbar Khan he called out, "Akbar Jana, *Aghai* Tallboot gave us his word!"

"*Baley,* Yes," Akbar nodded solemnly, "I only have trust in God and my own soul." He inhaled the last of his *beedi* and flicked the stub across the rocky ground. "If the word of an *Englees* was a bridge, no Afghan would cross. But now, it's worth a try, I'll believe it when I see it."

"To be frank, what we need is trust between us." A cynical smile twisted Colonel Adelbert Talbot's lips. "I don't see any issue for us to drink whisky together. But let us not reveal our private matters to anyone." He glanced at Sir Fitzgerald, "Isn't that true, Sir?"

"Of course. I agree," a sardonic smile tugged at the corners of his lips.

"Respectable *Aghai* Tallboot!" Lieutenant Mahmoud pleaded

like a vagrant beggar, "We have a saying in Afghanistan, no rose is without thorns. Meaning no one is perfect, we make mistakes and God always forgives us."

"Don't worry we have forgiven and forgotten too." Talbot reached into his pocket and took out his whisky flask. He took a couple of sips and handed the rest to Akbar. "Keep the rest and the bottle," he smiled. "This should be a binding trust between us." He shook their hands, "And don't feel ashamed of eating with your hand. Just like you, I sometimes eat with mine. I have no problem scooping a mouthful of pilaf if I feel like eating that way. You must ignore the utensils if you're uncomfortable using them." He gripped Mahmoud's shoulder in a friendly manner. "Let's get ready to welcome the Prince."

CHAPTER THIRTY-FIVE

At the most westerly edge of the Khyber Pass, at the border town of Landi-Kotal, Lieutenant Leigh of the British Army's Sixtieth Rifles was patiently waiting with his government-issued carrier pigeons to deliver the news of Prince Nasrullah's arrival.

Colonel Adelbert Talbot, an officer in the British Directorate of Military intelligence, was handpicked to escort Nasrullah and his entourage to England. A man in his late forties, Talbot was blue-eyed, wore round spectacles, sported a clipped mustache and parted his hair in the middle. While wearing a military uniform, he was the archetypal British official; the son of a decorated Royal Navy intelligence officer who had followed his father into the field of intelligence. In his undercover capacity, the Colonel blended in well with the average local Afghans, being fluent in both Afghan languages and well-attuned to the Afghan culture.

Sir Gerald Fitzgerald, was also handpicked to escort Nasrullah to England. He worked under Lord Bruce, the British Viceroy to India. As a British diplomat who had just entered his fifth decade, he had many years of foreign service experience under his belt, mainly in Turkey and Egypt. On casual occasions, Sir Gerald could be found wearing a plain coat of blue cloth, with a black velvet collar, and waistcoat. His convex gilt button bore a monogram of V.R. within a Garter surmounted by a Crown. When he removed his top hat, he revealed a gleaming bald pate that was offset by a well-groomed horseshoe mustache.

"Colonel Talbot," Sir Fitzgerald asked impatiently, "do we have any information yet about the arrival of the Afghan Prince?"

"No Sir!" With unblinking blue eyes, Lieutenant Talbot stared at him over his round-framed spectacles that had slipped to the tip of his nose. There was a note of irritation in his voice, "So far, no certain news has arrived. You'll be the first to know, Sir!" the Colonel spoke with a distinctive Yorkshire accent. The two men were seated on either side of a desk in the spacious office of the British cantonment of Peshawar.

Sir Fitzgerald folded his arms, his unlit pipe in one hand. "If the pigeons don't make it back here and the Prince suddenly shows up either before or after his scheduled arrival to board the train in Peshawar, what recourse do we have?" He paused, exasperation had brought the blood to his face. "The Prince was expected to be in Peshawar on April sixth, then it was the eleventh. We sent food, and essentials from Bombay to Peshawar, and everything spoilt. We threw that away and sent for a second shipment before his next arrival date, and once more we have had to discard everything. And, now, another shipment for April seventeenth?" His normally upright posture had slumped slightly under the frustration of the delays. He struck a safety match and lit his pipe causing a cloud of smoke to permeate the office. "It's already becoming too expensive to escort this young man to England and he's not even here yet!" His voice was so husky as to almost be inaudible. Wisps of silver-gray smoke curled and drifted away from his mouth and the pipe.

Talbot nodded, "I agree, Sir Fitzgerald. It was silly to invite this juvenile to Windsor, in the first place," he said tapping the arm of the chair with his long fingers. "Our squadron of the 13th D.C.O. Bengal Lancers have been waiting to receive the Prince at Torkham on the Afghan border since April 7th. A grand reception for the entourage, but a major inconvenience for the men involved. And I simply cannot imagine why these shipments of food and supplies were sent, and then tossed to the jackals and locals." He leapt to his feet and began pacing the office. "Our men in logistics have no clue to the conditions we face in this area."

"Colonel, this isn't a logistical issue, it's an intelligence issue. I wonder if Lieutenant Leigh is savvy enough with the pigeons? Or could it be that the Hindu-Kush hawks devoured them before they arrived to give us the report?" Smoke flared from his nostrils like a dragon in a cartoon.

"Sir, my subordinates in Landi-Kotal and Peshawar are well-trained officers of Army intelligence. I know that for a fact because I trained them. And, I personally know Lieutenant Leigh is one of the best officers in the force." Colonel Talbot removed his spectacles and began to wipe them with his kerchief. "Pigeons have an amazing sense of direction and a deep connection to their owners," he checked his spectacles, put them on, and leaned against the wall under a portrait of Queen Victoria, crossing his arms, "I have yet to see creatures more loyal than pigeons. No matter how far from home-base they are, or what threats they face, the birds stationed in our cantonments in India, by their almost flawless instinct, fly back to their keepers. They are worthy carriers in war, as well as in peace."

Lieutenant Liam Russell on the receiving end shouted in excitement. "There she is!" The British Colonel and diplomat ran out to where Russell was standing. He passed his binoculars to Talbot. A small dark body was soaring across the gray foggy skies of the Khyber Pass, its white wings just visible against the sullen sky.

After its thirty-seven-mile flight from Landi-Kotal to the British Army cantonment in Peshawar, Lieutenant Russell ushered the pigeon into the nesting box and gently brought it out again.

Colonel Talbot gestured towards the pigeon with his swagger stick, "If I'm not mistaken, this is pigeon CV-409, the one given to the British navy by Queen Victoria, am I correct Lieutenant Russell?"

Russell nodded, "Correct, Sir." He was holding the pigeon gently with his right hand, and its legs with the left, as he carefully removed the metal capsule containing the message. He handed the note to the Colonel, *"Two messengers of H.H. Prince Nasrullah Khan arrived in Landi-Kotal. Prince and the caravan are in Jalalabad. Will be in Peshawar Saturday noon."*

"I don't understand." Sir Fitzgerald said uncertainly. "What makes them think they'll make it to Peshawar in two days if they haven't left Jalalabad yet? It takes three days from Jalalabad to Peshawar."

"Must be his flying carpet," Colonel Talbot replied facetiously and chuckled. "I think we should head out to Landi-Kotal to escort the Prince to Peshawar's train station. Time is of the essence."

Not much later, wearing a rain poncho over his handsome hussar uniform, Colonel Talbot led the security cavalry towards the Pass.

∽◉∼◉∼◉◇

Thursday, April 18, 1895 -- Afghan calendar month: Hamal 29, 1274.

Landi-Kotal, India

Despite Prince Nasrullah's late arrival in Landi-Kotal, Colonel Talbot and Sir Fitzgerald were determined to carry out their diplomatic duties in welcoming him into the British military cantonment. The six-hundred plus men comprised of a battalion from the Sixtieth rifles, including Punjab infantrymen, and a platoon of Fifth Gurkha rifles made their way through the jagged mountain gorges to the outpost of Landi-Kotal

"Why is the Prince so provocatively slow?" Colonel Talbot demanded, an exasperated expression on his face. Has there been any news of his whereabouts? When will he arrive?"

"Sir," beamed the British Major of Landi-Kotal. "We just received

338

a note from the Major of the squadron of the 13th D.C.O. Bengals Lancers at the Afghan border town of Torkham. The Afghan Prince was honorably received by the Lancers and you can expect him here within a day. And Sir," the Major added, "Two men representing the Prince are here. They brought a note from the Prince."

"Call them in!" Sir Fitzgerald said with a bemused expression, wondering why the Prince would have sent representatives in advance. He removed his wet poncho, stroked his receding hair and horseshoe mustache, and clenched his unlit pipe between his teeth.

Raj, the short, stout, carroty-whiskered translator led the way into the tent with Major Akbar and Lieutenant Mahmoud close behind. Both men wore silver-mounted swords and cummerbunds. The swords were encrusted with gold and silver decorations. Their studded gems and floral motifs bore far more significance than their use as weapons, and such talismans were believed to be a powerful form of defense. Fine artistic calligraphy with Qur'anic passages and prayers were etched on the full length of the blade as an expression of piety and belief in the protection of the Almighty.

"Heelloo!" Raj greeted as he shuffled in, head bowed and palms pressed together; he was wearing a creamy *kurta churidar* and a brightly colored *pagri* turban. "This is Lieutenant Mahmoud Khan," he said brightly, in his singsong voice.

Mahmoud placed the palm of his hand on his heart and greeted Colonel Talbot and Sir Fitzgerald. "*Salaam Agha-hai Muhtarem!* Hello Respectable Sirs!" He took a drag of his *Beedi* as if it was a *chillum* packed with hashish.

"And this is Major Akbar Khan," Raj continued. "They're here to inform you of His Highness Prince Nasrullah Khan's arrival."

Colonel Talbot returned the greeting in Pashtu. "*Sheh Raghlast,* welcome." He flashed a smile revealing two gold-tipped crowns. Colonel Talbot and Sir Gerald Fitzgerald extended their hands to greet the two Afghans and ushered them to their seats.

"People tell me your patience is running out regarding the late arrival of Shahzadah." Lieutenant Mahmoud Khan said.

"There is a set schedule that was sent to the Prince for the boarding of the troopship in Bombay. He needs to be there on time," Fitzgerald managed to crack a smile.

"*Insah Allah!* God Willing, the Shahzadah will be arriving soon," Lieutenant Mahmoud Khan replied pursing his lips as he inhaled his cigarette. "He is the Prince and the son of our *Padshah*, King, his wish is Allah's wish, and his demand is Allah's demand. He's free to come or go anywhere, at any time." He turned to Major Akbar Khan, "isn't that right, *Grana* Major Sahib?"

"Absolutely," he agreed, lifting a hand heavenward, "May Allah spare our Shahzadah's life." He crossed his ankles, displaying as he did so, his boots covered in dried mud. "You can't rush him. Do you believe he has wings to fly?" His smile broadened ruefully. Discolored lower teeth attested to his love of *naswar*, which had caused his gums to rot. "I hope I'm clear to you *Angrez-ha*, British," his eyes suddenly bulged aggressively.

"Splendid, it should be fine if he's here tomorrow," Sir Fitzgerald said diplomatically, "otherwise, changes will have to be made to his itinerary, which will affect his schedule for the rest of the journey." His unease was clear to Talbot alone. "Of course, he's the Prince and the Amir's son, and the ship would probably wait for him to board because it's chartered.," he went on. "It would not wait for anyone else, even the viceroy! The next one will be the Pince's choice." He nodded and smiled. A shaft of afternoon sunlight penetrated the tent adding a shine to his balding head.

As an experienced diplomat, Sir Gerald was known for his attentive listening skills and ability to mend relationships during tough times. He was an outstanding example of the upper-class code of the Victorian Age; always mindful of his duty as a nobleman to act morally and honorably.

The large tent was pitched over red wooden poles that contrasted pleasantly with the faded canvas. In the corner, a dining area with a table for twelve was superbly decorated with grand candelabras, flowers, assorted fruits, and crystal glasses. It was prepared for British officers and delegations who, from time to time crossed into Afghanistan to meet with the Amir.

"Are you ready to receive His Highness tomorrow?" Major Akbar Khan asked almost gargling over the *Naswar* packed into his mouth.

"I beg your pardon?" Sir Fitzgerald croaked.

Akbar bustled out of the tent, spat out his green spittle, and dashed back in. "They told us not to trust a single *Angrez*, English. I want to ensure there won't be any surprises before His Highness arrives tomorrow." He lounged back in the chair, re-adjusted his silver buttoned corduroy waistcoat, and straightened his ornamental sword.

"And, if I may ask, who exactly told you we the British not to be trusted?" Colonel Talbot demanded.

"There's a saying in Afghanistan, *Dozd-Sar-e-khod par darad*, a thief has a feather attached to his head. What he has done many times makes the culprit stands out." Akbar pushed the flap of his turban back and rubbed his scarred face. "Should I remind you of how you *Angrez-Ha* toppled and exiled our beloved Amir Dost Mohammad Khan and installed your yes-man, Shah Shujah?" he snorted, "An incompetent donkey?" He regarded Sir Fitzgerald and Colonel Talbot slyly, "Was he admired and loved by you *Angrez-Ha* because he was wearing the Koh-i-Noor diamond as a bracelet? The same diamond that belonged to us Afghans and shone so brightly that you couldn't resist attaching it on your Queen's crown?"

"Major Akbar, *da ghalat da*, that's wrong," Colonel Talbot replied politely in Pashtu, "*Hess cha da khabara na manai*, no one believes that story. It will not help us to argue when our present business is to escort the Prince and his entourage to England," he looked across at the two men. "*Wobakhsha*, sorry, for my bluntness. I hope we are not going to waste our time talking about issues that will neither benefit the Amir, nor the Prince, nor Her Majesty!" He sprang to his feet and sauntered over to the bar table. Pouring a scotch from the crystal decanter for himself and Sir Fitzgerald, he turned to the Afghans, "Would you gentlemen like some whiskey? It will relieve your exhaustion after the long ride from Kabul." He handed Fitzgerald the amber liquid. "I've taken that tiresome journey many times to and from Kabul," He pulled a silver flask from his pocket. "I always carry this when traveling." He strolled back to the bar table, "You both deserve a little relaxation time."

Colonel Talbot was perfectly aware that Islam forbade the consumption of alcohol. But some drank secretly and he had no hesitation in testing their amenability.

"*Sharab?* Booze?" Lieutenant Mahmoud Khan asked, suddenly animated.

"Yes," Talbot replied. "*Da der khwand laree*, it tastes very good."

"I've never tried Hu'iski before, I would like to try some," Lieutenant Mahmoud glanced at Major Akbar Khan, nodded and raised his brows signaling him to follow suit.

"I will drink too, but only on one condition," the Afghan Major said cautiously.

"And what might that condition be?" Talbot asked, his blue eyes meeting Akbar's brown.

"That this will not be revealed to anyone." The scar on his face widened as he grinned, "Can this stay private between us?"

"Of course," Colonel Talbot replied, "But how do you hide from Allah?"

"It's between myself and Allah, but no one else. If I drink *sharab* I'll answer in *akherat*, the judgment day, and to no one else."

"Gentlemen!" Colonel Talbot raised a brow, "Are you sure you want to do this, doesn't Islam forbid alcohol?"

"Just like you and everyone else we're not perfect humans. We're sinful in countless wrongdoings," the Major said, but his voice cracked a little. "Adding another sin," he gestured toward the whiskey decanter, "makes no difference. We're not strangers to *sharab* but we always ask the Almighty forgiveness for our sins, and the Great Allah, undoubtedly grants us his compassion." He paused, "You didn't know the Lieutenant and I drink *sharab*? I go to Kabul's *Yahoodi Mahala*, Jewish quarter every so often, my *Yahoodi* friends make good *sharab* and sell me a bottle or two every so often. God always forgives me for my sinful act and he'll do the same now. Pour me a glass."

Colonel Talbot handed them glasses and lifted his in a toast, "May the Prince's trip be of success and a safe one. And, long live Queen Victoria and the Amir." Talbot and Fitzgerald clinked their glasses.

"May Allah return him home safely," Major Akbar Khan said. "Again! Will you give me your word not to reveal this to anyone?"

"You have my word. It will stay in this tent."

Both Afghans slumped onto a chesterfield couch, crystal glasses of whiskey clasped in their hands, hoping, as always, that the answer rested at the bottom of the glass, and the next, and the next. As first-time whiskey drinkers, they despised the taste but adored the feeling the amber liquid gave them.

"*More Shaaraabb Khwahesh mekunam!* More Hu'iski, please!" the Afghan Major pleaded in slurred Dari.

Colonel Talbot emptied the decanter into their glasses. Few words were exchanged between them and anything Maj. Akbar and Lieut. Mahmoud spewed out was becoming increasingly garbled and senseless. Unlike Colonel Talbot and Sir Fitzgerald, the two Afghan men had a low tolerance and high sensitivity to strong drink, and at this point lifted their hands and swayed their heads with less coordination than concussed boxers who just lost the fight in some tavern.

"Dinner is ready!" announced the Indian-born waiter.

"Gentlemen!" Colonel Talbot said. "Let's eat! You must be starving."

"*O'Baaacha! Bekhez!* H-h-h-heeey, boy! Get up!" Slurred Major Akbar Khan, jabbing a finger into Lieutenant Mahmoud Khan's chest. He cleared his throat as he slowly rose to his feet only to fall back on the couch at his first attempt. They finally managed to stand and stagger to the dinner table, gripping one another for support.

. The Indian waiters clad in teal British military outfits and turbans pulled out their chairs to seat them. Neither Mahmoud nor Akbar had ever experienced this level of hospitality before, but their tipsiness left them unimpressed. The table was set with assorted Afghan, Indian and European entrées.

"*Kooofftttaa Paallloowww!* Meatbaaaall Pilaaaafff!" Lieutenant Mahmoud exclaimed happily, swallowing back the saliva that threatened to ooze from his mouth. He drained the last of his whiskey. The glass tinkled sharply against the utensils as he set it down on the table. Leaning back in his seat, he placed his elbows on the arms of the chair and rested his face on his hand. "*Akbara! Tarjuman ta pushtana woka, dodai halal da?* Akbar! Ask the interpretor if the food is kosher."

Major Akbar's head swayed in slow motion like the repetitive movement of a praying mantis but he referred the question to Raj who was sitting next to him.

"*Agha Jan!*" the interpretor had tucked his serviette into his tightly buttoned *kurta* collar. He placed a hand before his mouth to direct his whispered reply to Major Akbar, "The food is prepared by Muslim cooks. It's kosher. Just don't eat the English food!" He raised his glass and drank a sip of water.

Major Akbar scooped up *a* large helping of *koofta* pilaf, his hand swaying like a cradle as he brazenly loaded his plate.

"Major Akbar Khan!" Colonel Talbot exclaimed, "did I overhear you asking if the food is kosher?" he placed his knife and fork on his plate, picked up his napkin, and dabbed his mouth.

"*Aghai* Tallboot," slurred Maj. Akbar Khan. "We only eat *halal* meat. *Jai Tashweesh nest*, don't be concerned." His eyes were bloodshot and his eyelids drooped as he stared vacantly at his porcelain willow-patterned plate filled with the pilaf.

"Mr. Akbar Khan, why are you concerned about halal meat and not alcohol? Don't you think it's a bit of hypocrisy on your part? Why this mucky, abhorrent bamboozle, this devilish serpent game? Does the Prince also drink like you?" Colonel Talbot demanded. Tensions rose sharply and the silence stretched like taut wires across the table.

"*Aghai* Tallboot, I'm not going to…"

"My apologies for interjecting," Sir Gerald Fitzgerald said calmly. "You must be excited about boarding the train in Peshawar and the ferry ship in Karachi for the first time?" He quickly cooled off a situation that had threatened to escalate out of control. There was a brief silence, like an indrawn breath, and then the clatter of utensils as the meal resumed.

"Yes! *Aghai* Fessjarwoold," Major Mahmoud Khan nodded contritely. "I am looking forward to the trip."

After years of bloodshed between Afghans and the British, Fitzgerald was eager to promote peace and mend fences with the Afghans and was particularly cautious about provoking the two Afghans regarding religion, culture, or their women, but still, Fitzgerald attempted a personal approach, "Do you both have children?"

"I have three grownup sons and two young girls," Mahmoud Khan replied, his eyelids almost shut. He was struggling to remember how to hold his knife and fork. He compromised, tore the meat with his hands, and spiked it with the fork.

"God bless them!" Sir. Fitzgerald said. Glancing at Akbar he asked, "How about you Major Akbar Khan?"

"I have t-t-two sons and one daughter from my first w-w-wife, three boys from my s-s-second, and two daughters from my y-y-youngest wife. We all reside happily together."

Fitzgerald was cognizant of the fact the two Afghans would not want to inflame the issue with an angry response for fear of attracting further attention to their drunken state.

"Akbar!" Lieut. Mahmoud Khan said in a slurred stage whisper directed at the Colonel's ear, "Remember not to eat with your hands, use utensils as we were told." He was still not sure whether to hold the fork with the right hand or left, himself. "We must have some self-control - don't exacerbate the problem or else, tomorrow, when the Shahzadah arrives, he'll order our execution right here, in Khyber-Pass, f-f-for drinking *Sharab*."

Major Akbar Khan's hand coordination was gradually slowing down. Holding the utensils loosely as he ate, his mood changed and he grew visibly anxious as he tried to cut the egg-size *koofta*. He muttered angrily under his breath. Suddenly the spring-loaded meatball catapulted off his knife and fell in a perfect trajectory across the table into Colonel Talbot's whiskey glass, splattering his face and military uniform.

"Are you new with utensils, Major Akbar Khan?" Colonel Talbot questioned laughing. He dabbed his face and uniform with the white starched napkin. "But I must say, you show superb talent in golfing, perhaps you could participate in the British Open when you're in London and compete against the champion, John Ball?" The entire tent erupted into laughter at that, even the attendants and servants giggled behind their hands. The Afghan Major's and Lieutenant's bewildered faces showed expressions of uncertainty as to whether to laugh uproariously like the rest, or apologize. Instead, they felt they were being humiliated, and this was seen as a mockery of their characters. Talbot's joke exacerbated their nervous self-consciousness. It was now clear that the two Afghans bruised easily and were becoming as skittish as horses bewildered by lightning.

"*Shoma A-A-Angrez-Hai Mordagow!* You pimp B-B-Brits!" the Afghan Major retorted drunkenly. He pounded his fist on the table causing his whiskey glass to tip over and spill. "A-A-Are you criticizing me with y-y-your laughter ju-ju-just because am not used to your da-dam-damn fo-fo-fork 'n knife?" He brandished the offending utensils. "*Koosmodar-ha*, Motherfuckers!" He slurred, each word and syllable blurring together until it became a single *padarlanatkharkoosha*.

"My dear friends!" Sir Fitzgerald interjected as the attendants cleared the table, "allow me to give you a word of advice." He filled his mahogany pipe methodically, "You were sent here in an official capacity to inform us of the Prince's arrival." Clenching his pipe between his teeth, he lit a match and moved the flame in circles over the bowl. After a few steady puffs, he went on, "How if we keep it in that official capacity and not turn this into a circus?" he nodded with a smile.

The interpreter tried to find the word for circus in Dari and tried, "*Bazeecha.*"

After a few periodic puffs to keep the pipe alight, the British diplomat continued, "Gentlemen, I'm truly sorry if we upset you. Please forgive us for our uncalled-for laughter, it was just a very funny scene but we didn't mean to humiliate you. How about if we keep this issue quiet between us?" He drew a hand over his receding hair, "I'm sure none of us want to turn this into something that could become troublesome." A thin wisp of smoke trailed up from his pipe. "It could so easily come to a point that our government in India and yours in Kabul would have to deal with."

As Raj interpreted, Mahmoud and Akbar's gazes flitted around the tent without settling on any object or person for long. Then they looked at each other, their hearts leaping in their rib cages. "*Ba-Ba-Baash! Saber-Kon! Wai-Wai-Wait!* Restrain, patience! *Khwahesh mekunam nakun!* We can resolve this in a friendly manner. Let's forget what happened tonight," Lieutenant Mahmoud Khan said fearfully. A perfect way to bring the two under their rule, using whiskey as their leash.

In preparation for Nasrullah's arrival in Landi-Kotal, both Sir Gerald Fitzgerald and Colonel Adelbert Talbot assessed the rehearsal of the Fourth Gurkhas marching band. As the final procession was about to end, the sounds of bugles, bagpipes, trombones, tubas, and drums echoed back at them from the mountains. The platoon of thirty-two men each contributed his full share to the volume of sound, the like of which had rarely been heard in the Khyber Pass before.

Colonel Talbot and Sir Fitzgerald applauded the men for their proficiency.

"Truly impressive work!" Colonel Talbot said as he shook hands with the stout middle-aged bandmaster. Both saluted respectfully. "I'm sure the Afghan Prince will be impressed." He glanced at Akbar and then Mahmoud as they were also observing the marching band, "What do you think of their performance?" he asked in Pashtu. "I believe we will give the Prince an honorable reception."

"I'm certain it will be memorable," Mahmoud responded with a tremor in his voice.

"You look despondent," Sir Fitzgerald said. "Is everything alright?" Looking over at Akbar, he added, "Neither of you seem to be in good spirits. I hope the alcohol last night didn't contribute to your melancholy, is there anything we can do to make you feel better? The Prince will be arriving soon and you both need to give him a good welcome."

"Can you keep last night's Hu'iski drinking incident a secret?" whispered Major Akbar Khan, uneasiness creeping into his voice.

"Major Akbar Khan," he puffed at his pipe, "you can count on Colonel Talbot and myself to keep this confidential, but how will you convince Raj?" he removed his pipe from his mouth and gestured with it toward the interpreter, "and more than ten other Indian servants not to speak about it?" He clenched the pipe between his teeth once more and allowed the smoke to drift. "Unfortunately, I can assure both of you," he said, studying the Afghan Major and then the Lieutenant, "that the entire encampment knows about last night."

"It's a topic of conversation and amusement among everyone here," Colonel Talbot cut in, "It won't be easy to contain it now." His blue eyes drilled into Akbar Khan's and Mahmoud's worried faces and panic made them prone to believe the worst was to come. On one hand, they felt as helpless as turtles on their backs, while on the other, they felt the tautness of the leash around their necks.

Dominance and control was Talbot's forte, and the two Afghans had fallen into his trap. They had just unwittingly joined his intelligence network and their job would be to eavesdrop and pass on information to Talbot regarding Prince Nasrullah's plans and state of mind. Fear and intimidation were useful tools in the Colonel's hands. Akbar and Mahmoud, sent to relay Nasrullah's time of arrival in Landi Kotal, found themselves caught up in Talbot's intelligence web with no other option but to abide by his rules. They were teetering on the edge of a cliff, as Talbot knew full well the Amir's response to his subjects exploiting the *haram* alcohol. They would face severe punishment, if not death. Lieutenant Mahmoud Khan spat his thickened saliva and it splotched on the arid ground.

"*Khodai de khwar nakee!* May God not ruin you!" the Lieutenant said. He praised Colonel Talbot and Sir Fitzgerald piously and obsequiously in Pashtu lifting his hands to the heavens. "You are both chieftains of this encampment. No one can disdain your word. You have vigor and weight to refrain anyone from spreading the story of our Hu'iski consumption." Both British men stood silent. Colonel Talbot tapped his swagger stick against his knee-high boot. Sir Fitzgerald with his hands on his waist and his pipe between his teeth puffed little clouds of smoke.

"You, *Aghai* Tallboot," Mahmoud continued, "invited us to drink Hu'iski with you." He pointed his finger heavenward. "Allah was our witness that we were forced to drink the *haram Sharab*. You made us believe it was like pomegranate water!"

"Perhaps you should remember your words when I poured the whiskey for you," Talbot replied, still tapping the swagger stick. "'We're sinful in countless wrongdoings. Adding another sin makes no difference. Remember?"

"This is the usual British trap to leash us Afghans like their dogs. This has been their trick for years," Maj. Akbar said bitterly. "When is this going to stop?

"*Bas!* Stop!" Colonel Talbot interjected, "I'll make a deal with you." He took off his round spectacles and wiped them with his kerchief. "We will make sure this matter is kept secret if you do the same for us." Hope arose and their panic and anxiety dwindled slightly; Mahmoud still trembled. His eyes shut and slowly opened in the direction of Talbot's newly cleaned spectacles.

"May the Almighty Allah be your safeguard," he breathed, clamping Colonel Talbot's hand in his. He knelt as if to kiss it, "Of course, we will keep your secrets private!" he grinned widely, flashing his greenish *naswar*-stained teeth. Throwing a glance back at Major Akbar Khan he called out, "Akbar Jana, *Aghai* Tallboot gave us his word!"

"*Baley*, Yes," Akbar nodded solemnly. "I only have trust in God and my own soul." He inhaled the last of his *beedi* and flicked the stub across the rocky ground. "If the word of an *Englees* was a bridge, no Afghan would cross. But now, it's worth a try, I'll believe it when I see it."

"To be frank, what we need is trust between us," a cynical smile twisted Colonel Adelbert Talbot's lips. "I don't see any issue for us drinking whiskey together, but let us not reveal our private matters to anyone." He glanced at Sir Fitzgerald, "Isn't that true, Sir?"

"Of course. I totally agree," he replied.

"Respectable *Aghai* Tallboot!" Lieutenant Mahmoud pleaded

like a vagrant beggar, "We have a saying in Afghanistan, no rose is without thorns. Meaning no one is perfect, we make mistakes and God always forgives us."

"Don't worry we have forgiven and forgotten too." Talbot reached into his pocket and took out his whiskey flask. He took a couple of sips and handed it to Akbar. "Keep the rest and the bottle," he smiled. "This should be a binding trust between us." He shook their hands, "And don't feel ashamed of eating with your hands. Just like you, I sometimes eat with mine. I have no problem scooping a mouthful of pilaf if I feel like eating that way. You must ignore knives and forks if you're uncomfortable using them." He gripped Mahmoud's shoulder in an expression of friendliness. "Let us get ready to welcome the Prince."

<hr />

Saturday, April 24, 1895 -- Afghan calendar month: Hamal 31, 1274.

Landi Kotal, India.

On this cloudy April day, Nasrullah and his companions rode wearily to their last encampment, about three miles from the British cantonment on the Khyber Pass. They were exhausted, dust-covered, sweat-drenched, and hungry. In advance of their arrival, bath tents had been pitched, cauldrons of water heated, and valises with clean clothes assembled. Boot polishers set out their beeswax, grease, and oven soot, and barbers equipped with blades and tools readied themselves to shave and trim beards. Everything was prepared for their well-being and comfort after the arduous twelve-day journey from Kabul.

After cleansing and ablution, dressed in a white cape and

turban, the fifty-six-year-old royal mullah, Shir Mohammad, literary meaning Lion Mohammad, led the congregation of Afghans in the late afternoon prayer to seek the Almighty's help for a successful outcome with the British. Everyone stood in neat rows behind him facing the sacred city of Mecca, side-by-side, shoulder-to-shoulder; obedience to Allah's divine law was of the utmost importance to their devout minds. As the prayer rituals proceeded, the full-bearded Shir Mohammad placed both hands on his ears framing a visage that bore a striking resemblance to poultry; but it was his ability to project his powerful roar, that could now be heard from the British cantonment, that was his leonine attribute. Shir Mohammad habitually used the word *Astaghfirullah*, seeking forgiveness from Allah, expressing shame, disapproval, and, ultimately, redemption for the repentant sinner. If he had known of Lieutenant Mahmoud's and Major Akbar's hooch-consuming habit, *Astaghfirullah* would have been bellowed forth multiple times with urgent requests to God to direct them on the right path before Amir invited them to the Kabul bazaar's gallows.

The congregation's steady murmur of Qur'anic verses was punctuated by simultaneous kneeling, standing, bowing, and pressing their foreheads to the ground while personally reflecting on prayer, paradise, forgiveness, and reward on the last day of judgment.

Finally, they reverently raised their hands in prayer for their bloodlines and families, both the living and the deceased.

Khairo, the head of Qandahar's Alakozai tribe, oblivious of those around him, mourned again for the loss of his only daughter, Malalai, and his brothers in the battle of Maiwand. His heartfelt plea was for England's destruction for she had authored the carnage and evil in his homeland. During this first leg of the journey, his mistrust of the British had heightened reckoning that the invitation to Prince Nasrullah was possibly another unconscionable belittlement of his nation under a thinly disguised veil of friendship. Khairo folded up his prayer rug and prepared to hide his bitterness and suspicion as he officially met Queen Victoria's proxies, Sir Fitzgerald and Colonel Adelbert Talbot.

At the Landi Kotal cantonment, a ceremonial display was presented the like of which no Afghan had seen before. As Fitzgerald and Talbot prepared to meet the Afghan prince, bugles were sounded and the British Twelfth Bengal Cavalry formed three mounted squadrons of gray, bay, and chestnut. As the five-hundred-yard advance began, the artillery moved into the open; first the chestnut squadron, then the three guns, then the gray and bay horses. On the Khyber road, they all paused. The artillery held up its position. A short distance away from the artillery, the cavalry assembled in two-deep formation and halted. The three guns limbered up in readiness for the salute. Nasrullah and his entourage thrust forward at a canter. The column dipped into a hollow and rose again on a crest. The British gunners moved swiftly into position, and, one after another, puffs of white smoke rose from the mouths of the cannons. One, two, three - twenty-one guns, and, with perfect timing, as the last one was fired, Prince Nasrullah Khan and his Afghan entourage officially set foot on British soil.

The Prince and his entourage dismounted. Nasrullah was wearing an ebony tunic for the occasion, adorned with a sash and epaulets with amber-striped black trousers, and long leather gloves—a credit to the English ladies for their assiduous work. He handed the reins to a groom. Colonel Talbot nodded at the bandmaster to begin the national anthem. The bandmaster and his subordinates were wearing patterned cloth helmets, scarlet tunics, and dark-blue trousers with a yellow welt. The bandmaster of the Fourth Gurkhas moved his mace in four sequential positions and finally lifted it high, signaling the band to start. Abruptly, the sound of drums, trumpets, and bagpipes broke the silence resonating throughout the cantonment alerting every British officer and Probyn's Horse to salute the Afghan Prince to the singing of God Save the Queen. At this point, the concept of a national anthem was entirely new to Afghanistan, so none had yet been composed.

"Your Highness!" Dr. Hamilton murmured to Nasrullah, "Please render a salute in reply. It's a gesture of respect and expected of you."

"*Baley!* Yes! Daktar Sahiba!" He held his salute as the union jack fluttered like a noiseless flame against the grandeur of the famous Pass. Flags of other empires had proudly danced and ultimately tattered here. Nasrullah and *Qomandan-e-Ala* Akram Khan took their position almost beneath the flag beside the two British men, with their close aids-the-camp behind.

Khairo wrapped his disfigured face with the end of his turban and stared intently at Colonel Talbot wondering why his face seemed so familiar. *Where have I seen this man, could it have been in Kabul or Kandahar?* he thought. Suddenly, a memory began to play across the surface of his mind like a part of an old nightmare.

Shortly after the salutation and the exchange of formal pleasantries between the British and the Afghans, Khairo implored Nasrullah with a furtive gesture.

"Shahzadah!" he said keeping his voice low. Concern was written on his partially covered face. He glanced at Talbot and back at Nasrullah, "*Eie Mard.* This man," he nodded furtively in Talbot's direction. A sob rose in his throat, "I am certain he was in Maiwand months before the battle started." He turned his face away and cleared his throat with a slight cough before looking back at Nasrullah, "I swear to Allah, he looked like a local Qandahari wearing a tattered *perahan* and *tunban* and a clumsily wrapped turban. I was suspicious of his blue eyes and his foreign appearance. I wondered then if he was an *Englees*." Khairo paused, "Just before the bloody onslaught in Maiwand he disappeared, but now I see him here. Trust me Shahzadah, I see the same features and dazzling blue eyes." He fell silent and cast another glance at Talbot. "And now he is wearing an *Englees* officer's uniform? Something is wrong!" As if to protect himself, Khairo tightened the flap of his turban more firmly around his deformed face.

Nasrullah stiffened, "I trust your judgment," he returned quietly, "But mistakes are possible. Are you sure of this?"

"I'm sure, Shahzadah!" Khairo said, unable to shake off the sense of foreboding that had come over him.

"I'm going to ask one or two questions," Nasrullah said. Don't worry, I will be cautious."

He sauntered over to Colonel Talbot with Raj, the interpreter, in tow' "Colonel Abdulbeert Tallboot!"

"Your Highness."

"It will be my pleasure to join you on this memorable voyage to *Englistan*."

"The pleasure is mine, Your Highness," Adelbert Talbot replied convivially.

"May I ask you a question?" Nasrullah straightened his tall karakul hat.

"Please, Your Highness, by all means."

"Why were we rushed to get here yesterday?" Raj echoed Nasrullah's question in his playful accented tone.

"Your Highness, there is no reason for the interpreter to translate word for word, I'm fluent both in Pashtu and Dari." Talbot's Dari was flawless with only the vaguest hint of an accent. His smile revealed two gold-tipped crowns. "Allow me to explain the reason we requested your prompt arrival, Your Highness."

Nasrullah raised his eyebrows hearing his reply, "You are certainly fluent in Dari!" he said as he signaled Raj to leave.

"Yes, Your Highness, and to answer your question, we are a day late for boarding the train in Peshawar, four days behind will affect boarding the ship in Bombay and ultimately the schedule for Your Highness's arrival in Portsmouth, where huge preparations are taking place." He smiled and tucked his swagger stick under his arm. "Another reason of concern is that the weather will be unbearably hot in the Indian Ocean if the embarkation is delayed any further."

Originally, the scheduled train route to Bombay was through Lahore, Amritsar, and Delhi a seventy-two-hour journey arriving on April 26th and departing on April 29th. Because of Prince Nasrullah's numerous delays for camel fights and other amusements, his schedule had been rerouted through Lahore to Karachi, from where they would be ferried to Bombay reducing the time to sixty-two hours. As Talbot explained the predicament of the departure and arrival, Nasrullah's mind was elsewhere, and the explanation went unheeded.

"We've made the necessary adjustments to Your Highness's timetable to meet the embarkation deadline and it should be fine if Your Highness boards the train in Peshawar tomorrow."

"*Besyar Khoob!* Very Good! We'll be up early and proceed towards Peshawar."

"Of course Your Highness!" He pushed his thin-framed spectacles back to the bridge of his nose.

"*Aghai* Tallboot, where did you learn to speak our languages so well?"

"Your Highness, I love learning languages, I speak other languages as well."

"And what languages are they?"

"I'm fluent in Arabic, Urdu, Russian, and German. I was hand-picked to serve you because of my fluency in Pashtu and Dari," he smiled again, "Our renowned diplomat, Sir Fitzgerald, and myself are to escort you to London."

"Aghai Tallboot, I don't recall ever hosting you in Afghanistan, but have you been there?"

"Briefly in Jalalabad, Your Highness," Talbot replied blandly. The lie left his lips as freely as a bird from a cage.

Khairo appeared to fix his gaze at something miles behind Talbot's head but he aimed his question at the man. "And where did you learn Pashtu, if I may ask?"

"*Zeh pa Quetta ke oseedelay.* I've lived in Quetta," the colonel replied, "I was stationed with 20th Mountain Regiment stationed in Chaman, close to Kandahar."

Khairo threw out another test of Talbot's integrity, "so you haven't been to Kandahar? A stone's throw away from Chaman?"

"Only briefly, right after the battle of Maiwand. We brought the dead and the injured to Quetta." He took a handkerchief from his pocket and dabbed the sweat off the wrinkles of his brow. His face reddened. He turned to Nasrullah, "Your Highness!" he bowed respectfully, "It is very hot out here and you must be exhausted after your long journey." "I am sure you all need to rest. We will be ready for your departure to Peshawar tomorrow." Switching the conversation to level ground, he smiled graciously, "Your Highness, relaying your arrival information via Lieutenant Mahmoud Khan and Major Akbar Khan was very thoughtful of you. I must add that Akbar Khan is very gifted in golfing. He did an amazing job tossing a meatball into my glass yesterday." He gave a broad smile flashing the gold crowns.

A profound silence followed, their unsettled eyes glanced awkwardly around the cantonment and avoided looking at each other; neither man knew what was being insinuated by this remark, but they wondered how they would endure a three-week-long voyage to London with Talbot. At length, Nasrullah cast an uneasy glance at Talbot, "well, you are correct *Aghai* Tallboot, we need some rest, we will retire for the night.

CHAPTER THIRTY-SIX

❦❦❦

Peshawar

Sunday, April 26, 1895 -- Afghan calendar month:
Sawr 1, 1274.

Peshawar, British India

Close to Peshawar, the arid, rugged hills of the Khyber yielded to alluvial, verdant farmlands resembling Jalalabad with picturesque fields of sugarcane, and citrus groves. They cantered through the city of Peshawar, a city of flat-roofed houses built from ochre colored bricks, wedged between wooden frames and coated with mud. But in the bazaars, the frames were painted a cerulean hue, and the bricks a glittering white. As they approached, the city was obscured from sight by a massive downpour.

Despite the incessant rain, on the road into Peshawar riders and those on foot moved aside to allow the Prince and his entourage to pass through. Most lined up along the road to hail the young prince and welcome him. Nasrullah raised a hand in greeting as he sat proudly on Baarfi who snorted and whinnied. The Afridis had turned out wearing their brightest embroidered costumes and their shouting could be heard from a quarter of a mile away, "*Zendah bad* Shahzadah Nasrullah Khan, long live Prince Nasrullah Khan." They cheered, waved, and applauded gustily. The nationalistic fervor of the crowd was driven by the belief that Nasrullah was spearheading the beginning of the end of British rule.

The progress of the caravan to the city's railway cantonment meant a three-mile-long skirmish through soft oozy sludge. As the enthusiastic gathering demonstrated its unwavering exuberance for Prince Nasrullah, a company of British Corps Military Mounted Police appeared to give added security to the young Prince. The cheering and waving went on as blocks of spectators narrowly flanked either side of Nasrullah's column.

Decorative arches were spanned and criss-crossed with bunting, gay rags, and flags, and Pashtu mottoes hung from balconies and windows showing their utmost jubilation for the young Prince of Afghanistan. They passed through the famous Qissa-Khwani bazaar, the Storytellers Market, in the center of the city, where tradesmen of Pathans, Hazaras, Turkomans, Uzbeks, Tajiks, and a handful of other tempestuous Afghans generally gathered and sat cross-legged in *Chaikhans*, *Chapli-Kebabis* and shared tales of their experiences from their journeys to Samarkand, Mashhad, Herat, Kashgar, Ashgabat, Kabul, Delhi, and other purlieus. Today, however, as Nasrullah was passing through, the public had forsaken their social gatherings and elbowed their way to cheer and applaud the Prince and his companions.

A deep anti-British sentiment prevailed in Peshawar. Rudyard Kipling aptly described Peshawar in his diary, as the *City of Evil Countenances*. Over time, it had changed hands from the Mughals to the Greeks, Persians, Afghans, Sikhs, and now, the British. When an Englishman passed by, they turned to glower at him and spat on the ground in disgust after he moved on.

A few miles away, clearly distinguishable from the city dwellings, English cottages and bungalows with tiled roofs stood surrounded by rose gardens and lush green lawns. Each house had its own watchtower with an armed *chowkeedar*, watchman, as a guarantee of protection to the colonial English families. *Ayahs*, nannies, pushed prams around the neighborhoods of the foreigners; servants walked English children on ponies. Punjabi and Sindhi coachmen drove their British masters to flamboyant social gatherings where the status of the colonies was discussed, the Paris fashions, jackal or leopard hunting, and the latest gossip was caught up with.

The jubilant crowd followed Nasrullah through the three-mile slushy roads to the railway cantonment. To ensure security, Colonel Zalmai Khan and his guardsmen stood cheek-by-jowl with the British Corps of Military Mounted Police to keep the jubilant crowd at bay. The entire railway station had been cordoned off to ensure there were no further disruptions to Nasrullah's already late itinerary.

Whilst the preparation for embarkation was underway, the Northwest Frontier's Commanding General, Sir Edmund Barrow, invited Prince Nasrullah and his regimental officers to dine with him in the station's regimental mess.

General Barrow was in his late fifties, a tall, handsome man of slender build, with dark hair streaked with silver and a fine handlebar mustache. Barrow was a colonel when, just after the Battle of Maiwand, he and General Fredrick Roberts led ten-thousand British soldiers to quell a rebellion in Kandahar. For his conspicuous bravery, he was awarded the Victoria Cross.

Among his subordinates, the ranks of which Winston Churchill was soon to join, the General was regarded as a maverick of his time. On this occasion, the General was dressed in a dark blue Hussar dolman with exquisite gold-laced scarlet sartorial confections attached to the shoulders by silken-wing-epaulets, black pantaloons with orange side-stripes. On his head was a feathery plumed bicorn hat, which gave him a vaguely Napoleonic appearance, although the front end of the hump-back bridge was positioned above his face and the back end at the nape of his neck.

At the entrance to the mess, six kilted sergeant-pipers greeted Nasrullah's men with wailing bagpipes. As Nasrullah entered the mess he whispered in General, Akram Khan's ear.

"These men dressed like women sound like howling dogs."

Akram Khan raised his eyebrows and grimaced.

As Nasrullah and the Afghan courtiers entered the regimental mess-hall, their faces washed blank with confusion for a split second as they attempted to grasp how different this British social gathering was from their own. Most scarlet-tunicked officers stood in groups chatting with a drink in one hand and a cheap cigar or Trichy cheroot in the other. The air was warm and smelt strongly of tobacco. Colonel Talbot, and Sir Fitzgerald, who was puffing contentedly on his pipe, were chatting to a couple of officers.

Instantly, as the Scottish pipers marched behind Nasrullah, the assembled officers, and their wives, fell silent, and the men stood to attention. The Prince was ushered to his seat, and the pipers completed their performance behind the royal chair.

Twenty long tables were set with crisp, white linen tablecloths. Fine glassware, silverware, and china plates embellished with the regimental crest gleamed under the luminescence of the candelabras and gasoliers suspended from the high ceiling. Tapestries, animal heads, and horns of all kinds were mounted on the whitewashed walls, some horns reaching over six feet long tip-to-tip.

Each table was occupied by some twenty-five uniformed British officers and their wives, most of whom were dressed in the latest European fashions, elbow-length gloves, and flowery hats, while others were elegantly clad in saris. A few of the ladies held long cigarette-holders made of ivory and silver, a mode that was fast becoming the height of fashion in Europe, and were smoking spiced Egyptian cigarettes.

To attract everyone's attention, General Borrow rose from his seat and clinked on a crystal glass.

" Your Highness, Ladies and gentlemen," he gave a slight bow in Prince Nasrullah's direction and raised his glass. "I request you to drink a toast to the Afghan Prince, His Highness, Nasrullah Khan, and to his father, His Highness, Amir Abdul Rahman Khan, who is a most faithful and loyal friend to Her Majesty, Queen-Empress Victoria." The assembly raised their glasses in Nasrullah's direction and drank. "I also propose this toast to Her Gracious Majesty, the Queen." There were some enthusiastic, "Rah, Rah's," at the drinking of this second toast, and then they took their seats once more. General Borrow launched into a brief speech of welcome to the Prince and his retinue. The Afghan guests, and the English members traveling with them, were seated at General Borrow's table. Behind the General was a richly carved mantelpiece, to right and left of which were two flags—the Union Jack and the British Raj—with their poles crossing each other. On the wall between the flags, hung an oval portrait of Queen Victoria, on a background of ivory, framed in richly carved silver, with an inner boundary of gemstones.

As soon as the dinner was over, Roma and Olivia thankfully made their way out to breathe some fresh air and stole the show as they walked across the room. Their dazzling latest European fashion and their youthful freshness and beauty turned everyone's heads. Olivia was wearing a gown that was a combination of black taffeta, cream lace, and blue silk net with an unusual broad panel at the back that formed the collar and a string of deep-sea pearls gleamed around her neck. Everything about the attire made her a *Beauté du diable*. Unlike Roma and the other ladies present, she was not wearing a corset or tight lacing of any kind. Her grandfather had disapproved of its use and shunned whalebone corsets for the health complications they caused, his stance eventually influenced the entire fashion industry.

Roma was yet to make the change. For the time being, she was still attached to her fashionable dresses that went along with various opulent corsets, although she complained regularly and was often not able to eat her favorite dishes. The corset she was wearing added a graceful line to her waist giving her figure hourglass femininity. The bell-shaped design of her skirt added to the illusion of a tiny waist. Her dress was accompanied by a dinner jacket elaborately embroidered in several shades of maroon silk. After the difficult first leg of their journey, the young women had chosen to bounce back to their graceful feminine look and were as bubbly as magnums of champagne. Several other English ladies followed Roma and Olivia to the foyer and engaged them in conversation. When they and ladies of regimental officers left the officer's mess together, Roma saw her opportunity to pay Zalmai a quick visit. Olivia was busy chatting to the spouses of the regimental officers who were interested in her association with Charles Worth. Suspicion would not be aroused as Roma would be presumed to be with the women. The ladies were ushered to another room where a fire burned brightly in the hearth.

Roma whispered hastily to Olivia. "I am going to see if I can find Zalmai. Please cover for me, if necessary."

Olivia nodded, "Don't be too long though," she warned.

As Roma left the building, she came across a young boy with a gun holster slung over his shoulder. He was leading Baarfi to the loading platform.

"Colonel Zalmai? You know him? Tall, very strong man?" Roma gestured Zalmai's height and physical description.

"Oh! *Dagarwal Sahib Zalmai Khan, Balay,* Yes." the boy replied, holding Baarfi's reigns in one hand, he gestured towards the regimental gate with the other. "*Hagha Halta dey,* he's there."

"Please ask him to come here."

"*Der Sha*, very good."

The boy led Colonel Zalmai across the premises of the regimental cantonment to where Roma was standing under the canopy, waiting anxiously, her hands tightly knitted together. Even from a distance, she instantly recognized Zalmai's distinguished silhouette and her heart lurched.

"You're dismissed!" Zalmai said to the lad, "No snitching regarding this meeting, else you'll be stripped of every privilege. Including that gun on your shoulder! Do you understand?"

"I don't know of any meetings *Dagarwal Sahib!* I'm blind and deaf," the young groom grinned.

Roma stared at Zalmai. He was soaked to the skin from the rain, which was still falling, and his copper-colored tunic and breaches were plastered with mud.

"Dear Roma Jan," he said with a warm smile, "I hope you finally had a break from the long ride." He removed his soaked hat, tucked it under his arm, and smoothened his dark hair with his wet hand. "You look beautiful," he said lightly. "Forgive me for my appearance, cordoning off the premises to hold back the crowd was a daunting task. Thank God, the people faded away fast after that."

"You look wonderful to me, Zal," she replied and reached up to rub a streak of mud off his chin. She gazed into his brown eyes and saw the flickers of light from the gasoliers in the nearby windows reflected there. They could hear strains of the Bohemian Rhapsody that was being played by the orchestra in the hall. A British regimental officer and his spouse walked by and greeted them casually. Zalmai scanned Roma's dress. The deep maroon brought out the hints of gold in her hair. "You've bewitched me!" His hand slid down her thin waist in a swift caress. She raised herself up on tiptoe and gently kissed his cheek. "You must be cold. Let's go inside, I've found a private room where we can be alone for a while."

"Where're those envious predators?" Zalmai whispered as he laced his fingers with hers.

Roma smiled. "The Prince and the cross-eyed Chief of Police are heartily feasting," she murmured. "I think they have been sidetracked by the flatteries of the British General. She held his hand and tugged him gently, "Come, follow me."

The foyer was empty and Zalmai quickly followed Roma through a dimmed corridor past the room where Olivia and the English officers' ladies were sipping champagne, and talking happily amongst themselves. Roma peeped through the door and waved at Olivia. Olivia waved back with a smile as she noticed Zalmai's face behind hers.

They walked a few doors down into an empty L-shaped room. The rain was pelting down on the small windows like liquid bullets, but the air inside was stifling. At the far end around the corner was a billiard table with three suspended lights shining dimly on its lush-green fabric. Two billiard sticks and smooth ivory balls were scattered on the table. The tapestries and horns on the walls were barely visible in the weak glow.

Roma stood next to Zalmai and briefly slid her hand over the gilded floral relief carvings on the side of the table where she stood. She leaned forward and nuzzled into his chest, and felt his stiff shoulders begin to relax. He ran his fingers through her hair and breathed in its perfume.

"You smell wonderful."

She said softly, "We have a couple of hours." And, drawing him by the hand, they slumped onto the leather sofa against a wall hidden and secluded from unexpected intruders.

"This is perfect," Zalmai whispered, marveling at the seclusion. A complete quietness settled over them like a fresh fall of snow. There was only the distant, muffled sound of the music through the brick walls.

Zalmai's gaze wandered over Roma's face. In the muted light he could see her cheekbones, the dark beauty spot below her mouth. His eyes strayed to her lips recalling to mind their memorable, sensual caress. Their eyes met and locked, it was as though he wanted her to read the urgency of his feelings, to intensely see into his soul. The desire for their lips to meet swept through her. She felt blissful quivers coursing through her belly. Her lips parted. Their faces were barely distinguishable in the weak luminescence from the lamps.

"Roma Jan . . ." His breath whispered against her face. "This precious momen. . ." " he trailed off, "I don't want it to fade." His fingers caressed the contour of her jaw, and he cradled his hand under it. "*Azizem* Roma Jan, my dear Roma. This moment is ours." He touched her with an intimacy she'd never expected from him. She lay beside him, transfixed.

Despite the discomfort of her tightly laced corset, she closed the gap between them. Zalmai breathed in the sweet smell of her lemony scented talc as she pressed her lips against his. She slid her hands behind his head feeling the cropped hair along the nape of his neck then upward to clutch the soft curls on the crown of his head.

He gently lifted her skirt along with her chemise; touched her garters, stockings and crotchless pantalettes, he had never imagined those before. He unbuttoned his mud-streaked breaches. His hands slid along her naked thighs, and the warmth of his mouth on hers shot needles of intimate desire all through her.

He swallowed as he dithered with her silken chemise. "I've¬I've never tried this before," he stammered.

"Me neither," Roma replied breathlessly, "but I desire it, with you. Now." Her eyes closed as Zalmai thrust inward. Suddenly, the world vanished, gyrated down to a complete void. Nothing mattered apart from the fulfillment of this desire and her exigency for intimate love. His fingers were like divine fire to her soul and their almost inaudible mixes of moaning and panting intoxicated them in this exploration of perfect unity. Their pulses and respirations raced to an urgent climax. No one had ever recognized her like this; he showed her the vigor of her own body, the beauty of her yearning. She envisioned with him all the unspoken longings of her soul. Then, moments later, soothing came in ripples; weightlessness as if levitating in space.

Zalmai opened his eyes from this euphoric sense of disembodiment. Roma leaned across his chest, kissing his cheeks, his eyes, his lips. There was a radiance that flowed from her, a luscious color of skin, and a delightful vivacity.

"I love you," she said. She fanned herself with a flutter of her hand and lifted her hair off her neck.

"This is just the beginning; our love is growing by the minute. I love you too, my dear Roma Jan."

It was pitch dark. At the center of the platform in Peshawar's cantonment railway station, under the smoke-stained canopy, stood a huge baggage cart drawn by two bullocks; and, around this, the tumult raged unceasingly.

"*Khabardar!* be aware!

"*Dursara Wogora!* watch yourself!"

"*Wodarieja!* Stop!"

The ear-splitting, shrill warnings of the haulers and movers, and the bellowing of frightened animals, it was just part of the general chaos that presided over the station that morning. The platform was strewn with goods and paraphernalia of all kinds, and crowded with horses, ready to entrain for the next destination—Karachi. Those on the platform were in constant danger of their lives from the flying hoofs of apprehensive animals. As the train drew in belching smoke and hissing steam it caused panic among the horses and initial alarm to those Afghans who had never seen a train before. They were appalled to see this massive iron horse with its many coaches screeching and squealing to a complete stop.

The intention was to clear the platform of some fifty or more horses belonging to Nasrullah's guards first. The Afghan men were fearless, and without a moment's hesitation, plunged into the midst of the rearing, kicking, animals to begin loading.

Talbot and Fitzgerald stood on the platform watching the tumultuous event with consternation, astounded at the complete lack of order. At the heart of the wild confusion was the Head of Logistics and Culinary, Major Akbar Khan, and his friend, Lieutenant Mahmoud Khan, who were hard at work attempting to urge everything haphazardly into the train. The state of their tipsiness was obvious: they were somewhat unsteady on their feet, loquacious, as loud as auctioneers at a sale, and their motor responses were sluggish.

Lieutenant Mahmoud Khan, guided by a single lantern, waded into the tumult. He directed, superintended, harangued and—from the tone of his voice—swore till the distressed beasts were set right. If one disorderly chestnut stallion could have spoken Pashtu, he might have said how mercilessly the Lieutenant had backed him into the train. The continuous protesting and snorting up the slippery gangway had become hugely entertaining for onlookers, Talbot and Fitzgerald.

"That whiskey flask I gave him the other day is doing a fine job," Talbot commented, "plenty of effort and exhilaration on their part...I fancy it won't be the last entertainment we will see on this journey! We'll keep them well supplied on the way." That reminded him to retrieve his flask from the pocket of his jacket; he uncapped it and took a couple of gulps.

Suddenly a cloud of steam from the train blurred the astonished and confused crowd.

"Look at their guards, they're as filthy as the mouths of fired guns," he tucked the flask back into his Hussar jacket pocket. "They have even stuffed dirty bits of cloth inside their Martini muzzles."

"Probably for protection against rain and dust," Fitzgerald replied lighting his pipe. "Their horses are also unkempt and have probably never been groomed," he puffed clouds of smoke and flicked the smoldered match away. "The Prince and his entourage ride fine beasts though." He checked his pocket watch, "Half-past eight. Despite everything, they are making good time so far."

Everything on the platform was wet and clammy to the touch, and with almost no visibility except for a few dim lanterns, and men stumbled across crates and baggage at every turn. More than one person fell headlong and was hoisted up by another fellow. Produced as a scene on canvas, it would be mocked as the product of an overly imaginative mind¬this capturing of a profound clash of civilizations in which Uzbek lancers were thrown together with a steam locomotive, apprehensive horses and their handlers, amid a ceaseless and relentless downpour.

"That little chap over there looks interesting," Talbot gestured with his swagger stick towards a young groom; his interest was piqued. He felt a touch of insobriety as he walked to where the boy was standing.

He was young, possibly only fourteen, and was keeping charge of a pack of *yaboos*, mules, laden with Amir's gifts for Queen Victoria. The boy wore a filthy *Perahan-Tunban* and strands of disheveled hair protruded from under his clumsily swathed turban. But he smiled and paraded congenially, displaying a Colt revolver strapped in a shoulder-holster over a grimy embroidered Qandahari waistcoat.

"Have you ever fired a shot with that?" Talbot asked bluntly in Pashtu.

"*Ho Sahib!* Yes Sir!" the boy replied with a cherubic grin, which portrayed an element of smugness.

"Can I see it?"

He handed him the Colt, "*Khabardar*, be aware," the boy warned him, "it's loaded. May Allah forbid that it goes off and kills someone."

Talbot noticed the loaded gun was as clean and smooth as a peeled onion, "Perhaps you should demonstrate your mastery," he suggested. "Target shooting sometime?"

"*Ho Sahib*, anytime you want. Maybe in Landan?"

Talbot smiled, "Maybe." He stretched his sturdy hand, "What's your name?"

"Gul Agha," said the boy.

Talbot felt the young boy's dirt-caked hand as he offered a light handshake; it was like sandpaper. "Your name means Mr. Flower," Talbot smiled, "You certainly sound like one."

After two-and-a-half hours hard work, Lieutenant Mahmoud Khan and Major Akbar Khan, soaked from head to toe, retired to catch a little rest before Nasrullah and his entourage boarded the train.

Finally, the wagons of animals and humans steamed off into the darkness. The angry thumping of the four-legged occupants could be heard for as long as the tail lights of the train remained visible. The Afghans may have been astonished and unsettled by the noisy locomotive, but they probably took some snuff and disguised their feelings. The horses, on the other hand, could only express their incredulity and alarm more forcibly.

Their next destination was Karachi along the Indus River. Inside the lavish saloon car, Nasrullah and his father's close courtiers assembled to marvel at their first train ride. As the heavy wheels of the train clacked between the flanges and the train rolled forward, the sudden motion caused a sensation as if their bodies were in space. Watching through the windows, they had an impression of self-motion as the train thrust away from the stationary platform. For the initial few minutes and miles, they were absorbed in taking in the astonishment of this novel experience, like children coming to grips with the thrill of a first arcade ride. A long deep silence fell between them.

As the constant thrumming settled to a speed of about forty-five miles-per-hour, it became as mesmerizing as the rolling and breaking rhythm of an ocean. Gusts of steam spewed from the sides of the train; black smoke puffed up into the sky; the smell of burning coal permeating the air; the long shrill of the whistle bouncing off the Indus valley, and the rhythmic swaying as they crossed road intersections; all this would remain ingrained in their minds forever. With all these progressions, with each new step in the evolutionary ascent, the world was changing for these Afghans. Their first journey to England might not bring change to the foreign policy of their homeland but would become a cultural shift as they contemplated a civilization outside their tribal cocoon. Apart from the guns, matchlocks, and other weapons produced in Amir's Mashin-Khana, time had frozen for centuries in their homeland. Every new experience would stun the Prince and his men, particularly as they witnessed the technological advancements of Europe.

As the novelty wore off, they began to discuss this adventure with their fellow courtiers in the swaying car. However, their attention was still drawn beyond the dark windows as silhouetted objects and visible lights bypassed them at a speed so much faster than their sauntering caravans.

"I wish we had trains too," General Akram Khan broke the silence. The General was so mesmerized by the motion of the train that he failed to slide his thick glasses back onto the bridge of his nose.

The regal saloon had been specially modeled for the Governor-General of India to resemble a stately home on wheels. It boasted an elaborate silk ceiling, an aquamarine velvet chesterfield, two wingback chairs, with a tasseled footstool in the same fabric; matching silk screens, tasseled lampshades, mahogany tables, a deep-pile carpet, and flowers beautifully arranged in metal vases attached to its walls. Indeed, the state of art swiveling carriage with six wheels under each coach was designed to produce a smoother motion on the tracks and added to the top-tier luxury.

Nasrullah glanced at Khairo Khan and asked, "Do you agree with my cousin?" He raised his brows inquiringly over eyes as brown as chocolate, "Khairo Khan..."

Khairo Khan was peering through the window hypnotized. "My apologies," he replied," I was in a reverie as I considered the speed of the train. I cannot believe the ingenuity involved in making such a fast-moving machine." He grinned, "I beg your pardon, would you kindly repeat the question?" His cheerful voice was slightly muffled through the flap of his turban. Khairo was on his feet with one hand tightly clasped on the brass handrail to control his balance against the lurching car.

"The General thinks we should have trains in Afghanistan, do you agree?"

"Yes, I agree with General Sahib Akram Khan. We are in dire need of sound transportation like this train in our homeland." His black pinstriped turban touched the padded wall. " Our caravans are slow. It would speed up travel time," he replied.

Amir Abdul Rahman Khan had set his policy with the British upon ascending to power. He bluntly banned railways and telegraph in his dominion for fear they would be utilized against Afghanistan in the event of a British or Russian invasion.

Nasrullah shifted his gaze to Field Marshal Hassein Khan and broached the same question. "Naieb-Salar Sahib, do you have any different thoughts?"

At that moment, the saloon door slid open and Prince Omar and little William zipped across the threshold. Their heads moved in all directions and their eyes took in everything at a glance. Prince Omar wearing his new pleated tunic and a pair of gray knickerbockers was already developing a British look. William wore a royal naval uniform with embroidered stars, anchors, and eagles with a big, white trim-lined flap behind the collar.

"Can we explore your room?" asked Prince Omar rubbing the brass knob on the door.

"Of course, you may," said Nasrullah ruffling the boy's neatly combed black hair. His accompanying Nannie had obviously spent quite some time grooming and dressing him. They both went to the window, cupping their hands like blinkers to peer into the dark night.

"There's a castle!" little William said excitedly.

Naieb-Salar Hassein Khan also peered through the window as the train passed the fifteen-century fort on the right and with the ferocious Kabul River on the left.

"I disagree with you both," he commented, reverting to their conversation regarding the advantage of railways. He was lounging comfortably on the chesterfield, his ample belly pressing against the restricting confines of his taut tunic. Medals of all sorts rested against his chest. The train's whistle echoed against the mountain as they left the fort behind. "That fort is a good example¬Attock—I'm sure some of you have heard the name before?" He gestured with a broad sweep of his hand, his onyx prayer beads wrapped around his fist. "It was built by Akbar the Great, a Mughal emperor. This fort was once part of Afghan territory . . . Our founding father, Ahmad Shah Durani captured it and halted the enemy from advancing north." He waved a hand in the direction of Afghanistan. "Yes, it was during the famous battle of Panipat, close to Delhi, in 1776." He crossed his feet and his stocky body swayed with the train's movement. "If there was no railroad or viable means of transportation for the Englees-Ha to reach Attock, or to Peshawa, which was also our city at that time, they wouldn't have been able to hold on to these Afghan territories for long. Not even for a week! We would have driven them out forcefully, as we had done many times from our land." He took a sip of his tea and set the cup back with a clink onto its matching blue saucer on the table next to him. "I'm twice as old as any of you." He glanced toward Parwana Khan who was seated on the footstool and was leaning against the wall, "No offense *Kotwal Sahib*, you and I are about the same age and I'm sure you know all this." He continued the story, "I have vivid memories of our history. I remember when the British extended the railroad tracks to Chaman, close to the border of Kandahar." He unwound his onyx prayer beads and started thumbing through them one by one. "Amir Sahib expressed his dissatisfaction by telling the Englees-Ha. 'It's just like pushing a knife into my vitals.'"

"What was Englees-Ha's reply to my father's comment?" asked Nasrullah, who was listening attentively.

"They didn't care about his comment. They even wanted to extend the railroad tracks all the way to Herat, Mazar-e-Sharif, and Kabul." Naieb-Salar Hassein Khan replied.

The train conductor shuffled into the carriage as though he was shackled at his ankles, he was holding a teapot in one hand while gripping the brass handle on the wall with the other. The crown of the rich yellow Banarasi turban he was wearing stood up like a pea hen's tail. He was obviously of mixed Anglo-Indian race; light brown curls that had escaped from under his turban graced a small fair-skinned face and blue eyes. He looked more like an average British soldier than an Indian. These white genes popped up occasionally in some families throughout India.

"Helloo! Sahib! Can I pour somore teea? " his accent was unmistakably Indian. He grinned showing off-white teeth and proceeded to skillfully fill everyone's cup without a spill, as the train swayed as gently as a cradle.

"So, Amir Sahib refused to allow the extension of the railroads into his dominion," Khairo Khan said.

"He bluntly told the Englees-Ha, 'No, you'll not extend an inch of your tracks inside my dominion'! Amir Sahib even ordered that a manual should be produced as to how to destroy railway tracks in the event of a threat of invasion.

"Yes, my father occasionally mentioned to us that he told the Englees-Ha, 'There will be a railway in Afghanistan only when the Afghans are able to make it themselves'," Nasrullah told them.'" As long as Afghanistan has not arms enough to fight against any great attacking power, it would be folly to allow railways to be laid throughout the country.'" Nasrullah echoed his father's sentiment.

But the British moved forward keeping one route into Afghanistan accessible all year round, allowing the immediate deployment of troops as far as Bombay, Calcutta, and Karachi to counter any threat to India from Afghans or Russians. The British ordered the construction of railroad tracks to Quetta, near the Afghan border and this would evolve into a plan to reach Kandahar at immediate notice should the order be given.

"*Naieb-Salar Sahib* Hassein Khan," General Akram Khan leaped to his feet and sat down next to Naieb-Salar Hassein Khan on the Chesterfield pushing his spectacles up his nose. "may I respectfully disagree with your notion of not having a railroad in Afghanistan."

Amir's chief of staff, *Naieb-Salar* Hassein Khan, raised a rugged hand and gestured politely, scrutinizing Sahib Khan closely as he spoke, "Please go ahead and say what you have to say, General Sahib."

"Thank you *Neib-Salar Sahib*," General Akram Khan set his teacup and saucer down on the mahogany table next to him. "Isn't it obvious that the Englees-Ha have already, to some extent made, and are still making, India one of the most progressive nations in the world?" Colonel Hassein Khan immediately perceived the direction of his amiable question. "Envision the subcontinent . . . Light years ahead of us . . . No doubt the Englees-Ha do benefit from India's advancement by building railroads and infrastructure but . . ."

"And the Indian is denied his right to run his own country!" Nasrullah interjected abrasively. "At what cost? And the bastard Englees spreads his genes? And like a slave, the Indian washes his masters' feet only to be sent across the border, or anywhere in the world, to fight and die for his Englees *Badaar*, English master? They steal India's resources and enrich Englistan to become a mightier and mightier colonial power?" Nasrullah stood to his feet and stared sightlessly at his reflection in the window. "I'd kill any bastard Englees child born out of wedlock in Afghanistan . . . and hang any Afghan who washes the Englees feet, or any Afghan woman who dances for them!" He turned to Neib-Salar Hassein Khan and said emphatically: "I agree with my father, no railroad for Afghanistan." Nasrullah changed the subject and cracked the knuckles of his long wiry fingers. "How much time is left before we get to Lahore?"

"There's about five hours left," replied General Akram Khan.

"Let's reassemble for breakfast in the morning. We all need to retire for the night," Nasrullah said.

CHAPTER THIRTY-SEVEN

❧❧❧

Whenever Nasrullah's British chartered train to Karachi stopped at railway stations along the Indus River to load coal and water, royal military bands and bagpipers blared their music on the platforms in his honor. Banners displayed at Lahore's railway station blazoned: "Welcome Shahzadah Nasrullah Khan." In Multan, Hyderabad, and Karachi: "Long live Great Britain and Afghanistan".

By altering Nasrullah's itinerary and rerouting to Karachi instead of Delhi, he and his entourage arrived promptly at the port of Karachi and embarked immediately for Bombay arriving there on April 28, 1895.

Bombay was the coastal metropolis on the Arabian Sea and the western gateway to India. Docked along its pier, the British troopship *HMS Clive,* was festooned along its railings and triple masts with blue and white flowers and vibrant banners welcoming the Prince. The *HMS Clive* was used to transport troops and their families on a round trip between Portsmouth and Bombay and carried as many as one-thousand-two-hundred people at a time.

From her starboard side, as she lay at anchor under the blameless warm morning sky, her chalky white hull, with a double row of portholes extending along its length, was reflected in the glassy sea. Nearby, the cawing seagulls skimmed the surface of the water like floating scarves as the climbing sun reflected off the vast ocean surface like molten gold. Here too, the music bands and bagpipes went on for some time, gnawing at Nasrullah like a silent poison. The grimace on his face and the constant clenching of his narrow jaw were signs that he despised the wailing of the bagpipes.

Before boarding the steamer, street entertainers and jugglers amassed on the pier to perform for the youthful Prince. He was particularly astounded by two of the many tricks that were performed: a dwarf mango tree was made to grow from seedling to fruit-bearing stage before his eyes in an incredibly short amount of time and his eyes widened in astonishment when he saw men swallowing daggers and thrusting swords down their throats. Prince Nasrullah, Prince Omar, William, and Khairo Khan clustered together mesmerized—even their food and drinks were served while they were being entertained. Nasrullah regretted that time constraints would cause him to miss many of these amusements, but still, his rapturous bravos for every trick echoed vociferously between the hull of the steamer and the buildings close by. Even under the shade of a canopied awning, it was unbearably hot. Nasrullah stripped off his tunic and astrakhan Karakul hat, handed them to the page, and rolled up the sleeves of his white cotton shirt.

Whilst Nasrullah was being entertained, a hubbub could be heard in the background as orders were yelled and commands were repeated. Hundreds of native Indian laborers hustled and bustled, moving portmanteaus, valises, and bits and pieces of paraphernalia belonging to Nasrullah, his entourage, and the Amir's English friends, into the steamer. The workers were clothed in white turbans and white cotton garments that extended below their knees and were tied at their waists by red sashes. The belongings of British officers and their families, stationed in India and now destined for Portsmouth, were being loaded at the same time.

Gul Agha, the young groom, tugged Baarfi onto the gangplank. With every yank, his oversized shoulder holster swayed like a pendulum. Many other grooms followed, walking the horses with a metallic clop-clop up to the ship.

The Head of the Culinary and Logistics, Major Akbar Khan, and his assistant Lieutenant Mahmoud Khan, both lightly clad in their flowing garments, presided over the cargo and livestock. With an abacus in hand, Mahmoud tallied the delivery of livestock that was ordered for consumption on the voyage. There were stacked cages of clucking and crowing chickens, a makeshift area filled with a bleating flock of about fifty sheep, four bellowing calves, and a cud-chewing dairy cow with a huge udder, to supply fresh milk for Prince Omar on the high seas, were all ready for loading onto the steamer. The animal feed and moistened hay ripened in the warm air. It looked remarkably like Kabul's open animal *naqash* market.

Colonel Talbot and Sir Fitzgerald roamed the pier to oversee the status of embarkation. As they approached Mahmoud, they were met with the same nauseating odor of the markets in Peshawar or Kabul. Mahmoud was chatting with vendors. Talbot appeared puzzled.

"Mahmoud Khan," he interjected, "the voyage is only about three weeks, but it looks as though you're foreseeing three months' food supply?" Colonel Talbot tapped his swagger stick on his khaki pantaloons. As usual, his appearance was dapper—the Crown and Bath star insignias decorated the shoulder epaulet bullions on a light military popper shirt still fresh despite the heat. Pomade had been applied to his neatly parted hair and his upturned pencil mustache was waxed.

Mahmoud spat his *naswar* mess of lime and tobacco onto the concrete pier. The ocean wind ruffled his thinning hair despite numerous attempts at smoothing it down with his hand.

"Tallboot Sahib," he wiped the greenish remnant of the saliva from his mouth with the cuff of his shirt. "Are you lacking math skills to tally how much food is needed for a little over a hundred of us Afghans for about three weeks' journey?" He held the abacus firmly with both hands making sure not to mix the beads. "So, if we face food shortages, will you be feeding us your salted pork and rock-solid biscuits on the voyage?"

"Is whiskey worse than salted pork for a Muslim like you? *Grana Mahmoud Jana!*" Talbot replied assertively with no change of posture. "Perhaps you have run out of whiskey?" he muttered in English for Fitzgerald's benefit. "Maybe another flask will make you a bit more subservient?"

"I'd be obliged to give him a bottle of my handpicked bourbon . . . London made, Barclay and Perkin," Sir Fitzgerald grinned, tucking tobacco into his pipe.

Lieutenant Mahmoud, who had not understood a word that had passed between the two men, nevertheless glanced about to ensure no one else was in earshot, knowing full well that he was the butt of the joke.

"What a *padarlant Englees* they are. *Koos modar-ha!*" he muttered, inaudibly. He dropped his chin to his chest and continued tallying.

Major Akbar Khan, who had overheard part of the interaction, joined Mahmoud.

"*Beradar*, Brother Tallboot, let me tell you something. . ." he cleared his voice and drew himself up to his full height. "We brought our own chefs and kitchen helpers, pots, pans, and food," he gestured toward the livestock, "to eat however we want and as much as we want!" The browbeaten look on his face seemed to emphasize his pitted smallpox scars. He set his Chitrali hat at an angle and scratched his head revealing beads of sweat that dotted his forehead. His nostrils flared, "Mind your own business, Sahib."

"Major Akbar Khan!" Colonel Talbot retorted, "I understand the livestock must be ritually sacrificed for you to eat," some squawling seagulls overhead almost drowned his words and one landed on top of a chickens' cage, "in six days, the vessel will stop in Aden to coal. Is it really necessary to fill the ship with loads and loads of livestock when you're able to procure more in Aden?"

"And how long is the coaling time?" asked Major Akbar Khan.

"A ship like *Clive* can take about ten to twelve hours."

"So while coaling in Aden we can wander around town and look for best fat sheep like these? And haggle with the vendors for the best price?" Akbar Khan lit up a *beedi* cupping his hands around the match against the ocean breeze. "No, that's not going to happen." He flicked the smoldering match away and took a long drag of the cigarette.

Sir Fitzgerald held his pipe to his mouth and puffed clouds of smoke into the air. He was shocked to observe a coffin set next to the makeshift sheep pen. *Is there a body in there?* he thought. *Why would they be loading a coffin onto the ship?* He traipsed away from the brouhaha between Akbar and Talbot and approached the casket. It was of bare pine and rough tawny wood and undoubtedly a coffin! He undid the latch, lifted the creaking lid, and gazed down at the contents in amazement. Inside, were mixed pieces of hard clay and terracotta. Fitzgerald removed his pipe and tucked it in his back pocket of his breaches, "I don't get it . . . why would this need to . . . "

Major Akbar Khan scurried toward the coffin, "Mistaar Jarwald!" He blurted out furiously, "Why are you *Englees-ha* so inquisitive about everything we Afghans do?"

"Just curious as to why bits and pieces of clay and terracotta are going to England. Can you explain?"

"Do you have to meddle in our private business? How and what we wipe our asses with?"

As the squabble now seemed set to escalate between Akbar and Fitzgerald, Talbot approached them calmly.

"May I have a private word with you, Sir Fitzgerald?" He gave Akbar a furtive hand wave. "Scat! Leave us alone please." As Akbar walked away Talbot muttered to Sir Fitzgerald. "Sir Fitzgerald," he nodded towards the coffin. "They use dried clay to cleanse themselves after they finished passing feces and urine. The Islamic tradition is called *istinja*," he explained quietly. "The new sanitary toilet paper, the *IZAL* disinfectant, that you and I use here in India and England, are unfamiliar to the Afghans . . . " The blast of an incoming troopship's siren sounded a long, deafening note interrupting Talbot's explanation. "Even we're new to toilet paper. Most of us are still accustomed to using newspaper and other means to clean ourselves."

The bleating of the sheep and clucking of chickens rose to a pitch after the blare of the ship's siren. "Turn a blind eye to the differences in culture and religion," Talbot said, raising his voice to be heard over the noise. "I assure you, there could be trouble if we poke our noses where they are not wanted. . . even to the point of affecting our relationship with the Amir."

"Can't they make use of water for cleansing themselves?" Fitzgerald pulled a silver pipe-reamer from his waistcoat pocket and emptied the pipe bowl of ash and dottle.

"Water would be the first option but it's often inaccessible."

"Does Dr. Lillias know about this?"

"I believe she does."

"What will be the options for the Afghans while on the voyage and in London?" He tucked fresh tobacco into his pipe bowl.

"I don't know," Talbot passed his swagger stick from one hand to the other. "I'd rather not involve myself regarding their sanitary needs . . . it's too sensitive . . . There are some things I would I rather not confront with the Afghans."

"Time is of the essence for them to learn . . . clogging water closets with pieces of clay and terracotta would make another perfect story for London tabloids. Doctor Hamilton should hustle up and tell them on the voyage what will be expected of them in London." Fitzgerald clenched his pipe between his teeth, struck a match, and inhaled a few times to allow the tobacco to catch.

"Yes, she has a better grasp of them than we have. I'd rather reach out to her or Frank Martin."

"Of course."

"What about the coffin?"

"Load it."

On the morning of April 29, 1895, the ponderous *HMS Clive* began to move and glide slowly out of the Bombay harbor, accompanied by jubilation and waving of kerchiefs from the spectators. The regimental band and bagpipers stationed on the pier played their tunes of adieu for Nasrullah who still found sound of the pipes intensely irritating; the British military men and their families on board also rang the cheerful atmosphere and blew their farewell kisses.

The colossal floating barracks was scheduled to make multiple stops on the twenty-five-day voyage before reaching Portsmouth, but even as early the following day, the Anglo-Afghan cultural divergences were put to the test. At half-past four in the morning, the shrill notes of the bugle resounded across the ship for the swabbing brigade to tumble out of their hammocks and start cleaning the decks. And the Afghan Royal Mullah, Shir Mohammad, with his throaty and boisterous voice sounded his call to prayer: "*Allah-Hu-Akbar*". From his waistcoat pocket, he pulled a very thin, fish-shaped, iron leaf and gently placed it in a bowl of water to determine the direction of Mecca.

"*Ooow taraf*, that way!" he declared in his Kabuli drawl. The men turned as one, in the direction of the sacred shrine of Prophet Mohammad, and the Mullah began to lead the congregation in prayer.

As first-time voyagers of the vast seas, some Afghans were excited about being aboard the troopship, others like Nasrullah, Parwana Khan, and *Naieb-Salar* Hassien Khan, had an intense, but unwarranted, fear of the ocean—fear of large waves, fear of distance from the land, fear of vast emptiness, and fear of cholera. Now onboard the ship and seeing the ocean for the first time, they were suffering from anxiety. Fear was their challenge and their demon to slay, although it had sprouted through their veins all their lives.

When the *HMS Clive* moved out of the harbor, Prince Omar, little William, and their newly-found coevals stood by the railings and noticed the cawing gulls flying both near the ship and in the distance. On occasions, they landed on the sea where they sat almost motionless in cozy clusters close to patches of coppery seaweed that tumbled over the slow-rolling swells with a motion like flying carpets. Often the seagulls flew very close and stared at the youngsters with black, beady eyes. Under their eerie, menacing, and unblinking probe, Prince Omar, little William, and other children jumped high and hooted playfully at them, shooing them away with fluttering hands. One gull confidently perched on Lieutenant Mahmoud Khan's brown archery hat, and the Lieutenant dashed like whirlwind across the deck toward the bow. The bird flew parallel to the steamer and did not gyrate or circle, but made a minute move as though they were in a ballroom dancing contest. The bird finally made a few short sidelong jerks in the air, its black eyes joylessly transfixed upon the Lieutenant's head. It gave one cry like a hurt child and glided away effortlessly from the ship.

Nasrullah, his close courtiers, and Amir's English friends were furnished with private quarters alongside the high-ranking British Military officers and their families. They also occupied the spacious, comfortable saloon, and the poop deck was also held solely to their tread. The lower-cast Afghans were accommodated in a huge room on the lower deck and were each handed a hammock to sleep on. They were utterly unfamiliar with the roped canvas net, in which they swayed like birds on twigs at every pitch and roll of the ship.

Captain Ebenezer Pattisson, a British naval officer who had taken charge of *HMS Clive* over half a decade ago, held an impeccable record for the steamer's operation. Seaworthiness, navigation, safety, and security were his highest priorities for the entire operation of the ship.

"I assure you," he glanced at the crowd on the deck. "I did not learn my seamanship on smooth seas alone, I've been exposed to situations in which I had to make difficult decisions." His competency was a vital component of character that gave anxious Nasrullah—and all those who had just met the Captain—a sense of trust and comfort. He was a tall, slender man, in his late forties, who walked the foredeck with a self-composed demeanor, either with hands clasped behind him, or one hand resting in the small of his back. He was calm, compassionate, and fair. As a thoughtful gesture, he handed William, Prince Omar, and each of the other children, a sailor's uniform. The Captain himself wore a frock coat with insignia, consisting of three rings of gold-braid with a loop in the upper ring, attached to his shoulders. His gleaming white trousers, buskin shoes, white gloves, and navy-blue feathery cocked hat distinguished him as Commander in the British Royal Navy.

"Ladies and gentlemen, let me introduce His Highness Prince Nasrullah Khan of Afghanistan," he announced to all on board the ship before setting sail and gestured towards Nasrullah with a bow.

Frank Martin whispered to Nasrullah, "Your Highness, please bow."

Nasrullah bowed with his hand on his chest. Immediately, a ripple of generous applause ran throughout the crowded deck. Nasrullah's entourage placed their hands on their chests and bowed graciously as well.

"Please make our distinguished guests feel at home throughout the voyage," said Captain Pattison to his sailors. The Captain then set the rules and regulations of the ship, while his steward, Lieutenant Commander Murphy, with a brass megaphone in one hand and a life buoy in the other, sounded them out and demonstrated the drill.

"First and foremost, if you see anyone, for whatever reason, fall overboard, immediately throw them a buoy! Buoys are attached to all railings within easy reach." Lieutenant Commander Murphy said.

"I will demonstrate an imaginary incident so you can witness every step, please be attentive. For a quick rescue mission," he continued, "one man is always on guard on the top deck, near the life buoy, and at any time, should he hear the cry of 'overboard', his job is to touch the spring, which releases the lifeboat into the sea."

Next to Lieutenant Commander Murphy stood a wooden manikin dressed in tattered clothes. Murphy tossed the dummy into the ocean and then the buoy. Through the megaphone, he called for a lifeboat to be manned and lowered into the water immediately, and for the ship to reduce speed. Within no time, the lifeboat was astern. The whole rescue operation took about half an hour, after which the Captain called for the vessel to resume speed. It was an eye-opening moment for many, especially the Afghans, as fear was evident in their eyes.

"That was quite a show you and the bird performed Lieutenant Mahmoud Khan," Sir Gerald Fitzgerald teased, "I've never seen anything like it before." His laughter could be heard throughout the mid-deck.

"You made an excellent team," Talbot agreed, chortling as he recalled the scene. The Afghan Lieutenant laughed with them; that gull had certainly taken a liking to him.

"Here's something I promised you." Fitzgerald handed him a small parcel wrapped in burlap sacking. "It's my favorite bourbon from London, Barclay and Perkins."

"Is it like Hu'iski?" Mahmoud Khan asked.

Yes, it's American whiskey, the name is different.

"Boorboon!" Mahmoud seemed content with the present and less bitter about the upset on the pier the day before. Tranquility changed his inner weather.

"Major Akbar Khan," said Fitzgerald, "don't forget it's yours too"

"H-H-H-Hide it . . . q-q-quick." Akbar stammered fearfully and looked around to see if anyone was watching.

"*Tashakur besyar zyad*, thank you very much," Lieutenant Mahmoud Khan scurried away to hide the bottle in his barracks.

Not long after *HMS Clive* steamed out of Bombay harbor, her maximum speed was increased to fourteen knots. The land vanished from the eastern horizon, signified at first only by a distant thunder of the surf. At length, a pale twinkling star appeared, rising from the sea. The striped golden hue in the West was swept away before the all-melding darkness, and the sea to the east grew shadowy and rapidly transformed to black. They had now begun crossing to Aden via the Indian Ocean and the Arabian Sea. Before long, hundreds of Edison lamps lit every deck, hallway, cabin, saloon, and mess hall on the vessel; so that from afar, it might appear as though strings of glowing pearls floated idly on the foggy air. It was the first time the Afghans had seen Edison lamps and they were fascinated to see some four-hundred of them illuminating the ship.

Frank Martin, explained to Nasrullah the concept of how a dynamo produced electricity and they wandered into the dynamo and switchboard room to witness how the potential energy of steam was transformed to kinetic energy and subsequently revolved the arm in the dynamo to produce electricity. Amazed by this invention, Nasrullah recalled his father's account when he hired the French electrical engineer, Mathias Jerome, who had demonstated a flashlight with a hand-cranked dynamo a decade ago. Mathias vanished after witnessing a few of the Amir's victims dangling from Kabul's gallows.

"If that *harami*, bastard, Jooroom had stayed in Kabul, Arg Palace would have been lit just like this ship by now, but unfortunately he ran away to *Faransa*, France," Nasrullah commented shaking his head regretfully.

As the British troopship sailed on, scores of chickens and eleven sheep were slaughtered in the Islamic way, and cleaned, cut, minced, tenderized, and, finally, sizzled on pungent coals. The aroma was inviting and whetted everybody's appetite. The air was hot and the warm ocean breeze carried mixed smells of the salty sea, kebabs, and other foods across the deck.

Major Akbar Khan, Lieutenant Mahmoud Khan, and their kitchen helpers including the ship's culinary squad were hard at work preparing the food on the poop-deck.

Captain Pattison and Lieutenant Commander Murphy had arranged a small musical concert. On the nearby dais, one sailor played the pianoforte while others accompanied him on cello, a viola, two flutes, a horn, a drum, and a fife. The music was enchanting and a pleasant change from the bagpipes.

The flickering lights of the lanterns on each table created wavering silhouettes of the passengers. Everyone was served with a meal of their choice, Afghan lamb or chicken kebabs sprayed with spices and tucked into *lavash*, bread, bangers and mash, or fish and chips. Captain Pattison had banned hard liquor aboard his ship as the result of a horrible accident that claimed lives a few years ago. Only beer, sherry, and wine were on the menu.

Lillias, Roma, Olivia, Mrs. Clemence, and the Martins shared a long table with their new British acquaintances. The conversation was exuberant as they exchanged stories of their travels and the excitement of heading home after a long stay in Kabul and India. Parwana Khan, Nasrullah, General Akram Khan, Naieb-Salar Hassein Khan, Frank Martin, Sir Fitzgerald, and Colonel Talbot shared the head table with Captain Pattison.

Roma constantly scanned the deck in the hope of seeing Zalmai. She longed to hand him a note she had written but he generally avoided the poop deck. For Roma also, not only was it inappropriate to search him out on the vessel, but if her actions were to alert Nasrullah or Parwana Khan, it would greatly endanger Zalmai.

Roma rose to her feet, "I'll be right back," she said to Olivia. "I'm just going to take a stroll."

Her pompadour-heeled shoes clicked as she crossed the wooden deck. She stood at the railings and pulled her wide-brimmed hat down to prevent it from blowing away in the breeze. She was wearing a white light cotton bodice with a high collar and narrow sleeves, and a full-length skirt that almost covered her black high-heeled shoes. She glanced down to what she could make out on the lower decks in the vain hope of seeing him. Her gaze lifted to the dark horizon and then to the myriad stars, the majestic zodiacal sprawl, "A sky of impeccable beauty," Roma murmured. After a while she turned to face the crowd again, leaning with her back to the rail.

Is that Gul Agha? she thought. He seemed only vaguely familiar at first. The young groom, now assisting the culinary squad looked remarkably clean. He was wearing a pin-striped white shirt, black pants, and a white cotton apron like the rest of the culinary helpers and had seemingly transformed into a young British kitchen helper overnight. Although he was engaged in other chores, a rather odd protrusion beneath his shirt and apron suggested he had not divested himself of his gun.

Roma stood by the railings hesitating to walk where Gul Agha and other kitchen helpers were.

"Gul Agha!" she called, but above the noise of the engines, the music, and the general hubbub, her voice fell on deaf ears.

However, Lieutenant Mahmoud Khan heard a female voice without recognizing the source of the call. He looked up to the top of the mast, and then looked vaguely around the deck. Roma's wave in Gul Agha's direction caught his attention. At that moment. the young boy's long apron caught under his foot and he fell to the floor with a thud.

"Steady on!" one immaculately uniformed helmsman grinned as he walked by on his way towards the bridge.

Lieutenant Mahmoud walked across to deck staggering slightly under the ship's motion, which was exacerbated by several sips of Boubon. He tapped Gul Agha's shoulder.

"*Oh Bacha!* Hey Boy! Sh-sh-She's calling you." He pointed unsteadily in Roma's direction and repeated, "she's calling you." He spun on his heel, exposing the same stained trousers he was wearing when he left Kabul three weeks ago.

As Gul Agha approached, Roma said urgently, "Zalmai! Do you remember him?"

"Oh! Zalmai Khan?" Gul Agha said, "*Baley! Balay!* Yes! Yes!"

"Please give him this letter, " she touched his shoulder reassuringly. "Do not show it to anybody else . . . Only to Zalmai. Do you understand?"

"*Balay!* Yes! *Besyar Khoob!* Very Good!" nodded Gul Agha, tucking the letter in his back pocket. He bowed gravely with a hand on his chest, spun on his heel, and walked swiftly away.

> *My beloved Zal,*
>
> *Sadly, the strict rules on this ship have parted us on this long journey. Although we are sailing together,*
>
> *I feel very melancholy and constantly reminisce about the times we have spent together.*
>
> *Olivia and I share the same cabin and keep each other company but I still long to have you near me.*
>
> *Our sublime but brief time together in Peshawar will always be embedded in my memory and I hope to spend more time with you soon.*
>
> *We have a twelve-hour stop in Aden and I would love us to meet for part of that time, if not the entirety,*
>
> *away from the ship. I realize you may have duties to perform, but send me a message when you are free*
>
> *and I will wait for you at the Grand Hotel De L'Univers across from the main square near Victoria Gardens.*

All my love dearest, and many kisses.
Your own, R.H.

Before calling it a night and descending to the hammock room on the lowest deck, Major Akbar and Lieutenant Mahmoud drained the entire bottle of bourbon Fitzgerald had given Mahmoud as a token of *baksheesh*. As they staggered into the cramped sleeping quarters, they were hit by the usual foul atmosphere of stiflingly hot, sweaty air.

"It's like a stuffy lion's den in Hindu-Kush," Major Akbar declared in a stage whisper.

Making their way by the weak glow of the lanterns attached to the side panels, they wove on tiptoe through the sleeping bodies on the floor and those suspended in hammocks as though walking through a minefield. Akbar found his hammock and clambered into it without mishap. But when Mahmoud attempted to follow suit, he not only hit his head against the low ceiling but the canvas-cradle rope failed under his weight and he fell. His fall was broken by the body of Gul Agha the groom, who, until then, had been sleeping peacefully underneath. In that moment of shock and panic, Gul Agha grabbed the gun from his holster and discharged it wildly. The blast woke everyone instantly— there were howls of panic, demands to know what was going on, and groans of protest from some. The noise was deafening.

"Is the ship going down? Are we sinking?" Gul Agha muttered, ashen-faced. He stood trembling with the gun swaying limply in his hand. Lieutenant Mahmoud staggered to his feet and blankly surveyed the pandemonium around him.

Colonel Zalmai tumbled out of his hammock, momentarily perplexed as he squinted and rubbed the sleep from his eyes. His bare shoulders and the hair on his chest glistened with sweat.

"Everyone! Shut up! Shut up!" he yelled raising both hands in the air. "Hand me the gun, you idiot jackass!" His hooded eyes widened,

"You shouldn't be carrying this."

The commotion became intense again as Gul Agha was identified as the perpetrator. The uproar alarmed the British sailors in the neighboring barracks and immediately the news escalated to the ship's chain of command.

Lieutenant Commander Murphy was notified of an apparent shooting in the Afghans' quarters and he and two officers of Royal Navy Regulating Branch—who maintained order aboard the troopships—immediately made their way below decks. They were met by Zalmai who reassured them that a weapon had been fired but no one was hurt.

"Who fired the gun?" Murphy's eyes scanned the dim room for an answer. He was barefoot and wearing only a sleeveless white shirt and shorts. He was also obviously annoyed.

Scores of hands pointing at Gul Agha.

"*Aan khar*, that jackass," Zalmai lifted the gun in one hand and pointed at Gul Agha with the other.

The barracks were unbearably stifling and, with scores of Afghans encircling them idly watching the spectacle, Lieutenant Commander Murphy signaled Colonel Zalmai Khan, Gul Agha, and Raj, to accompany him to the main deck for further investigation.

"This is a serious matter," Murphy said quietly, aware that many British sailors were sleeping on the deck because of hot nights. "Who should I consult with in your group?"

"That would be the chief of police, Parwana Khan," Zalmai replied. He leaned his back against the railing resting one arm along its length. In the other, he held the gun pointing downward. The warm ocean breeze ruffled his dark hair and he was relieved to feel cooler after the sweltering hammock room.

While Murphy waited for Parwana Khan to arrive, he jotted some of the details down in his notepad.

"What made you fire the gun?" Murphy asked looking straight at

Gul Agha as Raj interpreted the question quietly.

"Something heavy fell on top of me and crushed my bones, I thought the ship was attacked and we were sinking."

"Go on . . ." said Murphy, wagging the pencil in his hand.

"I shot blindly, without thinking. . . I then realized that Mahmoud had fallen on me and I praised Allah for missing him."

"Do you know why he fell on you?"

"No."

"I think we need Mahmoud here," Murphy said to Zalmai. "It all sounds innocent enough but it's worth checking every detail."

"I'll fetch him." As Zalmai sprinted down the stairwell, he almost ran into Parwana Khan who was coming down from the upper deck. His boot laces were untied, and, to cover his light-weight sleeping robe, he had wrapped a white sheet around his willowy body which partly covered his head giving him a ghostly appearance.

"Wait!" Parwana Khan snapped, "What's the rush? What's happened? Why do you have a gun drawn?" His voice echoed loudly in the stairwell.

"Murphy will brief you. I can't explain right now, remain on the deck with them. And keep your voice down, people are sleeping. I'll be right back," whispered Zalmai.

Within minutes, Zalmai and two of his guardsmen with curved daggers attached to their thick embroidered belts, escorted Mahmoud to the main deck. He was pale-faced and swaying on his feet. Seeing the Amir's executioner, he gripped the handrails to strengthen his posture and stop him from teetering.

"Sal-sal-salaam," he stammered, his eyes still droopy and unfocused.

"Explain in your own words what happened this evening," Murphy asked, pen poised over his notebook. Raj interpreted.

"I don't know," said Mahmoud lifting his unsteady hands with an expression of dubiety. "I've never seen a . . ." his head oscillated slowly and pensively against his chest . . . "what do you call that roped bed?".

"Hammock," Murphy replied.

"Hoomook. I've never seen a hoomook in my life . . . neither had my parents nor my forefathers." he slurred. He pouted his lips as though to emphasize the precariousness of the hammock. "A fall is expected from a hoomook when one like me" . . . gestured at himself, "is unfamiliar with it . . . " His *naswar* stained teeth were dark under the dimly lit Edison bulbs but Colonel Murphy caught a whiff of the whiskey on his breath.

"I believe Captain Pattison briefed everyone as we embarked not to drink heavy liquor. "Have you been. . . "

"I'll take it from here," Parwana Khan interjected. "Zalmai, your decision is my decision regarding Gul Agha, but I will take Lieutenant Mahmoud's investigation from here on." He gestured to the two guardsmen to bring Mahmoud, "I need a private moment with him . . . also, as the chief of police, I'll take possession of the gun." He darted a glance in Lieutenant Commander Murphy's direction. "I believe you are done. I will continue with the rest of the investigation and come back to you in the morning."

Murphy nodded and left with his officers. Zalmai handed Parwana Khan the gun and instructed the two guardsmen to accompany Parwana Khan and Mahmoud for further questioning.

"Go back to bed," Zalmai said to Gul Agha.

Gul Agha was about to ask whether he would get his gun back and then thought better of it when he looked at Zalmai's set expression.

Lieutenant Mahmoud looked into Parwana Khan's face and found the absolute ruthlessness of a man accustomed to carrying out executions without impartiality. His heart began to pound against his rib cage as he stared into those blank, sadistic, and dreadful eyes. He was known for being the tool of wickedness and an outstretched arm of demons. A cold-hearted murderer whose practice snowballed with the power and sanction of Amir Abdul Rahman Khan behind it.

It was pitch dark and well past midnight somewhere in the Arabian Sea. A beautiful night under the twinkling sprawl of the Milky Way. But Mahmoud was oblivious to the crisp smell of the ocean air, the gentle sway of the ship with the hypnotic sound of the waves slapping against its hull, and the swish of the sea against its bow.

Parwana Khan ushered Lieutenant Mahmoud Khan and the Afghan guards to a secluded and unlit area on the forecastle deck near the bow. Other decks were either occupied by sleeping sailors or off-limits to the Afghan guards and Mahmoud Khan.

The helmsman on the bridge could just make out a group of four Afghans sitting cross-legged and chatting among themselves and, as there was nothing unusual in that, paid them little more heed. The Royal Navy Regulating Branch officers often paced the decks to maintain law and order and ensure security for Nasrullah and his entourage.

Surprisingly, Parwana Khan brushed Mahmoud's arm in empathy. "Don't worry about anything," he smiled deceitfully. "I also have a fondness for *sharab*."

Mahmoud glanced at him uncertainly and nodded. The white bird of hope that had glided silently over his head for many years, suddenly reappeared in his imagination, signaling God's mercy to spare his life. The silent prayer seeking Allah's leniency was repeated with every heartbeat.

"I want you to keep this between us, of course," Parwana Khan's expression was unusually friendly. "I'll be asking you a few questions." In his inebriated state, Mahmoud missed the cunning undertone. "*Khoob ast?* Is that all right?"

"Of course *Kotwal Sahib*, by all means, I'm at your service," he replied submissively.

"Have you seen me drinking before?" he asked the two Afghan guards, "This conversation is also for you. Keep it confidential, what I am admitting is for your ears only." The guards agreed solemnly. He stared back at Mahmoud Khan. "Have you?"

"Never Sahib. Never!" he replied obsequiously. "I've never seen you drinking."

"Well, I keep it hidden because Amir Sahib hates *sharab*, he would burn me alive if he found out, but I would be keen to enjoy a few sips if you kindly offered me some."

"*Kotwal S-S-Sahib*," slurred Mahmoud, "I don't have any."

"Yet you have been drinking!" he smiled, "I am sure you have some to share." He tapped him on the shoulder. "This will be a long journey without something to ease the boredom. If you and I set off as good drinking pals, I will assure you a handsome promotion. Maybe you could become my assistant? Assistant to Kabul's chief of Police?" He gave him another friendly slap on the arm, "I have no doubt that Amir Sahib would agree to my proposal."

"*Kotwal Sahib,* I don't have any but I can get you some," Mahmoud partly confessed to what Parwana Khan eagerly wanted to hear.

"On this ship?"

"Yes."

"Who from?" Parwana Khan asked with an icy stare.

"Fessjarwoold or Tallboot."

"Very well. It's too late, they're sleeping now. Maybe a bottle for tomorrow night? Just you and me?"

"Of course."

As Parwana Khan spoke, his fingers were working silently and swiftly beneath the sheet that covered the light clothing he had worn to sleep in. He worked the laces out of both boots as he kept the conversation going, and tied them together, testing the knot to ensure it was sound. "

As Kabul's chief of police, Parwana Khan's prime duty was to secure the Amir's throne. For years he had eves-dropped, investigated handwritten records, interrogated people of all ages and ethnic backgrounds, planted informers and spies, and simply reinvigorated Amir's intelligence service to the best of his ability. His mastery of the business of spying and assassination came naturally to him. He knew everything about everyone of interest in Kabul, and had the Amir's blessing to eliminate anyone with or without justice being served.

The information from Mahmoud revealed Fitzgerald and Talbot's part in using Mahmoud as a spy in exchange for alcohol. But there was one vital piece of information missing.

"Well, *andeewaal,* my friend," he extended his hand, "the world is slipping by and we need to enjoy some pleasure. I'll have *Naieb-Salar Sahib* Hassein Khan join us tomorrow . . . I've been his drinking partner for years. How about Major Akbar Khan? Will he join us too?"

"I am sure he will, *Kotwal Sahib,"*

In one swift movement Parwana Khan sprang to his feet, the bootlaces wrapped once around each of his hands. Mahmoud's eyes widened in shock and he fell sideways under the force of the overwhelming assault. His mouth opened as the strand wrapped around his throat, but no sound emerged apart from a strangled gurgle as Parwana Khan tightened his grip.

Mahmoud gasped choked and kicked his feet as he fought for his life.

"Hold him!" the executioner ordered and the two guards moved into action, holding the struggling body down.

Parwana Khan increased the pressure on Mahmoud's jugular. "Tear the sheet," he ordered, "and push it into his mouth!" he was gasping and sweating now as he fought to maintain the pressure. "Die, you bastard, die!" he muttered beneath his breath.

Slowly, the fight went out of Mahmoud and his head lolled to one side. His body twitched several times and then stopped. Still, the executioner maintained the pressure. Seconds ticked by . . . minutes. Then he nodded to one of the men and tossed him the laces. "Tie his feet with this!" he snapped. "Be quick about it!" He was panting with exertion.

Parwana Khan bent down, picked up the sheet and tossed it to the second guard. Wrap the body in it," he said, "it will be easier to lift." He glanced up to see if there was anyone in sight on the bridge before helping them to drag the Lieutenant's body to the side. Between them they heaved Mahmoud's body up and rolled the shrouded body over the top railing. It disappeared into the pitch blackness and hit the water with a muted splash.

"We're done. Neither of you saw what happened here and you didn't hear a thing!" Parwana Khan said, his breath rasping, "This job was at the behest of Amir Sahib who gave me the authority to do what I just did."

"*Albata Kotwal Sahib*, Of course, Magistrate."

The helmsman on the bridge walked to a position where he could see the group of Afghan's who had met there earlier. Three men were walking away, quite hurriedly, he thought. *It seems they've decided to call it a night at last,* he mused, *I wonder what happened to the fourth chap?* He looked out over the sea. It was a quiet night and when these cool breezes came in to break the heat of the day, it made his night vigil quite pleasant.

Nasrullah endured mild sea sickness aboard the troopship. To maintain him in good health, Dr. Hamilton and Dr. John Bremner, the ship's physician, and three nurses checked him regularly once they set sail from Bombay.

Doctor Bremner, was a tall, willowy man in his late thirties with a thick bush of brown hair. He always seemed edgy around Nasrullah—like a cat observing someone from under the sofa—and left most of the checks to Dr. Hamilton, while he, in his white physician's coat with a stethoscope hanging out of the right pocket, watched from a distance.

"That boyish Afghan prince doesn't realize how privileged he is above all others on this ship," Dr. Bremner commented, looking at Dr. Hamilton over his round-framed spectacles. "We have lost scores of soldiers and civilians on previous trips for lack of sufficient medical resources and supplies!" He took the fountain pin from his ink-stained top pocket, scribbled on a pad tore off the page, and handed it to a nurse. "We would have to bury body after body at sea. The cholera epidemic has wiped out scores of people between Bombay and Portsmouth." He also gave a cynical account of quarantining *HMS Clive* for over two weeks for Nasrullah's safety, as was demanded by Lord Bruce, Governor-General of India. "With the continual movement of servicemen in and out of India, and lack of enough vessels, he's lucky to have had this ship stand idle for two-and-a-half weeks."

"That is because he's the Prince and has been invited by Her Majesty," Dr. Hamilton replied automatically. She paid no heed to his complaints but instead focused on the shimmering turquoise Arabian sea in the afternoon sun as wispy clouds drifted in the warm breeze sprinkling her pale skin with a fine spray of saltwater.

Cholera had been the Amir's main concern for his son and Dr. Lillias Hamilton had promised to give her utmost attention to Nasrullah's health on the voyage. With Amir's apprehension at the forefront of her mind, Dr. Hamilton watched Nasrullah continuously. She checked on him daily—his temperature, his heart, and bodily functions—always aware of her responsibility to his father. It was a daunting experience.

While Dr. Hamilton and Dr. Bremner set safety precautions in place to prevent Nasrullah from contracting harmful diseases, so Captain Pattison and Lieutenant Commander Murphy arranged various entertainments to relieve him of his boredom and uneasiness.

"Colonel Talbot," Captain Pattison proclaimed loudly, "I'm grateful for the wireless message you sent from Peshawar advising us to prepare ourselves to entertain a juvenile!"

"Bear in mind, my good fellow," Talbot moved his swagger stick with a sweep of his hand as though he was conducting an imaginary orchestra. "It's up to us to keep that Afghan chap of ours happy until he presents himself to Her Majesty." He glanced about to ensure no one was eavesdropping. " No one wants him to appear miserable, Captain, when facing the Queen at Windsor Palace," he smiled, exposing his two gold-crowned teeth. "I am sure, not even her little Pekinese dog, Looty, wants to see him sorrowful!" A great roar of laughter was heard from the poop deck where a cluster of Englishmen had gathered.

"In the past year, we've done an extraordinary job training him to present himself honorably in Windsor," Frank Martin said, smoothing back his caramel-colored hair that had become disheveled in the ocean breeze. He had taken to wearing a pair of tinted glasses with a leather nose-piece and side flaps. "It remains to be seen how he does."

"What I've noticed about the fella so far, Gentlemen, is that fun and entertainment are his priorities," said Fitzgerald, "he has never really grown up." He was shirtless, lying back on a recliner and basking in the sun with a glass of beer in one hand and his pipe smoldering in the other. Already with his fair complexion, his skin was changing color.

Captain Pattison asserted quietly, "The voyage with Nasrullah has been both daunting and tedious. So far we've managed to keep him entertained, but undoubtedly, it has been the hardest voyage from that point of view, we've experienced, ever."

Both top bosses of *HMS Clive*, Pattison, and Murphy, had proven enterprising when it came to keeping Nasrullah busy and amused. They formed an obstacle race around the ship run between groups of sailors, which made everyone burst out laughing—not least, Nasrullah! Prince Omar, William, and the other children jumped up and down, cheering the teams on, and laughing hysterically as the sailors attempted to climb the bridge from the deck on a well-greased rope. When they slid down on top of one another, Nasrullah shed tears of mirth. They organized duck races, sack jumping races, spoon and potato races, greased pillow fights, and, for the ladies, a candle race, and tug 'o war. At dawn each day, plans were made as to how to entertain Nasrullah. Without amusement, he would retire to his cabin and sleep as though suddenly overtaken by years of fatigue.

Whilst Nasrullah was being royally entertained, many of his courtiers, his horse, Baarfi, and many of the other animals aboard, showed wretched signs of distress—suffering the effects of foul odors and fumes, they were overcome with nausea, dizziness, debilitation, and seasickness.

Field Marshal Hassien Khan, General Akram Khan, and Khairo Khan, had not left their cabins and were unable to keep food down. They lay moaning in their putrid, vomit-reeking beds, feeling that the convulsions of their stomachs would never cease. Dr. Bremner had been as busy as an agitated squirrel; he was everywhere on the ship treating mostly the Afghans.

Even the Mullah was weak and could not congregate everyone to face Mecca, he tried but to no avail. "Allah will forgive the debilitation of the voyagers like me and others for not being able to pray," the bearded Mullah announced as he tossed his bucket full of waste, vomit, and used terracotta pieces of clay overboard. The ocean wind caused the end of his turban to flutter like a flag as he tilted his head forward and rested his body against the railing.

The veterinarian aboard the ship confirmed that Baarfi and a few of the other horses were sick as a result of being subjected to extreme temperatures, and defective ventilation. Two horses were in critical condition and Baarfi was showing signs of fatigue and stress. The vet professed that Baarfi's survival depended on his disembarkation from the ship while being coaled at the next stop in Aden. He also insisted that all the animals should be taken off the ship during long stops.

When Roma opened her eyes, both sea and sky were silvery under the approaching dawn; and soon, touches of scarlet and saffron were painted upon the waters. At last, the morning emerged in its grandeur, with the sky a sheer turquoise blue and the sunshine emblazoning the crests of the waves. She shielded her hand to deflect the sun from her eyes. On the horizon, amid black and gray hills, was a smattering of white and red houses. As the ship moved closer to shore, a street could be discerned and beyond that, the sea again and a dilapidated marina with hundreds of rickety masts bobbing up and down like aquatic pistons. As *HMS Clive* drifted into the bay and finally anchored near a hefty embankment, Captain Pattison blared into his megaphone from the bridge.

"Ladies and gentlemen we have arrived in Aden. Please ensure that you return to the ship within twelve hours for re-embarking."

In the last six days, Roma had lapsed into melancholic boredom with longing for Zalmai. Since writing him the letter requesting a rendezvous in Aden, she counted every hour to their arrival. Any thought of the meeting with Zalmai at the Grand Hotel De L'Univers changed the tempo of her heartbeat.

Roma, Olivia, and other English officers' wives and children were the first to disembark in the early morning after docking in Aden. This was Yemen's dustbowl, the stepping stone of the British empire to her colonies. From a distance, it appeared a to be picturesque city surrounded by breathtaking views of the mountain. As they docked, white storks could be seen flying around the city's tall minarets, but animal dung and rotting refuse made the air malodorous and Roma and Olivia soon forgot the charm of the panorama. Their arrival at the Grand Hotel De L'Univers disillusioned them further. The name had evoked a vision of a pleasant palace set amidst tranquil rolling lawns adjacent to spectacular sandy beaches, but that wasn't the case. The three-story hotel was fronted by whitewashed arches and a façade from which paint had peeled in layers. It stood like a huge square shell, which at first seemed deserted and desolate. The only positive thing it had to offer was the newly designed Victoria Garden across from it, but that too seemed to be on the verge of dying, exposed as it was to the pitiless glare of the African and Arabian peninsula's sun with little or no water.

"Honestly, this place looks like hell," Roma said as she expressed her deep disappointment. "I took Lieutenant Commander Murphy's word about it, but he clearly has not seen it himself to judge its condition."

"How about a nice *douche* in the hotel before we do anything else?" Olivia suggested.

"You read my mind!" Roma replied. "I feel as though ants are crawling over my body, feasting off days of accumulated dirt and sweat."

Before climbing the wide stairs to the long, narrow lobby, Roma and Olivia were surrounded by a swarm of money-changers and beggars, both young and old. The hotel porters shooed them dismissively. As they walked into the open-aired lobby the clatter of their footsteps awoke the dozing concierge behind the check-in desk.

"We would like a room," Roma said briskly.

The concierge rubbed his eyes and sprang to his feet. His face was pock-marked, and, with a flash of a smile, he revealed multiple broken and missing teeth. Olivia looked at him with distaste as placed his hands on the desk exposing unclipped grimy nails. She took in the tattered clothes, and the turban, like an old bath towel, that was stained with dirt and sweat. In his belt, he wore a dagger with a silver hilt.

"Room number thirty-two, third floor, up the stairs to your right." He rolled his words in broken English with a deep, throaty Arabic accent. Pointing at the rickety stairs at the end of the lobby, he handed the key to the porter. "Please follow him."

There, near the staircase, Amir's executioner, Parwana Khan, was seated cross-legged on a tall-backed Egyptian straw sofa, flipping the pages of a Harper's Weekly Journal. Obviously, unable to read English, he was amusing himself with the illustrations.

"The bastard is spying on us," Roma said as she glanced at him, her heart pounded with shock knowing Zalmai might soon arrive and fall into Parwana Khan's trap. "I'm sure he has followed me to try and catch us together!" As she glanced again at Parwana Khan, he peered over the magazine at Roma and then scanned the area outside to see if anyone resembling Zalmai was approaching the hotel.

"He's like a blood-hound tracking his prey," Olivia said under her breath, "he's the sort of man who won't give up!"

They both knew enough about Parwana Khan to realize he would be undeterred by fatigue, hunger, or sweltering heat when obsessed by the excitement of a chase. His object was simply to shed blood and kill. But this game of cat and mouse between the executioner and Zalmai was becoming stealthier by the day. Parwana Khan had the determination, calmness, patience, and zeal, to hunt down Colonel Zalmai Khan upon whom he had had his sights fixed since leaving Kabul and saw as a trembling imbecile, an unwary feeble victim deserving of death. It was obvious that he was waiting for that moment of *in flagrante* between Roma and Zalmai to close in against him.

"Is there another staircase to the third floor?" Roma asked the porter quietly.

"Yes, at the opposite end, in the very back of the building but it is a bit further to your room." The concierge said something in Arabic to the porter. "He'll show you the other way. Please follow him."

With the clatter of their thick heels and the rustle of their long skirts, Roma and Olivia followed the porter with their valises relieved not to have to catch the eye of the executioner at close range. The dark-skinned porter with unkempt curly hair was a youth, probably in his mid-teens. His baggy khaki shorts, from which his knees protruded like two hard-boiled eggs, were belted around his skinny waist. The flip-flop leather sandals he wore revealed dirty, cracked heels to the women following him up the stairs. From the open windows in the room on the third floor, a warm ocean breeze flapped the net curtains. A double bed was flanked with nightstands on each of which was an oil lamp. The glass of one was cracked. The bedspread was red satin with multiple stains.

Olivia leaned down to smell and wrinkled her nose., "*Mauvaise odeur*! I wonder when this was last washed?"

The bathroom was a cubicle in which a tin water tank was hung by a rope from a beam; on the underside of the can, was a dripping nozzle coated with scum and green slime. The bather was expected to stand on the slippery cement floor and pull a string to allow the water to gush over his head and back.

"I'll endure the rusticity of this hotel and take a bath anyway," said Roma after inspecting the crude shower arrangement.

"*Moi aussi*, me too," Olivia said chuckling, "*Bonne baignade.*" She went first.

As Olivia bathed in the bathroom of Grand Hotel De L'Univers, Roma could hear the splash and gurgle of the water as she stood by the window undoing her chignon. She shook her hair loose and felt it brush her shoulders. The warm breeze blowing off the peninsula caressed her skin, which was damp with perspiration. She dabbed her face and neck with her flowery kerchief, as she looked anxiously across the Victoria gardens for Zalmai, but could see no one resembling his appearance.

What if he comes, Roma thought, *there is no way of warning him about Parwana Khan. But perhaps that young groom failed to deliver the note to Zalmai? Is there any way Zalmai might be aware that he is at the hotel? If only he would call off his surveillance mission and disappear. . .and that Zalmai will be able to see me.*

There was a confident rap at the door. Roma's heart skipped a beat—could it be him? But it was the young porter who handed her a note and held out his hand for *baksheesh.*

"Wait!" Roma said, "Let me read this." The handwriting was scribbled hurriedly and was almost illegible, only the letter "Z" at the end made her believe it was Zalmai. She rummaged into her valise and pulled two Egyptian *Qirsh* coins. "Is the man who gave you this note downstairs?" she pantomimed, as she handed him a single coin. He nodded. "I'll give you another coin if you bring him here."

"*Shurkran.* You wait . . . I bring for you him."

Olivia vacated the bathroom, a bright towel wrapped around her petite figure. She stood next Roma behind the fluttering curtains and they watched the executioner hurry down the wide stairs of Grand Hotel De L'Univers. He stood for a moment, straightened his tilted tasseled hat, and looked carefully about, examining his surroundings with care, a spy seeking his counterspy. Then he abandoned his mission and left for the ship.

"Olivia!" Roma said melodically.

"*Oui, mon cheri.*"

"I'm expecting him soon! Please could you get dressed and wait in the lobby? Ask Zalmai to wait in the room while I'm in the shower?"

"*Oui, bien sûr,*" smiled Olivia. "I'll order some wine and have something to eat until you come and join me. *Très bien?*" She kissed her cheek and closed the bathroom door behind Roma.

When Roma walked out of the bathroom, Zalmai was standing at the window, arms crossed. As he turned towards her, she dropped the towel and Zalmai drew a sharp breath. He felt a rise of intense passion as he admired the subtlety of each curve and contour of her body, her exquisite form, her vivid complexion, her flowing hair. He took her gently by the shoulders and looked deeply into those blue eyes then reached down and kissed her gently.

He gathered her closer and pulled her naked body into his embrace. He felt her soft, round breasts against his chest and longed to cradle them in his virile hands.

She drew away and unbuttoned his shirt and nestling her face against his chest. Zalmai took her by the hand and lead her to the bed and she lay watching him as he stripped off, taking in the newness of his naked masculinity. Then he lay with her and, for the first time, they experienced complete privacy to explore the pleasure of this union without the anxiety of imminent discovery.

Each time they met was harder than the last, but their feelings ran deeper as they discovered this more intimate relationship, and they dared to think, in each other's protective cocoon, of the means to extend their emotional and physical intimacy for a lifetime. Roma already knew she loved Zalmai as if he were the last of her kind.

They lay flat on their backs, slicked with sheens of sweat, panting from the intense sexual release they had just experienced. At first, complete silence permeated the room, then Zalmai propped himself up on his elbow and looked down at her contented face framed by disheveled hair in the tangle of the sheets and rumpled pillows. Her hand brushed the hair on his chest.

"*Dostat daram*," somehow the words needed to be said in his own language.

"Interpret for me," she smiled, but she knew. She had read the message in his eyes.

It was only as they dressed that Roma remembered to ask the question. "How did you manage to get passed that cross-eyed bastard downstairs?"

He chuckled. "I'm always a step ahead of him."

"How?"

"Easy," he smiled. "He follows you to catch me, I follow him so that he doesn't catch me. He knew we had the chance to meet outside the ship," he went on, "So, I let him disembark first and I let Gul Agha, the groom boy follow him. . . He's my eyes and ears. He tells me everything about him and his whereabouts." His voice was clear and he looked relaxed, "I would just like to get his gun back from the *Kotwal* Parwana Khan."

"He took his gun away? Why?"

"Yes, he fired it in the barracks, luckily there were no fatalities." Zalmai gave the full account of what took place and the very confidential issue involving Lieutenant Mahmoud Khan. "He was murdered and thrown overboard but you must please keep it to yourself . . . Only two of my guards witnessed this horrible killing of Mahmoud and I don't want them to lose their lives for leaking the information."

"He killed him on the ship?"

"Yes."

She gasped, "But it must be reported to Captain Pattison."

"I believe he knows something about Mahmoud because Lieutenant Commander Murphy interrogated him first. He would have had an eye on him and must realize he is missing."

"He must be exposed! We must think of something," she was back in his arms and laid her head on his chest, feeling the soft motion of his breathing.

"I agree, but with great caution, we must not jeopardize any other lives . . . He's a killer."

"I'm worried that someday he might harm you too," she rubbed his forearm. "How long do you think you'll be in London?"

"I don't know, maybe a few months. Why do you ask?"

She averted her eyes, "Just curious."

"Are you coming back to Kabul with Daktar Hameeltoon?"

"No, I will be with my mother in London . . . That's home," she said, blinking back tears so that Zalmai would not notice.

"Maybe you could come back to Kabul and stay with Daktar Hameeltoon again next year?"

"I don't think so, my mother needs me."

She could not imagine a future without Zalmai being part of it. She was afraid for him, immensely worried about him around a despot like the Amir, and his executioner, a cold-blooded murderer who was probably seeking a reason to eliminate him even now. Already Roma knew she would miss him immeasurably when he left for Kabul. For him to bid adieu with a cavalier wave would break her heart. She couldn't bear to lose him.

"Roma my love," said Zalmai placing his hand over her heart, "We need to leave, your friend, Olivia is waiting for you downstairs."

The first thing the passengers noticed when they returned to the troopship, was that everything on the vessel was blackened with coal dust. It clung to the faces, hair, and the once white uniforms of hundreds of sailors; it caked their shorts, shirts, and hats. The men were hard at work scrubbing and mopping the decks, polishing handrails, and wiping down cabin doors and portholes to rid everything of coal dust. The passengers crunched pieces of coal underfoot as they walked up the gangplank.

The gangplank was raised, and before the ship's horn was sounded for departure, Lieutenant Commander Murphy called the roll and discovered one Afghan was unaccounted for, Murphy remembered the name well. Lieutenant Mahmoud Khan, who had undergone interrogation by the Amir's executioner was missing. He made the call again.

"Lieutenant Mahmoud Khan!" Murphy blared through the megaphone. When the call was again met with silence, he shouted a third time. "Has anyone seen Mahmoud Khan?" There was no reply. He asked Raj to translate into both Pashtu and Dari in case his British accent was not understood but there was still no response from the crowd.

When the roll-call of all passengers revealed that Mahmoud Khan was missing, making it clear that Zalmai and his guards who feared Parwana Khan's retribution were cleared of having spoken to the British, Roma secretly reported Zalmai's account of the murder to Captain Pattison and Lieutenant Commander Murphy.

The departure of the vessel could no longer be delayed, Pattison took control of the ship's wheel to navigate through the treacherous Red Sea, whilst Lieutenant Commander Murphy prepared to ask the Amir's Chief of Police, Parwana Khan, a few pertinent questions. Murphy asked Frank Martin, Colonel Talbot, and Sir Fitzgerald—who were Nasrullah's chaperones to England and back to Kabul—to participate and witness the process.

"Where is Lieutenant Mahmoud Khan?".

"I don't know," Parwana Khan replied, smoothing and straightening his brown, double-breasted jacket. The medals attached to his jacket¬bestowed on him by Amir for his accomplishments—clinked importantly with every move he made. But Kabul's chief of police was desperately nervous. His jerky behavior made it appear as though he had a cockroach crawling up his back.

"Several of the men who know him said he has not been since you took over his interrogation on the night the shot was fired," Lieutenant Commander Murphy said.

Fitzgerald intervened, "I hear you interacted with him last and took him away with two Afghan guards. Thereafter you returned without him from the forecastle deck near the bow. That account was given by the helmsman on the bridge. Where is Mahmoud, Sir? We need an answer!"

"Shouldn't *you* answer where he is since you gave him the bottle of *sharab*?" he retorted with narrowed eyes. "Perhaps he fell overboard because he was too drunk?" He smirked furtively.

"Then let me ask you this simple question, Mr. Chief of Police," Talbot commented astutely, "it's obvious from the report we received that four of you were on the forecastle deck, but only three of you returned. If he accidentally fell overboard and you were there to witness it, why did you not call for help or report the matter?"

Murphy said, "We did the rescue drill before sailing from Bomb . . . ."

"*Bash! Bash!* Wait! Wait!" Nasrullah interjected. "So, it was determined that he consumed *sharab* and violated Allah's will? He drank something that we Muslims despise?"

"Yes Shahzadah," nodded Parwana Khan suddenly alert and attentive.

"If I was in the shoes of *Kotwal Sahib*, Parwana Khan, I would have tossed that son of *harami* into the sea, to be consumed by creatures of all kinds, myself!" Nasrullah declared loudly.

Frank Martin stepped alongside Nasrullah and had Raj translate to him in an undertone, "Your Highness, what you just said is wrong. You cannot order someone's death by tossing him overboard. This is a British ship and it's definitely not acceptable under British law."

"Well, that idiot Mahmoud was my own Afghan and we are entitled to the final word on whether he lived or died," he retorted, nostrils flaring. "Regardless of whether he was on this ship or the moon—I decide his fate." He gave an indignant snort through his aquiline nose and clasped his hands firmly behind his back.

"Your Highness," Sir Fitzgerald said, "with your permission, I would like to have a private word with Lieutenant Captain Murphy and Colonel Talbot. If it's no trouble, Your Highness. It will only take a few minutes."

"Of course, *boro*, go!" Nasrullah gestured with a dismissive wave of the hand.

As Talbot, Fitzgerald, and Murphy stepped outside to engage in their private conversation, Parwana Khan, Nasrullah and Frank Martin stood by looking at one another wordlessly.

"Gentlemen!" Fitzgerald declared, "This is likely to result in an incident that none of us will be able to control," he struck a match to light his pipe cupping his hand around it to block the breeze. "If this murder story is leaked to London and the European tabloids it will result in grave repercussions for all of us. We will regret it if this exacerbates to a point beyond repair." He puffed out a cloud of smoke from his pipe, shook the match and tossed it into the Red Sea.

"Especially as Her Majesty is expecting him in Windsor in a couple of weeks, if this story blows up into an international incident, we will pay for it dearly." Talbot looked towards the sunset on the African side of the Red Sea.

"So far, we're not getting any information from the killer. He's denying it and the Prince is taking his side," said Lieutenant Commander Murphy. "We don't have much choice . . . this must go away. What do you suggest, gentlemen?" Murphy removed his hand from the pocket of his white twill pants and straightened his peaked cap. "Bear in mind that the list of the manifest from Bombay will show his name. In Portsmouth, they will have to be told that one man is missing." His eyes shifted back and forth between Fitzgerald and Talbot.

"Well, we will have to declare him missing, cause unknown " Talbot answered thoughtfully tapping his knee with his swagger stick. "Discard the first report and make a new one, missing—cause unknown."

"Are we in agreement gentlemen?" asked. "Shall we sweep this under the rug?"

Murphy and Talbot nodded their agreement, "I don't think we have a choice," Talbot said.

Sir Fitzgerald acted as spokesman when they re-convened the meeting.

"Your Highness, we'll consider this a case of missing at sea, cause unknown," he said. "The case will be closed." He leaned forward with his hands on the desk in front of him. "But, Your Highness," he said, "please ensure that no one else falls overboard during the remainder of the journey!"

"I warn you not expose any of my men to your filthy *sharab,* ever again!" Nasrullah pointed his finger at Fitzgerald abrasively.

"It will not happen again, Your Highness."

∿✑∾✑∾✑∿

Roma knocked at her sister's cabin door, "Lily!" she called her sister by her sobriquet as she often did when she was in trouble. Lillias opened the cabin door to find her younger sister wrapped in a blanket and looking pale and uncertain.

"Can I come in?"

A vestige of morning light was in evidence through the cabin's porthole.

"Are you ill, Roma?" Dr. Hamilton asked with concern.

"Not ill, but I am worried, I need to speak to you."

"All right, sit down. The steward brought a pot of tea a few minutes ago, I'll pour you a cup," Lillias replied. "I can only think this must be urgent for you to have come so early, and not even properly dressed yet, Roma!"

She busied herself with pouring the tea and handed a cup and saucer to her sister.

"Now," she said firmly, "what is the problem?"

"I think my menstruation has stopped."

"You think your menstruation stopped?" Dr. Hamilton repeated her words and squinted at her with a vexed expression. "What do you mean, 'you think' How long has it been since your last period?"

"I am nearly three weeks overdue," Roma replied miserably.

Lillias raised her eyebrows. "This relationship with Zalmai. How far has it gone?" she demanded. Roma, have you been intimate with him?" She leaned across from where she was sitting and gripped Roma's free hand.

"Yes."

"I'm appalled!" she unclasped her hand from Roma's immediately and stood up. "How could you not think rationally?" she demanded as she paced the small cabin back and forth. "How could you be so selfish? Don't you realize that this will affect my job and my relationship with the Amir? Apart from that, if indeed you are pregnant, what about your future? Have you stopped to think of anything at all?" She donned a warm jacket and walked out towards the poop deck with Roma in tow. "I don't want anyone eavesdropping on our private matters." By Lillias's thumping footfalls as she climbed the ship's stairwell to the deck, Roma knew her sister was furious.

"I hate this. I just cannot believe what you've done!" She stood by the handrail gripping her jacket collar closed against the strong north-easterly wind blowing towards the English Channel. "You've caused trouble for both of us!"

" The seagulls' cries were ceaseless as they glided easily with the speed of the ship. Lillias looked towards the horizon and calmed down a little. "I knew from the very outset when Zalmai haggled for the necklace in the Char-Chatta bazaar that this relationship would end up in disaster. I should have put a stop to it then!" She looked back at the rolling waves of the Atlantic Ocean. "Are you in love with him?"

"Yes."

"Roma," Lillias's lips had tightened to a thin line. "You are only twenty-two and you have many years ahead of you. Could you not at least have given the outcome of this relationship some rational thought?" The moist early morning weather was damp against her face, she saw fog on the horizon, ship sirens frequently blared from all directions. She looked sternly at her sister as the professional side overtook the emotional. "Do you have any symptoms?"

"Yes, for a week now."

"And what are they?"

"My breasts are tender, and I have dizzy spells." she thought for a moment, "I have no desire to eat anything and I've also vomited a few times—in the morning, mostly."

"Urination has increased?"

"Yes."

She felt unable to express to Lillias how much Zalmai meant to her, to find the words that could describe the love she had for him. And currently, with his child growing inside her belly, she was overwhelmed with love, there were moments that she wanted to shed tears of joy.

"Lily, I want this life. I want to raise this child," she said firmly.

"How many sexual interactions have you had with him?"

"Two."

"When?"

"Last time in Aden on May 6th, first time in Peshawar April 26th." Under the grey morning skies, her eyes were like faded lapis lazuli.

Dr. Hamilton did a quick reckoning based on the dates Roma had given her. They were due to arrive in Portsmouth on the following day, May 22nd. "It's been about twenty-seven days," she said, "there's a high possibility that you're expecting." She unclenched the handrail and spun on her heel heading back to her cabin. "Let's check you thoroughly."

It was too early to expect fetal movement but there was a change in her uterus. "Have you told Zalmai you're possibly pregnant?"

"No."

"Then please don't tell him until you are sure."

"Lily, I am carrying his child. I know that."

"Roma, it's too early, don't spread news we can't be certain of." She placed her stethoscope back in her bag and rammed it irritably into the overhead bin.

"If you are pregnant," Lillias said sitting down on the bunk-bed opposite her sister, "How do you imagine you are going to raise the child as a single parent?" She reached out and held Roma's hand. "You know Zalmai is going back to Kabul and you won't be able to go with him, particularly if you are pregnant—it would ruin him— and it may even cost him his life! And our Mum needs you in London . . . Have you thought about that?"

"Lily, I haven't reached that point yet. I'll deal with it when the time comes," she said, sounding a little desperate under her sister's interrogation.

"The time is now, if you think you are carrying his baby."

"Our love is deep and I believe he'll accept anything that is best for me and his child," she said softly.

"Let me assure you, Nasrullah will not leave London without him."

"He and his gang of murderers are not like Zalmai. He can tell them to go to hell. He can stay in London with me . . . and his child."

"Roma, Are you out of your mind? You hardly know him! What about the choices Zalmai will have to make—his parents, work, and way of life. You are only thinking of yourself! And what about my situation—how will I be able to return to Kabul after such news! This is work that I care about. It is not just about the Amir, but the poor people of Kabul, and the clinic I started."

"Lily, when we arrive in London, let's talk with Mum, together. I'll introduce Zalmai to Mum."

"Just don't speak to him yet," Lillias pleaded, "Allow him to keep

416

his mind on serving Nasrullah. You know very well that Zalmai has a crucial task in keeping him safe while he is in London."

PART TWO
CHAPTER THIRTY-EIGHT

Thursday, May 23, 1895 - Afghan calendar month: Jawza 3, 1274.

Portsmouth, England

The sky was cloudless and the sun shone with blazing splendor as Nasrullah disembarked from the *HMS Clive* and set foot in England amid a thunder of salutes from the ships and land batteries at Portsmouth.

A grand welcoming ceremony of British naval and military brass, clad in parade uniform, awaited the Afghan Prince on the jetty. Nasrullah was attired in a brilliant uniform, richly embroidered with gold, and wore a blue sash attached with an order of his father. Olivia Worth and all the English ladies who had worked expertly and tirelessly on his clothing were the indisputable heroines who vouchsafed him a stately appearance at this, and many functions to come.

Subsequent to inspecting the troops, Nasrullah was escorted to the parade-ground at Southsea, where prior to the arrival of this young Afghan Prince, no such ceremony had been afforded to any Eastern sovereign. High-profile British dignitaries wearing frock coats of the latest styles, doffed their high hats and removed their white gloves to shake his hand. At first glance, observing his personal appearance, countenance, regal stature, and erect figure, they were not given the impression of him as a neophyte, but a young man with a profound understanding of Victorian intellect and etiquette. He was received as a Habsburg or Tsar prince might have been, as one who stood out as exotically different, but possibly intellectually and socially on their level

He was ushered onto the dais, where he was faced with six-thousand troops standing in immaculate military formation below him representing all the arms of the British Armed Forces. As he stood before them, three immense drum rolls sounded accompanied by trumpets, and, as they paused, a bugle band struck up the anthem of Old England: "God save the Queen". And then repeated it a second time as there was no national anthem for Afghanistan. No one appeared to have thought of that lack of before leaving Kabul, nor even thought to design a national flag. Just the Amir's plain black flag fluttered next to the Union Jack. Nasrullah failed, at that stage, to notice the puzzlement among the dignitaries that the absence of a national anthem had caused, and possibly, among some, derision.

After these formalities, Nasrullah and his entourage were driven to the Government House where luncheon was served. There, Lord Falmouth, Munshi Abdul Karim Khan and Sir Rafiuddin anxiously waited to greet him.

Sir Fitzgerald made the introductions.

"Welcome to England, Your Highness." Lord Falmouth said as he removed his tall hat and one of his white gloves and shook Nasrullah's hand gravely; his bald pate gleamed in the late morning sun. "Her Majesty specifically instructed me to be at Your Highness's service."

"Thank you Lord Faalmoot, it is a pleasure to meet you." A smile stretched across Nasrullah's face, "I will be consulting with you every step of the way, Lord Faalmoot."

"By all means, Your Highness."

Nasrullah turned to face Munshi Abdul Karim Khan, Queen

Victoria's Indian secretary.

"Your Highness," Munshi smiled, clasping and shaking Nasrullah's hand in both of his. "*As-Salamu Alaykum*." The medals—bequeathed to him by Queen Victoria—on the proud thrust of his chest clinked against one another as he embraced Nasrullah three times in greeting. I'm obliged to see Your Highness in person." Munshi Abdul Karim's pagri turban was of Banarasi silk adorned with an egret's plume, which the sea breeze oscillated like a boxing speed bag. An embroidered cloak was draped over his shoulders. "May Allah deliver you safely to London . . . "May you not be tired." He held him in arms-length. "It is good to see you, my dear Shahzadah."

"*Tashakur,* Munshi Sahib," Nasrullah smiled. The fringes of his embroidered epaulets swung idly as he moved. "I've brought Baarfi, my horse, with me. Thank you for both horses you procured through Sultan of Bahrain for us."

"We'll go for a ride at Your Highness's pleasure."

"Of course." He then turned to face Sir Rafiuddin.

With a rustle of his long Indian dress, Rafiuddin stepped eagerly forward to greet Nasrullah, "My eyes are brightened to see Your Highness," he said. "You have arrived with the grace of Allah." He hunched his back in submissive gesture and held Nasrullah's hand with both hands for longer than necessary. A smile passed across his bearded face like a quiet storm.

"Rafiuddin Sahib, I'm looking forward to a time when we can converse privately," he said including both men in a meaningful glance.

Rafiuddin straightened his black embroidered cape over his shoulder, "We are at your pleasure, anytime, Your Highness," he assured him.

After luncheon, Nasrullah was taken by coach to the dockyard where a special train was waiting to take him to London. His arrival at

Victoria Station had been eagerly awaited by large crowds and he was plunged into the midst of spectators who wanted a glimpse of him, before being ushered to a reserved space on the platform where he stood facing a guard of honor with a band wearing regimental colors. It was drawn up in open order as for royal salute, comprising a hundred men of the First Goldstream Guards. In attendance, was also a captain's escort of First Life Guards. Moments after Nasrullah's arrival, Lord Carrington, representing Queen Victoria in his capacity as Lord Chamberlain, ascended the platform wearing the Windsor uniform.

"I'm honored to receive Your Highness to the United Kingdom," he said as he bowed.

"Thank you Lord Carrieton, the honor is mine," Nasrullah declared as he shook his hand.

When they finally left the station, Victoria street, Wilton Road and the entrance to Buckingham Palace was congested and almost impassable with people in horse drawn carriages, omnibuses, and on foot all hoping to catch sight of the Afghan Prince.

Nasrullah and his entourage were ushered through the crowds in a cavalcade of sumptuous carriage to Dorchester House in Mayfair where he would be residing for the duration of his stay in England.

As the column of horse drawn carriages snaked its way out of Victoria, through Grosvenor Place and Piccadilly, to Park Lane, the horses pranced and held their heads higher. It was as though they sensed the significance of the procession through the excitement of the crowd. Great numbers of people had amassed on the streets waving and cheering in welcoming the Afghan Prince. The cavalcade passed Hyde Park Corner, and for a moment caught the sweet scent of mixed flowers that had drifted up on the warm twilight breeze. Further down on Park Lane and the adjoining streets, lamplighters, carrying ladders with which to climb the poles, held torch sticks to light the gas lamps. As the carriages rode on, the streets behind them shone like strings of pearls.

The clatter of the horses' hooves were silenced as the carriages halted under the lofty Portico and along a semi-circular sweep of guard railings in front of Dorchester House. The entire mansion was lit up with gas lamps like a birthday cake. On its stairs leading to the main entrance, menservants and attendants clad in frock coats and white gloves stood to welcome Nasrullah.

"*Qasr-e-*Bokingum? Buckingham Palace?" Nasrullah asked Lord Falmouth doubtfully.

"Your Highness, this is Dorchester House, it is just as elegant as Buckingham Palace," Lord Falmouth replied. "This great mansion was once the Embassy of the United States and the Ambassador who resided here boasted that 'it was the most magnificent Embassy in Europe, or the whole world for that matter.' The Ambassador was further quoted as saying, 'There are many fine Embassy buildings in the various capitals belonging to the powers, but none can compare in point with the beauty of architecture and gorgeousness of Dorchester House.' Your Highness, if I may humbly request, please consider looking inside." Raj's translation was left a few phrases behind when Lord Falmouth stopped speaking.

An attendant opened the carriage door and unfolded the step for Nasrullah to alight. The young Pince's glance at Lord Falmouth was disdainful.

"I hope I won't be subject to British ridicule for staying in this chicken coop?"

"Not at all Your Highness," Lord Falmouth doffed his high silk hat and bowed in respect. "The British people have tremendous respect for Afghanistan, His Highness the Amir, your brother, the Crown Prince, and Your Highness as well. Please accept my sincere apologies if we could not offer better than what Your Highness is about to see." he gestured broadly toward the building.

"So, Laard Falmoot," Nasrullah stared at Lord Falmouth, "I am not as equal to Naser al-Din Shah who was housed in Bokingum Palace?" He stepped down, glanced at the façade, and ascended the flight of steps leading to the massive double doors. The two men crossed the chequered marble floor in the colossal rectangular foyer with Raj, the interpreter in tow. Nasrullah walked purposefully, hands clasped behind his back.

"Your Highness, The Shah of Iran paid a visit to Great Britain about twenty years ago," Lord Falmouth said pointedly. He allowed himself to fall behind Nasrullah for a moment, he surreptitiously opened his gold snuff box, tapped some snuff onto his knuckle, and quietly sniffed it into each nostril, "If the Shah had been offered a choice between Buckingham Palace and Dorchester House, he might have chosen Dorchester House."

"Choice?" Nasrullah looked down his nose at him. "Was it his choice that *Malika* Weektorya appointed him a Knight of the Order of the Garter? She appointed an utterly disgraced idiot who spent his time in *fahesha-khana-hai*, brothels, of Paarees, Paris, before his arrival to visit her in *Qasr-e*-Weenzor?" His nostrils flared, "I am sure there won't be similar choices granted to a Shahzadah like me, but only to a disgraced womanizing Shah of Persia?"

As he crossed the foyer, his footsteps sounded harshly on the marble floor. He spun on his heel to examine the splendid three-story high walls and the stately grand marble staircase leading to picture galleries with open arches above. He was secretly impressed by this masterpiece of Italian architecture.

Lord Falmouth led the way into the library, "Please Your Highness."

Nasrullah marveled at the magnificent rooms overlooking the western terrace and the manicured lawns beyond. Rows of lofty bookshelves in frames of inlaid rosewood contained orderly collections of rare, valuable books. The vaulted ceiling was charmingly painted to resemble a tapestry. Gilded furniture was arranged in every room and foyer. A broad flight of steps led down to the wide western terrace where a huge marquee had been erected on the lawn. The spacious balustraded stone terrace, which occupied two sides of the mansion was an eye opener for the Afghan Prince. Back in the galleried hall the two men ascended the grand staircase—a unique monument to the excellence of its designer some forty-two years before—at a more leisurely pace. The gallery above surrounded the staircase on all four sides, lofty pillars in clusters of two and three, of the purest white marble, supported the deeply-recessed soaring ceiling, which was rich in gold mosaic work. Nasrullah trailed a hand over the walls of grand staircase impressed by its smooth stone surface.

"Your Highness, they're the rarest marbles in the world, straight from the quarries of Carrara in Italy."

"Interesting."

Lord Falmouth with a slow tapping of his cane conducted Nasrullah from the contemplation of the staircase into the dining-room where attention was drawn to the marble mantelpiece. Two male figures carved from the whitest marble appeared to support it on their bowed heads.

"Your Highness the mantelpiece in the ball-room is similar but supported by women."

The sculptured women were topless and each had, what appeared to be, a thin sheet of cloth covering their privates. The artistry of those unique figurines was like a border of flowers along the course of civilization.

"I prefer not to look at these idols," Nasrullah declared abruptly, "Sorry, Lord Falmoot, we Muslims are not fond of idols and statues." He shook his head and abruptly left the room.

Nasrullah's thoughts were drawn to his father, the Amir, at that moment. At the behest of his favorite wife, he had destroyed the fifth century Buddah in Bamyan by blowing off its legs. The Muslim conquest in the seventh century had resulted in the first desecration when its face was sliced away.

"At Your Highness's discretion," said Lord Falmouth nodding respectfully. "Your Highness, could I draw your attention to these wonderful oil paintings?" He pointed to the first, "This is Philip IV Of Spain by Velasquez, and this is the Duke of Olivarez, also by Velasquez."

Nasrullah glanced at them with complete disinterest—they held no more importance to him than a flea.

"Well, Lord Falmoot, my stepmother likes hanging paintings of my father and her father, but I have no desire for such portraits."

"At Your Highness's discretion," Lord Falmouth repeated and bypassed the other more valuable paintings by Rembrandt, Paolo Veronese, Van Dyck, Claude, without elaborating further.

After being shown through many of the grand rooms of Dorchester House, Nasrullah opened the door to a toilet.

"This is the water-closet Your Highness," Lord Falmouth explained as he saw the quizzical expression of the Prince.

"*Hamam?*"

"Similar, Your Highness."

He looked into an exquisite fixture attached to the wall, the art work fascinated him—a lion's head at its pinnacle, and colorful flowers and tree branches painted on the surface.

"And what is this?"

"This is a ceramic urinal, Your Highness, attached to indoor plumbing." He showed him the flush toilet with its elevated water tank and the cast-iron bath and basin encased in wooden fixtures. Nasrullah turned on a tap and was intrigued to see water gush out.

"Your Highness, these features are very new and were only recently installed in Dorchester House. Only a few homes have these amenities in London and, in fact, throughout Europe."

"Interesting," said Nasrullah.

They returned to the gallery and stood at the balustrade looking down over the foyer.

"I'll accept it, Lord Falmouth but on two conditions. No, make it four," he said. "One, bring in arch lighting to replace all the gas lamps. Two," he raised two fingers, "remove the furniture from the parlors and replace them with cushions and bolster pillows on the floors. Three, remove the portraits and cover the statues under the mantelpieces. Four," he continued to emphasize the points by raising his fingers, "dismiss all butlers and servants, except where there's a real need for them."

"Of course Your Highness, we will set to work immediately."

"It looks as though we are in agreement," Nasrullah nodded. He shook Lord Falmouth's hand and ordered his retinue to carry their luggage into the splendid mansion.

CHAPTER THIRTY-NINE

"What do you mean that it will be costly?" Nasrullah demanded in a tone like the grating of ice. He was ensconced cross-legged on the mattress in the parlor in Dorchester House.

"You said in Kabul that his face could be restored, but if I remember correctly, you never mentioned a cost attached to this!" He removed his Astrakhan hat and ran his fingers through his oil-slicked hair. "I demand the Englees-Ha should pay the cost! They were responsible for disfiguring his face in the battle so they should bear the cost."

"Your Highness," Dr. Hamilton said quietly, "War is a terrible thing, and the consequence is loss of lives, injuries of all kinds and life-long psychological damage to anyone on the battlefield," she sipped her tea and surveyed Khairo over the rim. "Khairo knows that the entire British force was decimated in the battle." She set her cup down on the table next to her.

"Daktar Hameeltoon," Nasrullah rested his elbows on his crossed legs and tilted forward to emphasize his point. "My father staunchly resisted Khairo's travel to Landan, but I insisted only for one reason . . . to repair his face." He threw a glance at Khairo. "I don't want to go back to Kabul without having his face repaired." Dr. Hamilton met his glance and nodded.

"I've consulted with a longtime acquaintance who is now professor of prosthetics in Lahore, Major Hugo, a graduate of Barts, which is a teaching hospital here in London. He doesn't think there will be a high price incurred with the surgery, but the designing and engineering of the mask to fit snugly on his face is done by a manufacturer in France, which will incur costs."

"Is, . . . how do you say his name . . . here in Landan at the moment?"

"Major Hugo, Your Highness. Yes, he's here for a family visit and leaves for India again next month."

"Is there any chance he can see Khairo?"

"I'll ask him and let you know."

"Daktar Hameeltoon, I'll pay for his costs," Nasrullah said, glancing once more at his friend who had chosen to remain silent during this interchange. There was something more to Nasrullah's generosity than nervousness in facing the Amir on their return. Reaching into his pocket to help Khairo may have been intended to ensure his loyalty as a tribal elder of a powerful clan in Khandahar. Or to buy his help in the future to destabilize India if Queen Victoria denied Afghanistan's full autonomy. Whatever the case, Nasrullah intended to gain something in return.

They were sisters by birth and sisters by soul, Lillias and Roma had always been close in the past but their relationship had become strained by what Lillias perceived as Roma's careless attitude to this untimely pregnancy. Both women needed to gain a greater perspective of their issues by stepping back and seeing the wide angled version.

Knowing that the Amir would be furious once he learned of the intimate relationship between his Head of Security and Roma, Dr. Hamilton was forced to think of the consequences. It was quite possible that she would lose her job as his physician. She cherished her work at Arg Palace and had always given herself to perform every task with one purpose—to spread love and emotional support to the

Amir and all she served in Kabul. But she had begun to realize that things would never be the same again in the court of Amir Abdul Rahman Khan.

Before leaving Kabul, the Amir's suspicion had grown as he contemplated her motive for writing the novel, "*A Vizier's Daughter: A Tale of the Hazara War*". The book was due for publication shortly and would almost certainly sever her ties with him for revealing his atrocities against the minority ethnic Hazaras in Afghanistan. Now of course, there was Roma's relationship with Zalmai and the more Lillias considered the options, the more she knew that Zalmai's only chance of survival would be to stay in England with Roma.

The last time Roma and Zalmai had spent time together was in Aden and on casual occasions aboard *HMS Clive* and there had no opportunity for Roma to speak to him in private.

For the past two days, since her arrival in London, Roma had moved back into her parents' four story home with her three brothers, and three sisters including Lillias. The house had been built in the Italian renaissance style in Marylebone's neighborhood, which was just a stone's throw away from Dorchester House.

Roma knew she was carrying Zalmai's child and did not need anyone to her confirm the pregnancy. More than anything, she longed to tell Zalmai the news, but had sure way to reach him. Asking for him directly was an invitation for disaster and Lillias refused point-blank to convey messages between the pair when she visited Dorchester House to check on Nasrullah and Prince Omar.

Now that he was in London, Nasrullah had a tight schedule: there were meetings with British Royalty, dignitaries, attending events, and soon this would involve visits to arms and machinery manufacturers, and prominent Muslim leaders. Zalmai was daily involved in escorting the Prince from one side of London to another, so unless Roma came up with a proper plan to meet with Zalmai, the chances were that she could no longer see him before his return to Afghanistan.

As she fretted with the emptiness and loneliness she felt without Zalmai, she received a calling-card from a childhood friend.

Elizabeth Cochran had heard that Roma was back from Kabul and wanted to pay a visit

◆◇◆◇◆◇

"Elizabeth!" Roma exclaimed in delight when her friend arrived the following morning, "This is such a wonderful surprise!"

Elizabeth Cochran was Roma's childhood friend who possessed all the charm and beauty of her Scottish bloodline. Her hazel eyes were gentle but possessed with a spark of humor. Roma embraced Elizabeth fondly and then held her at arm's length admiring the way her chestnut ringlets were restrained above her high brow, yet formed a perfect frame to her face. She was wearing a blue brocade with long skirt and a light turquoise crepe bonnet and sturdy high-heeled shoes.

After exchanging pleasantries over tea, Roma suggested they enjoy a stroll in Hyde Park.

"It's a beautiful day," she said as she tied the ribbons of her bonnet, "far too good to waste it indoors."

They walked to Marble Arch and sauntered down the path parallel to Park Lane towards Hyde Park corner.

April showers had brought May flowers and the lovely mid-morning breeze permeated their sweet fragrance. The sun peeked through the new leaves of the trees and choruses of bird song welcomed Roma and Elizabeth, to the Park.

As their light-hearted conversation continued, they shared the pathways with men of the Liver Brigades—some on horseback—who greeted them with a doff of their silk hats; nurses dressed in white pinafores strolled with babies in their high-wheeled perambulators. There were governesses and adolescents and children carrying little

430

bags of crumbs to feed the ducks and the swans. Hyde Park was the playground of London's rich and poor alike.

Coincidently, Roma saw Prince Omar and little William Martin running in the direction of the Serpentine Lake. Both were appropriately dressed in sailor suits, and each had a toy boat in hand. Prince Omar's nanny scurried to catch up with them.

To Roma's surprise, they had no intention of stopping when she called them, "Please wait, I have a question." Roma called again and this time they reluctantly stopped.

"Good morning," William said politely.

"Salaam," Prince Omar added. Both boys were short of breath.

"Do you boys know, by any chance where Colonel Zalmai is?" Roma asked.

"He's with Baarfi . . . over there," he gestured with a wave of his hand towards the Rotten Row stables.

"Thank you."

They paused after answering Roma's question and dashed when she dismissed them with a laugh.

"So who is this Zalmai?" Elizabeth asked perceptively

Roma's face colored. "It's a long story, Elizabeth, and I'm not sure you will understand." she replied hesitantly.

"Well, you will never know whether I will, or I won't, if you don't tell me," her friend replied bluntly.

Roma walked slowly in the direction of the stables and poured out her heart to Elizabeth.

"Do you think dreadfully of me?" she asked when her confession was met with silence, "I know Lillias does."

Elizabeth stopped and turned to face Roma. "What I think is no matter," she replied, "but you are my friend, and you are in a grave situation, so I will stand with you. It doesn't mean I approve of what you have done, mind you!" But she softened her words with a smile. "I can see you need to see this man, so we should hurry in case he leaves before what must be said, is said."

Roma's eyes brimmed with tears. "Thank you, Elizabeth," she said, "This is too big for me alone. I am in need of a friend I can trust to tell me the truth but still loves me, despite everything."

"Come now," Elizabeth said briskly, "Dry those tears and let's see if we can find this person!"

Roma and Elizabeth reached the end of the path and continued walking towards the Rotten Row bridleway, a favored spot for wealthy equestrians to show off their steeds and their horsemanship, and for the women to parade their beauty before eligible gentlemen.

The walls of the large two-story building had recently been whitewashed between the blackened beams. The upper half of several stable doors were wide open allowing the horses to put their heads out and bask in a little sun. As Roma and Elizabeth walked along the cobbled aisle that was flanked by long wide stables, a white chisel-faced Arab horse—with gleaming black eyes—poked his head out. The stable smelled of damp hay, grain, leather, and acidic horse urine.

"I'm sure that's Baarfi," murmured Roma. She walked closer and felt convinced it was Nasrullah's horse. There were metal gratings between each stall and she could see the horse from the next stall was being groomed outside. The groom boy, Gul Agha, with the empty holster still strapped to his shoulder, had a grooming cloth in hand, had given a final shine to the coat, and was wiping the face of a horse belonging to Zalmai's guardsmen.

"Is that you Gul Agha?" Roma called.

"*Baley*, yes!" he spun around and saw Roma. "Salaam," he smiled. He was clad in the same cutlery uniform that was issued to him aboard *HMS Clive*. Now, however, it was wrinkled and filthy. "You want see Zalmai?"

"Yes. Do you know where he is?"

"*Bya*, come."

CHAPTER FORTY

The carriage stopped at the main public entrance of Bartholomew Hospital—fondly known as Barts—on West Smithfield; at the far end of the building, the beautifully rounded dome of St. Paul's Cathedral rose majestically above its rooftops. In a niche above the arched gate stood a statue of King Henry VIII, while on either side of him were small statues of a sick man and a lame.

Dr. Hamilton rummaged in her bag for a sovereign and deposited the coin in the heavy red donation box attached to the wall. As an institution that served the poor, Barts was dependent on donations for its survival and the box was designed to encourage generous handouts. Khairo tightened the end of his turban around his face.

"Let's go in," Dr. Hamilton said, aware of the Afghan's unease in these foreign surroundings.

They walked towards the white ornate stone building passed a gurgling fountain in a small garden, and entered the hospital through some rather bulky weather-worn doors.

"How may I help you?" the receptionist asked in a chirpy voice.

"I am Dr. Lillias Hamilton and I am here to meet Dr. Hugo . . . we have an appointment regarding Mr. Khairo."

"Please have a seat, I'll let the doctor know you have arrived."

Minutes into their wait, Professor Hugo walked into the reception hall. He shook hands warmly with Khairo and then with Lillias.

"So this is the gentleman you mentioned . . . severely injured in the battle of Maiwand?" She nodded. "*Kya Ap Urdu Janta Hey?* Do you know Urdu?" He asked in Urdu.

"*Tohra*, little," Khairo replied. His voice muffled under his turban.

Hugo grinned. "I offer you my heartfelt condolences for the loss of your beloved daughter and brothers. I was briefed by Dr. Hamilton--"

"Khairo doesn't converse in English, Dr. Hugo," Dr. Hamilton said, "but I am certain he understands your sympathy."

He smiled, "I believe he does," he said, "Please follow me."

Major E. V. Hugo, Professor of surgery and prosthetics in Lahore, was a graduate of Barts school of medicine. He was a well-respected alumnus whose close affiliation with the school's faculty and President, the Prince of Wales, allowed him a greater advantage to perform as a guest lecturer and surgeon. He was deemed a man of superior ability in his field of medicine, both to serve the public and impart his knowledge to the students. He was a tall slender man in his early forties with bushy eyebrows that all but hid his deep-set eyes. His face—framed by a good head of hair and side-whiskers—reflected lucent intelligence. He practiced medicine at the Mayo Hospital in Lahore and was fluent in the Urdu language. At this meeting, he came dressed in black trousers, a starched white shirt with an upturned collar, and a black cravat.

He ushered them into a conference room next to a medical library, "Please make yourselves comfortable," he said and sat down across from them at a gleaming desk with not a single object atop. "So, he has come all the way from Kabul to have his face repaired?"

"Yes," Dr. Hamilton replied, "it was a painstakingly long journey and a first experience for him and many others."

"I was told at the faculty meeting the other day, that His Royal Highness, the Prince of Wales, had said that a faceless Afghan would be requiring surgery and had elected me to conduct the procedure."

"Yes, Dr. Hugo, I mentioned you to His Highness, Prince Nasrullah, who conveyed the request to His Royal Highness."

With a congenial smile, Dr. Hugo turned to Khairo, "Could you please remove your turban?" he asked, gesturing with a twirl of his hand.

He examined him closely. "I see the side of his face has been greatly deformed by a depressed fracture of the cheekbone," he commented, "and the loss of the eye." He seemed completely absorbed in his assessment of the extent of the damage. "Any thoughts as to what weapons were used?" he asked, staring intently as he moved Khairo's face from side to side.

Dr. Hamilton pressed a hand to her mouth as she considered her reply, "I'm assuming it was a gunshot along the left jaw and cheekbone, which also blinded his eye. And, possibly, a saber cut to his mouth." She stood up and pointed to the periphery of Khairo's jaw.

Dr. Hugo nodded his agreement. "We would probably need to raise the bone here," he said, "where the interior wall of the sinus has been crushed in. The bones, and any rebuilding found necessary, would have to be precisely adjusted to the undamaged structure and held in position. "If you have a look here, Dr. Hamilton, these wounds differ from the others. This could be shell wound damage." He pointed out places on Khairo's nose and cheeks where parts of maxillae had been torn from the bone and displaced. "Much will have to be done prosthetically," he ruminated, "and, of course, we will replace the eye with an artificial one, which will lessen the disfigurement."

Dr. Hamilton agreed. "I presume that in the case of differences in the size of the eyeballs, because one eye perhaps congenitally too small, some cosmetic improvement may be made by lessening the palpebral aperture of the larger organ by increasing that of the other by tightening the muscles or ligaments that give support to the outer corners of the eyelid.

"Yes, that's a canthoplasty procedure that may be necessary in his case. Once all the bone adjustments are done, we will set the eye in place and make the mold for the mask that will replace the lost portions of the face."

"How is the mask made?" asked Dr. Hamilton.

"With a plaster mold, an impression of the deformed face,"—he tilted and moved Khairo's face in various directions. "Forming the mold and the making of the mask will be costly."

"Prince Nasrullah agreed to pay those costs," Lillias said with a smile.

"Excellent! You won't be using your turban to hide your face anymore," He grinned at Khairo. "No more!" he emphasized with a shake of his head. "No more!" he said again twirling his forefinger in the air.

He then set the appointment for the surgery.

Gul Agha, the groom, escorted Roma and Elizabeth through the corridors of Rotten Row's stables to an open area where Zalmai and his guardsmen were polishing and buffing carriages to a flawless shine. An Open Amempton, a Double Brougham, and two Sociable Landaus with interchangeable heads, had been bestowed by courtesy of the British Government to Nasrullah and his entourage for their use in London and Lord Falmouth had also approved the accommodation of the stabling of their horses.

"*Oona* Zalmai," Gul Agha said, nodding in his direction.

Roma's and Zalmai's eyes locked in a passionate stare, and the feeling inside Roma unfurled and burgeoned.

"Finish the rest. Squirt some oil on the wheels and joints, I'll be right back," Zalmai instructed and dried his hands on a cloth as he walked over to the two women.

Roma introduced them. "This is Elizabeth, my childhood friend," she said, "and Elizabeth, this is Zalmai, I call him Zal." Roma smiled. Her full rosy cheeks and fair complexion were glowing with the pleasure of the moment.

"Very nice to meet you Zalmai," Elizabeth said with a brief curtsy, and she stretched out her hand to shake Zalmai's.

A bit of confusion clouded Zalmai as her hand hovered in the air, he was unsure how to respond to this polite gesture from a woman.

"Very nice to meet you Eleezabet Jan," he said, bowing and holding his hand to his chest. He glanced back at Roma, "Preparations are being made for Shahzadah-e-*Eglistan*, Prince of Wales, and the Royal family of *Englistan* to receive Shahzadah Nasrullah in *Qasr-e-*Weenzor tomorrow. We are readying the carriages."

"Do you have a moment to spare now? I have something important to tell you."

"We are testing the carriages. Would you and Eleezabet Jan like to ride with me? We can talk too."

"Of course," Roma said immediately.

"They're harnessing the horses, the carriage will be ready shortly,"

Zalmai assisted Roma and Elizabeth into the Brougham carriage and Roma slid the window open to allow the midday breeze to pour in. With a snap of the whip, and cries of hoy! hoy! from the coachman, the horses took them away from Rotten Row towards West Carriage Drive.

"What is it you wanted to tell me?" Zalmai asked taking Roma's hand. "Is there a problem?"

"Zal, there is no other way to tell you this," she said, "I'm pregnant."

His eyes widened with shock. "You're pregnant?" he muttered.

She nodded unable to tell if he was happy or not. She glanced quickly at Elizabeth who was seated opposite but her friend's expression told her nothing.

Zalmai gave Roma's hand a quick soft squeeze, and he looked out of the window at the lush sprawling lawn leading down to the Serpentine Lake where swans, ducks, and other aquatic birds swam.

For a moment, he went into a reverie glancing at the happy children running and playing under the willows and poplars, as the carriage swayed gently on its path. Then he looked back into Roma's eyes.

This was very hard for Zalmai to digest knowing an intimate relationship without being married would not be well received in his culture or, as he understood it, in Roma's either—let alone a child out of wedlock. He had deviated from the Afghan norms and his religious beliefs, and Roma's revelation had brought everything home to him inescapably. Zalmai was tormented between the love he had for Roma and the culture he practiced that had been part of his life's evolution and still, he believed, remained strong and fortified. But it was only now that he understood the boundary had already been crossed and there was no way back.

Roma was undergoing turmoil of her own as she attempted to assess his reaction.

"Are you very angry?"

He moved closer to her on the tufted velvet seat and put his arms around her.

"I am still having a hard time believing this." He lifted her hand and brushed it with a soft kiss, "I'm going to be a father? We're having a baby?" His voice was almost inaudible, wanting to shut Elizabeth's presence out of such an intimate moment.

"Wonderful." He met her eyes again.

Roma nodded again and said softly, "Yes." Tears sparkled in her eyes, "Isn't it amazing?"

Her attitude cheered Zalmai. "Yes!" His loud response attracted the attention of a group of bystanders as the carriage turned right on N Carriage Drive.

"But I also have bad news," Roma said.

He winced and his sturdy muscular physique slumped, "Tell me."

"Lillias may not be going back to Kabul."

He immediately understood the reason. "Because of us?"

The horses' hooves clattered on towards Marble Arch.

She nodded. All the joy had gone from Roma's face. She removed her bonnet and touched her chignon, "She's angry with me and specifically disappointed in me for severing her relationship with the Amir."

"I understand," Zalmai said bleakly.

"Lillias is certain the Amir will terminate her employment because of our relationship," she said, "and once he knows I am expecting your child, that will be the end." The breeze blew a whisp of hair across her cheek and she tucked it behind her ear. "And I'm sure that cross-eyed evil man will hold your feet against the fire."

"Of course, he'll find a way to kill me, right here in Landan once he knows the full story." His face turned pallid and his large Adam's apple moved in his lean throat as he swallowed. "He stabbed and tossed Lieutenant Mahmoud's body overboard for less than this, and he warned me multiple times not to get caught with you." Rubbed the back of his neck. "Nothing will stop that cold-hearted killer from slitting my throat once he knows I have made you pregnant?" Shook his head anxiously. "He has already sentenced Major Akbar Khan to death; he will face the gallows the moment he arrives back in Kabul."

"What for?"

"For drinking alcohol with Lieutenant Mahmoud," he looked out the window and saw the Marble Arch and the crowds of gaily dressed women and men, and, for an instant, the bustle of London diverted his attention from the dilemma that he might face with Amir's executioner.

"I won't let him hurt you!" Roma blurted out, "You must stay alive for this!" Roma gestured at her womb.

"What choice do I have?"

"Hide with me."

"Where?"

"Let me think."

"Perhaps this is where I come in," Elizabeth interjected. Roma and Zalmai had been so embroiled in their dilemma that they had almost forgotten her presence. "I could offer you a place to stay in our family home in Scotland until Prince Nasrullah leaves England," Elizabeth suggested warmly. She looked at Roma, "My sister, Kirsten, and her husband, Kevin will be glad to have you over for as long as you need." Her eyes widened eagerly, "We could leave almost immediately— today if you like! It's a huge farmhouse, my Dad helped my Granddad to finish the building." She was as sincere as sunlight.

"Oh, Elizabeth, that would be wonderful," Roma exclaimed, "But Zalmai, I need to know what you think. You will be forsaking everything if you do this. It will change your life completely and you may never again be able to return to Afghanistan."

His expression was resolute. "Everything I want or need is here in my arms," he said. "Go back home. I will send Gul Agha with a message when it is safe for me to meet you."

Munshi Abdul Karim Khan and Sir Rafiuddin Ahmed—known as Moulvi—made their appearance in Dorchester House ahead of the Prince of Wales who would be receiving Nasrullah on the following day.

For the time being, they brought Muslim Indian chefs to prepare *halal* food for the Afghans. They also brought sheep, and baskets filled with a variety of poultry, for their consumption. Makeshift pens were built to confine the animals in the well-tended and immaculate yard of the mansion. Early the following day, the fastidious aristocrats of the Mayfair neighborhood, were not only awakened not only to an unusual bleating and crowing but to the loud prayer call of the Mullah. Five times a day, from dawn to nightfall, he stood and faced Mecca on the balcony above the portico and chanted the *adhan* for three to five minutes, summoning faithful Muslims to attend the prayers. Quite possibly, the only Muslims in the area were the occupants of the Dorchester House, but still, his enthusiastic voice could be heard blocks away. However, according to the London tabloids, Park Lane had been transformed into a primitive environment as quickly as the midnight clouds raced across the moon.

The benevolence of Munshi and Moulvi to bestow cattle and poultry was not their only intention, but also, to enlighten Nasrullah of Queen Victoria's state of mind regarding his father's quest for full autonomy of his dominion.

"Shahzadah, we've tried our utmost to convince the Queen to accept Amir Sahib's request for Afghanistan's representation in the court of St. James's," Abdul Karim informed him, "but to no avail!" He was seated crossed-legged in the parlor, teacup in hand. The lilt in his voice was not much different from Raj's, except it tended, at times, to whine with self-pity like an Indian street beggar. His high, tubular turban appeared as though it had been wound around a tall hat.

As night fell, the pageboys lit the gasoliers throughout Dorchester House. Since a great deal of the fine furniture had already been prudently removed, its new inhabitants made themselves at home lounging on cushions and bolstered pillows set on the floors of every room. The luxury hand-carved thirty-six seat dining table had been replaced by a *destarkhwan,* tablecloth, laid out on the floor.

"I can attest to that." Rafiuddin agreed, who was also comfortably sitting crossed-legged, his folded black robe on his lap, hands clasped, elbows touching his knees. "Yes, we both heard Her Majesty's refusal when we asked her intention," he reported, rocking to and fro.

"Let me make this clear," said Nasrullah with calm determination, "She will be convinced once she reads my father's letter and received his *baksheesh*!" he leaned against the bolster pillow and rubbed his stubble. "We all know, *Englistan* needs us more than we need *Englistan* and they would rather pay us trivial subsidies to defend their Crown Jewel than lose it to Russia."

Abdul Karim glanced at Rafiuddin, perhaps wondering whether

Nasrullah's intense nature was inseparable from his fantasy. Desire and determination alone would not make his goal achievable. And they knew, that pacifying the Queen with Amir's gifts—as though she was a youthful child—would not work. Nasrullah was on the wrong trajectory to achieve his father's goal and was as doomed to failure as an unreplenished stream.

"While Your Highness was on the voyage, we informed his Highness, Amir Sahib in Kabul, via Sheikh Isa Al Khalifa that the Queen was not changing her position. His Highness replied with this note. Abdul Karim pulled the folded wireless from his embroidered waistcoat and handed it to Nasrullah.

The message read:

Nasrullah should remain in London until the Queen grants Afghanistan full autonomy.

"That might have to be our last option if all others fail," Field Marshal Hassein Khan said. His onyx worry beads were wrapped around his wrist, and his hands laced over his rotund belly.

"Agreed," Nasrullah replied but without any conviction that such an eventuality would arise.

General Akram Khan nodded in approval, "Let's present the Queen with Amir Sahib's letter before we consider changing our position." The lights shining from the gasoliers reflected off eyeglasses. "We only came ashore a couple of days ago, so there is no need expect a negative response as yet." His newly stylish trimmed beard—courtesy of a barber in Piccadilly—gave him the distinctive appearance of a higher ranked officer, which suited him well.

"My apologies for intruding into Amir Sahib's business," said Khairo, his muffled voice sounding faint behind his tightly wrapped turban. "As you know, I'm only in Landan at the behest of His Highness, *Shahzadah*," he gestured politely towards Nasrullah, "to the have surgery on my face," he said apprehensively, "But if, as we have been told, Malika-Weetorya had already decided to refuse the

Amir's request before the *Shahzadah* had even seen her, our mission is doomed!" he blurted out with unexpected boldness. "Never trust an *Englees* until you verify his intention."

At that moment, the young groom, Gul-Agha was shown into the parlor disrupting the conversation amongst Nasrullah and others. He asked permission to speak.

"What is it?" Nasrullah demanded angrily.

"We can't find Colonel Zalmai Khan," he said, "he has been missing since this morning." For the first time he was not wearing his holster. "His valises are gone too," he stammered.

The Amir's executioner sprang to his feet, and dashed to the door.

"Follow me!" he yelled at the groom.

CHAPTER FORTY-ONE

❦❦❦

Khairo lay on the operating table that stood in the center of a horseshoe of elevated galleries from which the students and internal Barts' surgeons could observe the full procedure. A cluster of four lamps hung unevenly from the ceiling; their purpose was to bring about the best possible visibility to every part of the operating room.

Dr. Hamilton and close associates, some of the more senior surgeons who had worked with Dr. Hugo over the years, were accommodated on horse-hair chairs to witness the operation in close proximity to the table.

Against the wall were shelves filled with various operating instruments and on either side of Dr. Hugo, dressed in white robes, stood two masked scrub nurses who were arranging the surgical tools on the tables next to them.

Once the final preparations were made under strict hygienic and sterilization rules, and a general anesthetic was administered, Dr. Hugo turned to each nurse individually looking directly into their eyes, "Ready?"

They nodded and began to hand him handing him the appropriate tools for the first incision. Dr. Hugo's movements were quick and efficient. His hands moved to and fro as he operated, changing methodically from one surgical tool to another. He was intently focused on every stage of the operation. The instruments he sought were immediately handed to him by one nurse while the other wiped the blood from the used tools and sterilized them again. The incisions were precise; bones were pegged, elevated, and adjusted; the damaged eye was replaced with the artificial one. Dr. Hugo's murmured requests to the nurses and the occasional clinking of instruments were the only sounds heard in the theatre. Hours passed before the final stitches were in place and Dr. Hugo was able to straighten his back. There was clapping from the galleries and student doctors gathered in informal groups to discuss what had taken place.

While Zalmai's whereabouts was a mystery forcing the Amir's executioner to leave no stone unturned in finding an answer, Parwana Khan was fully aware in his own mind, as to why Zalmai had gone, and whom he had absconded with. But it was still necessary to question every groom, guard, culinary worker, and anyone else remotely associated with Zalmai. It soon became evident that the groom boy, Gul Agha, was the last one who interacted with him.

"When and where did you see him?" asked Parwana Khan.

"This morning at the stables." Gul Agha answered, his face pallid. "He went with Daktar Laila's sister," he added voluntarily . . . in that carriage." He pointed at the double Brougham.

"Who drove?"

"The *Englees* man, Fraidoon," Gul Agha had adopted an Afghan name for the groom and coachman, Freddie Collins.

Freddie Collins frankly revealed the address he had taken Elizabeth and Roma to when Raj asked him on the executioner's behalf, 29 Queen Ann Street, Marylebone he told Raj. And the gentleman had stepped out some distance from the stables—and no, he did not know where he went after that.

"Shahzadah, I knew the *haramzadah*, bastard, would do something like this." Parwana Khan declared bitterly when he reported to Nasrullah later. He rubbed the back of his head and blew out a series of short breaths, "He'll face the gallows in Kabul if I don't manage to behead him here in Landan." His eyes protruded, and he clenched and unclenched his fists, "I just need to find him!"

"I should have reported his roguish behavior to my father when I caught him with Roma in Kabul," Nasrullah said shaking his head in regret. "He would have rotted in the deep well by now."

Nasrullah immediately promoted Zalmai's assistant to lead the cavalry for the royal visit to Windsor Palace on the following day. He also briefly informed Colonel Talbot and Sir Fitzgerald of Zalmai's disappearance but it was not reported to the metropolitan police, and, understanding it was an *affaire de Coeur*, they lost no sleep over the matter.

Dr. Hamilton was summoned and questioned by Nasrullah, but as her sister Selena had secretly informed her that Roma and Zalmai were already on a train heading up North, she swore she knew nothing about Roma's whereabouts.

"Daktar Hameeltoon," Nasrullah warned sternly, "when you do receive information, please tell your sister that I'm not going back to Kabul without Zalmai!"

A torrent of invitations had almost overwhelmed Nasrullah when he came ashore. Several royal banquets, balls, concerts, as well as formal meetings with Queen Victoria and the Prince of Wales had been arranged; then there was the Lord Mayor's welcome at Guildhall; a luncheon with the newly-appointed Under Secretary of the British Foreign Office, George Curzon and his wife. The ones he most looked forward to were a closed-door meeting in London with *Anjuman-i-Islam*, and Abdullah Quilliam, *Sheik-ul-Islam* of the British Isles, had invited him to visit the British Muslims in Glasgow. There were various important appointments with armories, arms manufacturers, and factories throughout England. In addition to all those scheduled events though, there was still ample time for Nasrullah's personal entertainment. Everything was fresh and exciting. He became well acquainted with the Punch and Judy puppet shows; the bare-knuckle prizefights in some of London's neighborhoods; performing animals; Organ-grinders, Hurdy-gurdy and white mice; and multiple other diversions that held higher precedence over almost anything else for the youthful Afghan Prince.

In a preliminary introduction, Queen Victoria, the Prince of Wales, and other royal family members had received Nasrullah in the Green Room at Windsor Castle on the previous Saturday, and his father's presents of benevolence were bestowed on her as a gesture of friendship from Nasrullah. They were all neatly packaged and transported to Windsor Castle. Seven-hundred-and-fifty finely handwoven Afghan carpets and one-*Kharwar* (five-hundred-sixty-kilograms) of dark blue crystals of *lazhward*, Lapis Lazuli. The Queen was grateful. But the precious casket manufactured by Frank Martin's men, containing the autographed letter from his father, was to be presented to Her Majesty at today's State Reception, Monday, May twenty-seventh.

Nasrullah wore one of his richly-embroidered scarlet tunics and dark trousers that Olivia had designed, and a black astrakhan fez ornamented with a splendid diamond star. He also carried a scimitar sheathed in a gold-mounted purple velvet scabbard. He looked confident but a bit distracted, unsure of what to expect when he handed his father's letter to Queen Victoria. He and Frank Martin had rehearsed the etiquette of greeting the Queen beforehand.

General Akram Khan was in full uniform that bore a resemblance to an Ottoman Turkish senior officer. He looked quite overwrought. He continually dabbed away the sweat that beaded his brow with his kerchief and pushed his thick glasses back even more frequently than usual.

As Nasrullah's interpreter, Colonel Adelbert Talbot stood a

short distance behind Nasrullah, composed and smiling. The Queen held Talbot in high esteem for his remarkable intelligence work in Afghanistan and the north-western frontier areas.

For this occasion, Frank Martin wore a frock coat, a starched white shirt with a stiff upturned collar, and black satin cravat. He looked proud and excited to be meeting the Queen for the first time. Frank was in possession of the black velvet box containing the precious casket he had designed for Queen Victoria. In it was the Amir's missive to Her Majesty. The casket itself held no pleasure for him since the brutal execution of the ten men who helped him manufacture it.

They arrived at Windsor Station, where they were met by Major General McNeill and multiple footmen clothed in scarlet waistcoats adorned with gold, scarlet knee-breeches, white stockings, and powdered white wigs.

Major General Sir John McNeill was a senior British Army officer and Scottish recipient of the Victoria Cross for his gallantry in the Egyptian war. He was a tall, priestly-looking gentleman of about sixty, a Scottish Highlander, a favorite of Queen Victoria's who deemed the Highland identity as her own. McNeill's striking blue eyes were emphasized by his neatly combed metallic-white hair and drooping mustache. Victoria had given her sovereign stamp of approval to metamorphose the Highlands into a major cultural anchor in the minds of Victorian Britons and Canadians. General McNeill had been chosen to meet and accompany Nasrullah and his retinue to Windsor Castle.

Nasrullah and his attendants were led to waiting carriages and escorted by mounted cavalry to the Castle. The clatter of horses' hooves grew louder as the cavalcade passed under the *porte cochere* of George IV's gate and crossed the quadrangle where they were saluted by a guard of honor of the First Scots Guards. They alighted at the state entrance tower and from there were ushered through the long corridor with its handsome vaulted ceiling supported by banded columns. A central crimson runner drew the eye up the grand staircase to the landing above where two Royal Army Officers clad in Scots Guards uniforms met them and led the visitors to the vestibule where Queen Victoria was to receive them.

Exactly at the scheduled meeting time, Munshi wheeled the Queen in through the tall double-doors.

"*Oulyahazrat*, Your Majesty," said Nasrullah in Dari, "I'm honored to see you."

"Your Highness." She gave a quick smile, "Welcome to Windsor again." She stretched out her hand. On her wrist was an exquisite diamond and emerald bracelet and pinned to her black silk dress she wore her favorite brooch bestowed by the Prince Consort on their wedding night—an oblong sapphire surrounded by twelve large diamonds.

Nasrullah approached her, knelt, held her outstretched hand lightly, and brushed it with his lips. He stood up and bowed.

"I'm honored to see you again *Oulyahazrat*." He glanced at Frank Martin who gave him a brief smile and nod of approval.

Queen Victoria seldom extended her hand to be kissed, and then only on special occasions, doing so for Nasrullah was a rare privilege. Many courtiers at Windsor Palace may have wondered why the Queen granted Nasrullah the privilege of kissing her hand, but no one seemed to know for sure.

It was clear Nasrullah did not yet understand that Colonial Britain had been ruled for almost sixty years by a woman with a strong disposition, who was able to petrify royalty by simply walking down the palace hall, and whose empire was considered "The World". Nasrullah had assured his brother before leaving Kabul that he would lure Queen Victoria to his father's demand, as though he believed she could be enticed into Aladdin's cave. He had been openly disparaging of the petticoat rule of Arg Palace by Queen Sultana, and if that wasn't a lesson to be learned, he would soon discover that matriarchy could overrule men.

"Shall we proceed to the Grand Reception Room?" General McNeill asked after the usual pleasantries were exchanged. "Your Majesty. Your Highness. Please." He ushered them forward warmly extending both hands in the direction of the room.

In the weeks whilst waiting for the prosthesis to arrive from Paris, Khairo's face had begun to heal.

"Look, we have your new face!" he lifted a strangely shaped mold from the shipping box and held it up for Khairo to see. Dr. Hugo set to work fitting and securing it into place and when he was satisfied with the result, held up a mirror for Khairo to see.

The delight on his countenance shone forth with all the vibrance of a new dawn. Although one side was static, it was no longer deformed and unsightly. For the very first time since the horrific battle, Khairo deemed it unnecessary to hide himself from the world behind the cloth of his turban any longer. He gazed into the mirror and marveled at the miracle of the restoration. It was even difficult to tell the difference between the real and artificial eye at a distance. Underneath the prosthesis, hooks like ice-tongs had been used to raise the fractured portion, while chromicized catgut sutures were introduced through drill holes, and sterilized ivory pegs and tacks were applied to hold the bony structures together. The French manufacturer had demonstrated exceptional skill in producing a large portion of the face mask from metal to rebuild the nose, cheek, chin, and eye socket. It was held in place with springs, pegs into his nasal cavity; a pair of spectacles fitted to his ears. By applying electroplating and artistic coloring, the final result was extraordinary.

Khairo's pleasure was palpable. He examined and re-examined his new features in the mirror and running his fingers over the smooth planes of cheek, jaw and chin. He laughed at his lopsided smile. But when he looked into Doctors Hamilton's and Hugo's eyes, his one good eye welled up with tears of gratitude.

"You have your face back," said Dr. Hugo. "No more wrapping your turban around your face." Twirled his hand in circles.

Khairo nodded and smiled. "Thank you," he said in English, "Thank you! He could not express his true feelings in a foreign tongue, but in Pashtu his feelings were expressed loud and clear, "*Der Ala! Der Ala!* Exceptional! Exceptional!" He sounded at that moment, as if he were the star of his own show! "*Tashakur Daktar Sahib Oogo wa Daktar Sahiba Liala Jan.*"

It would be better to leave it there.

Sir. General McNeill led the way as the Queen was wheeled through the Grand Corridor and into St. George's Hall. Nasrullah walked alongside the Queen with is retinue at his heels. As the footmen opened the set of tall double doors to the Grand reception Room, Victoria rose from her chair and leaned for a moment on her walking stick. Indubitably, signs of general physical deterioration were noticeable in the seventy-six-years old monarch.

The Grand Reception Room was the most elaborate and elegant of all the state apartments in Windsor Castle, with expensive and subtly carved Parisian *boiseries*, or wood panels, lining its approximately hundred-foot-long walls. They were like enormous tapestries of rich yet artful colors, its sea-foam verdant walls embellished with frosty and shimmering rocailles. The garlands, cherubs, and festoons reflected the renaissance depiction of George IV's reign. Indeed, the room was like a poem without words.

The Reception Room was filled with Her Majesty's courtiers, the prime minister and ministers of government, lord chancellors, field marshalls, admirals, generals, and their wives.

"Ladies and Gentlemen!" a footman announced, "Her Majesty, the Queen, and Prince Nasrullah Khan of Afghanistan!"

She was escorted to a low armchair by two equerries while a brass quintet struck up the familiar refrain of *God Save the Queen*. Frank Martin had set the jeweled casket, still in its box, across the table from where Her Majesty was seated. A footstool had been placed before her and Princes Beatrice, who was seated at the Queen's side, took her cane.

Her Scottish-born doctor, Sir James Reid, stood nearby to ensure the sovereign did not become over-tired or stressed, and to be on hand if any unexpected health issues should arise.

Lately, Victoria had withdrawn from large functions, incapable of bearing the effects of crowded or overheated rooms. It was understood that her stay during this event might be curtailed at any time should she experience discomfort or a headache.

Victoria had continued to remain in mourning in the thirty-four-years since Prince consort Albert died. Despite the encouragement of her family to leave her widow's weeds behind she steadfastly dressed in black and a white cap in memory of her husband. Despite her loss, she continued to make decisions and carried out the affairs of the state, which demonstrated her emotional acceptance and intention to continue her life as congenially as possible.

During functions such as the one in honor of the Afghan Prince, Victoria may have experienced unbearable emptiness, which today would be understood as geriatric depression.

An equerry held the chair for Nasrullah to sit across from the Queen while behind him, Colonel Talbot readied himself to translate.

Prince of Wales declared to the assembly: "To the health of the Sovereign and our guests of British Royalty now assembled here, welcoming you in my name."

KHALIL NOURI

A silence fell, as everyone knew the Queen was about to engage in conversation with Nasrullah. "Has Your Highness found London pleasant?" she asked.

"Yes, *Oulyahazrat*, and there are still many places and things for me to explore during my stay," Narullah replied. The golden fringes on his epaulets swung incessantly as he turned from the Queen to Colonel Talbot for translation and back again.

"I trust His Highness Amir Abdul Rahman was in good spirits?"

"Yes, *Oulyahazrat*, by the grace of Allah he was fine." He glanced towards the casket, "My father has conveyed his highest honor and respect in an autographed letter contained in a gift for Your Majesty." He looked at Frank Martin who immediately stepped forward.

"With Your Majesty's permission," He slid the casket from its black velvet case and set it on the table before the Queen.

It took a second or two for the dazzling beauty of the casket to sink in, even though it was right before her eyes.

then Victoria's eyebrows arched in amazement at the intricacy of the work displayed in that magnificent gift—solid gold lavishly embellished with diamonds, rubies, emeralds, and other precious stones on its exterior, all of which were considered absolute specimens of brilliancy, purity of color, and perfection of cutting. The entire casket was valued at 6,000 pounds.

"Impressive!" she exclaimed, "most impressive! Is this your design, Mr. Martin?"

"Partially, Your Majesty, but it was suggested by His Highness the Amir himself. I, along with ten others, brought it to its completion." No mention was made of the men who had perished, and if the Queen had become aware of the reason for their execution, it is doubtful that she would have accepted the casket. However, she was well aware of Amir's reign of terror and had always looked the other way when it came to his methods of maintaining rule over his dominion. "Indeed, the Amir is greatly talented as well as a clever ruler. I have full

453

confidence in him," she said, and a rumble of agreement was heard around the room. "I thank you and the men who worked tirelessly to complete this delightful artifact."

"I'm honored, Your Majesty," Frank Martin, replied. He bowed and stepped back.

Sir General McNeill reached inside the casket and retrieved Amir's missive which was addressed to Her Majesty Queen Victoria and Empress of India. It was to have been handed to the Lord-in-Waiting before placing it before Queen Victoria. The Lord-in-Waiting paused and appeared troubled, he was instantly aware that the envelope was not properly wax-sealed as it should have for a sovereign. But, far worse, it appeared to have been deliberately wetted all over by someone's tongue!

Reportedly, a ceremony had been most religiously performed on the Amir's missive by Nasrullah before he delivered it to Windsor Castle. The Mullah had stayed up the entire night before, reciting the Qur'an and blowing prayers onto the letter so that the Queen of England would be compelled to grant Amir Abdul Rahaman's wish for full autonomy. Why the licking of the missive had been carried out, no one was prepared to say.

The Lord-in-Waiting held the missive gingerly, openly showing his disgust as he approached the Queen and quietly explained the circumstance. The Queen regarded the damaged letter with a dubious eye.

"Please take it away," she said quietly.

After some hesitation, the Lord-in-Waiting spoke privately with Frank Martin and Colonel Talbot who agreed that Nasrullah should read the missive to the Queen himself. There was a bewildered hubbub in the room. No one was sure what had caused the sudden halt in proceedings. Even the Prince of Wales, and the Dukes of York and Saxe Coburg, were showing their impatience.

Nasrullah agreed to read the copy of the missive in Dari while

Colonel Talbot translated it for all to hear. Nasrullah stood and read it clearly, conveying his father's congenial request for his country's direct representation in the Court of St. James's, instead of through the British government in India.

Frank Martin endeavored to remain calm as he conveyed Her Majesty's instructions to Nasrullah later, but inwardly he was mortified and enraged. A new copy of the letter per the sovereign's protocol, sealed and locked, was to be sent to Windsor Palace immediately.

"After which," he told Nasrullah through gritted teeth, "the Queen will give her response."

CHAPTER FORTY-TWO

❦❦❦

Thursday evening (July 11, 1895)

"May it never cease to flourish as a lasting emblem of the unity and loyalty of my Empire", said Queen Vitoria at the opening of the Imperial Institute in 1893.

The Imperial Institute was a large conspicuous building situated in South Kensington that was at once a center of the advancement of Britain's imperial interests and was built in honor of Queen Victoria's Golden Jubilee.

On Thursday evening, July 11th, Prince Nasrullah attended a reception given in his honor at the Institute. Nasrullah and his retinue were ushered through the arched entrance of the grand vestibule to where they were received by Lord Herschell, Queen Victoria's top judge and the Lord Chancellor. Lord Herschell was in his late fifties, balding, with a chiseled jaw-line and clean-shaven apart from long side-whiskers. His mouth and eyes conveyed a sensitive yet determined nature.

"Your Highness, it's an honor to welcome you to the Imperial Institute," he declared with a bow and a handshake. He gestured politely towards another section of the hall. After the salutation by the First Life Guards in the central foyer, a quavering voice announced: "His Highness Prince Nasrullah Khan of Afghanistan."

Nasrullah glanced briefly at the vaulted ceiling and the grand staircase, which seemed to hang in the air as though it belonged to a fairy-tale castle. They passed two couchant marble lions flanking the flight of stairs that lead to a long high corridor and then to an enormous hall. There, he was received by Queen Victoria who was seated in her wheelchair with her walking cane across her lap. She was dressed in an evening dress of black silk adorned with jet beading and lace applique and wore the Koh-i-Noor diamond as a detachable pendant. Years before, it had graced her regal diamond tiara.

Munshi stood in attendance behind the Queen ready to push her wheelchair. Her Majesty was surrounded by the royal family, with the Prince of Wales, Princesses Beatrice and Louisa on her left, and to her right the Prince of Wales's son, George, Duke of York, and his betrothed Princess, Mary of Teck. Queen Victoria was engaged in conversation with an immaculately dressed gentleman and paused as she noticed Nasrullah approaching.

"Your Highness, Prince Nosroollah, I'm pleased to see you again."

"I am honored to be received by Your Majesty," Nasrullah bowed and stretched out his hand as he had been taught, with Colonel Talbot acting as translator. General Akram Khan and engineer Frank Martin followed suit.

"Did you see the Koh-i-Noor *almas*, diamond?" Nasrullah spoke quietly out of the corner of his mouth.

General Akram Khan acknowledged his words with a slight nod.

Queen Victoria turned again to the man who had stood by during the introductions. "Your Highness," she said, smiling in Nasrullah's direction, "may I introduce you to Herr Strauss who is here from Vienna at my request to conduct the orchestra tonight. I am told he has a surprise for you."

"Herr Strauss," she asked in her rusty German, "please remind me of the name of the composition you've prepared for His Highness?"

"It is called the Shahzadah march, Your Majesty," Strauss stated politely in his heavy German accent. Eduard Strauss, was the son of the Austrian composer, Johann Strauss I. He, with his two brothers, made up the Strauss musical dynasty. He bowed before Nasrullah but remained six paces away. "Your Highness, I am honored." Strauss was of medium height and build, and his light complexion contrasted with a dark goatee, a neatly upturned handlebar mustache, and curly hair. He looked more like a Mexican revolutionary than the conductor of an orchestra. An order with multiple medals adorned his immaculately tailored frock coat.

The circular galleried hall seemed neither to be a concert hall nor an opera house. The orchestra was set on a raised dais at the center and the audience was seated about it enabling clearer vision and a greater sense of participation in the proceedings.

Nasrullah and his retinue were ushered to seats in the same section as the British royals and had an excellent view of the orchestra. Over a thousand British dignitaries dressed in their finery, filled the hall hoping to get a glimpse of the Prince of Afghanistan. The ladies were dazzling in their decollete evening gowns, in silks and satins of every color and shade, and their jewelry caught the light of the enormous chandeliers.

Herr Strauss emerged amid tumultuous plaudits, stood on the dais and faced his orchestra of around forty musicians. Then silence fell and expectancy rose. The orchestra stood by in readiness, the first page of the song score was opened before the conductor, each musician observed him intently, and the faces of the audience were focused on Strauss alone. He waited—the white wand rigid in his raised hand— just then, the lights in the concert hall dimmed. That was the signal for which Herr Strauss had been waiting. The baton moved into play, the musicians swayed to the signal, and into the semi-darkness streamed the inception of the overture. The strains of *God Save The Queen* burst powerfully forth in Viennese waltz timing; and as the audience simultaneously rose to their feet in honor of the Queen it felt as though the very ceiling and the walls shook. Nasrullah had, at first, remained firmly seated, until Colonel Talbot—who was seated behind him—whispered in his ear, "Your Highness, it is expected that you should stand."

Frank Martin also gestured mechanically signaling him to stand up.

The Prince stood uneasily, avertinh his drowsy gaze.

When everyone was seated once more. Herr Strauss led the orchestra into the *Shahzada march*. He was transformed as he dived into the ocean of sound and emotion, painting with his baton, as elegantly as any artist with a brush. The march was written to impress the United Kingdom's guest of honor. But to Nasrullah's untrained ear, it meant nothing. He had grown up listening to local Afghan or Indian dance tunes, and this was his first introduction to European Classical music. He appeared bored and unmoved, even unimpressed with the theme Herr Strauss had composed in his honor. It became increasingly difficult for him to concentrate during the second half of the concert. Sleepiness threatened to overtake him and he was unable to suppress his yawns. During the performance of *The Blue Danube*, Nasrullah's eyes closed and he fell asleep. His mouth opened, and his head inclined more and more to the right until, finally, his chin found a resting place on his chest. Many people nudged one another and trained their opera glasses in his direction for a clearer view. He had the look of a child after too much carnival.

Talbot again whispered in his ear, "Shahzadah, the concert is coming to an end, please stay alert."

Martin rolled his eyes.

Nasrullah leaned forward, fidgeted, and straightened his embroidered frock coat, "I am awake," he mumbled, but he was caught between wakefulness and slumber as though partially anesthetized. The next day London's taverns, coffeehouses, newspaper tabloids, boulevards, and parks, bubbled with mirth as they detailed His Highness's weariness.

The weather was fair and warm, and a fine brush of cirrostratus in the early evening sky parted to reveal the crescent of the new moon near the northwest horizon.

Nasrullah donned his splendid state outfit—a tunic of green satin, embroidered with gold flowers. The invitation to Buckingham Palace to meet with the Queen and the Prince of Wales was scheduled for eight o'clock and the young Prince decided to utilize the few remaining hours to further explore the city before making his way to the Palace. As he crossed the foyer to the porte cochère of Dorchester House he instructed his newly appointed Head of Security, Saboor, who had replaced Zalmai, to prepare the escort.

Saboor was a huge bear of a man, a born rider and lancer, who had grown up as a *Buzkash* in a well-known family of four generations of horsemen, who strove to win every *Buzkashi* game in the name of their bloodline, to retain the prize and the fame. Saboor's enormous hands and his powerful handshake could have fractured every bone in the hand of one who greeted him if he chose to do so. Saboor had been known to rip the flesh or limb from a headless carcass of a goat while riding and playing this unruly game. He was middle-aged and shorter than Zalmai, with Northern Afghan features showing him to be of Uzbek descent.

Before long, Baarfi and a thoroughbred were hitched to Nasrullah's horse-drawn Sociable Landau, and seven guards of mounted lancers rode before and behind the royal carriage.

Lord Falmouth and other English assignees assisting Nasrullah in his stay while in England, were astonished by Nasrullah's guards who were little inclined to concern themselves with pomp and ceremony, or even a spit-and-polished turn-out, as long as they were provided with a good supply of cartridges for the loaded carbines they carried. As Lord Falmouth said, "fortunately the English crowd is unmistakably gentle and pacific, otherwise the suspicious and hawkish behavior of Nasrullah's guards over their prince might have had fatal results."

The clatter of horses' hooves alerted the Mayfair neighborhood of the Shahzadah's presence. He was haughtily ensconced in the carriage with one arm hanging over its side. They clattered through Regent Street to Piccadilly and on to the High Street. At the corner of Bond Street and Hughan Road they were brought to a halt by a jam of carriages, horses, and carts.

A teenage boy furtively waved and passed flyers to anyone showing an interest and he approached Nasrullah and handed him one.

"Sir!" the boy said, "You'll enjoy the fight. It's starting in ten minutes." he pointed to the flyer again realizing Nasrullah couldn't understand. "Italian and Irish boxing match," he hunched over and balled his fists.

"Wait! Stop!" Nasrullah yelled to his coachman who looked as though he was prepared to take a gap through the traffic.

"There!" the boy pointed to the entrance where the match was to take place.

Three of Nasrullah's guards, including Saboor, followed him to the entrance where he was obliged to pay for all four to gain admission. The building seemed to be a music hall or a theater; some two-hundred people were seated around a makeshift boxing ring of about twenty to thirty feet in diameter under dim lighting. Everyone's head turned like windmills, in awe at seeing the Prince of Afghanistan in a prizefighting hall. Two fighters with bare knuckles clenched, and hands raised to waist height, posed pugnaciously for the benefit of the crowd, glaring at each other. Nasrullah and his guards were congenially ushered to first row seats usually reserved for London's better class supporters of the sport.

Already the crowd was yelling like demons; the deafening sounds of whistlers, howlers, stompers, and squawkers resounded throughout the hall. Nasrullah looked on, as eager as a morning hawk for the game to begin. One massive boxer, six feet tall and weighing about two-hundred-and-twenty pounds—Mickey to his Irish fans—stood square, legs bent, one foot ahead of the other, with torso leaning forward and fists close to his face. The Italian, "Big Tony", was a bit stouter, olive-skinned with greasy curly hair—a big lump of flesh, bone, and muscle. He stood firm and sized Mickey up from head to toe. Big Tony was billed as an untamed stallion who could kick and split a ten-inch log in one blow. The short, leather-faced referee held up a wad of money and shouted at both bare-knuckle contestants, "Are you in agreement as you enter into this contest that the victor will take this money?" He waved the stack of hard cash in his hand.

"Yeah!" both replied in unison.

"Are you in agreement that my decision is the only decision and final?"

"Yeah!"

The contestants recited something to each other but the frequent applause and cheering made it difficult for anyone to hear. The doors to the hall were closed and locked to prevent the intrusion of police. Bare-knuckle prizefighting was illegal as anything was considered fair game: there were no written rules; headbutting, punching, eye-gouging, and choking were all permissible in the ring.

The fervor of the spectators reached fever pitch and the noise rose to a crescendo as the bell rang.

Big Tony permitted Mickey to work him into a corner where he was supposedly at his mercy. The Italian see-sawed a bit, waiting for a good opening, and to assist his opponent to seek it, he dropped his hands loosely and gave his green-white-and-red boxer shorts a hitch, all the while watching Micky intently. The Irishman fell into the trap. He was moving in to swing for a knockout blow when the Italian seized his opportunity. Big Tony's head dodged neatly to the left avoiding the punch and at the same moment, swung a punch with brute force to Micky's kidneys that sent the Irish boy groaning to the floor. Nasrullah stood and cheered wildly with the best of them. Round followed round until both prizefighters were swaying on their feet; blood trickled from cuts around their eyes and their mouths were filled with blood. People bellowed, yelled, cheered, and whistled. Nasrullah was completely absorbed. The scheduled meeting with the Queen and the Prince of Wales at Buckingham Palace was forgotten or blithely disregarded. He appeared not to have checked his watch, nor to have been informed by his guards that he should have left the arena. Any sense of responsibility had departed when the fight began.

Before leaving Kabul, his brother, Crown Prince Habibullah, had warned Nasrullah: "Your undivided attention is vital in Englistan, do not deviate or get consumed by your own pleasures and amusements." It appeared he knew his younger brother well.

Nasrullah was sent to England for only one reason: to promote the desire of his father to free Afghanistan from the talons of the Crown. Punctuality therefore should have been at the heart of his business, and his behavior such as would bestow his respect for the most powerful woman on earth, Queen Victoria.

As his carriage and guards passed the gates of Buckingham Palace about forty-five minutes late for the assigned meeting, Nasrullah was given a particularly chilly greeting by the Lord Chamberlain at the portico.

"Your Highness, I'm afraid Her Majesty has already retired for the night!" he said. He turned away deliberately and walked back to the palace steps.

Nasrullah, Frank Martin, Khairo, the royal Mullah, and Raj the translator, were looking forward to the tour of England. Khairo no longer felt the need to cover his face. The surgery had had an uplifting effect on his confidence and left him feeling like an emerald among pebbles.

They were to inspect prominent arms and machinery factories; to make purchases of lathes, drill presses, bandsaws, and other essential machinery for the *Mashin-Khana*; and to take samples of new arms and munitions to exhibit for the Amir. Also, in Liverpool, Nasrullah was to meet with the Muslim convert, Henry Quilliam, who had been successful in recruiting several British nationals into the religion.

Before making the trip, Nasrullah had sent his father's letter to Queen Victoria. Unlike the previous attempt presented to her in a thoroughly licked envelope, Frank Martin and Lillias Hamilton oversaw the process. The new missive was authenticated and affixed with the Amir's signet—engraved in a circular blob of red wax—on a new envelope. Lord Falmouth and Sir General McNeill had carried it by hand on June the sixth, the day before the party left. Nasrullah still spoke confidently of his petition being granted, but inwardly he remained anxious, remembering Munshi and Sir Raffuidin's remarks.

It soon became evident to all that Nasrullah's interest was in the manufacture of guns and ammunition, and shipbuilding, rather than glassworks or cotton mills, which he considered dull and unimportant. There were stops in Birmingham, Manchester, Glasgow, Carlisle, Newcastle, Liverpool, and Leeds.

In Newcastle, he was received by Lord Armstrong the founder of Elswick Ordnance Company, a British armaments manufacturer of the famous Armstrong guns and rifled breech-loaders. Lord Armstrong was an engineer, industrialist, inventor, philanthropist, and eminent scientist. Nasrullah had the pleasure of staying with the Lord at his Craigside mansion, a country house near Rothbury in Northumberland, where he had also entertained the Shah of Persia, and the Prince and Princess of Wales, and other high profiled guests. His was the first house in the world to be lit by hydroelectric power.

Upon Nasrullah's departure from Newcastle, Lord Armstrong bestowed some of his newly designed guns on the Amir. All were packed in a huge box and shipped to Dorchester House. Nasrullah expressed his gratitude for the Lord's generosity.

"Thank you Lord Armstroong, I'm sure my father will place a mass order once he examines your samples."

At Liverpool Station, Nasrullah was met by Abdullah Quilliam, who was accompanied by some of his newly-recruited Muslims, all wearing Muslim garments. Quilliam was tall, lean, and middle-aged with fair skin and blue eyes. He still had a full head of brown hair and had grown a luxuriant rounded beard and mustache in keeping with his adopted faith.

"*As-Salaam-Alaikum*, Your Highness," Quilliam said as he bowed and stretched-out his hand to shake Nasrullah's. His voice had a natural humility and his demeanor was quiet and respectful. He had opened the first functioning mosque in Britain on Christmas Day, six years before. Some time later, the twenty-sixth Ottoman Caliph, Abdul Hamid II, granted Quilliam the title of *Sheikh al-Islam* for the British Isles and Nasrullah's father had also recognized him as the *Sheikh* of Muslims in Britain, while the Shah of Iran appointed him as the Persian Vice-Consul in Liverpool. Some British had shown their displeasure at the awarding of these Muslim titles and denounced him as a traitor.

"*Wa alaykumu s-salam*, my brother, *Shaikh* Abdullah." Nasrullah returned Quilliam's greeting with a handshake and then hugged him tightly three times. Abdullah Quilliam bowed again, and held Nasrullah's hand wishing to kiss it. Nasrullah instantly drew his hand away and said, "Honorable *Shaikh* Abdullah, it's my place to make obeisance to you," he smiled, somewhat shocked that a dignified religious man should think to kiss his hand. "Religion," he added, "comes before everything."

A communal banquet had been prepared at the mosque in Brougham

Terrace in honor of Prince Nasrullah's visit.

It was past midday and white starched dining cloths, *desterkhwans*, were laid out in several rows on fine carpets under a blameless sky. Men bustled about setting the food under a large tree. All halal as it was announced. Birds sang and chirped incessantly.

The Bishop of Liverpool was among the invitees and was deeply annoyed about the banquet given for Nasrullah.

"Your Highness, let me remind you that England is a Christian land, and that, to Christianity her greatness is due!" he declared bluntly.

Khairo said something in a low voice.

"The greatness of England is due to the resources of her colonies and blood of those, like us Afghans, who protect the Crown," Nasrullah returned sharply. The Bishop's eyes locked onto Nasrullah's and for a moment a chill descended.

Quilliam walked between Nasrullah and the Bishop.

"You are both our guests of honor and equally respected," he interjected quietly. Thereafter, no further discussion was exchanged between them.

Nasrullah took his valise from Khairo, called Abdullah Quilliam aside and handed him two-thousand-five-hundred pounds in cash planned as a gift for the occasion.

"This is the charity from my father to the Liverpool Muslim Institute," he said.

"Your Highness, we are more than grateful for your generosity," Abdullah Quilliam announced openly, setting the bundles of cash on a nearby table.

He took Nasrullah's hand, "What a coincidence and a blessing with the Grace of *Allah*," he said lifting both hands towards the heavens, "may His Almighty reward you for your kind benevolence!" His eyes glistened and danced as he looked at Nasrullah. "Today, the mosque premises were put up for sale by auction because no funds were available . . . Yes, today!" He scanned the listeners whose rapt faces expressed their amazement and delight. "Two buyers have made offers, but now, through the help of *Shahzadah,* we have the funds and we can prevent the sale. Not only can we secure the property, but we will also be able to add two neighboring properties for our children's school to study the Qur'an and the sacred religion of Islam." He gestured towards Nasrullah with both hands, palms up. "Thank you, Your Highness!"

"It's our duty as Muslims to help you whom God has sent to build the Islam faith," he replied as he took a glass of water from the tray offered by a helper. "I must also confess, the credit also goes to Munshi Abdul Karim Khan and Sir Rafiuddin Ahmad who reminded us to make a pledge."

The news of Nasrullah's timeous donation to the cause of Islam in England spread like wildfire. Over time, plans were drawn up to adapt the premises for the Muslim Institute's purposes.

In Birmingham's Small Heath area, Nasrullah visited the Small Arms Works (BSA). Only a half-hour was alloted to this stop but he persuaded the Train Master to delay the train so that he could make a full study of the manufacturing processes of rifles.

"I will be here for two hours and perhaps longer," Nasrullah said. And here too, he was given some military sniper rifles and small arms. He delayed the train another hour or two in order to inspect Kynoch's Ammunition Works, and here too, he acquired boxes of cartridges of all kinds to exhibit in Kabul.

In Birmingham, as his tour neared its end, a crowd gathered at the station to see him and increased as time went by. The scheduled time of departure was 4:10 pm but he only boarded the train at 5:50 pm. Expressing his obvious frustration, the Train Master was reported to have said, "this was the most unpunctual potentate I have ever had to deal with!"

❧❧❧

London newspapers and tabloids buzzed with reports of Nasrullah's daily activities, meetings, conjectures and rumors and anything deemed to be of interest to the English public. One story surfaced in The Times stating, *"Those fortunate people who live near enough to Dorchester House to get a view of the gardens and terrace, had a unique opportunity of entertaining themselves and their guests."*

The noisy calling to prayer began before dawn and continued at intervals to nightfall. Nasrullah and his men practiced their devotions like good Muslims and congregated behind the howling Mullah on the terrace above the portico, or the lawn. Some in Mayfair were not aware of this Muslim practice and were disturbed to the point of informing the police. As soon as the news spread, however, bedroom parties were organized by neighbors that overlooked the property.

The public was intrigued by the daily deliveries of sheep and chickens. Thirty to forty headless fowls would instantly flutter away once the axe fell. Bleating sheep pleaded for mercy when the time came to be sacrificed and consumed. The animal's throat was cleanly cut and the name of *Allah* was twice pronounced while it bled to death; after which the dripping carcases were carried up that magnificent marble staircase, through the beautiful reception room, spoiling carpets, splattering the walls and turning the place into a perfect shambles before arriving in the kitchen where it was to be stewed or tucked in a rice caldron for a hearty chicken or mutton pilaf.

Another of London's tabloids reported, *"The Afghans Live with Extreme Frugality."* One set of meals was prepared for all. The hundred-plus men of Nasrullah's retinue and attendants sat cross-legged around a tablecloth in clusters of four or five, including Nasrullah, and ate with their hands from one dish.

Nasrullah who had by now mastered with precision the art of holding and eating with utensils, still slept on the dining-room floor

468

among his retinue, because, in the old Afghan myth he was certain that no self-assured man could sleep in a bed and survive the night. It could be an open invitation for midnight assassins to take the opportunity—perhaps even Jack the Ripper? He and his retinue simply turned Dorchester House into a barracks.

Londoners were informed of the technological advances made in Dorchester House. Nasrullah's aspiration was met when Lord Falmouth cut the ribbon for the installation of electricity and called for Prince Nasrullah to do the honors.

Nasrullah flipped the switch and the whole Italianate mansion was illuminated like daylight. The shock held everybody spellbound. The Afghans looked up at the dazzling chandeliers and bulbs as if they were the most wonderful thing they had ever seen. That night, the story concluded, a few of them attempted tried blow the bulbs out as though they were candles before going to sleep. The installation of the supply plant and motive power was completed just before Nasrullah was due to throw a reception party.

The mentioned opening ceremony of electricity in Dorchester House encouraged Queen Victoria to approve the resumption of the electrical installation in Windsor Castle. A decade ago she had ordered electricians to install lights, but only in selected rooms. When one of the technicians suffered a frightful shock that almost killed him, she had ordered all work to stop.

"What's the Afghan Prince's view about the English ladies?" The Londoners—especially the women—were anxious to hear his view.

It was a triumphant evening for him, a charming ball had been thrown in his honor in Buckingham Palace, at which London's ladies who mixed in royal circles turned out in their flamboyant outfits and expensive jewelry. The orchestra was once again masterfully conducted by Edward Strauss playing the enchanting Viennese waltzes. As the crowd gathered on the ballroom floor of the Hanover Square Rooms, the maestro conducted his father's tune dedicated to Queen Victoria in 1838, *Hommage a la Reigne d'Angleterre*, couples began to follow the smooth graceful movements of the dance. The ladies, stepping and twirling in perfect time with their partners, were the picture of elegance. Nasrullah was watching from an armchair fascinated with the function. His eyes were on a young lady whose slender waist was encircled by an azure-blue sash, who seemed to possess both the fresh innocent beauty of face and grace of movement. A question from the Duke of St. Albans broke Nasrullah's reverie.

"If I may ask Your Highness a question."

"Please," said Nasrullah.

"What's Your Highness's view of our English ladies?"

Over the next couple of days, the London tabloids published the following: *"The Shahzada is not at all impressed by the beauty of English ladies. He says that the young ones are altogether too thin, and that their figures constitute an insuperable defect, while the ones which conform more to his idea of beauty in the way of plumpness are invariably too old."*

He reportedly did not speak English well, and did not make a good impression on the local press. A reporter from the Cumberland Pacquet newspaper described him as "a stolid, impassive, and greatly bored youth."

CHAPTER FORTY-THREE

❦

Thursday evening (July 11, 1895)

After returning from his tour of provinces, Nasrullah authorized the attendants to cache the boxes of guns and munitions in Dorchester House. He then immediately shuffled through a two-week long stack of post, to see if Queen Victoria had replied to his father's letter. "Is there any response from *Qasr-e-Weenzor*, *Malika* Weetorya, while I was away?" His voice echoed throughout the galleried foyer. But there was no response from anyone.

His patience was dwindling, knowing that the Queen had had ample time to reply and informed Lord Falmouth that he required the Queen's reply immediately. Lord Falmouth returned with the answer that Her Majesty was still consulting with her ministers. This, despite the fact that she had decided to refuse Amir's request before Nasrullah set foot in England.

For the British Government, the more pressing problem was how to get rid of Nasrullah. His stay in England had already been far too lengthy and his maintenance was costing an inordinate amount of money in grand receptions, sumptuous banquets, flamboyant balls, elaborate concerts, and luxurious travel arrangements, apart from housing and feeding his large retinue. The functions, however, were viewed by the young Afghan Prince to have been such a prodigious success that he unhesitatingly looked for more. He had been handed a blank check for a prolonged grand sojourn.

Consequently, the Queen decided that something must be done to cut this undesirable expenditure. She and her advisers considered the most tactful approach was to send Nasrullah word that per her doctor's advice, she must soon proceed to her residence on the Isle of Wight, for her usual vacation. Could Nasrullah kindly call on her at Windsor immediately to bid farewell? To the Queen's satisfaction, Nasrullah took the bait delightfully and the meeting was scheduled for Saturday, July 20, at Windsor Palace.

Queen Victoria and a number of British government officials took part in the farewell ceremonial event for Nasrullah in Windsor Castle's Red Drawing Room. Shafts of afternoon sunlight flooded through the room's mullioned windows, enhancing the sumptuous scarlet, white and gold decor. Lavishly carved gilded sofas and matching chairs nestled among ebony cabinets and consoles topped with silver candelabras, vases, and military trophies.

General McNeill—clad in a braided dolman, knee-high boots, with a sword at his side—stood and read the Queen's note to Nasrullah.

"Your Highness," his distinctive Scottish accent was deep and clear. "The Shahzadah's trip to England was provided with the purpose of strengthening the British alliance with Afghanistan, a martial and powerful state which remains the only barrier between the British and the Russian dominions in Asia. Needless to mention, as we all know, Afghanistan's regal sovereign, Amir Abdul Rahman, is regarded as being among the most brilliant and shrewd of the world's rulers." He lifted his gaze from his script to Nasrullah again. "Your Highness's visit to England has been significant in strengthening the British position in India against Russian rivalry. There can be no doubt," the General continued, "that the visit of Your Highness to Britain has proved a most successful stroke of policy in our relations between Great Britain and Afghanistan."

Although Nasrullah's declared hatred of England prevented him

472

from much outward display of his feelings, inwardly, he had been delighted with his reception and regarded Britain as a far more wonderful place than he had anticipated.

Before leaving Kabul, his brother, Prince Habibullah had hinted that he must produce something of value, something worthy of his highest efforts, something to give him a sense of healthy pride. But so far, it seemed, his visit to Queen Victoria had produced nothing of lasting value.

Princes Beatrice set the envelope addressed to Amir Abdul Rahman Khan on the table in front of her mother and Queen Victoria handed the sealed envelope to Nasrullah who was sitting next to her.

"Your Highness," said the Queen amiably, "Please convey my best wishes to my friend, Amir Sahib. This is the reply to His Highness's letter. "Nasrullah's heart beat a little faster as he glanced down at the envelope with British Royal red wax stamp and another similar stamp bearing the Queen's name and initials, Victoria R.I.

"I will, *Olyahazrat*. We're grateful for the hospitality we received during our stay in *Englistan*."

Nasrullah tucked the letter into the pocket of his frock coat and stood to shake the Queen's hand while she was still seated. Princesses Beatrice and Louisa stood and shook hands with him and bade farewell, "I hope England was pleasant for Your Highness?" Louisa asked.

"Certainly, *Shah-Dukht*, Princess," Nasrullah replied with a bow.

The cavalcade of carriages from Windsor Castle to the train station carried the Duke of Connaught, Prince Henry of Battenburg, General McNeill, and other British officials. The Prince of Wales and Nasrullah sat in the leading carriage with Colonel Talbot present as the interpreter.

"Shahzada Nosroolah, I trust your visit cemented the Anglo-Afghan alliance, we have had an unwavering relationship, which, I'm sure, will continue to grow. We appreciate you making the long journey to England." He tapped Nasrullah on the shoulder, "I would like to plan a visit to Afghanistan one day." The melodic clatter of four sets of hooves was amplified briefly as the cavalcade passed through the castle gates. "You could show me around. I'd be interested in seeing the country for myself."

Since Nasrullah's arrival in England, he and the Prince of Wales had enjoyed one another's company. Despite a thirty-year age difference, they developed a pleasurable relationship around common interests— going to derbies, shooting pheasants and ducks, and attending house parties. There were obvious differences. Nasrullah's deep Muslim faith restricted him from drinking alcohol or mingling with women whose behavior was indiscrete. Ultimately, the friendship was based on light-hearted fun, and mutual benefit, but had little depth.

"Of course, Shahzadah Edword," Nasrullah mispronounced the Prince of Wales' name as usual. He had heard him called Bertie, and tried "Burdie" a few times, but, in the end, was asked to call him Edward. "We can forge a solid relationship directly between our countries."

Inevitably, crowds gathered to watch, waving and cheering, as the royal coach made its way through the streets of Windsor, and lined the road towards the station.

When they arrived, the Duke of Connaught, in his uniform of the Scots Guard, Prince Henry of Battenburg, and Lord Carrington all bade farewell to Amir's son as he prepared to board the special train to London. But the Shahzadah handshake, as it became known in London, was reserved for Prince Edward. Nasrullah half raised his hand as though to salaam, paused halfway, and slapped down on the outstretched hand of the Prince of Wales. Nasrullah's boyish farewell turned a solemn occasion into laughter.

Upon his return from Windsor Castle, Nasrullah's Brougham stopped under the portico of the Dorchester House, he dashed from the carriage and shouted for Raj who ran down the marble staircase as if the devil was behind him.

"I'm here at Your Highness's command!" he panted, eyes wide.

"Translate this word for word," Nasrullah said as he tore open the sealed envelope and handed him Queen Victoria's letter. "Quickly!"

"Of course, Shahzadah!"

> *Queen Victoria to the Ameer of Afghanistan.*
> *Windsor Castle, 19th July 1895.*
>
> *My good Friend,*
>
> *I have received at the hands of your Highness's son, the Shahzada Nasrullah Khan, the friendly letter of your Highness dated 20th Shawwal-ul-Mukarram, 1312 Hejira, and I am much gratified at the expressions of goodwill contained therein.*
>
> *I have received with pleasure also the beautiful casket which contained your Highness's letter. I shall gladly retain the casket as a memorial of the gratification which it has given me to receive as my guest the son of such a sincere ally as your Highness.*
>
> *On my part, I shall always desire to hear of the health of your Highness and of the prosperity of your Dominions.*
> *I'm, Your Highness's sincere friend and ally,*
>
> *Victoria R. I.*

Queen Victoria's letter did not mention anything about direct diplomatic relations between their respective nations. It said nothing that Nasrullah was hoping to hear. For him, the disappointment arrived with a deep sense of grief—a finality that necessitated a helping hand to draw him from the rapids of despond, which were freeing his grip on rationality. As the promising sunrise became starlight for the Afghan Prince, the failure of his mission evoked mixed feelings of deep shame and re-awakened old feelings of contempt for the British who had trodden him down.

He read the Queen's letter over and over but the answer he sought was not there. Before leaving Kabul, he had promised his brother, and those who had high hopes for him, that he would not return home empty-handed. Life suddenly held nothing for him; his race was run and he could envision no ray of light upon the horizon. The youthful Nasrullah could simply not see a way forward.

He kept his father informed by telegram, which, on arrival at Peshawar, was forwarded on by special barefooted runners who arrived at the Arg Palace within a day. The Amir was bitterly disappointed at his own failure to establish direct relations with the British Government. "It is the custom," he said, "not only among the aristocracy but among our poorest people as well, that a guest should never return in despair at his request being refused, even if he be an enemy. But my son, who was the son of a sovereign and the guest of another illustrious sovereign, was returned with a dry but polite refusal to my request."

There was a disconnect in Amir's expression of his feelings. His deep sorrow for his son as well as his country was obvious, but expecting the British Sovereign to apply the Afghan culture of hospitality—the code of Pashtunwali—was an elusive dream.

According to Afghan custom, it was understood that guests should show their appreciation of a feast by reciprocating in some manner. This "smiting their guest's mind" expected something in return—a concept that would be repugnant to most Western thinking.

While the British had no intention of accepting the terms and conditions of the Amir's request, they justified spending thousands of pounds on the Afghan Prince to remain in his good graces. To wind up by telling Nasrullah to go home seemed to exhibit both the virtue of hospitality and the science of diplomacy in a new light. A blanket refusal would have been perceived as hostile, diplomacy was intended to ameliorate the blow.

Nasrullah had already outstayed his welcome in London. Three weeks had passed since he received the refusal letter and was ceremonially bidden farewell, but still no date had been scheduled for his embarkation and the situation was becoming increasingly unpleasant.

Life in London had become unbearably dull. As the days and weeks passed, so his boredom heightened. He was no longer on visiting terms with Royalty, there were no more Ascot races with the Prince of Wales, no Epsom Derby days, no entertainment by hosts eagerly desiring his company; the endless round of official visits, reviews, and amusements completely ceased for the Amir's son. He spent whole days in seclusion at Dorchester House, slept in late, or went back to bed several times a day. He had fallen so low as to be glad to accept an invitation promising an evening's recreation at a shilling exhibition. Over time, his mood changed dramatically—from the elation he experienced when he descended the gangplank of the troopship in Portsmouth—to despair and misery as he knew he was being forced to leave.

Then the Park Lane snitches informed Colonel Adelbert Talbot of clandestine activities at Dorchester House. There were late-night meetings, the constant egress and ingress of carriages of unknown individuals, and armed Afghan guards vigilantly patrolled the premises around the clock. With Talbot's informer, Lieutenant Mahmoud Khan having been tossed overboard and Major Akbar Khan under Parwnana Khan's strict surveillance, Talbot could not enter the mansion without Nasrullah's permission and had no other informant within the Mayfair residence to understand Nasrullah's state of his mind. Talbot's hands were tied.

The London tabloids and newspapers began to speculate as to why the Shahzadah had not left England. Rumors became rife: "*Shahzadah falling for an English woman*" or "*Enjoying the luxury free life*". Even the Punch and Judy puppet show entertained Londoners with: "*The Shahzadah must go to Papa.*"

But inside Dorchester House, Nasrullah had become a hurricane of wrath: "By God!" He yelled, his voice reverberating throughout the galleried foyer, "I will not leave *Englistan* until our freedom is fully granted!" He paced with Queen's letter clasped in his hand, reckoning and strategizing a plan of action and, just as rapidly, discarding it.

He shook the offending letter in the air, "This will not stop us from obtaining our freedom!" he declared to General Akram Khan and Naieb-Salar Hassein Khan, "You will be joining me to visit Niekolass, the *Amparator-e-Roosya*, Emperor of Russia, on my way home . . . we need his help! Enough is enough of these Satanic games the bastards *Englees-ha* are playing with us."

"Shahzadah!" Hassein Khan said calmly. He was sitting cross-legged on a cushion, elbow on one knee, thumbing his onyx beads; a ribbon of blue cigarette smoke wafted from the ashtray next to him. Hassein no longer smoked *beedi* but the new English cigarette brand, 555. "I and others," he gestured with the sweep of a hand at General Akram Khan and Parwana Khan, "have been deeply affected by this decision of *Englistan*." The smoke continued to curl from the ashtray. "Our hopes are shattered, and we have no solution to this unjust decision by the *Malika* Weektorya except to go home and discuss it with the Amir Sahib." He took a long drag from his cigarette, set it back in the ashtray, and discharged a long stream of smoke through his nostrils. "As your counselor and elder, I suggest we take advise from His Highness, Amir Sahib."

"Neib-Salar Sahib," Nasrullah's brow creased. "My utmost

respect to you, I've always regarded you as my elder and I've taken your advice just as my father's. But, I cannot bear the humiliation and dishonor of going home empty-handed. It is not an option for me!" His thin lips curled in disdain, "I'll let my heart lead me."

Nasrullah had begun to view every honor that Britain paid him with suspicion, "I will support the frontier tribes and topple the satanic British in India. Yes! I'll seek help from the Afridis, Waziris, Momands, the Duranis, and every tribe on the Frontier to rise against them in the name of *Allah* and kick the bastards out of Hindustan."

A book of instructions had been given to Nasrullah by the Amir to simplify certain unforeseen circumstances and guide him to follow throughout his journey. However, the book did not mention what action should be taken in the case of a refusal from Queen Victoria. For the second time, Munshi Abdul Karim Khan and Rafiuddin Ahmed privately assured Nasrullah that his father had approved his decision to remain in England until the Queen agreed to full autonomy for Afghanistan. On several occasions, one or the other of them came at night, or sent trusted men as emissaries to carry messages on their behalf.

"Shahzadah, the last option to bring a resolution to this issue is to let Windsor Palace know of your plan . . . " said the Munshi.

" . . . Precisely, Munshi Sahib," Nasrullah interrupted, "I'll notify Lord Falmouth to pass the word to *Qasr-e-*Weenzor immediately."

Nasrullah was distracted when Dr. Hamilton, who frequently stopped by to check on his health, arrived with another woman. A brief silence permeated the foyer like an indrawn breath.

"Your Highness, this is Mrs. Kate Daly, a longtime friend, and a medical associate. She will be traveling with us to Kabul to serve the Amir Sahib and the . . . "

" . . . Daktar Laila Jan," Nasrullah blurted out irritably, "we don't even have a set date for leaving Landan until I clear up some issues with *Malika* Weektorya!" He turned to Kate Daly and said, "*Khanum*

Dulee, I hope I am not wasting your time but your journey will have to wait until further notice."

Dr. Hamilton saw immediately that Nasrullah was fidgety and consumed with anxiety and anger.

"Your Highness," Kate Daly's smile widened. "I've packed my valise and portmanteau, ready to depart at any time, but I am able to wait until you are ready." She was a fever nurse in her mid-thirties who had completed her general training at Whitechapel Hospital, London. One of the main reasons she had decided to become an expert in her field had been to nurse her ailing father. She was tall, well-attired with an almost enduring smile hovering around her thin lips. Kate Daly was also a gifted artist and a competent-proficient pianist who enjoyed playing Schubert's and Bach's sonatas for her circle of friends and family.

"Your Highness, I can see there's a problem," Dr. Hamilton said quietly as she took Nasrullah aside. "Can I be of help?" She noticed the tension in his jawline, and his face revealed anger and extreme fatigue.

"By God!" Nasrullah said, punching a finger heavenward, "I will not fail!" He sat down on one of the gilded chairs with his elbows on his knees, and cradled his face in his hands. "I will not leave until she hands me full autonomy."

"Did Her Majesty refuse the Amir's request?" Lillias asked hesitantly?"

"She has dismissed us!" he declared bitterly, "but we are not leaving London without getting what we came for!" Dr. Hamilton listened sympathetically to his arguments without much comment except to stand in agreement with Hassein Khan's suggestion that they return to Arg Palace to discuss the situation with the Amir. But General Akram Khan, Munshi Abdul Karim Khan, Rafiuddin, and Khairo all joined the chorus in support of remaining in order to force Britain's hand. Had Frank Martin been present, he would also have opposed their plan. Nasrullah changed the subject abruptly.

"Daktar Laila Jan, is there any news from your sister and Zalmai?"

"No, Your Highness, their whereabouts are still unknown to the family, but if there's any news, I will not hesitate to share it with Your Highness."

"I want Zalmai back in Kabul," Nasrullah ground out, "his betrayal is punishable by death!"

Lillias left feeling that Nasrullah was standing on the edge of a precipice.

Perhaps to an extent, she mused, his father should bear the burden of guilt for having chosen his young, inexperienced son to bind a delicate and sensitive diplomatic agreement between two vital nations each holding in their hands the fate of the jewel in the crown.

∾⊚∼∾⊚∼∾⊚∼

It took three days for Lord Falmouth to convey Queen's reply to Nasrullah's ultimatum, during which time, Nasrullah's anger grew and he bristled with restless energy that gnawed at him like a quiet poison.

Falmouth alighted from his carriage and removed his silk hat revealing his shining bald pate. With the tap-tap of his walking stick against the marble floor, he was ushered across the foyer to the drawing-room where Nasrullah was staring absently through the arched window into the lush green garden.

"Your Highness," greeted Lord Falmouth as he bowed and shook his hand. "Apologies for my imposition."

"Hello! Lord Falmoot, no imposition at all . . . is there any news from *Qasr-e*-Weenzor?" Nasrullah rubbed a hand over his stubble and surveyed Falmouth coldly.

"Your Highness, I've conveyed your message to Her Majesty and she instructed Princess Beatrice to write this letter for Your Highness's eye." He handed him the envelope, which was sealed as always, with the royal emblem and the Queen's initials.

Shortly after Lord Falmouth left Dorchester House, Raj translated Queen's letter:

> *Her Majesty Queen Victoria to His Highness, Shahzadah*
> *Nasrullah Khan*
> *Osborne, 20th August 1895*
>
> *The Queen has received the Shahzadah's verbal message*
> *via Major General, Lord Falmouth on the 17th, and she*
> *fully understood His Highness's request.*
> *   The consultation with Her Majesty's ministers is still*
> *being debated.*
> *   Should the final decision be made, His Highness, the*
> *Amir will be informed Immediately in Kabul. Meantime,*
> *The Queen wishes His Highness's safe journey home.*
>
> *Victoria R.*

Even though her response was polite, it was a firm refusal to be blackmailed into a decision she was not prepared to make, and yet another attempt to send the Afghan Prince home.

Nasrullah plunged deeper into rage, "The *macha-khar*, female-donkey, lied again!" His painful bellow filled the entire mansion as he stormed down the marble staircase. Shaking the Queen's reply above his head he roared, "By *Allah*, I'll set Landan on fire if my demand is not met."

"What was her response?" General Akram Khan asked as he came through to the foyer with Khairo Khan to see what the noise was about.

"The same thing again! She told me to go home and she would deal with it later." He called for a glass of water.

"Sweep it under the rug . . . unfortunately our plea means nothing to her," Khairo Khan said. He looked a decade younger after the work done on his face and was possessed with renewed vigor.

"Preposterous!" General Akram Khan said. His newly framed glasses no longer slid down to the tip of his nose. He had adopted the look of a London gentleman, with a tailored frock coat, cravat, and even a silk hat, but his upturned shirt collar fitted him like a lobster shell.

At this crucial juncture, Nasrullah's thoughts were chaotic. Not long ago, he had felt as important as a cabochon ruby in the eyes of the Queen. He had seen himself as royalty on her level, but now he was being dismissed like a naughty child sent home to his father. It made his head spin in bewilderment and, always, the dark shadow of failure mocked him.

"Your Highness's protest has not made a sliver of difference to the Queen," Khairo observed, "but perhaps there is another way . . . I haven't forgotten that these bastards killed my family and shed the blood of thousands in Maiwand. We should not let go of this easily."

"What do you propose, Khairo?" General Akram asked, as he handed his hat to a page and sat down on a gilded chair nearby. Nasrullah and Khairo sat on the sofa opposite.

"I beg you not to reveal to Amir Sahib that this suggestion is mine, or else, he will pronounce my death sentence."

"Don't worry, Khairo Khan," Nasrullah assured him, "The trust between us is mutual and solid." General Akram Khan nodded.

"Use the guns and munitions you stashed here," Khairo said.

Nasrullah glanced at him in alarm, "How?" he demanded, "do you expect us to go into the city and start shooting indiscriminately until the Queen submits and agrees?"

"No, that's not my proposal." He fidgeted and leaned forward.

His good eye danced. "Very simple," he said. "Create an atmosphere of terror from here," his forefinger pointed downward. "From here. From right where are now!"

Khairo had never allowed his hatred for Great Britain to be transformed into the more positive emotional side of indifference, it was a constant poison to his soul. And for those like Nasrullah and, to an extent, General Akram Khan, bitterness remained in the back of all their minds. But if they were to follow Khairo's plan in a last-ditch attempt to use intimidation to force their will on the Queen, it would no longer be a request, but a demand on Nasrullah's terms.

"How?" Nasrullah asked again impatiently.

"It could be easily done," the ironclad Kandahari replied. "How many guns do we have?"

"I don't know." Nasrullah turned to the page. "Go and fetch Saboor." As the page scurried off, he glanced back at the others, "As Head of Security, he will have a correct account of the guns and munitions," he explained.

Khairo knew Britain's hands would be tied if Nasrullah and his men fired volleys of bullets into the air from Dorchester House. Queen Victoria could not take the risk of killing or injuring anyone without inflaming relationships permanently between Afghanistan and Britain, and particularly the Amir's son, who had been invited by the Queen herself.

"We all know Afghanistan is vital to British-India's security," Khairo said as he wrapped up the outline of his plan, "*Malika Weetorya* will have no choice but to make the concession!"

"It's brilliant!" Nasrullah accepted Khairo's proposal without hesitation. He grinned and slapped his friend's shoulder.

"This will make that *Macha-Khar* reconsider." He looked from Khairo to General Akram Khan, "Let's do it," he said.

CHAPTER FORTY-FOUR

As the lamplighters in Park Lane lit the street lamps, Nasrullah, General Akram Khan, and Khairo stood under the portico of the Dorchester House and faced the retinue of security guards, cooks, pages, grooms, and other Afghans who had been summoned to hear Nasrullah's announcement.

"Our Head of Security, Saboor!" he gestured at him with a wave of his hand, "has enough munitions for you to display memorable *atesh-bazi*, fireworks, here in Landan. He will issue each of you with a new *tufang*, gun . . . those who were already issued with a *tufang-e-dan-pur*, muzzle-loaded gun, need to exchange it for the new *tufang*."—he lifted the Lee-Enfield above his head so that everyone could see it. "All you have to do is load ten rounds into each cartridge," he unclipped the cartridge, held it up, and placed it back in the gun. "Cock-and-fire, cock-and-fire, until the ten rounds are finished." He demonstrated the cocking with an unloaded Enfield, passed it to Saboor and picked up the long-barrelled Musket. "You don't have to fill the gun powder and round in the muzzle like you did with this old *tufang*. Put that aside, and with the grace of Allah you'll never use them again!" He turned to Saboor and asked to give him an exact count for the munitions.

"Shahzadah, we have over one-hundred Enfield rifles, one Maxim, and some Armstrong machine guns." He stood next to the stacks of wooden boxes that were labeled 'FOR AMIR OF AFGHANISTAN', courtesy of the British manufacturers of arms. "The rounds are here," he set his long, powerful arm on the box next to the stack, "We have plenty."

"No need for the *masheendar*, machine guns," Nasrullah said, "*We're not going onto the battlefield.*"

As the announcement was delivered, Nasrullah heard Naieb-Salar's shuffling footsteps approaching him from behind.

"Do you really want to do this?" murmured the Naieb-Salar anxiously, "Why does this have to end in such an unnecessary fashion?" He looked at Nasrullah intently, "Intimidation will not work *Shahzadah*, and May *Allah* forbid, what if there are fatalities?" He thumbed his onyx prayer beads nervously, "This is a dangerous prospect that may cause more harm than good." Faced with Nasrullah's set expression, Naieb-Salar drew on his 555 brand cigarette and exhaled wearily, the smoke drifted across his flabby face.

"Perhaps you're right Naieb-Salar Sahib, but as I said before, I can't go home empty-handed and face humiliation by my own Afghans." Nasrullah turned back to his men and Hassein Khan's footfalls faded away gradually.

As an experienced soldier who made simple but calculated choices, Naieb-Salar had learned to be flexible on certain occasions and assertive on others. His public persona reflected a mild version of the Amir's, and the shrewd sovereign saw the passion in a man who had served him loyally for decades. As the most entrusted protégé of the Amir, he had been appointed as head commander of the Afghan army and accompanied Nasrullah as a trusted adviser in the absence of his father. But he was walking a fine line in his wish to intervene in this rapidly escalating situation between Nasrullah and the Queen. He had been informed that the Amir had given his stamp of approval for Nasrullah to prolong his stay until the Queen accepted his request, but he knew that he was unaware of his son's plan to coerce the Queen by firing off rounds of bullets into London's night sky. Knowing he would not be able to deter Nasrullah when all the others were enthusiastically behind the plan, Naieb-Salar chose to speak his mind and then walk away rather than face a complete breakdown of his relationship with the Prince.

"Every one of you must take orders from Saboor or our Chief of Police, Parwana Khan," shouted Nasrullah. "They will tell you to only fire at the sky and nothing else. . . Again, let me repeat, aim only for the stars!" He scanned the group of men before him, "They will also give the order to ceasefire." He raised both hands as though in submission, "I will be firing the first shot and thereafter you follow suit . . . is it understood?"

"*Baley!*" Everyone roared in unison.

After Nasrullah's announcement to take arms, Saboor and Parwana Khan bustled through the premises ordering the Afghans to take their position and open fire soon as Nasrullah fired the first shot. Ample amounts of bullets were dispersed among all armed men and pages had been instructed to collect the empty shells and help load cartridges with fresh rounds. Sentries stood guard at the gates to hinder any intrusion. Windows were opened and muzzles were drawn. Soon, the whole of Mayfair, Hyde Park, and Buckingham and Kensington Palaces, would believe themselves under siege from an unseen enemy.

To add a little more firing power, Parwana Khan handed Gul Agha's Colt revolver back to the young groom, saying, "Just aim for the stars. Not at people. Not at neighbors, houses, trees, birds, or anything else. Just the sky," He turned his cross-eyed gaze upwards, "up there, see the twinkling stars?"

"*Albata*, of course, *Kotwal*, Magistrate, Sahib," Gul Agha replied importantly as he holstered the gun. "May Allah grant you higher dignity for giving me the *tufangcha*, gun, I'll do as you wish." He glowed with happiness as he walked to the window humming a tune. He sounded like a bee in a bottle.

Prince Omar was not present to witness the upcoming frenzy. Mercifully, he, William, and the Martins were having a wonderful time at the south coast resort of Bournemouth.

Nasrullah stood on the balustraded balcony and aimed the gun at the dark sky. His first shot sounded deafening, but it was immediately followed by the rattle of hundreds of intermittent rounds from other rifles that split the air like sparks from a volcano. Within moments, the whole wide area of Mayfair and beyond was plunged into confusion.

Carriages and people on Park Lane in the vicinity of Dorchester House were terrified. Women screamed. Pedestrians fled, and coachmen tried desperately to control panicked horses. The ear-piercing noise disturbed the birds roosting in trees in the area and they fluttered in confusion and flew blindly into the night sky. Further afield, people out for an evening stroll saw mysterious lights raining down from above. To the city inhabitants, the scene was quite unimaginable, in fact, stupefying. Hundreds of bullets were being fired, and, at first, it was difficult to know where they were coming from. Minds swayed in shock as they sought to comprehend the images of mayhem. London had not experienced anything like it in recent Victorian times. It was utterly shocking!

A detailed account was given by a carriage driver whose horse-drawn carriage was cantering southward on Park Lane. He witnessed a stream of stray bullets whistling through the air like a meteor shower and one, with its terminal velocity, hit his horse causing a deep flesh wound in its hindquarter. With a painful scream, the horse reared causing the carriage to topple like a rolling ball. The coachman heard more expended rounds tinkling as they rolled down the tiled roofs nearby. Had Nasrullah not thought that when things rise they also fall and could have caused fatalities?

As the shooting continued unabated, the Metropolitan Police blocked off Park Lane from Hyde Park Corner and Marble Arch, as well as all the side-streets leading into Mayfair, including east of Hyde Park from West Carriage Drive.

Mayfair was still being pounded with the perpetual mind-numbing cacophony of gunfire. Thus far, although police had moved into the area, there had been no return of fire. As Khairo had anticipated, the situation was far too sensitive for any hasty counter-action to take place. The news was quickly spread throughout London and was telegraphed to other major cities in England. Queen Victoria was notified later that night on the Isle of Wight where she was vacationing. She immediately delegated Lord Falmouth, Colonel Talbot, and Sir Gerald Fitzgerald to bring the tumult to a peaceful resolution with Nasrullah. So far, Khairo's plan for Queen to make a deal with Nasrullah was working.

All three men approached Dorchester House under police escort. They stopped at a distance, lanterns flashing to attract attention. A police officer stepped forward, a white flag raised above his head and waved it to and fro.

"Ceasefire! Ceasefire!" Nasrullah shouted, but his voice was not heard above the ceaseless roll of bullets. He raised both hands, the Enfield in one, and Parwana Khan responded immediately with the pre-arranged signal. The firing stopped and the men looked around at one another, exhausted from the effort—the silence was deafening! Nasrullah motioned to the sentries to let the men to advance, and take their names before allowing them into the compound.

As an experienced warrior, Khairo Khan had muffled his ears, once again using the end of his turban. "I think they are here to make a deal," he said to Nasrullah, his good eye sparkling in anticipation. "Your Highness, ask them first and foremost for a full Afghan independence, and then the return of our Koh-i-Noor diamond."

Nasrullah touched both of his ears and asked Khairo to speak louder. As he repeated himself, Nasrullah clapped him with his famous Shahzadah handshake and grinned broadly.

"You're on the mark! he said loudly. "Those are our first demands, my friend." he rested a hand on Khairo's shoulder as they went down the stairs to the lobby. "The third one is to hand Zalmai to us. Can't leave without the *padar-lanat*, cursed his father. He should face execution for his betrayal."

"Agreed!" said Parwana Khan who had overheard the last comment. "By the sacred book of Qur'an," he swore solemnly. "I should have killed the *Haram-Zadah*, illegitimate son, before he left . . . right here in Landan." Shook his head regretfully.

Nasrullah greeted Lord Falmouth, Sir Gerald Fitzgerald, and Colonel Talbot in the parlor.

"Your Highness . . . " Talbot began.

"You will have to speak a bit louder," Nasrullah interrupted.

"Of course, Your Highness," said Talbot in his accented Pashtu. There was a wry twist to his mouth that might have been interpreted as a smile. He raised his voice. "We weren't aware that you were having a celebration tonight." Diplomacy dictated a roundabout approach rather than hammering home the facts immediately. No one was under any real illusion that this had been some sort of peaceful Afghan celebration. He removed his visor cap and tucked his swagger stick under his arm. "A pity we weren't invited, Your Highness."

"*Aghai* Tallboot," Nasrullah looked him directly in the eye, "This so-called celebratory event will continue every night until our demands are met," he replied bluntly—and a little more loudly than necessary. Already, the art of blackmail began to fit him quite comfortably. His words were met at first with complete silence. Fitzgerald and Talbot glanced briefly at each other and then at Falmouth.

Lord Falmouth broke the silence as he retrieved his gold snuff box from his waistcoat pocket, tapped some snuff onto his knuckle, and sniffed it into each nostril.

"And what might those demands be, Your Highness?" Fitzgerald asked.

"Just a moment!" Lord Falmouth set his silk hat on the table and tucked his snuff box away. From the pocket of his frock coat, he produced a pen and a pad. "Please continue Your Highness.

"I hope you will understand, Lord Faalmooth, that I came to London for a purpose that has not been met. Nasrullah sat down on the sofa, exhausted from the shooting, crossed his legs, and took a gulp of water from the glass that had been poured for him. "So my first unconditional demand is exactly what I came to *Englistan* for. To seek Afghanistan's full Independence. And again I say, the people in Landan will not rest peacefully until our demands are met!" He glanced at all three men. "My second demand is the return of the Koh-i-Noor diamond, which rightfully belongs to Afghanistan." He asked for a refill of his glass, "And there is a third demand. I want you to find our man, Zalmai, who has run away with an English woman. Parwana Khan will provide you with his details. You have until tomorrow to respond, failing which the shooting will continue throughout the night, and the next, and the next."

"Your Highness we will get back to you soon as we have answers . . . But we implore Your Highness to hold off on the shooting. The Queen will be consulting with her ministers and that will take a bit of time," Lord Falmouth cautioned.

"As I said, you have tomorrow. All day," Nasrullah returned coldly. There was exasperation in his voice; stress was beginning to take its toll.

Queen Victoria remained silent. Nasrullah's demands simply went unheeded. Another night came and the starry sky seemed overpowered by the trailing lights of flying bullets manifesting webs of fire over Mayfair. As the shell fire grew hotter and the Enfield blasts greater, Nasrullah continued to hope that Queen Victoria's tenacious refusal—to meet the exaction of his demands—would change. But, as the following day passed without any response, that hope dwindled, like a sail that diminished at the horizon.

CHAPTER FORTY-FIVE

The Queen was furious. Explosive and irritated by turns whenever she was informed of the latest news from Dorchester House. To make things worse, Bertie had arrived from London to Osborn intending to persuade his mother to find an immediate solution to halt Nasrullah in his tracks.

"What has been done to stop this, Mother?" Bertie's nostrils flared like those of a mad horse, "We cannot have Mayfair held to ransom by this young upstart! London had been brought to a standstill by his actions. What has been achieved so far?" He nagged her with a barrage of questions. "It is completely embarrassing!"

"Bertie," the Queen arched her pale eyebrows and narrowed her eyes,"You and I both know how sensitive this matter is. It could flare up at any moment into an international incident. You were the one who took 'this young upstart' to house parties, and introduced him to those so-called actresses and dancers. You know him far better than I do! What would you do to stop him, if you were in my place?"

"Mother," Prince Edward prickled at the Queen's usual judgment of his personal life and raised his voice a bit higher, but still in a deliberately controlled manner. "What did you hope to achieve by inviting him in the first place? You knew the Amir's expectation was for self-determination for Afghanistan and you were never going to agree to it!"

"I invited his father but when that changed, I could hardly refuse his son!" she retorted. But her pale complexion had become paler under Bertie's accusations and her voice cracked.

"Mother, the Indian Governor General advised you, and in fact, your own advisers said many times, that Nosroollah was a volatile person, but you went ahead and asked Beatrice to send the invitation." He lifted both hands and nodded as if encouraging the Queen to accept full responsibility for the current situation. "But I suppose," he said, "we can be mildly thankful that sooner or later his ammunition will run out!"

"Bertie, I'm too frail and old for these back and forth debates with you," she said, wringing her hands. She turned to her lady-in-waiting, "Helen dear, please could you call for some tea, and bring Looty, when you come."

"It would have been preferable to invite Crown Prince Habibullah."

"I tried, Bertie," she said as her lady-in-waiting sat Looty on her lap. "I obviously would have preferred to invite him, but his father didn't want him to come for some reason."

"So, mother, who have you spoken to so far in order to bring this fracas to a conclusion?" Bertie asked in a quieter tone of voice as he accepted a cup of tea.

"A number of people," Queen Victoria said as she stirred her tea, "Lord Falmouth and Col Talbot first of all, and then the Head of Scotland yard who is working with the police on this. I have also spoken to General McNeill and Lieutenant Colonel McCormick. She patted Looty and picked up her cup and saucer.

"What about Munshi? I'm sure he is in cahoots with Nosroollah! Has he given his advice?" It was another barb intended to hurt the Queen and she knew it.

"I have asked him because he understands the mind of the Afghans better than we do."

"And what did he suggest?" Bertie asked but without attempting to reduce the heavy irony from his tone.

He didn't have an answer to the problem," the Queen said defensively, "he said what you and I know already, that Nosroollah does not want to go back without a direct answer to his demands. He said it would be the cause of shame and humiliation for the prince."

"And so, he holds us all to ransom! The young fool! I could happily wring his neck right now!" Bertie banged his cup down on the table. "What have you asked the police to do? We need some immediate action to put an end to this havoc. It could easily turn into carnage."

"Which is what I don't want, and neither do the police," Queen Victoria said, raising herself up in her chair. "Much more than local trouble, it could cost Britain another war with Afghanistan—and that is what I am trying my utmost to avoid, Bertie." She shook her head firmly, "No! No more. The loss of lives in the first and second wars were too much. No more bloodshed." She met Edward's eye, "But neither will I be blackmailed into giving in to the Amir's request, nor to Nosroollah's demands. This situation requires delicacy and that is the sort of answer I am seeking!"

Prince Edward regarded the Queen with just the hint of a smile, "You are right of course, Mother," he said. "If I were you, I would call in the people the Prince knows and seems to respect. Perhaps, among them, there will be someone who is able to negotiate with him."

There was a sudden release of tension in the room and Victoria smiled at her son. "That is good advice, Bertie," she said approvingly, "I'll follow it up immediately."

Her Majesty called for a glass of scotch on ice and gave Looty a hug.

The Queen's relationship with Bertie had been fraught with difficulty from his youth. She had been a distant parent who had failed to meet the needs of a sensitive child and his response was rebellion that was chiefly aimed at hurting his mother. Bertie's incessant gambling and inappropriate connections with a number of women, both married and unmarried, caused scandals and had created deep rifts in the relationship between Queen Victoria and her son. For years she had suffered from depression over the loss of Prince Consort, Albert, and silently blamed Bertie's behavior for his death. Lately though, both Queen Victoria and Prince Edward had worked at repairing their relationship. With the Queen's encouragement, Bertie was actively preparing himself for his future role as king. Private squabbles would arise, but the public face of the Crown must be maintained.

⁕⁕⁕

Hours later, a list was drawn up of those who might conceivably hold some sway over Nasrullah, and an urgent meeting was arranged.

Dr. Lillias Hamilton, engineer Frank Martin, Lord Falmouth, Sir Gerald Fitzgerald, Colonel Adelbert Talbot, Munshi Abdul Karim Khan, and Sir Rafiuddin, were summoned to Osborn House for an impromptu conference with the Queen and the Prince Wales.

As they walked down the corridor that led to Queen's favorite room, the Durbar Room, known as 'The Queen's India', those that were new there glanced up at portraits of Her Majesty's Indian servants and other Indian artwork that adorned the lilac walls. But the focus was on Queen Victoria who was seated on a gilded chair with her little dog on her lap. Bertie sat on her right and Princess Beatrice on her left side. The room glowed with candlelight that was intended to portray a relaxed ambiance, but the atmosphere was troubled. Both Lillias and Frank Martin felt they should have realized something of this nature was about to happen when Nasrullah was thwarted in his request, and that preventative action could have been taken.

They were shown to a long table, draped in starched white cloth, and the Queen was assisted to take the seat at the head. The Prince of Wales sat at his mother's side.

The Queen's advisers General McNeill and his assistant Lieutenant Colonel McCormick had already arrived and both were in officers' uniform.

"I'm grateful that you were all able to make the journey at short notice," the Queen said. "I've had no choice but to call for this urgent meeting because our distinguished guest, the Prince of Afghanistan, is a bit on edge." She glanced at Lord Falmouth and continued. "As Lord Falmouth mentioned, Prince Nosroollah has made certain demands which the Crown is unwilling and unable to meet, particularly, as we feel England is being held to ransom. The Prince and his men are prepared to continue their onslaught in Mayfair until these demands are met." She glanced round at one face after another. "We have brought you here in the hope of bringing some sanity to the situation we find ourselves in," she said. "The firing of guns in any public area cannot be tolerated and must be stopped immediately. Prince Edward and I believe one of you will be able to negotiate with Prince Nasrullah to bring about a ceasefire." She touched her white cap and laced her fingers together above Looty's head. "Some of you have dealt with the Prince and know him far better than we do. You know his nature and may be aware of his habits . . ."

Initially, there was silence, but then Frank Martin spoke up. "Your Majesty, on behalf of the Amir, who would, I am certain, be grieved to hear of this outcome, I would like first of all to extend an apology. I feel a certain responsibility as I was sent by His Highness, the Amir, in part to oversee this mission and to guide the young Prince. I think he may be acting on bad advice from some of his men in my absence."

"Thank you, Mr. Martin," the Queen replied, "Do you think you may have any power to quell this uprising?"

"Doctor Hamilton and I have discussed that possibility, but we doubt that our influence would be felt in dissuading the Prince from his present course of action," he replied. "but failing any other option, we would be prepared to try."

The Prince of Wales turned to Munshi and Rafiuddin, "Would either of you gentlemen consider speaking to Prince Nasrullah?" he asked, "you may not be closely acquainted but you share some common ground."

Neither Munshi nor Rafiuddin had any desire to stop Nasrullah. A positive outcome of Nasrullah's rebellion fully aligned with their interests, as they knew a free Afghanistan would more than likely lead to a free India. For a moment there was complete silence in the room.

The Prince of Wales looked at him with irritation, "Well! Surely you have some thoughts, Munshi?" he asked coldly. There was no love lost between them.

"No, Your Highness. This was my first meeting with the Prince, so I really don't know him," Munshi replied in his rhythmic cadence.

The Queen set a hand on the Crown Prince's knee and muttered, "Bertie, please let me handle this." She had never liked Bertie's disdainful attitude towards Abdul Karim Khan. The Queen went on to say, "As you all may know, this is a particularly delicate matter and we have to walk a fine line to prevent things from getting completely out of control." Her face appeared pallid in the candlelight. She leaned back in the chair. Looty stood up, turned around on her lap and settled down comfortably again. "We obviously cannot use force to subdue Nasrullah's men without causing an international incident. This is an extremely awkward situation and I need your assistance," she stopped any further explanation and looked around the table. "Any thoughts? Dr. Hamilton?"

"Your Majesty, as Mr. Martin said, we are willing to try to dissuade the Prince, but he is unlikely to accept our plea," Lillias answered. She was well-attired, having found a dress in London exactly to her taste. It was a sapphire blue satin embroidered all around the hem with a border of flowers and gold and silver leaves in chenille and silk.

"Munshi, you have already answered to Edward, but can you, Sir Rafiuddin, and Munshi, as Muslims, think of any way Prince Nasrullah can be stopped?"

"Your Majesty," Raffiuddin replied, "I have little understanding of his character, and would not be sure how to approach him. I'm also in the same position as *Munshi Sahib*." The Munshi nodded sagely—careful not to upset his tall spotless white turban as he did so.

Bertie stared at both Indian men and his face reddened, "Do neither of you have a thought on how to stop him? Then perhaps, at the very least go and condemn him! Is that too hard for you?"

Both men gazed submissively down at the table.

His mother set his hand on his again and said quietly, "Bertie, please be calm." While neither the Queen nor Bertie wanted another flare-up, especially in the presence of others, the Crown Prince resented the way his mother always stepped in to protect the Munshi.

Frank Martin raised a hand.

"Mr. Martin?"

"Your Majesty, I think I know of someone who might be able to help," he said thoughtfully.

"And who would that be, and why?" asked the Queen anxiously.

"Your Majesty, you rightly thought of appealing to Prince Nasrullah through a fellow Muslim," Frank Martin said, leaning forward respectfully. "The Prince is an ardent Muslim and deeply respects Islamic Law. The one person in England who could conceivably help is Henry Quilliam." His blue eyes met the Queen's. "While in Liverpool, I noticed they both showed deep respect for one other. Prince Nasrullah's offering of a substantial amount of money towards the building of a meeting place for Quilliam's ministry was very well-received. Their mutual faith bonded them instantly." I was personally impressed, Your Majesty, when Quilliam bent to kiss the Prince's hand, but Nasrullah wouldn't allow him to. He was uncomfortable with a man of Quilliam's stature, submitting to him in that manner."

The Queen contemplated for a moment and glanced at Bertie. She was hesitant to show her deep disdain for the Muslim convert who appeared to be recruiting destitute men and children into the faith of Islam. Bertie gave a brief nod of approval. Queen Victoria broke the silence in the room. "I am open to your idea, Mr. Martin, perhaps he is indeed the one to stop the Prince." She glanced around the table once more, "Does anyone have anything to add to that?" she asked. There was no response. "General McNeill?"

"I am fully in agreement, Your Majesty.".

"Then you have my authorization to brief Mr. Quilliam and request his accompaniment to Dorchester House!" She turned to Frank Martin, "Mr. Martin, would you be so good as to meet with Mr. Quilliam at the same time. He may need your persuasion."

"Of course, Your Majesty," Frank Martin replied and bowed low before the Queen and the Crown Prince.

A wireless message from General McNeill requesting Henry Quilliam's presence in London was relayed from Osborn immediately after the meeting with Queen Victoria. Quilliam left Liverpool before dawn, just as the morning light had begun to challenge the dark sky. He arrived at Victoria Station within six hours, where he was met by General McNeill, Lieutenant Colonel McCormick, and Frank Martin.

Quilliam had had plenty of time to think on the train from Liverpool to London. The head of the Muslims in Britain had learned of Nasrullah's escapade via the newspapers and was deeply concerned. Such parochial behavior toward Britain was a dark blot on the Prince that would be remembered for a long time to come. The more Quilliam thought about it, the more he grieved for the young man who had set out with good intentions, had been exceptionally well-received upon his arrival, and had become since the shooting began, a pariah to the British public at large. He was saddened as well for the British Muslims who had held him in high regard. They had not forgotten his generosity in donating thousands of pounds to their cause, but now they too, were disillusioned. Abdullah Quilliam wanted this to end immediately.

After introductions, Quilliam was briefed over tea at the station.

I don't fully understand what all this is about," he said, "I am aware that it has something to do with Prince Nasrullah and the shootings at Dorchester House, but I don't quite know where I come into it. I would welcome an explanation?"

"Certainly, Sir," General McNeill said. They were an ill-assorted group seated around a table in a rather dingy tea room. Henry Quilliam was wearing a flowing Muslim garment, a coat, and a lambskin hat, while the General and his Lieutenant were uniform, and Frank had not had an opportunity to change out of the frock-coat and high collared shirt he had worn the previous night. None of the men had slept much.

The teas and coffees all looked and tasted as though they had been poured from the same pot, but they were warm and wet, which is as much as they could have hoped for at Victoria Station. Quilliam placed his valise on the floor beside him.

"Mr. Quilliam," said General McNeill in his distinct Scottish accent as he removed his military peaked cap, tucked it under his arm, and smoothed back a shock of white hair. "I am sure you are aware of what is going on in Dorchester House?"

Quilliam nodded, "I have seen the papers, Sir."

"Her Majesty authorized me to work with you in stopping the Afghan Prince from the ongoing shooting. It has to be done in a peaceful manner and Her Majesty, the Queen, believes you may be the man to achieve that."

Abdullah Quilliam looked him in the eye, "Why me, Sir?"

"I think Mr. Martin might be better placed to answer that," McNeill replied.

"Mr. Quilliam," said Frank Martin, "I've known Prince Nasrullah for years, but he would look the other way if I tried to persuade him to do this. But that day when I accompanied the Prince to Liverpool,

I saw the intense spiritual bond between yourself and Nasrullah. I've never seen anything quite that sincere in his manner before. Not even with his father. I believe you have a good chance of convincing him to stop."

"It may not be that simple," Quilliam said slowly, "but of course, I am prepared to do my utmost. *Allah* will hear my prayer in advance and I believe he will answer it. His kindness is very near to us. I have no idea how this unfortunate outburst in Mayfair can be stopped, but the Almighty is the one we can turn to for assistance."

Although he was surprised to have been called in to help, Quilliam willingly agreed to do what he could to dissuade Nasrullah from any further disruptive behavior and to persuade him to leave England immediately. Beyond any doubt, both Quilliam and Nasrullah were deeply devoted Muslims, and the sacred connection between them through *Allah* and Islam were paths to a good result.

A carriage was waiting for them outside the station and Frank accompanied Quilliam through one of the side roads towards Dorchester House.

"You will need to walk from here," he said. "I wish you all the luck in the world."

Quilliam set his valise down on the road beside him and raised both hands in supplication as the carriage turned back the way it had come.

"O' *Allah*, may my request be in Your obedience and help me to seek Your satisfaction and direction in all I say and do . . ." His prayer trailed off, he picked up his valise and walked the block to Dorchester House.

༄༄༄

Quilliam's Salaam, bow, and hand on his chest allowed him to be welcomed without hesitation into the mansion.

"*As-salamu alaykum*, I'm Abdullah Quilliam," he said—using his

Muslim first name."

There was an instant buzz of excitement. This was the British convert to the Islamic faith that Nasrullah had spoken about so often. It explained his curly brown hair and sky-blue eyes and why an *Englees* should be wearing a Muslim garment.

"I am here to see His Highness, the Shahzadah," Quilliam said. At that moment, he saw a familiar and unforgettable face, "Khairo Khan!" he called out as Khairo approached to see what was going on, "May *Barakat-ullah*, blessings of the Almighty, be upon you and your family. If you recall, we've met before in Liverpool, you were with Shahzadah.".

"Yes, of course I remember you with pleasure!" Khairo replied immediately, "*Shaykh al-Islām, As-salamu alaykum*, brother!" Khairo Khan replied, using Abdullah Quilliam's title. Khairo called Raj to interpret. "We are blessed of Allah to see a dignified man of God like yourself, again. May *Allah* always bring you." He hugged him three times in an expression of love and brotherhood. Khairo sent a page to fetch Nasrullah, ushered Quilliam into the parlor and ordered tea. "I trust you are not too tired *Shaykh Sahib*. His Highness, the Shahzadah will be here shortly."

Minutes passed and the word of the Shaykh's arrival at Dorchester House spread, Mullah Shir Mohammad and Naieb-Salar Hassien Khan hustled down the marble staircase to greet him and engaged him in conversation with Raj's help until Nasrullah arrived. The Prince had reverted to Afghan dress and had wrapped a shawl around his chest and neck. He looked exhausted and struggled to keep his eyes open fatigued and he greeted Quilliam with obvious mixed feelings, knowing immediately that the Shaykh had come on a mission. After the previous night's rounds of gunfire had once again unsettled Mayfair, he had become assuaged with self-doubt. This was not working . . . the Queen had offered no response to their actions . . . perhaps he had even disgraced his father. Once again he saw himself as a failure.

"*As-salamu alaykum*, Shaykh Abdullah."

"Your Highness," Quilliam approached Nasrullah. "*As-salamu alaykum*," He stretched out his hands, clasped Nasrullah's hand, and again bent his head to kiss it. Nasrullah pulled away. "Please *Shaykh Sahib*, I'm mortified, it would be sinful for me to allow an exalted man like yourself kiss my hand!" He dropped clumsily onto the couch across from where Quilliam and Khairo were sitting. Hassein Khan and the Mullah sat nearby.

"Please excuse me . . . I had very few hours' sleep last night . . ." Nasrullah said wearily. He felt like an aged sentry exhausted by a long retreat from battle.

"May Allah give Your Highness strength. Please forgive me also for stopping by unexpectedly. My primary reason was to pay my respect to Your Highness, but I was also prompted by the news of the shootings from Dorchester House that has become the main topic of conversation throughout England."

As Raj translated a sudden silence descended on the room. Nasrullah winced at Quilliam's blunt opening, lowered his eyes, and fiddled with the edge of the shawl he was wearing. "Is there anything I can help with the will of *Allah* to resolve the issue, Your Highness?"

Under Abdullah Quilliam's gaze, Nasrullah had no stamina remaining to explain his rage, and what had seemed righteous justification in his own eyes for his actions. He saw, without being told, how he had damaged the Islamic movement in Great Britain. He had arrived in Liverpool as a Prince and a benefactor, and now he had shamed the faith he came to uphold and strengthen. He owed Quilliam, Britain's head of the Islamic movement—a reason—an answer for his actions—but now he felt he had none. It was also important to Nasrullah that he maintain face before his men. He could not allow them to feel his disgrace.

The page brought tea. There was the tinkling of cups in the background and, as their guest, Abdullah Quilliam was served first.

"*Shaykh Abdullah Sahib*," said Nasrullah, "Let me say this briefly." Nasrullah was handed his cup, "I'm very disappointed as to how *Englistan* treated us. We Afghans never treat our guests like what we've experienced here." He lowered his head and stared at the cup in his hand. The smell of freshly brewed black tea and cardamom reminded him of home. But even as he looked down at the steaming cup, he was reminded of how he was received when he stepped ashore, of the pomp and ceremony of the visit, the balls, and the visits—had he forgotten it all? Was he a child still, who demanded more when granted much?

"May *Allah* grant Your Highness a very long life," Quilliam stroked his beard, and caught Nasrullah's eye. "Your Highness is well aware that our holy book of Qur'an says we should refrain from disappointments as it they are a useful tool for the devil. The devil is delighted and well-satisfied when he sees Your Highness disappointed. It's also said in a *hadith*," Quilliam continued shrewdly "'evade from disappointments because it impedes and even halts one's development.'"

Quilliam had reasons of his own for deterring Nasrullah from expressing his rage and holding England to ransom through these nightly shootings. As a spiritual man, the *Shaykh al-Isl*ām of England saw the benefit of convincing Nasrullah to go home. If he were successful, his gesture of goodwill, might result in the Queen's good grace towards England's Muslims. Secondly his peaceful mission to deter Nasrullah from this violent protest—one Muslim to another— would increase his stature in the eyes of the Ottoman Caliph, the Egyptian monarch, and the Shah of Persia who all gave him the title of Head of Muslims in Britain, but throughout the Muslims worldwide.

"*Beshak*, no doubt, *Shaykh Sahib*, we must respect the will of Allah," Khairo agreed. He looked at Quilliam with his one good eye and blinked.

The tubby Mullah, *Shir* Mohammad used his habitual word,

"*Astaghfirullah!*" An expression of redemption, shame and disapproval, and slowly rocked back and forth on the chair stroking his long gray beard.

Naieb-Salar Hassien Khan who had been against the shootings from the very outset, said, "*Beshak!*" His onyx prayer beads clicked in every stroke of his thumb. A box of 555 brand cigarettes was, as usual, tucked into his waistcoat pocket.

Nasrullah agreed with a defeated nod, and mumbled, "*Allahu Akbar*. God is great."

Nasrullah was a faithful Muslim himself and had genuine intentions when it came to the religion,

"*Allah* commanded the *Iblis* out of Paradise, and regarded him as *Shaitan*," Quilliam continued, seizing his advantage, "an evil spirit who disobeyed *Allah*, possessed bodies and made them destroy their spirits and love for the Almighty *Allah*." he paused, "The Satan must be evaded at all costs."

"*Ameen!*" Nasrullah and the Mullah muttered in unison. A silence followed, broken when Nasrullah mumbled something inaudible.

"Demons and *Iblis* operate where there is shame, sorrow and repentance, the only path back is to make peace with your good self and relinquish the unnecessary demands," Quilliam urged." He stood, opened his valise, and took out a Qur'an; he kissed the book and rubbed it on both of his eyes, "Your Highness . . . "in the name of this holy book," . . . he proffered the Qur'an to the Prince, "I implore all of you to stop the *Iblis* from possessing you for his own good. Defy him bravely with all your might and let the Almighty rid the Satan and send him to hell. Again, I implore you to ceasefire and make peace with yourselves and others," He set the Qur'an on the table, knelt down and pressed his head humbly on the floor near Nasrullah's feet.

Nasrullah was suddenly electrified, springing from the couch, he bent down, and raised him up. "*Shaykh Sahib*, please, I beg you to stop," he said, deeply embarrassed.

"Your Highness, please accept my plea."

"I will, *Shaykh Sahib*," Nasrullah answered humbly. He swore an oath, *qasam*, upon the name of *Allah*, and, lifting his both hands, made a pledge to God that he would return home.

A thank you letter from Windsor Palace signed by Queen Victoria was addressed to Frank Martin which included the following: "What you have suggested was beyond astonishing, you have my sincere thanks and so does Britain. You are accredited for your steadfast loyalty to Britain."

CHAPTER FORTY-SIX

෴෴෴

When Nasrullah crossed the English Channel and set his foot in France on the third of September, the New York Times published an article titled: "At Last the Shahzadah Goes Away".

No doubt, Queen Victoria gave a great sigh of relief feeling as though a mountain had been lifted off her chest. Even the Punch and Judy puppet show cast him as a heartbroken prince who had departed from England without the Koh-i-Noor diamond. The amusing performance displayed in skillful movements of the puppet's hands, arms and limbs, covetously holding a diamond. The puppeteer impersonated Nasrullah's heavy Afghan accent as he hid the diamond under his karakul hat. Mr. Punch's sharp eyes detected the priceless gem, "What's that dazzling English monocle shining through your lambskin cap, *Shahzadah*?" he demanded to know.

"It's not a monocle Mr. Punch, but a rarely found shining potato that will go home with me," responded the puppet. The spectators' roared with laughter every time the show was played in towns and cities throughout England.

En route to Kabul, Nasrullah and his retinue marveled at the sights in the cities of Paris and Rome before boarding the *HMS Clive* in Naples. They arrived at Karachi about three weeks later and at Kabul at the end of February, the following year.

Nasrullah left England profoundly disappointed, despite Quilliams's encouragement. It worked through his system like a poison with the realization that the golden opportunity to secure an independent Afghanistan had failed miserably. It tortured Nasrullah to know that the tables had been turned on him, and he would have to endure embarrassment when he arrived home.

He was not feted along the way from Kandahar; and few of those who came out to witness the return of his entourage along the route towards Kabul cheered as before.

On his more muted arrival at Arg Palace, Nasrullah would not admit mea culpa, but the responsibility for his misadventure was passed off to others. His straight arrow had become a boomerang that would continue to torment him with more failures and defeats throughout his life.

Major Akbar Khan's death sentence for his consumption of alcohol on board the ship was upheld by the Amir and carried out by Parwana Khan shortly after their arrival in Kabul.

Prince Nasrullah persuaded his father to pursue the British government for the extradition of Zalmai to face prosecution for his betrayal but the authorities showed no interest in interfering in a private matter mutually agreed upon between a couple who were now legally wedded; when no crime had been committed.

They had been officially pronounced husband and wife shortly after their arrival in the town of Dunfermline, Fife, a peninsula in eastern Scotland where Roma's childhood friend, Elizabeth Cochran's sister, Kristen, and her husband, Kevin Brown, lived with their two young children. They welcomed Roma and Zalmai into their large vernacular-style farmhouse. According to the account of Roma's sister, Selena Hamilton, who made the trip to see the couple in Dunfermline, she was gratified to see her younger sister's happiness. The restlessness of this young woman, who had wanted nothing more from life than travel and adventure like Lillias, had lifted like a cloud of morning mist after sunrise. Zalmai always said that their marriage had been written in their eyes from the first day they met. It was a bond inextricably embedded in them, their protector and defender. Roma was about four months pregnant and the bloom of motherhood rested comfortably on her. She and Zalmai were caught up in the miracle of life, the making a new person, and had already embraced this sentient-being into their hearts and souls.

Roma helped Kristen in her chores, while Zalamai and Kevin worked together on the farm, raising cattle, cultivating crops, and doing the other essential farm work that their livelihood depended upon. As a devoted Muslim, Zalmai never missed his prayer five times a day. He was the only Muslim in Dunfermline but was, before too long, welcomed by the neighbors and the town's inhabitants.

Lillias Hamilton, Kate Daly, and Frank Martin accompanied Nasrullah on his return to Kabul. But, upon their arrival, Lillias, knowing she could not defend her writing about the atrocious massacre of the Hazara population in her novel '*A Vizier's Daughter: A Tale of the Hazara War*' that was about to be published in London; neither could she deny knowing beforehand of her sister's love affair with Zalmai realized it was time for her to leave. It was obvious that these events had scarred the relationship, and that she and the Amir could no longer be in accord with each other. It was a heartbreaking moment for an uncommonly gifted and caring physician. She was the only one, possessed with the warmth of a daughter's eyes, who could calm the raging Amir, deemed difficult by her predecessors such as Dr. Alfred Gray and other physicians. Lillias had coached Kate Daly to follow the same medical procedures for the Amir as she had done for the past year-and-half. She emphasized that keeping her patience with him was paramount. She pointed out that he responded and recovered faster when he felt loved and emotionally supported, and would be less inclined to react by ordering the execution of his subjects—an explanation that Dr. Daly took completely in her stride!

It was time for her to leave with a heartfelt curtsy and a kiss on Amir's forehead. The Amir's eyes welled and in a weakened voice said, "Daktar Liala Jan, *tashakur* for everything."

The ladies of the Harem-Sarai sobbed like abandoned children when Lillias introduced Kate and revealed that her time in Kabul had come to an end. But Gulrez's sorrow gave way to delight when Lillias gave her the box of Pears Soap that she bought for her.

"*Khanum* Gulrez, this is the best soap in England! I'm sure you will see the difference in your complexion and feel the softness on your skin." Dr. Hamilton smelled the bar of soap and then brought it to Gulrez's nose, who was at once enchanted by the flowery perfume.

She bade farewell to Queen Sultana in her apartment and gave her a bottle of honeysuckle and lavender perfume, from London. The Queen's almond-shaped eyes filled with tears and her mascara smeared a little as she held Lillias in her embrace. "I shall miss you a lot," she said, "you'll be remembered forever! Thank you for the kind gift and for bringing my son safely back to me. I will never forget your kindness, Daktar Laila Jan."

Frank Martin continued presiding over the Mashin-Khana for another five years. He and his factory workers assembled and put to use the machinery he had assisted Nasrullah in purchasing from England. The production of the factory doubled and tripled through his hard work as years went by.

The English veterinarian, Thomas Clemence, also stayed for a few more years before he was notified that his wife was dying of cholera. He left Kabul immediately but only arrived in time for her burial. He never returned.

Despite Nasrullah's failure to achieve all that the Amir had wished for Afghanistan, the young Prince was not condemned in any way on his homecoming; on the contrary, he received a higher salary from his father. Ironically, shortly after his return to Kabul, Prince Nasrullah built himself a mansion, which was considered the finest in Kabul. His father, the Amir, was there to cut the ribbon at it's ceremonial opening—Prince Nasrullah had built for himself a true replica of London's Dorchester House!

Four years later in 1901, both Amir Abdul Rahman and Queen

Victoria died.

Nasrullah remained staunchly opposed to British policy in India and Afghanistan. He, Khairo, and Barakatullah, an Indian revolutionary, attempted and failed, to topple the British government in India. Queen Victoria sent a letter to the Amir stating: "His Highness, Prince Nasrullah is suspected of conniving with the tribes along the Indo-Afghan frontier. I request Your Highness to prevent your subjects from destabilizing India."

Despite his frail health, the Amir prevailed over Nasrullah and put a stop to his rebellious mission. He responded to the Queen, "Rest assured, Your Majesty, my dominion will continue to be thoroughly friendly to the British government." His swift action may have prevented another bloody war with England.

The friendly Anglo-Afghan policy continued under Crown Prince Habibullah, who succeeded his father after his death by the right of primogeniture. But, when World War broke out, Nasrullah—and the religious factions he represented—supported the German-Turkish side in direct opposition to Britain. Amir Habibullah's declaration of Afghanistan's neutrality infuriated Nasrullah who threatened to remove his brother from power and take charge of the frontier tribes in a campaign against British India. But later the German Kaiser, Wilhelm II called it fruitless and abandoned the mission. Habibullah's eighteen-year reign was marked by congenial relations with Britain. He was assassinated, and the prime suspect to his brother's murder was Prince Nasrullah. He assumed power for a week before Habibullah's son, Amanullah was enthroned.